ALSO BY

The Brass Machine

The King's Sun

The King's Fear

The King's Time

THE WAR FOR HEAVEN

ISAAC GRISHAM

COOPER BLUE BOOKS, LLC

This is a work of fiction. Names, characters, places, and incidents either are the product of the author's imagination or are used fictitiously. Any resemblance to actual events, locales, or persons, living or dead, is entirely coincidental.

Cooper Blue Books, LLC

www.isaacgrisham.com

Edited by Kristen Corrects, Inc.
Cover art design by Dissect Designs

First edition published 2026

ISBN 979-8-9917410-2-6 (ebook)
ISBN 979-8-9917410-3-3 (paperback)
ISBN 979-8-9917410-4-0 (hardcover)
ISBN 979-8-9917410-5-7 (audiobook)

for John “Ace” Grisham

We miss you. Every day.

At once a sound of crying fills the air, the high wails
And weeping of infant souls, little ones denied
Their share of sweet life, torn from the breast
On life's very doorstep. A dark day bore them off
And sank them in untimely death.

from Aeneid, Book VI
translated by Seamus Heaney

CHAPTER ONE

ANGELS DESCENDED FROM HEAVEN. They radiated color, bathing the earth in brilliant light.

The trumpets are overkill, Damian thought as a brass proclamation assaulted his ears. He'd been lying in a patch of lush grass, savoring a fall breeze. His exposure to nature was usually limited to open car windows while driving between work, classes, and a tiny apartment. The fanfare intruded upon this rare moment of appreciation.

Why did angels have to arrive in this *park? Or here in Minade of all the obscure places?*

Damian glanced at his vehicle, a 1993 Buick Century that refused to die. It rested a few yards away, the engine still warm and ticking. Grime clouded the windows, but he found his reflection. He appeared blank, unimpressed. Thinner than he realized he was. The expression summed up his sentiments about the Buick.

In high school, he'd dreamed of sitting behind the wheel of a pony car. With the power of a V8 engine at his fingertips, nothing would keep him from escaping his small hometown of Minade. Nothing except his parents' finances. By his seventeenth birthday, they'd scraped together enough money to gift him the old sedan.

"The Century's design was outdated when GM built them, but it was—is—very reliable," Damian's father had said in the driveway after the grand reveal. A slight, bespectacled man perpetually dressed in worn khakis and a sweater vest, he beamed with pride at what he considered the best kind of present: a bargain. "Take good care of her, and she'll be with you for years."

"Thanks, Dad." Damian fixed a smile on his face, but his heart felt as heavy as the three-thousand-pound car parked in front of him.

"You will appreciate what your father and I have sacrificed for you," his mother said, her sharp eyes seeing through his fake smile. "We expect you to take care of it, and to pay for gas and insurance."

"Of course, Mom." Damian peered up at her imposing figure. Though thin, she was a head taller than him or his father. As always, she'd pulled her long hair up into a tight bun. The simple style emphasized her sharp features. "Can I take it for a spin?"

His father tossed him the keys. "Beautiful evening for a drive around town. Be back before sunset. It may be your birthday, but you still have school tomorrow."

As his father ambled back into the house to catch the evening news, his mother crossed her arms and watched as Damian climbed into the Buick and started the engine. She motioned for him to roll down the window.

"Mind your father." She leaned over so she could peer inside the sedan. "And don't go all the way out to your friend's place."

Just now, or ever again? he wanted to ask, knowing she'd be pleased as punch if he never saw his best friend—his only friend—ever again. "Don't worry, Mom. I won't be gone long."

She gave him a tight smile. "Happy birthday, Damian."

A figure paused and glanced down at Damian, her body blocking the angels' lights.

"Don't worry. They're coming," she said, glancing back at the other people congregating in Minade's only park.

"I know." The intrusion irritated him, but he smiled up at her. The expression felt pleasant, so he kept grinning after the woman turned away.

Like any town in rural Illinois, an ocean of corn surrounded Minade. After two years of community college, Damian had finally escaped. Sadly, instead of driving a Camaro, he took a train up to a university in Chicago. The distance had concerned his parents, but they couldn't produce an argument against the generous scholarships he'd earned.

They found other ways to maintain their control over me. A hundred miles of corn and soybeans wasn't enough to escape Minade's grasp. He'd wanted to pursue a degree in creative writing, an outlet he'd used to express himself since learning the alphabet. Even better, he was good at storytelling. Devoid of much imagination themselves, his parents dissuaded him.

"If you're going to be frivolous with your future, you won't receive another cent from us for expenses," his mother had said one night after dinner. He'd marched into the living room to argue the case for his preferred major. His mother was doing needlework, and his father watched FOX News while working on a crossword puzzle.

"Frivolous?" He'd come armed with ambitions of becoming a writer and scholarships that would allow him to hone that craft, but his parents seemed unconcerned with a future that would make him happy. "How is pursuing a dream frivolous?"

"It's foolish to think you'll be able to support a family off writing." She set down her needlework and focused her gaze on him. "Especially here in Minade. The only paper worth reading is the church newsletter, and they don't pay writers."

Damian was speechless. *She assumes I want children—that I want to spend my life in Minade!*

"Study something practical. Something you can live off." His father removed the spectacles from his face and a handkerchief from the pocket of his sweater vest. As he spoke, he wiped imaginary smudges from the lenses. "You can always write in your spare time. It's not a hobby you need a degree for."

"A hobby, Dad? This school's creative writing program is amazing. Lots of their graduates have successful careers."

"It's too bad about the car," his mother said, looking over at his father. "If we'd known he'd only use it for a couple years... Do you think we can get anything for it?"

"The car's in *my* name!" Damian huffed in frustration before disappearing back into his bedroom.

In the end, unable to bear the cost of living in Chicago independently, Damian bowed to their demands. Two years later, he graduated with a degree in business. By that time, his parents had other reasons to be disappointed in him.

While attending university, Damian had met Alena Bucket. Her intelligent outlook and face full of freckles enraptured him. She seemed taken with Damian as well—*still no idea why*—and the two had fallen in love. He insisted they marry immediately. Though he had no ring to offer her, he got down on bended knee one evening in her dorm room.

"Absolutely not!" She brushed him off, taking the proposal in good humor. Seeing his dejected look, she pulled him up off the floor to sit beside her on the bed. "You may have been raised to expect marriage so quickly—and that's fine—but I wasn't, and I have to remain true to myself, too. I don't want to tie the knot until I'm done with college."

"Even if you know I'm the one?" He was baffled.

"It has nothing to do with how we feel about one another." She rested a hand on his forearm. "We're both in school for our own goals, and we shouldn't let ourselves get distracted from them."

Damian considered how dull his statistics, economics, and management classes were. Meeting Alena was the best thing to happen to him in years, and most of his life goals now revolved around making her happy. "If you say so."

"Besides, you can't afford the distraction of living with me," she said, simultaneously teasing and closing the matter. She grabbed the book he'd brought over with him to study and tossed it in his lap. "As your calculus grades prove."

Damian's willingness to continue a relationship outside of marriage illustrated how the Windy City opened his mind to the wider world. He slept in on the weekends. Went drinking with classmates. If he'd taken the Buick to the city instead of the train, he and Alena would've regularly fogged up the windows.

They eventually graduated. Damian had two options: return to the ocean of corn with his degree or remain in Chicago. When Alena at last accepted his marriage proposal, the choice was obvious. Together, they launched their careers. Alena started at the *Tribune* as a copy editor, while Damian accepted a position as a junior programmer for a small software company.

Like many young newlyweds, they enjoyed themselves and their successes. Not everything was perfect. Even after living in school dormitories, he found their small apartment claustrophobic. Alena thought it charming. To compromise, she encouraged spending their extra money on vacations, fleeing the cold Chicago winters when possible.

We should've taken more trips.

Tragedy struck in their late twenties. In an accident involving a pen, Alena died.

A cumulus cloud filtered the sun's light, casting a shadow over the park. Damian's smile wilted as a soft wind shook red and orange leaves from nearby maple trees. He could hear their fallen brethren crunching as people walked around him.

The death of Damian's wife had been the second devastating loss in his brief life, and it felt as though the pillars supporting his existence crumbled. In Alena, he'd found a partner from whom he drew strength. She opened his stubborn Midwestern mind. Pushed him to think beyond the confines of his upbringing. Helped him step out of his parents' shadow.

Did I build my confidence on our relationship? Rely on her for my identity? He didn't suppose that to be entirely true. But when she died, his spirit had crumbled as well.

Grief-stricken, Damian rarely left home. He lacked the energy to brave the crushing masses on the city streets or trains. Work allowed him to program remotely. His manager, noticing his social anxiety increase over the next year, suggested he move out of Chicago.

With little money or direction in life, Damian returned to Minade, back to where a Buick Century waited under a tarp behind his parents' house. The town was a solid and immutable fixture—still a prison from which escape was near impossible, but a prison in which he hoped to find a modicum of comfort. *The safety of my origin.*

It was only after he settled into a cheap apartment that he realized exactly how enduring his hometown was. How much *he* had changed in the interim.

Relocation had allowed him to regroup. To distract himself, Damian reenrolled in night classes at the community college. This time, he maintained a focus on creative writing, still hoping to one day pen a novel. Alena had encouraged him to explore his genuine passion, especially when he expressed disillusionment with his chosen profession.

With luck, I'll dedicate a book to her one day.

Damian frowned. The woman who had glanced down at him earlier was back. Others accompanied her, and they all wore grim expressions.

Why is everyone gathering in the park? Then he noticed colorful lights reflecting off wet faces. *Ah yes, they're here for the angels!*

That his parents weren't among those peering at him was remarkable. *Mom would rub this theological proof in my face!* They'd been pressuring him to return to church. To start a new family. To take his future seriously.

They meant well, and Damian appreciated their concern for his eternal soul—even if their actions did little to soothe his wounded morale. His mother had never liked Alena, determining his wife led him astray. She'd been tactful enough to keep her disapproval quiet since the accident, but she wasn't silent about his path forward.

"Don't worry, young man." An elderly gentleman, grasping a wooden cane with a gnarled hand, kneeled in the grass next to Damian. "They're almost here."

Of course they're almost here, he thought. *I can hear them!*

To his parents' chagrin, Damian no longer accepted the reality of an afterlife. Not that he'd turn down immortality. He wanted Alena's soul to exist in blissful perpetuity, beyond the threat of devastating war, virulent biological agents, and hairy spiders.

"I want to believe in eternity," Damian said while visiting his family before ending up in the park. They were sitting in their living room. The news was on. "It would be great to see Alena again one day. And Colin, too."

His mother grimaced, missing a stitch in her needlework.

"Imagine an end to the constant earthly battles. The back and forth, black and white," he continued, ignoring his mother. "Nothing but peace. Even if the afterlife is eternal sleep, what an amazing rest it will be."

In a rare moment of conversational awareness, his father turned away from the FOX News anchor. "What do you mean?"

"We all love a good sleep, right?" Damian wasn't used to being questioned by his father. It was his mother who usually dug for details. He pointed to the television. "You like the news. Imagine being able to watch the news all the time. Nonstop. Wouldn't that be enticing for you?"

"Damian," his mother whispered. She'd set aside her needlework, blood having drained from her face. "This talk of death is troubling."

"What?" He looked up at them both. "What do you mean? You think I want to kill myself?"

"You should speak with the elder. He'll know what to tell you. It's supper-time, but I'm sure he'll accommodate us."

She got up to search for the church elder's phone number, but Damian refused to be lured into a theological conversation. He wouldn't let religion trap him again.

"I still have some writing to do tonight for class." He got off the couch and headed for the door. "And work in the morning. I need to get going."

His father nodded, as if simply having things to do was enough to dissuade suicidal tendencies.

"Damian?" Drawers opened and closed in the kitchen, his mother frantically trying to find the church's contact tree. "Damian, where are you going?"

The angels trumpeted their arrival, causing several people in the crowd to jump. Their bright lights reflected off the Buick's windshield. Damian craned his neck to get a better view of the vehicle, noticing several oddities. Neither celestial beings nor clouds reflected off the glass. Instead, it was dark green, and intricate patterns had etched their way across its width. *Is the car...upside down?*

It occurred to Damian that his thoughts, like his red Buick, were not entirely intact.

After leaving his parents' house, he'd driven down Main Street toward his apartment. Throughout Minade's quaint downtown block, fall festival signage adorned lampposts. As he passed under the town's only stoplight, wreathed with colorful fake leaves like garland, he gritted his teeth at his parents' assumptions. He wasn't suicidal. Even if he was—*and who isn't a pinch morbid now and then?*—it was tough to abandon the idea that purposefully ending one's life was a one-way ticket to the wrong side of the ethereal tracks.

In the spasm of irritation, he failed to notice the combine harvester lumbering ahead of him. When his eyes refocused, he was close enough to read a sign affixed to the back: how's my driving?

I've never seen one on the back of a harvester. Is there a legitimate concern out in the cornfields? Dirty and aged, the number to call was no longer legible.

Damian had cut the Buick to the right to avoid rear-ending the green machine, watching in fascinated horror as he careened past the metallic appendages folded up toward the front. Relief flooded through him.

Then he hit a pumpkin stand set up at the city park's entrance.

The crowd parted as the angels bore down on Damian with the same ferocity he'd shown the winter squash. Their lights and trumpets amplified their glory. Only, they weren't angels. They were ambulances.

Damian couldn't recall when or how his car overturned, or what forces ejected him from the vehicle. *They must've been strong to be rid of my chubby figure. Perhaps I crawled away in case it caught fire?* As the fall breeze and green grass slipped from his senses, he glanced at his trusty Buick for the last time. His reflection glared back at him.

When the harsh-colored lights dimmed and sirens dulled to a whisper, Damian closed his eyes. The time had come to discover what, if anything, came next.

His second-to-last thought was of Alena.

The final was pumpkin pie.

CHAPTER TWO

BLEEP...BLEEP...BLEEP...

The monotonous sound pulled Damian into the conscious realm.

I was in an accident, he remembered, struggling to shake off remnants of darkness. From that void rose the image of a BMW wrapped around a telephone pole, its roadworthy days over. *No, not this time. I was driving the Buick.*

Another memory—Damian's dead-eyed reflection in the Buick's window—chased away his recollection of the totaled BMW.

Bleep...bleep...bleep...

I'm alive, he thought, recognizing the all-too-familiar chirping of an electrocardiogram. The heart monitor sounded ancient. A lethargic *bleep* instead of a crisp *beep*.

Damian imagined the ECG's plastic casing had yellowed over a decade ago, though he couldn't bear to open his eyes and verify. That same imagination painted gruesome states in which he might discover himself. *I must be at Minade Hospital.*

The local institution was not-for-profit. Church-operated for over a century. The facility had twenty-five beds and a reputation for issuing more harm than health to those who stepped through its doors.

Damian had never been to Minade's hospital. His parents dedicated themselves to the church that funded it, and while they certainly couldn't afford much health care, they were cognizant of the institution's notoriety. Unwilling to risk the welfare of their only offspring, they always took him to Peoria for any medical needs. To one of the big hospitals.

The ones with machines that go beep...beep...beep...

Alena's death had been quick, sparing her a lengthy hospital stay. The last time Damian spent time in a medical facility was after the BMW met its end.

"Colin..." he said.

"Your name is Damian Craig Hartter," said a voice into his right ear, sounding as though it had passed through sheaves of loose paper. Despite the dry tone, the accompanying breath was wet and bitingly cold against his face.

Damian opened his eyes, lids sluggish in their response. A bright light greeted him, making it difficult to see his surroundings.

An operating room? he wondered, grateful he couldn't confirm his mind's bloody scenarios. *Why would they wake me in the middle of surgery?*

Several figures leaned over him, cutting into the harsh illumination. As Damian's sight adjusted, he found three beautiful women staring down. The one who'd spoken into his ear had pale skin rarely caressed by the sun's rays. Another stood on his left, considerably shorter than her counterpart, with a face glowing with golden tones. The third woman, positioned at the crown of his head, reminded him so much of Alena that his breath caught in his throat.

The trio were nurses, though not of the variety he'd seen outside of television. Dressed in crisp white skirt uniforms, they'd tucked their long hair neatly under caps. The attire had all but disappeared by the 1980s, years before he was born, replaced with unisex scrubs. As alluring as his attendants were, the overly starched clothing emphasized an inhuman element about them. The lines of their faces were too sharp. Their eyes too focused. *Do people cosplay Nurse Ratched?*

Bleep...bleep...bleep... The languid sound continued its rhythmic pacing, not once changing. Damian thought his heart rate would've skyrocketed. Then he remembered ECGs didn't make noise unless there was a problem. An irregularity.

Like Colin.

The pale woman leaned back down to his ear. The light swayed behind her cap, revealing her pinned hair to be gray. Damian found that strange because she otherwise appeared youthful. Likely younger than himself.

With her ruby-red lips parting, he felt an icy breath against his skin once more. "Colin Eugene Cherry first passed through these halls many years ago. Your name is Damian Craig Hartter."

Damian choked. Neither Colin nor his family would've stepped foot inside Minade Hospital. They had the means to pursue only the best health care.

I'm not thinking straight. I have a concussion, he thought, straining to see past the figures. The harsh light caged his vision. All he sensed was the uncomfortable surface he lay upon, more like a metal table than a bed.

The shorter woman slammed her fists down, missing his face by an inch. The overhead light shifted until it hovered over her, highlighting more gray hair. "You are Damian Craig Hartter!"

Damian shrank under the fiery heat of her breath. It occurred to him that the statement was actually a question.

"Yes," he said, nodding with vigor. "Yes, I'm Damian."

The trio backed into Damian's peripheral vision, apparently satisfied. The harsh light darted away with them, leaving him in near darkness. With an unobstructed view, he expected to make out doctors in surgical masks and latex gloves, trays full of barbaric instruments, and that damn ECG. But nobody huddled around illuminated X-rays. No monitoring machines bleated out rhythmic bleeps.

What he saw just past his feet was a dull-gray wall with three rows of perfectly aligned, shiny square panels.

I'm in the morgue? Bile rose in his throat. Bile, or possibly... *It's not embalming fluid, you idiot*, he told himself.

"There's been a mistake," he called out to the nurses, his voice hoarse from the acid he kept swallowing down. He could see their vague outlines, but they did not respond. "Why am I here?"

Damian cautiously rolled his head back and forth. An emergency exit sign glowed to his left, now the only source of illumination. To his immense relief, he realized the panels on the wall were not the stainless-steel doors of a refrigerated mortuary cabinet, but flat-panel televisions.

I'm at work! He recognized what the company's owner called the Wall of Production.

Elation at not being in a morgue quickly burned itself out, replaced by the same dull ache he felt in his soul every time he walked by the screens. Each department's work was on display for all to see in statistical form, as well as data on how it all tied into profit. All employees had to pass by it each time they arrived and left work, went out for lunch, or used the restroom.

Damian considered the wall an incredible waste of money and resources, and he hadn't missed it once since he started working remotely.

Bleep...bleep...bleep... The rhythmic pattern was not electronic. Water pooled on the linoleum floor, fed by a leak in the ceiling.

I should get ahold of management. That needs to be fixed before it damages all those televisions.

The belief that a car accident had left him critically injured kept him still, and the thought of being shoved into a body-sized refrigerator froze him in terror. He couldn't conjure a reason the three women had transported him to Chicago, but assumed it meant his bodily harm was minimal. Management's number was at the receptionist's desk, so he made to sit up and hop off the table—and found he was paralyzed from the neck down.

"Help!" he choked out. His chest tightened, and nausea made the televisions spin. "Come back! What's going on? Why am I here?"

The trio returned, taking their former positions around his head. With them came the bright light, blotting out the array of screens. The luminescence cast long shadows over the nurses' faces, making it difficult to identify their distinguishing features. *Odd. They seemed so vivid a minute ago.*

Then it struck him, and it seemed impossible. He couldn't make out the women's appealing details because the features were no longer present. Smooth skin and sharp lines had aged decades, wrinkles and crevices creating the jagged shadows now darkening their faces.

Damian couldn't look away from them, refusing to believe their transformation. Even as he stared, though, the women's papery, translucent skin crumpled into swirling dust. Their entire bodies lost cohesion, held in place by the stark white nursing uniforms. The caps couldn't contain their pinned gray hair, which came undone and draped haphazardly over lumpy shoulders.

The hair of old crones. As the thought crossed his mind, portions of the living dust clouds reconstituted into leathery skin, phasing between solid and amorphous.

Very old crones! He wasn't even certain they were women or anything natural. Worst of all, once their eyes swept away into the grime, they never again solidified, leaving only hollow caverns for him to stare into.

The crone to his left squatted down, sooty lips solidifying as they brushed against his ear. The golden tones of her skin had disappeared, replaced with layers of folded flesh and swirling gray ash. Her breath remained hot. When she spoke, the harsh light once again drifted over her head.

"When were you born?"

Damian wanted to answer. It was a simple question. His own lips refused to move, and all he managed was an unintelligible grunt.

"When were you born?" she asked again, her voice returning to a thunderous boom.

"Ma-March 18, 1991," he finally said.

The light source shifted directly over Damian's face as the woman straightened. All three figures appeared to study him, though it was difficult to be certain now that they didn't have eyes. Damian thought—wished—one of them would hold up a hand and ask how many fingers he saw. It was a last-ditch hope he was suffering a debilitating concussion. That he was imagining or misinterpreting this entire experience.

Perhaps I'll get some Jell-O when this is over, he wondered, his thoughts unraveling. *Do they make pumpkin Jell-O?*

What the trio ended up doing, the question they asked, he never would've foreseen. "When did you find faith in the Creator?"

Damian fumbled with the query. Medical personnel didn't ask such things. Not in such a strange fashion, at least. Minade Hospital assumed you were born into faith.

"I-I'm not sure." He stumbled for the answer as the crones drew in close. They increased in size, loose flesh falling away into currents of grit. Afraid they would unleash a wave of fury, he said, "I really don't know. I just grew up with it."

I hope they don't ask when I lost my faith! He remembered that clearly. He'd been lying next to Alena when—

The nurse at the top of his head, the one who had reminded Damian of his wife, bent over so her hollow eye sockets hovered above his face. The light gave her a luminous crown. She whispered, "Have you ever seen Satan?"

"What?"

"Formerly known as Lucifer."

"The TV show?" Damian asked, brows furrowed. Without eyes to connect with, he fought the urge to squeeze his own shut. He was certain that if he did, something would crawl out of the caverns and drop onto his face.

"Have you ever served Satan?"

"Wha-what?"

"Are you a member of the opposition?" the crone bellowed. Her breath was a combination of the others', simultaneously hot and cold.

"No!" Damian said, his bewilderment erupting under a mountain of panic. If his bladder hadn't already contracted, he was certain the three women would soon slip across the linoleum floor.

"Have you ever spoken to them?" she asked, still screaming.

"Of course not!"

"Have they ever spoken to you?"

"No!"

The woman on his right squatted, joints audibly popping. She whispered into his ear, though he couldn't tell if she was being sinister or seductive. "Did they send you here in the guise of Damian Craig Hartter?"

"Here?" he said, trying to gesticulate at their surroundings. When his arms failed to move, he settled for rolling his eyes around. "Sent to this shit-hole place?"

The trio continued peering down at him. They made no noise. Only the wet *bleep...bleep...bleep...* serenaded them.

Finally, he hissed at them through gritted teeth, "I am myself."

"That is for us to ascertain." The three fell silent. As if they'd exhausted the energy it took to maintain cohesion, each started to fade away. The overhead light darted between them in a frantic pattern, obscured by the women's scattering dust.

"Why am I at work?" Damian whispered, afraid his exhalation would hasten their disintegration. Halfway through the question, his mental faculties abruptly dulled.

Did they drug me? A chill made its way through his body, and a disturbing thought occurred to him. He glanced down toward his toes, verifying he was on a solid surface and not submerged in a tub of ice.

"Are you stealing my kidneys?" It was difficult to form words.

"We did not take your kidneys," the crone to his left said with indifference. "They are intact and may continue to function for many years."

The one at his crown chimed in, "As will several of your other organs."

"Why do you envision yourself at work?" said the one to his right. "That is a question you must ask yourself. The plane in which you are located is distinctly different from the one you are accustomed to, and much of what you perceive and experience here is of your own making."

"Collectively speaking," they said together.

"Who are you?" The darkness from which his mind had escaped minutes ago threatened to overtake him once more.

"We are the Gray Ones, and we watch the way in."

"The way into where?" he said, words slurring.

What remained of the trio disappeared into the shadows. Even if they had responded, Damian wouldn't have heard. Waves of exhaustion overwhelmed him, pulling him further from the conscious world.

"No, wait... I don't..." he said into his shoulder as his head rolled to the side. All his muscles went slack, and heavy eyelids closed.

The single energetic light blinked out. As the dark depths enveloped his mind, Damian uttered one more question. "Am I in?"

The only answer was a damp *bleep...bleep...bleep...*

CHAPTER THREE

DAMIAN SAT STRAIGHT UP in bed, screaming at visions of webbed glass and vaporous clouds. Sheets and blankets tangled around him. He fumbled and rolled, trying to shake himself loose.

"Calm down, Damian," said a voice from the other side of the bedding. A steadying hand pressed against his back, saving him from tumbling off the mattress.

"What's going on? Where am I?" Calmness was a hard state to attain, even as the nightmarish imagery receded into the hazy memory of dreams. He trembled as someone peeled away layers of linen. "Did I make it in?"

A small parting in the blankets appeared before Damian. He dove toward it with both hands, widening the hole and pulling his head and body through.

"Yes, you made it in." The voice came from behind him. It was familiar, gentle, yet firm. "You're going to be fine. You're home."

As Damian turned, he knew he was not home. His place was tiny and cramped, with a single window overlooking a parking lot. The bedroom he was currently in was spacious, with high ceilings and several windows providing a view of magnificent trees and distant mountains. *The Midwest is flat. Not a mountain to be—*

For a terrifying moment, Damian believed he'd left one horror only to enter another. One of the beautiful nurses had manifested in this new space. The one who reminded him of his wife. At least, before the monstrosity had lost its eyeballs.

The woman hadn't styled or pinned back her brown hair. Rather, she'd pulled it back into a hastily tied ponytail, highlighting a pretty face sprinkled with freckles and a set of dark, present eyes.

This *was* his wife, not a trick of light or deceit. Her posture, her casual confidence, the comforting hand on his back... He could only associate them with Alena. No impostor could've replicated all her characteristics.

But if she was here, that meant he was...

"A pen?" Damian blurted out. A choked laugh escaped him as he grabbed her other hand. The skin was warm and smooth. "A *pen*?"

"Well, it was more original than a car accident," said a smirking Alena. "You haven't seen Colin in over a decade, and yet you're still imitating him!"

Damian stared at the grin, not wanting to look away from her face again. He thought he should be in shock. Frozen in consternation. His zombie wife sat healthily in front of him, appearing exactly the way she had the last time he saw her, down to the jeans and oversized maroon hoodie.

Instead of panic, he found himself pleasantly bewildered. Equally surprising was the giggle he couldn't contain. He covered his mouth with a hand as laughter burst through his lips. It built upon itself, and he nearly rolled over in a fit. Alena pulled him into a tight embrace, sheer delight on her face.

"I—I can't believe this," Damian said once the laughter subsided. "I never thought I'd see you again."

"Really?" She peered at him quizzically. The smile never left her face, and it was the most beautiful thing he'd ever seen. "You believed in this, though. You were prepared for it."

"I used to." He interlaced his fingers with hers, relishing her touch. He remembered the nurses—the Gray Ones—asking when he found his faith. "But I lost that belief, Alena. I remember when it happened."

The moment came shortly after he and Alena had graduated from university, but before the wedding. They'd gone to bed early, getting extra rest before job interviews the next day. Alena was already asleep, snoring softly, and he'd just finished reciting his nightly prayer.

And then it hit him. Concrete certainty that his words, the thoughts he'd been sending into the ether every day, were actually going into a void. No one was listening to him. Nothing was going to answer.

"No." Alena shook her head, a few strands of hair falling out of her ponytail. "You remember when you made a conscious decision to push back against things you grew up believing, but the journey to that point took place over a long time."

Even before Damian had left for Chicago, the statutes by which he lived were crumbling under their own demanding weight. By the time he was sleeping next to Alena, he questioned exactly where those decrees originated. Even then, he told himself that, no matter the implausibility of a higher power, organized religion was something worth participating in. He still sent up the ritualistic prayer every night. A force of habit, an act akin to carrying a lucky rabbit's foot.

Might have been something to all that after all.

"But you never believed in life after death, and I let go of that fantasy." Damian gestured at the enormous room. "Are flames about to consume us?"

"Of course not! You've made it to the good side." Alena stood up, pulling him out of bed and toward the nearest window. The grand vista struck him with wonder. Snowcapped purple mountains graced the skyline. At their base was a serene lake surrounded by a forest of giant coniferous trees. "But you should set aside your assumptions about the Afterlife. This place is nothing like you expected. Even while much of it is of our own making."

"The Gray Ones," he said, lowering his head.

"Hmm?"

Damian shook his head, attempting to clear the fog from the pool of dim memory. Like trying to recollect a dream, the more he sought to recall the details, the fuzzier they became. "The Gray Ones said something similar. About how everything we see and experience here is our own doing."

"I've never heard of them." Alena frowned. "After my death, I woke up in my grandfather's arms knowing where I was and that everything was okay."

"Maybe it was a hallucination. My brain trying to make sense of what was happening." He gave one last attempt to piece it all together. He could understand the mortuary cabinet, but not the Wall of Production or...

Something about my kidneys? And what does any of that have to do with a car accid—

"Oh, shit!" Damian turned away from the view. "They're going to think this was a suicide."

"What? Who?" Alena had been heading toward a door, but looked back in concern.

"My parents. I was with them right before it happened," Damian said. "I mentioned something about how I'd love to see you and Colin again. They weren't sure where the thought was coming from—or leading. Caused a bit of an argument."

"Your poor mother!" She pulled open the door and stepped through. He followed suit, finding himself on a spacious and brightly lit second-floor landing. Despite the apparent space for multiple rooms, there was only one other door. Tucked away on the side, it was closed. Without even knowing the purpose of the room it led to, Damian felt an unexpected animosity toward it.

"I don't understand why you're still defending her." He followed Alena down a sweeping staircase. "You realize she hated you?"

"Your mother didn't hate me. She never liked me, true. Disapproved, certainly. But not hate. She was only concerned for your well-being. And who could blame her? You look just like her. Not as tall, but somewhere in the face."

"Alena." Damian trailed behind as she made her way through an open foyer. A library lay beyond one archway, and another led to an elaborately set dining table. Though this was his first time walking through it, the floor plan rang with familiarity. "Where are we? What is this place?"

Alena glanced back at him, a sparkle in her eye and the usual smirk on her lips. Then she stepped through the back of the foyer into his favorite room of any house: the kitchen. As he took in the ample space filled with modern appliances, skillets and pans, and an array of cooking utensils, she wrapped herself around his left arm. "We're home, babe."

Over their earthly years together, the couple spent Sunday mornings drinking coffee on the couch and discussing their future. They dedicated much conversation to the type of home they would grow old in. It had been a bonding exercise. A way to get to know each other better. Their wants and desires. *Alena has made my ideal home a reality.*

As she continued the tour through the house, though, what he *didn't* find occasionally dismayed him. The bathroom, for example, was as large as the bedroom and equipped with a whirlpool, a soaking tub, and a walk-in shower with twelve nozzles. Of all the amenities the bathroom contained, it lacked a toilet. Alena told him there were no toilets in the entire household. The need for one didn't exist.

"Unless you're into that," she said with a shrug before moving on with the expedition.

Other than the kitchen, the library enamored Damian the most. Bookshelves lined every wall, crammed full of texts. A wooden ladder was close at hand to peruse the loftier manuscripts.

"You'll find all your favorite books on that shelf." Alena gestured to a readily accessible area. "Even the silly one about dinosaurs."

"Michael Crichton is *not* silly, and neither are his books!"

Alena ignored him, pointing to the next shelf over. On it sat around thirty leather-bound books. "More importantly, there's your autobiographical series."

"But I didn't write my biography."

"Technically, no. Nobody writes this type of series," she said. "But they're automatically created and filled as your earthly thoughts and events occur."

Damian cringed at the idea. "Must be the most boring work ever written."

"Not the chapters I'm in." Alena gave him a sly look, walking over to a similar shelf with another set of books, presumably her own series. Selecting a volume at random, she absently flipped through its pages. "These really are interesting, though I'll warn you not to reminisce too long over your past life. My grandfather... Well, I'm grateful he took the time to welcome me here."

While Alena read through some paragraphs, Damian wandered around the library, scanning the spines of a hundred books. None of the titles stuck out, though his mind was in a daze. Not as much as he expected after crossing the barrier between life and death, for waking up to a nonchalant tour of his dream home by his wife, but his mind was still parsing this new reality. It kept circling back around to a bump in logic. His brain, trained after years of programming, took issue with a faulty line of code.

Unable to identify the source of his brain fog, he asked, "I'm guessing this isn't everything?"

Alena snapped the volume closed, returning it to the shelf. "No. Today is for you to adapt to the Afterlife. Your end was traumatic. Not everyone reacts as calmly as you have. For now, enjoy the things you dreamed about in life."

Damian waited for the—

"But," she continued. "There's so much more ahead of you. For both of us! As great as this home is, sitting around waiting for family and friends to arrive would get tedious. No, there's an entire world out there to interact with and jobs to perform."

"But I don't want to work!" He was immediately skeptical. Part of his notion of perfection was exiting the soul-crushing machine that was the American dream.

Alena shrugged. "You don't have to, but work is available for those who need something to do. Can you imagine billions of souls aimlessly milling around? Utter chaos."

"What have you been doing? I don't suppose there's a flourishing book market here."

"As a matter of fact—and you'll be interested to know—our authors can't create new works fast enough to keep up with demand. But no, I didn't pursue editing." The impish look that seemingly always graced the corner of Alena's mouth disappeared, replaced by exuberance. "I work in childcare."

This revelation did not surprise Damian. His wife had always adored children and possessed the mothering instinct. However, that desire—that drive—was the one constant rift in their relationship. Alena's strong personality gave her an edge in their disagreements, and she usually got her way. When it came to having kids, though, Damian never budged. He didn't want them.

The bump in logic, the faulty line of code, suddenly crystallized in his mind. The spacious home with the gourmet kitchen and expansive library was *his* dream, not hers. Alena would've been content with a space the size of the bedroom.

"Fewer rooms to clean, the better," she'd say over their Sunday-morning discussions. "Less space for clutter to creep."

Alena's pursuit of a career in childcare made sense. It fed into a want he had steadfastly denied her in life.

She created this home for us, knowing it would make me happy. But at the expense of her own joy? How can our expectations overlap? Or the wishes of billions of people?

Damian's thought process circled back on itself, going round and round. At the center of that whirlpool was the second door located off the upstairs landing. That door wasn't for him.

"It's sad," Alena said, interrupting his mental crash. The sorrow in her voice was palpable. "Many of the children I help have been around for hundreds of years. They're not allowed to mature into adults until a member of their family arrives, which can take a while. Sometimes, it never happens."

"That's terrible! Why aren't they allowed to grow up?"

"It's a strange rule that's always been in place." Alena's voice was bitter. "These children have been separated from their relatives, and now they're not allowed full access to the Afterlife. Some people think they should only mature with family guidance. I think that's ridiculous, especially for the kids who've been here for centuries. It's not fair to them! Especially when there are plenty of folks willing to take them in."

Damian drew her into an embrace. Alena could be passionate about a cause, but she rarely revealed the emotions an issue stirred within her. Instead, she channeled that energy into solutions. "Sounds like you have a very important job."

"I like it." She took a deep breath, gave him a squeeze, then pulled away. "You'll be able to pick any line of work you want."

"Where do I even start looking?"

"You might get some ideas tomorrow morning at the Orientation of the Dead." Alena took hold of his arm and urged him toward the foyer. "It's in the Celestial City. I know how much you hate getting up before ten, but it's early in the morning."

"What kind of afterlife allows such travesties?" In truth, with terms like *Orientation of the Dead* and *Celestial City*, his earlier cognitive disarray was giving way to imaginative flare. "What will this presentation cover?"

"It's an *orientation*, not a presentation," she said, still tugging on his arm. "Getting used to this place can be a process, and there are certain dos and don'ts. You'll learn some things that'll help you acclimate. Stuff I would never remember to tell you. Like peregrination."

"Peregrination?"

"You know, I don't remember being this inquisitive when I first arrived here." Alena let go of his arm and made her way up the stairwell, fingers trailing on the banister. "You may not feel it yet, but you're probably overwhelmed by all this. So don't worry about tomorrow. Just relax for now. Tell me all you've been up to. It's been a very long time, and I've missed you."

You have no idea. Damian forced his concerns and questions aside as he followed her up the stairs and back to their bedroom. It *had* been a long time, and he was eager to continue their reunion.

CHAPTER FOUR

"Is that... Is that mine?" Damian stood on the front porch, a cup of coffee frozen halfway to his lips. He'd gone straight for the kitchen to brew a pot after rolling out of bed. Fatigue wasn't an issue. Never had he been more awake and alert. Few things brought him more joy than starting a new day with a good cup of joe.

Inhaling rich aromas from the mug in his hand, he'd stepped outside, intent on examining the grounds surrounding their house. The view was spectacular. Tall grasses sprawled for acres, bordered by enormous trees in the distance. The atmosphere possessed an autumn hue, though nothing was dying. Not a single crisp leaf littered the ground, nor was there a patch of brown grass. Deep colors saturated the surroundings like morning dew. Even the sky itself radiated an amber hue.

Despite the light, the horizon was devoid of a rising sun. *I suppose the Afterlife isn't on a planet. And light doesn't require a source?*

And then Damian's gaze had fallen upon the—

"I certainly didn't get it for myself!" Alena appeared beside him. She held a cup of her own, filled with steaming Earl Grey. "Went my entire life without one, and there's no need for them here. Still, I'd say it's *ours*. I thought you'd like it."

"I *love* it!" He jumped off the porch, coffee slopping over the sides of the mug, and strutted toward a black Chevrolet Camaro.

After it had been absent from the market for years, Chevrolet redesigned and reintroduced the pony car in 2010. Damian fell in love with its predatory lines. He imagined racing the SS trim down country roads, the growl of a V8 engine startling crows in the fields.

Once he escaped Minade, Damian hadn't followed the Camaro's yearly tweaks and upgrades. Still, he could tell the model currently parked in their driveway was a recent design. The lines were more refined, though its rapacious disposition was uncompromised.

"Your orientation begins in a few minutes," Alena said, interrupting his third circuit around the vehicle. "I put some clothes on the bed for you to change into."

Damian pouted, wanting to inspect the car's interior. Through the window, he could see it was unlike the Buick Century in every way. Power seats and locks. Premium leather trim. Windows without screwdrivers jammed alongside to keep in place. *I bet the engine doesn't require five attempts to turn over.*

"How'd you get ready so fast?" He noticed her gray slacks and blue sweater—clothing she would've worn to the *Chicago Tribune*. She'd released her hair from its ponytail, letting it drape over her shoulders. "Er, I mean, you look really nice."

"Thanks." She rolled her eyes behind the tea's steam. "We can change clothing with a thought. The trick takes time to master, and we need to get going."

"Okay, okay. I'll be right back." Damian scooted inside the house, returning his cup to the kitchen before heading to the bedroom. He took the stairs two at a time, pleased the exertion didn't leave him out of breath.

A pair of jeans and a Henley waited for him on the bed. Not as chic as what Alena wore, but she always felt most comfortable in public dressed professionally.

Give me comfort any day of the week, he thought while changing clothes.

Back outside, he stopped short halfway down the driveway to the Camaro. Alena sat behind the wheel, and he sputtered in protest.

"You realize this car isn't actually a car? That its wheels won't hit true asphalt? Take a seat, babe. You don't know how to drive this thing yet." She gave him a crooked smile through the open window. "Besides, you don't know where we're going."

"The Celestial City, duh." He opened the passenger-side door. Before settling into the bucket seat, he noticed the lack of a fuel hatch along the side of the vehicle.

No need for gas or an oil change. It was difficult for him to accept that the car, like the light in the sky, could run without a source of energy.

"We live in the boonies, thousands of miles from the city." Alena slipped on a pair of sunglasses. She pressed the engine's start button. The resultant roar brought delight to Damian's ears. After maneuvering out of the driveway, she accelerated down the open road. "I'm not even sure where the city is."

Damian gripped the sides of his seat as they drove around a series of hills, the wheels hugging the twisting road without slowing. "Isn't the orientation about to start?"

"You're right." She glanced at the dashboard clock. With a firm grip, she took hold of his left wrist. "We don't want to be late. Ready to peregrinate?"

"You said that yesterday. What exactly is—"

The hills and trees lining the road disappeared into a smear of green, gold, and purple. The road twisted and turned until he no longer knew what direction they headed. Alena's hands no longer held the steering wheel, which jerked left and right of its own volition. Momentum built, and his body pressed deep into his seat. Moving was difficult, and speaking was useless. The scenery drowned out his words as they whooshed by.

Then the vehicle snapped back to normal speed, and a massive wall exploded into view in front of them.

"That's peregrination." Alena's usual smirk was now a full-on grin. "You'll notice we didn't fly out of the car at the end. I know that's your specialty."

"You're superbly hilarious." Damian's hands clutched at his chest. He forced himself to relax, mildly disquieted to discover he had no heartbeat. With his chin, he indicated what lay ahead. "What's that?"

The road led them out of a dense forest and right up to a set of thick wooden doors, the only visible passage through a wall of what appeared to be diamond.

Thirty feet high, the barricade stretched across the horizon. The polished stones shimmered with every color, dazzling his eyes. Its surreal beauty looked out of place in the middle of the woods.

"The Celestial Wall and, naturally, the Celestial Gate."

Even she's put off by the lack of originality.

"Diamonds are the strongest rocks on Earth," Alena said. "Here, they represent the city's impenetrability."

"And what exactly are they?" Damian nodded at a pair of creatures standing on either side of the gate. They were like humans, though nearly twice as tall and gaunt. Dressed in flowing robes of dark, muted colors, they stood as still as statues.

"Guardians," Alena said. Then, lowering her voice: "They're the closest things to what we think of as angels. Just don't call them that. Guardians are warriors, protectors of the city."

The two Guardians looked like kings of old, complete with ornate crowns on their heads.

Old kings suffering from severe malnutrition. Definitely not the chubby, cheery cherubim I'm used to seeing in art.

"No wings?"

Alena shook her head, then shrugged. "I haven't seen a pair of wings, but that doesn't mean they don't have them."

Damian studied the Guardians as she drove forward. The forlorn pair tilted their heads toward the vehicle, considering them in return, then turned and pushed open the thick doors.

After spending a quiet day surrounded by forest, books, and coffee, Damian was ill-prepared for the Celestial City. Its scale daunted him. Miles of structures built on top of one another. On the outskirts, buildings were elementary in design—simple boxes lined up next to one another. But closer to the center, they became larger and more intricate. A mammoth castle, featuring bastions, barbicans, and buttresses that could've inspired a hundred fantasy tales, stood at the heart of the city. He admired the architecture, though puzzled over the defensive elements.

Thousands of structures filled Damian's view, though their matching design impressed him. White stone walls, trimmed in gold, caught the soft amber light. Only one building differed. A smaller castle sat next to the massive central one. It had the same defensive features, but its stone was plain gray.

The streets were brick, each piece painstakingly laid. The sheer number of people flocking across them, even at the edge of the city, put Chicago to shame. Within his view, hundreds of individuals walked in and out of shops, sipped drinks on pavilions, or congregated in large groups. He gawked as they passed by people from hundreds of Earth's cultures and time periods. Some wore capes. Others, tall hats. A few wore nothing at all.

As Alena drove through a myriad of avenues and lanes, the most striking individuals were those who couldn't have come from any of Earth's cultures or time periods. Green-skinned folk, gelatinous blobs, and walking lampposts mingled in the crowds.

"What is that? Who are they? Are you telling me aliens exist?" Damian kept up a steady stream of questions, face pressed against the Camaro's narrow window. Alena only smiled in return, keeping her eyes fixed on the road ahead.

The Celestial City possessed one characteristic Damian found lacking in other urban municipalities he'd visited: cleanliness. With throngs of people walking the streets, he expected to see trash, dirt, and general wear. Instead, everything was astonishingly immaculate. No cracks marred the mortar holding everything together. He deeply associated tidiness with beauty.

After a few minutes of navigating, they arrived at an immense building covering several city blocks. Round and squat with a domed roof, it resembled a sports stadium. Numerous entrances lined the exterior wall, people lining up by each.

The place looks like it seats over two hundred thousand. Damian wondered what the average number of daily deaths was.

Alena parked the car in a small, vacant lot, then they joined a line. It took only a minute before they entered a curved stone hallway running the perimeter of the building. Mounted torches lined the wall, but the interior was dim. Damian's eyes took a moment to adjust. The main auditorium was no better.

Hundreds of sconces zigzagged along the walls, their illumination unable to penetrate the darkness of what he assumed to be the concave ceiling.

"Over there." Alena pointed to a row of empty seats near a small stage at the massive room's center. The dais was the only well-lit area, meant to focus eyes on the imposing figure standing there. The twelve-foot-tall Guardian wore elegant maroon robes of the same style as the two at the Gate. Braided dark hair hovered a few inches off the ground and was topped with a single-jeweled crown.

Before Damian could suggest a more distant alternative—he was never the student sitting at the front of a classroom—Alena was already heading down a set of stairs. As he hurried to catch up, the murmurs of the crowd caught his ear. He kept hearing the same questions again. Some of them were familiar. He'd been asking them himself.

"Do you know why we're here?"

"Will the Creator show up?"

"How did you die?"

"Damn motorcycle came out of nowhere!"

As though waiting specifically for Damian and Alena, the Guardian spoke as soon as they took their seats. "Welcome, and good morning. My name is Athan, and this is my associate Mai."

The gaunt figure turned and gestured toward another individual Damian hadn't noticed. Standing just outside the light bathing the dais, Mai shared the starved features of the other Guardians, as well as their style of dress and long, braided hair. The shadows etched across Mai's face portrayed displeasure at being there.

"We will be the orators of this Orientation of the Dead."

Athan's voice was monotone and devoid of emotion, reminding Damian of his university statistics professor. *She was just as likely to doze off from her own dry timbre as the students.* Damian hoped to make it through this new discourse fully conscious.

"Every one of you woke up within the last seventy-two hours in the Afterlife, a wholly distinct reality from that to which you are accustomed." Athan turned slowly, head bobbing as though trying to look each person in the face. "It may appear and feel familiar to your senses, but it is an illusion. The fabric of the Afterlife's reality has been translated into something your mind can comprehend."

An ingratiating fella, Damian thought. He shifted in his chair—or at least what appeared to be a chair.

"This being your first excursion into the city, you were likely confronted with the fact that humanity was never alone," Athan said. "The only universe in which you were at the center was the one inside your own minds."

Mai stepped forward, gesturing toward the middle of the dais. Millions of tiny golden lights burst into view. They swirled around the Guardians before coalescing into a semi-transparent facsimile of the Celestial City. The glittering castle at the center loomed over hundreds of miniature buildings. Damian could see that the wall encompassed the entire city, and that the gate appeared to be the only way in or out.

"Are you seeing this?" He nudged Alena. "It *is* a presentation!"

"The Celestial City sits at the center of all Creation. All planes of existence intersect here." Athan walked around the model. "You can move about within your reality, the human Afterlife."

With a flick of Mai's wrist, a sheet of golden particles drifted away from the city, forming a flat, thin disk. It briefly reminded Damian of the icy fragments orbiting Saturn, but the specks of light continued drifting out into the audience. People reached out, grabbing at the particles, disappointed when the gold dots passed right through their hands.

"Thousands of separate planes exist alongside yours," Athan said. Additional particle sheets appeared, eliciting gasps as the entire auditorium lit up. Damian had just enough time to notice the room's ceiling was concave before his eyes fixed on the brilliant flecks in front of him. They weren't just spots of light, but moving representations of stars, worlds, and creatures. He grabbed at a diorama of a gorgeous waterfall in the middle of a forest, but the image defied his form as easily as everyone else's.

I always thought that if an omnipotent being pulled the universe's strings, then it was too creative and powerful to dedicate all its energies to humanity. Damian believed such an entity would have multiple planets—perhaps universes—populated with intelligent creatures. Each project would be distinct from one another, revealing different facets of its creator's mind.

"Interaction between planes is prohibited, except where they all intersect within the city." The delicate layers of light were so tightly packed together around the room that Damian couldn't see the dais. "It is here at the hub of Creation that the Embassy assists in collaboration between geneses."

The concentric disks dissipated, withdrawing their light from the outer reaches of the auditorium until just the miniature of the city remained.

Alena leaned over while Athan continued speaking, whispering into his ear, "The Embassy is billions of years old, created long before humans. It fosters social events and cooperative undertakings. As the number of projects increased, they added additional branches to accommodate them. Most planes now have their own."

"Sounds bureaucratic."

Alena nodded. "The Embassy has taken on more duties over time. I don't know a lot about the other branches, but ours regulates activities and keeps tabs on individuals' whereabouts—whether here or on Earth."

"Here or on Earth?"

Before Alena could explain, Athan coughed abruptly. Both of them glanced at the dais, startled to find the Guardian staring back. Dark, scrutinizing eyes looked over them, made more intense by the sudden quiet in the auditorium.

"The Embassy plays only a small part in the social fabric of your Afterlife. Some of your new abilities, like peregrination, have been purposefully limited to encourage interaction with others." Athan resumed a slow pace around the stage. In the background, Mai waved a hand, disappearing the light particles. "One of your new gifts is the ability to materialize simple, practical items. All you need to do is visualize the object in your mind and..."

The Guardian lifted an arm. A carpenter's hammer phased into existence in the palm of Athan's hand. Another round of delighted gasps, and thousands of people reached out their hands to attempt the trick themselves.

"Unless you are a Guardian, you cannot materialize objects within certain spaces. This building is one such location."

Damian swore he saw the corners of both Guardians' mouths twitch upward at the disappointed groans from the crowd.

In the same expressionless voice, Athan explained the fuzzy line between what they could and couldn't forge with their minds. The more intricate and useful the item, the more likely it was they'd have to find it outside their homes. *An introvert's nightmare.* Social interaction was, as the Guardian put it, the bedrock of society.

"The general edicts by which you lived are the same ones you will continue following," Athan said, explaining that they couldn't slander, maim, or kill one another. Damian wondered over the latter, considering they were already dead. "While these rules are formally in place, there is little need to enforce them. It should seem unnatural for you to consider acting contrarily. You are the good human souls, after all."

Damian thought of Gregory, a Yorkshire Terrier that lived in the Chicago apartment neighboring his and Alena's. The tiny dog barked shrilly at two in the morning, every morning. And every morning, Damian imagined chasing the canine off the building's roof. True to the Guardian's word, he couldn't conjure a murderous thought regarding Gregory. After a few moments, he wondered why he was even trying.

"We understand everyone makes mistakes, accidentally breaks a decree now and then." Athan peered sternly into the audience. "If we believe a penalty is deserved, imprisonment within the Dungeon of Darkness will be implemented."

Mai gestured from the shadows, and light particles burst into view again. Rather than producing a replica of the Celestial City or highlighting the cosmos, the specks formed an image of a monolithic golden rock. It covered the entire stage, stretching up to the ceiling like a skyscraper. *Is the display broken?*

Others in the auditorium shared Damian's sentiments, and their jubilant murmurs pivoted to concern. Damian wondered what situations might arise that would lead to incarceration. *The stern Guardians, mighty protectors of the Celestial Gate, must exist for a reason.*

"Rest assured, the dungeon has not been needed or used since before the Great Ascension, and I have no doubt it will continue to be unused for the foreseeable future. I should also warn you," Athan said, words laced with a hint of annoyance, "not to enter the dungeon of your own accord. Not unless you plan on spending a great deal of time there."

The Guardian continued to speak, but Damian's mind wandered. His adventurous side, the part that loved to explore every street of Chicago and try each restaurant he came across, was kicking in. He knew with certainty that he would visit the Dungeon of Darkness. It sounded mysterious. *So un-celestial.*

"Before we adjourn this Orientation of the Dead," Athan finished, "we encourage you to sign your name in the Grand Book of Appointments. It will be your only chance to meet the Creator and ask your one question."

Athan strode off the dais and disappeared down a dark hallway. Mai quickly followed, appearing eager to escape attention.

"My one question?" Damian asked, but tens of thousands of people standing and shuffling toward their exit drowned out his words. The building was better designed than most stadiums, with dozens of stairwells, ramps, and outlets. In a matter of minutes, they were standing in the outer hallway.

"Over here." Alena tugged at his arm. She directed him to one of the several lines forming throughout the dim hall. At the head of each was a podium supporting an enormous book.

"What's this for?"

"Weren't you listening?" Alena craned her neck, looking back into the dark auditorium. "You need to make an appointment to meet with the Creator."

Damian gulped. "I actually get to see the Creator?"

When she didn't answer, he repeated himself.

"Hmm? Oh, yes. A personal one-on-one. You'll be able to ask one question—anything at all—and it'll be answered."

A flood of queries consumed Damian. *What's the meaning of life? Where do lost socks go? Why do people feel the need to ruin desserts by putting fruit in them? Except pumpkin pie. That's always delicious.*

He wondered what Alena had asked. The distant look in her eyes told him now was not the time to ask.

"What's up with you? You seem preoccupied."

"Something said during the orientation." She pushed him forward as the line advanced. "I'll tell you about it in the car."

A minute later, Damian was peeking over the shoulder of the woman in front of him to get his first look at the Grand Book of Appointments. It appeared to be old and dusty, with thick pieces of yellowed paper. As he watched, names scrawled into existence next to corresponding dates and times. He guessed some kind of magical network linked all the books throughout the building. *Predecessor of the Internet.*

The woman, having signed her name, turned and handed him a large fountain pen. He flinched, reminded of the device that had cut Alena's life short, then accepted it. The first open slot he found in the book was eleven days away. He quickly signed his name before someone else could take it.

Back in the Camaro, Alena finally opened up. "Something about the presentation struck me as odd."

"You mean *orientation?*" Damian poked her arm.

"Shut up, Damian. You remember Athan saying all planes intersect here in the Celestial City?"

He nodded.

"It's not an untrue statement, but it's not wholly accurate." Alena held out her hand and stared intensely at the palm. After a few seconds, two Lincoln pennies appeared. They were joined as a single object, one running perpendicular down the other's middle.

"Imagine that each penny represents a plane of reality. You can see they meet at the center. But they also intersect along this entire line." She ran her finger along one of the ninety-degree corners. "Outside the Celestial City."

Damian's eyes widened, though he wasn't sure what his wife was insinuating. If they weren't supposed to interact with other planes beyond the wall, surely there were other safeguards in place.

"What does it mean?"

"I don't know." The pennies vanished. "It's probably nothing, though it feels like a basic lapse in logic."

The way she said it, Damian doubted it meant nothing. When she started the Camaro, though, the roar of the engine drove her concerns away from his mind.

CHAPTER FIVE

Alone at the house, Damian stared into a wall mirror in the foyer. *One of those mirrors people check for bits of food in their teeth before rushing out.* He wasn't looking for masticated salad, though. Instead, he alternatively reached out and touched the glass, cool against his fingertips, and caressed the warm skin of his face. Both surfaces were solid, as expected. But his skin—his true, original body—was in a mortuary freezer in Minade Hospital, *as cold as this mirror.*

The perfection of his body's reproduction unsettled Damian, but its detailed accuracy also disappointed him. While Alena had metabolized through any meal with ease, his increasing waistline forced him to buy new pants every year. It was another reason he never understood claims of resemblance between him and his mother. She was tall and thinner than Alena. His height was average, weighed down by a belly that would one day droop over his belt.

Would have drooped over my belt. Damian pinched his side. *Vanity, it seems, is not exclusive to the living.*

When he was a young churchgoer, he often imagined what the afterlife would be like. Actually, since the elders preached of golden streets lined with precious stones, he mostly thought about what he'd be able to *do* in the afterlife. Fantastical abilities like peregrination. In all the tales he dreamed up, he never considered repeats of earthly concerns like body image.

Damian saw in his reflection a piece of paper clutched in his hand. It had brought him as much delight as waking up to Alena after death, but it also created the same mental discord he experienced during the tour she'd given of their home.

Minutes prior, Damian had been enjoying a breakfast omelet at the kitchen island. The doorbell rang halfway through the meal. He leaped from his seat and made for the front—checking his teeth in the foyer mirror before opening the door.

On the porch was a wiry old man dressed in a light gray button-up shirt and blue slacks. A sweater coat of the same azure hue, fastened with brass buttons, gave the man an official look.

"Hello!" Damian said.

"Well, hello to you, too," said the visitor in an equally jovial tone. A bushy handlebar mustache bobbed as he spoke. "My name is Jim Parsons. Thought I'd introduce myself. I'm your mail carrier."

Damian blinked, certain that Jim was going to pull a Sears catalog out of the leather messenger bag hanging from his shoulder. *Do failed corporations live on in perpetuity, too?*

"Somebody needs to deliver the mail," Jim said when Damian asked for clarification. "No matter how little of it there may be."

"Of course, I'm sorry," he said, though Jim seemed too buoyant to take offense. "Can I offer you some omelet? I just made a fresh pot of coffee."

"I sure would love to stay and chat over some coffee." The mail carrier gave a wink. "But your neighbors over the mountain are expecting a delivery of fresh cream—possibly for their own java—and they're always paranoid it'll sour. As if anything here could go bad!"

Jim's mustache wobbled as he laughed. Damian gave a polite chuckle, though he wondered about the character of his neighbors.

The old man fished around inside the messenger bag, finding and handing over several envelopes. "Your mail for the day, Mr. Hartter."

"Thank you. Nice to meet you, Mr. Parsons."

"Likewise! Perhaps I'll have time for coffee next time." With a salute, Jim turned and ambled toward an ancient Ford Model A mail van idling in the driveway. Next to the Camaro—next to any car Damian had ever seen—it was an antique.

Back in the foyer, Damian rifled through the mail. Most was for Alena. The envelopes had her name scrawled across the front. No address or sender, just her name. Only one had his written across crisp white paper in exquisite calligraphy. He ripped it open and pulled out a carefully folded letter.

Flame,

It's only been fourteen years! I didn't expect to see you around these parts for another couple of decades. You could've at least attempted to make your death more original. Alena—now there's a way to go!

I've made lunch reservations for us at Messie Bessie's Tea Room in the city. They make excellent pumpkin squash soup. Tomorrow, noon!

Until then,
Avenger

The note was from Colin. Flame and Avenger were code names they'd given themselves in elementary school. The two had also developed a secret language so they could pass coded messages to one another. Nothing an adult couldn't figure out, but sophisticated for a couple of fourth graders.

As excited as Damian was to see his best friend for the first time in many years, unease took root in his stomach. He felt the same way each time he encountered a new bump in celestial logic—*the faulty lines of code*. The continuation of his and Colin's childhood adventures would be a welcome addition to his own perfect afterlife. Back when he imagined outlandish stories while sitting in church, though, he'd never factored in his friend. Colin never believed in the great beyond, and everyone *knew* belief was required to get in.

After reading through the letter once more, Damian set the rest of the mail down on the hall table under the mirror and stepped into the library. The silver text along the spines of his autobiographical series gleamed in the ambient light. One volume for each year of his life. Except for the last installment, the more recent the book, the thicker the spine. Still, the one labeled *The Eighteenth Year of Damian Craig Hartter* felt heavier than it should have when he removed it from the shelf. Sitting down in a reading chair, he flipped through the pages until he found the section he was looking for.

A car horn sounds from the driveway, drawing me out of the book I'm reading, Damian read, startled when he actually heard the horn's blare in his ears. He could even see the cover of the novel: *Next*, by Michael Crichton.

"That's new," he said to himself, uncertain if he liked this twist on books. The quiet of reading was one of its perks, and the subject of this chapter was not one he really wanted to see or hear again. Still, he continued.

"We're off to the movies, Mom!"

Leaving the book on my bed, I race through the kitchen to the laundry room for my jacket. It's mid-April, and the air still has a chill.

"Don't forget to call us when you get there." My mother, a frying pan full of sizzling eggs in one hand, turns away from the stove. She towers above me, and I'm suddenly aware of how often she uses her height to her advantage.

"Yeah, sure," I say, my excitement ebbing. Resentment rushes

to take its place. It's only because of her stature that I even answer.

"You're sure you don't want dinner? Your friend can join us."

"We'd be late for the movie." I wince at the whine in my voice and force more acerbity into it. "After the last time Colin had dinner with us, I'll be lucky if he ever steps foot inside this house again."

"Why is he driving, anyway?" She turns back to the stove. I roll my eyes—of course she ignores my jab. "Didn't he just get his license?"

"Really, Mom? Given how often you and Dad let me take my own car out, he's driven way more than me."

Chunks of egg fly out of the pan as she spins. "Watch your mouth, or you won't be seeing any movies." She chews on her inner cheek as though debating what to do with me. Finally, shaking a spatula, she says, "Don't forget to call this time. I don't want to phone all the theaters again."

I cringe at the memory of a disgruntled employee searching each row of the theater for me while my mother waited impatiently on the phone. It's one of the most embarrassing moments of my life. Probably one of those things I'll laugh at far in the future.

Damian chuckled in remembrance. The incident itself wasn't particularly humorous, but the indignant look on his younger self's face was comical. It also contrasted with the hurt in his mother's eyes at the comment on driving, which he hadn't noticed at the time. He regretted his words. Doubly so, now knowing his parents only meant to protect and not punish him.

The car horn sounds again. I storm out of the kitchen, softening my steps as I make my way through the living room to the front. Dad is watching the television, shaking his head as a news report rails against President Bush and the ongoing war in Iraq.

"Don't call if you get arrested." My dad's usual comment whenever I leave. My idea of a fun weekend is playing Xbox 360 at Colin's house, staying up late, and drinking too much soda. Police intervention is never likely. Still, I give Dad a chuckle before pulling the door closed behind me.

"What took you so long?" Colin steps out of his new car. The BMW M3 is a beautiful vehicle. Parked next to the Buick, it appears three times more expensive than it really is.

Damian gasped as the volume produced an image of Colin in his mind's eye. The last time he'd seen his friend, Colin had been but a shell of himself. Withered and much too thin. Here, he was tall and muscular, eyes twinkling beneath a mass of curly black hair. Next to him, the seventeen-year-old version of Damian was a head shorter and paunchy.

"The usual. My mom," I say with an air of gloom, motioning for him to get back in before either of my parents change their minds and pull me back indoors. "Let's get out of here."

"You shouldn't be so hard on your mom. You're more alike than you think. Come to think of it, you even look alike."

"Fuck off!" I punch Colin in the shoulder as he backs out of the driveway and accelerates down the street. "But don't let me forget to call her in half an hour. I can't have her phoning around."

Colin pulls up at the stop sign at the center of town. Rumor has it the city is going to install a light, which would be a first for Minade. "Why'd you lie to your parents about where we're going? My cousin's a good guy. We're not doing anything wrong."

"You clearly don't know my parents as well as you think. It's not easy for me to just go see a movie. Takes a week to convince them I won't sneak into an R-rated showing. I'm lucky they let me go into Peoria at all."

"All the heathens?"

"As if there aren't any heretics in Minade!" I throw up my hands in exasperation, then continue. "If I mentioned your cousin, they'd want to know more about him. Call his parents. Know where he lives. See if he's like...like you." I dig myself deeper into a hole.

"I see."

"My parents aren't like yours." I fish the cell phone out of my pocket. "This is what they give me, and I'm punished if I don't use it. Yours gives you a new car!"

"Hey, they didn't just hand me the keys." Colin punches down on the accelerator as we leave city limits, a little more aggressively than I thought necessary. "I have to pay for the insurance."

I snort. "From the bank account they keep depositing money into?"

"I worked for that money."

He glowers, and I know I should drop the subject. I just can't help myself, though. "Sorry if I don't count tending the family pumpkin patch as work."

Colin's only response is to drive faster. The sun dips below the horizon of harvested corn stalks—it'll be another month before farmers till and plant the fields—and he switches on the BMW's headlights. We fly over the top of a hill and down the steep decline on the other side. I usually love the sensation of my stomach defying gravity. Right now, it makes me feel sick. We've been friends for so long. I know in my heart he's as touchy about his family's money as I am about my parents' lack of it.

"Look, Colin. I'm sorry. I didn't mean that. You know I'm just jealous."

He remains silent, and I eventually look over to see how pissed he is. The depth of thought and unease his eyes convey surprises me, as does his lack of words. Colin is smart. Too smart. He runs circles around our classmates with his wit. Right now, anger is present too. Not at me, though. Not entirely.

"You don't know how hard it is for me, Damian," Colin says, breaking the quiet.

"Care to fill me in?" Before I can bite my tongue, I add, "From my point of view, you seem very well-off."

"Yeah, my family's got money. We're one of the few families in this town that's well-off. And the only Black family. I'm the rich Black dude at school." His voice is even, but I hear the leather of the steering wheel creak as his fingers tighten. "The rich, queer, Black kid."

"Nobody cares about that," I say, but the words lose themselves in the new silence settling around us. The statement is false, and I know it. If I had Colin's money and charm—and this BMW—I wouldn't be on the outer perimeter of the school's social structure. My friend has all those things, and wants to be at the center of the crowd, but only geeks like me accept him. At least, before it came out that he's gay.

When word got around to my mother, she descended upon me with religious zeal. It took weeks to convince her that I was straight. That Colin and I were not fucking around. That she needed to stop calling his parents. Then, despite her disgust, she kept inviting him over for dinner. I was shocked the first time, and was equally dismayed when she tried to change his mind about being gay. She's adamant in her insistence that he can simply cease such abhorrent behavior, and he now refuses to step foot inside my home.

I'm not sure what to say about the matter regarding Colin. All I know is that he chose me to be a friend. Even though he longs to be a part of a larger social circle—even one that will never accept him for who he is, which I don't understand—I believe he values our friendship as much as I do.

Even though I have no qualms about Colin's sexuality, I also believe no amount of money grants access to what awaits after death, and that our friendship is limited to our time on Earth. I will never tell a soul, but I cling to that fact with ardor. It's the one thing I have over Colin. One thing in which I will prevail. The only thing that truly matters.

"Wow," Damian said aloud, grimacing at his past self-righteousness. "Such an ass."

"Don't forget about Wayland's Curve," I say as the vehicle flies over another hilltop. My stomach goes weightless again, the sensation pulling my mind back to the present. We had to be going at least eighty-five miles per hour.

"Oh, don't worry." The glint in Colin's eyes reveals his usual mischievousness. "I know what's coming."

Damian looked up from the book, not requiring its help to visualize what happened next. The sequence of events had haunted him ever since that night. One more hilltop stood between them and the end of their journey. When the car passed the crest and began its steep descent on the other side, the BMW's headlights flashed over an orange reflective triangle. It was fastened to a slow-moving tractor with a planter attached to the back.

Jeez, I really wasn't original at all.

The BMW's velocity was too great to stop in time, so Colin had opted to swerve left. They careened by the farm equipment, inches away from scratching the new car's paint. *It was a fine idea. Would've worked too, if it wasn't for Wayland's Curve.*

The road's sudden sharp right took many drivers off guard after coming over the hill. Fifty yards after the turn, the road took another quick twist to the left. Wayland's Curve was notorious for accidents.

It was only once Colin had passed the tractor that he realized how close they were to the first bend in the road. He turned the steering wheel clockwise so hard Damian was certain it would wrench off. The car whipped around the corner, their bodies straining against the seat belts. For a moment, it seemed things were going to be fine, but then Colin tried to guide the vehicle back into the proper lane.

Damian remembered little of what happened next. He considered looking down at *The Eighteenth Year of Damian Craig Hartter* to relive the experience, but chose instead to close the book. The police report had stated that the left wheels caught on the edge of the road. When Colin finally wrested control of the vehicle, the second turn was upon them. Colin swerved left, but it was too late. The BMW raced off the road, through the ditch, and flipped before finally smashing into a telephone pole.

Damian placed the book back on its shelf, returning to his chair with *The Nineteenth Year*. He didn't open it, but sat staring into space.

Colin hadn't died that night. Another year would pass by—*beep...beep...beep...*—before he succumbed to the injuries sustained in the accident. Most people found relief in the death by reciting to one another, "He's in a better place now." Damian despised those words. According to his beliefs, Colin *wasn't* in a better place. Most everyone in the community would've agreed, despite the mantra. Even Damian's mother shook her head in silence, presumably disappointed she'd been unable to convince Colin in time of the error of his ways.

By the time Colin passed, Damian had lost his pious attitude about immortality. He no longer reveled in his assured place in what lay beyond—that he'd be the one with riches. All he wanted was to chill with his best friend again. To drink caffeine all night and play Xbox. Chat about girls—or boys. It didn't matter.

My wish has been granted! Damian glanced at Colin's letter, which he'd placed on a side table, and willed away the sadness welling in his chest. *No reason to be gloomy. I'm back with my wife, and I'm having lunch with my best friend tomorrow.*

The crux of it all, what had placed him in a melancholy mood the moment he'd opened the letter, was that the three of them didn't belong here. At least, not according to what he believed fifteen years ago. With time, Minade's religious majority may have learned to tolerate Colin's homosexuality, but they would've run him out of town—*and the rest of his family?*—if it was legal. Alena, who described herself as an agnostic atheist, would never have found a place in their hearts, either.

Then there's me, who lost faith. And losing faith is just as bad as never having had it, if not worse. So then, how did we make it in?

Damian pondered for a minute, recalling Alena's concern from the previous morning. *Maybe there's nothing wrong here, but the Afterlife is so radically unlike anything we predicted—possibly to the point of disgusting Mom!*

Damian stood and stretched. *It'll be a while before I crack open another of these volumes. I see how Alena's grandfather became obsessed with the past.*

As he returned the book to its proper place, a shadow fell across the room. With a start, he turned to find a round face in the window. A high-school-aged girl with short, flaming red hair had her nose pressed up against the glass.

"Hey!" Damian shouted, more out of surprise than distress. He stepped over and pulled back the curtain, but the rotund girl had left the window and was climbing onto a shiny green bicycle. She used only one hand to hoist herself onto the bike. In the other, she held... Damian had to squint to make it out. A cigar.

His morbid past now forgotten, Damian laughed as he moved to the porch. He didn't hurry. The kid had harmed nothing—*other than my sense of privacy*—and could peregrinate once she reached the end of the driveway. Still, it was one of the more puzzling things he'd seen: a heavyset teen out cycling while smoking a stogie.

Probably a neighbor, he thought. *Maybe even the ones Jim Parsons delivered cream to.*

He'd ask Alena about it when she returned from work.

Damian headed back inside. Instead of the library, he returned to the kitchen. The omelet he'd abandoned earlier remained, still warm. After pouring some coffee, he dug back into it, all the while wondering why anyone would spy on him.

CHAPTER SIX

DAMIAN SAT BEHIND THE wheel of the Camaro idling at the end of the driveway. He'd flipped the turn signal on out of habit. Now the rhythmic blinking light on the dashboard mesmerized him. *You can do this. Alena showed you how. Peregrinating is easy.*

Peregrination was a simple process. All Damian had to do was imagine his intended destination and mentally express a desire to be transplanted there. Alena explained that they couldn't jump into institutions like the Embassy or others' private properties. Only Guardians and the Creator were immune from that rule.

Damn! I could've intercepted the cigar-smoking kid, Damian thought. The disappointment didn't last long. He found joy in peregrinating from one room of the house to another. Alena made him stop after he appeared naked in the bubble bath she'd been soaking in.

The description of the girl who'd peered through the window didn't remind Alena of anyone she knew. Her brows furrowed as she considered Damian's concern. "Most of our neighbors are old, even by our standards, and they look it."

"Should I report it? Tell a Guardian?"

"What kind of scandalous behavior do you think she was up to? Watching you read about our sexual escapades?" Alena shrugged off any concern. "I doubt the Guardians would throw her into the dungeon. Crime is basically nonexistent."

"If there isn't any, why's there a dungeon at all?"

"I think the only crime in this circumstance is overindulgence in weed." She pointed out that any mind-altering substance could've been in the cigar. "She probably forgot where she lives!"

"If weed is a crime, then how many sentences have you served?"

Alena stuck out her tongue. "I prefer shrooms in my tea!"

Of more interest to Alena was Colin's letter. She reminded Damian twice before leaving for work not to forget the lunch reservation. He got the feeling she wanted him to get out of the house and explore.

The Camaro wasn't necessary for peregrination—it was actually easier to transport one's body alone. But Damian wanted to show off the vehicle to Colin, who likely drove something with more class, perhaps an Aston Martin. Colin would know what the pony car meant to Damian, though.

Finally breaking free of the blinker's hypnotic effect, Damian turned right onto the road. He sped up past ninety miles per hour, hoping to take the disorienting edge off peregrination this time. With a firm grip on the wheel, he closed his eyes—*don't have to worry about Wayland's Curve*—and concentrated his thoughts on the Celestial City.

A tingling sensation spread throughout his body, then a sudden burst of velocity slammed him back into the seat. Smeared colors, whooshing wind, and a disquieting lack of motor control nearly overwhelmed him. Amid the chaos, he thought he recognized the towering Celestial Wall and two Guardians hastily opening the gate for him. The car then snapped back to its previous speed.

What Damian failed to consider was that the Camaro would still travel at ninety miles per hour after transportation completed. Crowds of people cried out in alarm as the black Chevrolet appeared in the street, darting for the sidewalks as it careened by. A gelatinous, lime-colored blob, presumably sentient, wasn't able to dodge in time. It splattered against the vehicle's grill, green goop spraying in all directions.

Damian let out a screech as he slammed on the brakes, bringing the car to a halt. The bucket seat allowed him to hunker down in embarrassment. His eyes bulged as he glanced in the rear-view mirror, trying to locate the remains of the stricken blob. Thousands of water droplets obscured his line of sight.

Did I kill them? Is it actually possible to be killed here? He remembered Athan saying something about murder still being outlawed in the Afterlife.

As he scanned, the dots of condensation slid across the surface of his back window, drawn to one another like magnets. They joined to form larger spherical droplets tinted bright green. Before long, there were only a hundred drops, then a couple dozen. Finally, two clear green orbs slowly merged into a single enormous mass. Back to its original size, the lime-colored blob rolled off the back of the car and ambled away.

I need to work on this. Damian waved apologetically at the creature. Then, with a sigh of relief that no disgruntled shoppers were coming after him, he drove for several blocks before parking on the side of the road. Shops lined the street, each with a large picture window featuring its wares, most of them bakeries, restaurants, and candy stores. He grinned, knowing he could now eat all he desired and not gain a single pound.

The general height of the buildings in the neighborhood, upward of five stories, suggested that Damian was midway through the city toward the center. Over the rooftops to his right, he saw the peak of the civic center where Athan and Mai had oriented him. Straight ahead stood a massive building he hadn't noticed on his previous visit. Its neoclassical design and immense size projected authority despite its being constructed with the same whitewashed material as every other structure.

The Embassy? He wondered how much office space the building provided, how many cubicles were crammed inside.

Halfway between Damian and the behemoth structure, a black sign with gold lettering swung back and forth outside one store: Messie Bessie's Team Room. The clock on the car's dashboard told him ten full minutes had passed since he'd entered the Celestial City.

Only a few minutes late. He hoisted himself out of the bucket seat and joined the bustling crowd on the sidewalk. *Totally normal for me.*

A bell rang as Damian opened the door to the tearoom, announcing his arrival. The interior wasn't as cute as the name suggested. Thick wooden beams supported a high ceiling, itself plated in bronzed tin. With only a single large room for seating, it had the vague feel of a church sanctuary, albeit with small round tables and petite chairs instead of pews. Teapots of all shapes and sizes lined the walls, dispelling solemnity. The clinking of china and the din of chatter—*and those delicious smells*—cemented the eatery's comfortable atmosphere.

"May I help you?" a lady as old as time itself greeted Damian.

"I'm meeting a friend of mine. He made a reservation. Colin Cherry? I'm a little late."

"Oh yes, Mr. Cherry!" Her face lit up, making her appear at least two hundred years younger. She pointed a gnarled finger toward a table at the rear of the restaurant. Damian felt a shiver of excitement when he recognized the back of his friend's head. "He's waiting for you in the corner."

"Thank you," he said, trying and failing to outdo her magnificent smile. *She's had a thousand years to perfect it.* Then he weaved through the tables, most of which were surrounded by cheerful patrons and covered with teapots, pastries, and quiches. At the last moment, Colin turned his head and looked right at him.

Damian gasped. He wasn't sure what he'd expected to see, but it wasn't this. Colin didn't appear a day over sixteen. Compared to the last time Damian had seen him in the flesh, he practically glowed with health.

"Look at you, Damian!" Colin said, leaping to his feet. Several neighboring diners glanced up. "You grew up on me!"

"Grew *out*, maybe," Damian replied as the two embraced. Just as when he woke up to his wife, he felt awestruck to be in the company of a friend he thought he'd lost forever. "Still shorter than you."

Colin wore a deep blue button-up shirt and a light gray sports jacket. It would've been casual attire at the Chicago office Damian used to work in. On Colin, who might've been playing hooky from high school, it looked too mature.

Dressing like the rich kid he is. Damian was immediately ashamed of the thought.

"Sit, sit," Colin said. He plopped down in his seat. A young waitress appeared, setting down menus and glasses of sparkling water.

"I know you didn't like the Buick. Told me often enough when you visited me in the hospital," Colin said after they'd been told the special of the day—rainbow quiche. "But you didn't have to destroy it, and yourself in the process!"

"Nah, I couldn't take it anymore. It was the only thing my parents were leaving me in their wills." Damian leaned forward as though they were conspiring across a lunchroom table. "But what the hell happened to you? You left us all with a lot of questions."

"Unfortunately, I don't have any answers for you. The folks we have in the DoD—sorry, the Embassy's Department of Death—are at a loss, too. They're all from the eighteenth and nineteenth centuries, though, and don't trust the medical practices of our time. Thought I was lucky I survived the crash at all."

"With all you endured afterward, I wouldn't say you were lucky." Damian tapped the table with his fingertips. He wondered how many conversations similar to this transpired each day. "The emergency response team had to cut away parts of the BMW before they'd even try to move you."

Colin barked a laugh, drawing a few bemused looks from other tables. "Yeah, it looked like the car was trying to make love to the telephone pole and wouldn't let go until it succeeded."

Damian sat back in his chair, beyond thrilled the Afterlife had restored his friend to his former self. While he'd escaped the accident with nothing more than a few bruises and a guilty conscience, it had left Colin mangled and disfigured. The impact broke nearly every bone on the left side of his body. He'd been in a coma while the doctors did their best to set everything back in its proper place.

Six months after that ill-fated night, Colin's eyes fluttered and opened. He appeared to recognize everyone in the room, anyone who came to visit. Injuries had reduced his verbal skills to grunts, and he retained even less control over locomotion. Out of a sense of duty or contrition—*I never figured which it was, or which was stronger*—Damian spent every free moment of his time by Colin's side. Just as he had before Colin gained consciousness, he shared everything happening at school and events from around the world.

Whether it was Colin's personal strength, Damian's one-sided conversations, or the doctors' ministrations, Colin continued to make rapid progress. By the time the anniversary of the accident rolled around, Colin had regained the ability to convey messages. Only short bursts of speech or gesturing, but it was more than anyone ever expected. He even moved around the room on his own for short periods of time.

Which is why it surprised everyone when, while undergoing minor surgery to remove pins from his left arm, Colin died. The doctors could never adequately explain what went wrong.

"Anything catch your eye?"

Damian blinked, glancing up from the menu to the young waitress. Lost in his reverie, he hadn't actually reviewed his options. Rather than look a fool, he ordered the special. Colin did the same. "And the tea of the day, too!"

After the server whisked away, it was Colin's turn to hunker down over the table, looking at Damian mischievously.

"Do you recall the pact of our youth?"

The answer was obvious, and it presented itself at the forefront of Damian's mind. But when he went to answer, the words wouldn't form. The response, and all the memory and knowledge it contained, dissipated. His mouth hung open stupidly as his mind dipped into sudden freefall.

"What'd you say?" he asked when the wave of disorientation passed.

"What've you been up to the past few days?" Colin gave a crooked smile. "Out there in the sticks in that big house of yours."

"Oh." Damian mentally pushed away the remaining discomfort. "Just relaxing. Spending time with my wife. Done a bit of reading."

"Ah, yes. Alena Bucket-Hartter. She's been stirring up a ruckus lately. Making quite a name for herself."

"Really? What about?" Damian frowned. Alena had always stood her ground or made herself heard if need be. *But making a ruckus?*

"From what I've heard, she's pushing for reforms in childcare." Colin took on a formal tone Damian was unfamiliar with. "Especially with how the system processes children with no family."

"Processes?"

Colin nodded, then shook his head in disappointment. "These kids are basically placed in a room, stuck in a kind of limbo, and forgotten about."

"It's rather odd, isn't it? All of it, I mean." Damian leaned forward again. This time, it wasn't out of boyish covertness. He laid out his concerns, everything from childcare to how the Afterlife included him, Alena, and Colin. He flushed when he included Colin's posthumous placement on his list of peculiarities.

"Believe me, I was as surprised as you." Colin waved away Damian's embarrassment. "Way more so, I bet. Humans invented countless versions of the afterlife throughout history, most of which were ploys to control the living. The truth is the dead have much more control over eternity, though I'm still trying to grapple with oddities such as myself. After being on the defensive for so long in Minade, it's taken me a while to relax here and allow the acceptance of others. To accept myself."

"If you're an oddity, I'm right there alongside you." The revelation surprised Damian. Colin had always been so self-assured, so solid when facing opposition.

"Point being," Colin continued, "there's a lot going on here, much of it nuanced. I've been doing a ton of work to understand everything."

"What kind of work are you doing? Stirring up a ruckus of your own?"

Colin's dark eyes twinkled. "Nothing of the sort! I found a job at the Embassy."

"Really? What do you do?"

"I work in the Department of Satanic Investigations."

Damian blinked.

"What? I find the work fulfilling. It adds a bit of an edge to my existence here."

"What exactly does one do in the...Department of Satanic Investigations?" he asked. "I mean, apart from what's in its name."

Colin waved a finger as if to say, *Ah, ah!* Then he leaned back. The server had reappeared, balancing two large plates, each holding an entire rainbow quiche, and a large teapot shaped like a pumpkin.

"It's a hot black tea paired with sweet raspberries," she said before leaving them to their food. Any tea would've suited Damian just fine. Alena was the connoisseur.

Colin continued talking as if the waitress hadn't interrupted. "Most of my work requires special clearance to know about. The details, I swear, would blow you away. Actually," he said, pointing a speared yellow pepper at Damian, "you should think about working at the Embassy. I know so many people throughout all the departments. You could be in there by tomorrow afternoon if you wanted."

"Then would you be able to tell me about your investigations?"

"Only if you worked within the DSI. I can't otherwise. Literally." He scooped a generous helping of eggs and vegetables into his mouth, then pressed the fork to his lips. "Even if I tried to divulge anything, the words wouldn't come out. But a tour might appease some of your curiosity."

"Really?"

"We'll have to clear it with security first, and I can't show you the entire place. Haven't seen it all myself. There are departments with names even more sinister than mine."

Damian finally took a bite of his dish. He enjoyed the cheesy dough, but he barely noticed the vegetables and spices on his tongue. Possibilities swam around his mind. *I haven't had time to think about my future. Thought I'd finally do some writing, though I suppose I have eternity for that. The Embassy might help me understand the faulty lines of code I keep running across—and the girl at my window.*

As the food disappeared and the teapot drained, Colin spoke of how he spent the rest of his free time. Not only had he picked up where he left off on

Earth, playing games with all the nerdy crowds, he'd built up a large core of acquaintances. Everyone wanted to be his friend, and he wanted to be theirs.

He seems to be part of the crowd now! Damian thought, glad for Colin.

"I even have a boyfriend! His name's Anthony. We've been living together here in the city a couple of years. Would've invited you and Alena over for dinner before now, but I wasn't sure if you two were still making up for lost time."

"Have been and will be!" Damian said, and they drew looks with their boyish snickering. "But we should meet soon. Just because we have all the time in the universe doesn't mean we should waste it. I can't wait to meet Anthony."

Once they'd consumed every morsel of food, the two thanked their waitress and the hostess, then left the tearoom. It felt odd to Damian that no check arrived, and they made no payment. The staff was simply pleased that they were pleased.

Back out on the busy sidewalk, the Camaro drew the desired reaction out of Colin. "Wow! I forgot how much you wanted one of these. I understand your attraction. It's aggressive and sexy. How's it handle?"

"It's the best thing I've ever sat behind, though a golf cart would've been an upgrade from the Buick." Damian beamed. "Scared a crowd half to death peregrinating into the city."

Colin chuckled, peering through the window of the vehicle much like Damian had when he first discovered it in his driveway. "Keep in mind that most people here never saw a car during their lives, and they prefer to keep their current existence as simple as possible."

"I don't want to think about a future when newcomers view us as Luddites." It unsettled him that, though he wouldn't age another day in appearance, there would always be a way in which he grew older and obsolete.

Damian moved to get into the Chevy, but Colin placed a hand on his shoulder. He pointed up the street at the massive building that dominated the horizon. "That's the Embassy. A quick walk. One reason Bessie is always so crowded. I want my first ride in this beauty to be out on the open road. We'll make sure there's no farm equipment lurking around."

The crowds got thicker as Damian followed Colin to their destination, eventually stepping foot on the grounds of the Embassy. Regal trees, bushes, benches, and walkways populated a lush green lawn not unlike that upon which Damian died, all surrounded by a wrought-iron fence. Though impressive, the grounds couldn't compete with the expansive building sitting on them. Complete with two wings expanding from a central main building, a gigantic dome topped the Embassy. The building seemed alive to Damian, staring down with contempt at the specks of life peregrinating on and off the lawn.

"The grounds act as a peregrination hub for Embassy employees," Colin said. "Lucky thing the grass refuses to be trampled."

The two made their way through throngs of officials and up a flight of stone steps. At the top was a pair of massive ornate doors made of solid wood. They reminded Damian of those set within the Celestial Gate. The Guardians standing silently by helped with the visual.

"Athan?" He recognized the long maroon robes and jeweled crown. Mai, stationed on the other side of the doorway, wore a deep frown that discouraged interaction. Up close, the pair appeared more inhuman than they had during the Orientation. Their hair was thick, each strand perceivable, while their limbs—what Damian could observe through their robes—seemed too thin.

"Damian Craig Hartter." Athan spoke in the same monotone voice as before, neck craned to peer down at them impassively.

"You know my name?"

"I remember everyone who goes through our orientation."

Damian turned to Mai. "You, too?"

"Mai has taken a vow of silence," Athan said, drawing Damian's attention back. "It has been many thousands of years since they have spoken a word."

"We're headed to security," Colin said, rolling back on his heels. "Want to give him a tour of the building."

Athan nodded with great deliberation. Then, with Mai's help, they opened the heavy doors before them. Colin stepped through, but the Guardian grabbed Damian by the shoulder before he entered. Robes fluttering, Athan said, "You should know what you endeavor."

"Huh?" was all he managed, still amazed anyone could remember his full name, especially when they hadn't actually met. Before he properly enunciated a question, a heavyset creature with three twisted horns protruding from its neck bumped between the two, pushing Damian forward into the building.

The palatial foyer seized Damian's attention, dispelling Athan's cryptic words. A grand stairwell led to the upper levels, and multiple hallways branched off in a myriad of directions. The room was strangely empty for the number of people peregrinating outside. He counted only fifteen walking determinedly through.

Colin noticed his bewilderment. "Not much time for milling around."

Never would've guessed by the decor. The foyer was dimly lit by an elaborate chandelier peppered with hundreds of candles. Dark-red velvet curtains hung over tall windows. Vertical panels of the same color covered each wall, lined with gold, silver, and bronze. Each wooden panel had unfamiliar symbols etched into it.

In the middle of the foyer, directly beneath the chandelier—*and where one might find a fountain or statue in a more pretentious location*—was an oddity Damian couldn't identify. Hundreds of thin panels, similar to those on the walls, lined up next to one another, wrapping around in a circle. They hovered above the floor and rotated slowly, like a carousel. Each panel had its own unique inscription and what appeared to be a keyhole at the top, just above eye level. Like those on the walls, Damian couldn't understand the symbols, and he couldn't imagine what the keyholes unlocked.

"What is this?"

When no answer came from Colin, he looked around to find his friend opening a door tucked away in the back corner of the room. Hustling over, he saw it led to a narrow staircase going down.

"Getting clearance from security is not a pleasurable experience," Colin said, heading down the rickety steps. "It may be one of the worst things you'll endure in the Afterlife."

Damian stopped short at the doorway. The passage down was adorned with the same design as the foyer, but it somehow looked ominous.

"Of course, the worst experience here would be a picnic back on Earth."

Encouraged, he followed Colin down. After an unusually long descent, another door blocked their path. A plaque on the wall read The Graeae.

Colin knocked, and the door opened slowly. A raspy voice Damian found familiar said, "Enter."

Dim light from the hallway briefly illuminated the room before darkness swallowed it up. In that moment, Damian saw a refrigerated mortuary cabinet, a wall of flat-panel televisions, and a puddle of water on the floor fed by a leaky ceiling. *Bleep...bleep...bleep...*

Three figures stood about the room, a faint ball of light floating overhead. Damian immediately associated them with nurses, which wasn't right at all. They were large, dark billowing clouds of moldering mass, more akin to a thunderstorm than health care personnel.

Memory of his previous visit to this room suddenly hit Damian. The terrifying and confusing interview by the Gray Ones. Anger surged through him, and he opened his mouth to demand answers. Before he spoke a word, an overwhelming urge to sleep hit him, and he slumped over into Colin's arms.

CHAPTER SEVEN

In high school biology, Damian learned that an increasing number of people were born whose jaws never formed wisdom teeth. Some scientists theorized this to be further evidence of continued human evolution. As the brain cavity enlarged, the jaw diminished, ridding itself of the unnecessary third molars. Damian wasn't a scientist—neither was the biology teacher, who scoffed at the idea of evolution—and couldn't say if the theory was well-grounded. He didn't care either way. His mouth had the usual extraneous teeth. At seventeen, during the time Colin was in a coma, he had them removed.

He hadn't been fearful of the surgery. Nervous, yes. So shaky he thought his body would wobble right off the chair. Still, he refused to be afraid of a procedure people underwent every day without incident. It wasn't the subsequent pain that made the event unforgettable, either, for his mouth resumed its usual state of being a mere two hours after returning home. Instead, the nitrous oxide got to him.

With a mask pumping gas into his lungs, Damian had stared dully at the ceiling, trying not to imagine teeth being pulled from his jaw. He slowly noticed how familiar the ceiling tiles appeared. Square, not rectangular, with beveled edges. The more he considered them, the more positive he became that he'd seen these exact tiles in a dream just a few nights prior. The nightmare had ended with his brutal murder.

Damian moved to get out of the chair but found he couldn't budge. Nor could he speak. The gas paralyzed him, leaving only his eyes with the ability to look around. This he did with fervor, trying to capture the attention of a passing hygienist.

A dental assistant walked into the room, flaming red hair curling about her shoulders. He blinked rapidly, trying to draw her attention. As she sauntered over to a counter and pulled on a pair of latex gloves, he remembered she had been a part of the nightmare. In fact, he was certain she was the one. The assistant was going to kill him.

The woman stepped beside his chair and fiddled with some sharp-looking instruments. Panicked, Damian strained to move. He'd never wanted to kick and scream more. Yet all he could do was watch.

But witnessing his own demise wasn't what he'd woken up wishing for. Instead, he let the gas take him to a faraway place.

I foresaw my death. Waves of darkness overtook his conscious mind. *Then I walked right into it.*

In reality, Damian had already been in a faraway place. Everything he'd seen—the hygienist, the ceiling tiles, the shiny doorknobs—was real. His brain had conjured up the past nightmare, the recognition, and knowledge of impending death, courtesy of nitrous oxide. The threat had been imaginary, but the fear was extreme.

In the Embassy's basement, at the door marked The Graeae, horror seized Damian. This time, the situation was real, and it felt just as dire. It made him wish for the dentist's chair, for the dulling comfort of the gas.

Perhaps I am *back in the care of a doctor. I'm having more teeth pulled. I'm under the influence of nitrous oxide, and I've made up everything about the Afterlife.*

He was now paralyzed from the neck down. He sensed the three shadowy individuals suffocating his movement with their will. The creatures—*the Gray Ones*—radiated a specific *feel*. Like strep throat or the flu.

"Hey, Damian! Talk to me. Can you hear me?" It was Colin's voice. Fuzzy at first, gradually becoming clearer.

"What..." he said, taking several deep breaths. As his senses returned, he realized Colin had broken his fall and now sat on the floor, cradling his head. He rolled his eyes toward the plaque on the wall. "The Graeae?"

"They're our security. Don't worry, it's common for those who meet them a second time to faint."

"I did not faint!" he said.

"You most certainly did." Colin chuckled. "I passed out on my second visit, too. It's not really fainting. Their will smothers you. Overrides your motor functions."

"Paralyzes you," Damian said. "Why did we have the first visit with them?"

"Only a select few have that meeting. They all have something in common. I can't tell you more about that, though. Not yet, anyway." The mischievous expression returned to his face. It wasn't the first time Damian had found it immensely irritating. He could think of a hundred things the two of them had in common. They'd been best friends, after all.

One of the three figures from within the room stepped—*floated?*—forward, followed by the room's single source of light. It gestured with a cloudy appendage, pointing toward what looked like an electric chair used for capital punishment. In an icy voice, the entity said, "Colin Eugene Cherry, place Damian Craig Hartter on the cot."

"They call that a cot?" Damian whispered.

"It's what *I* see in the room. During my first encounter, I thought I was in an asylum. A place Minade sent kids like me to be...rehabilitated. The Gray Ones appeared as hot guys dressed in security uniforms. They were how my cousin—the one in Peoria—used to describe his school's cops to me. In my mind, they weren't guarding against delinquent kids, but keeping the queers hidden away."

Colin appeared distant for a moment, as though that memory drew him back. Then he shook his head, put his arms under Damian's shoulders and knees, and lifted. "Oof, buddy, you've gotta lose a few pounds!"

"Shut up," Damian said with a growl.

"They've got fancy names I can't remember. Doesn't matter. You can't tell them apart," Colin said as he stepped over the threshold. Hesitant at first, he then moved quickly to deposit him on the cot or, as Damian saw it, in the chair. "Point is, they'll use dread and horror to alarm you and get the answers they want. Just remember, they're a bunch of smoke and can't do you any harm. You'll be out of here in no time."

The smothering will of the Gray Ones dissipated, but before Damian could move an inch, leather straps wrapped around his legs, arms, and forehead, immobilizing him against the chair. He wanted to cry out to Colin as his friend backed toward the exit. To ask him to stay—*hold my hand*—but kept quiet. Colin had never lied to him before. Never led him astray.

This is just like having a tooth pulled. Happens all the time without incident. And this could end with a job that answers some questions—and shapes my eternity.

"Yes, we're only smoke. We can't hurt you," said one figure as the door clicked shut. The Gray Ones drifted closer, huddling around the chair as they stared at him with eyeless faces. The one speaking had been the angry nurse with hot breath and golden hues on her dark skin. "Let us resume."

"You are Damian Craig Hartter." The statement—*question*—came from his right. He felt moisture freeze against his cheek as he strained against the leather strap to turn his head.

"Yes, that's my name," he said before their tempers flared. He could see his breath in the wobbly light hovering above. *They know this already. Next they'll ask when I was born.*

The harsh light darted over to his left. Dusty lips, framed by layers of ashen flesh, solidified into a devilish smile. "Where were you born?"

Damian froze, thrown off by the trick. He'd been born in Peoria, not at Minade Hospital. Of that, he was certain. Peoria was home to two major hospitals. Both were respected institutions, both religiously affiliated, and their sprawling campuses nearly overlapped one another. Only a single road divided them.

The answer came to him just as the entity directly in front of him lifted its arms, preparing to slam them down on his lap. "Saint Francis Hospital!" he cried out, mostly in relief. For good measure, he added his birth date.

The creature leaned forward until their noses nearly touched. He had nowhere else to peer but into her empty eye sockets. "When did you *lose* faith in the Creator?"

"What?" Damian choked, thinking they'd caught him in a trap. "You know that?"

"Our sight is limited," the three said in unison. The ball of illumination circled rapidly between them. "But we see all that comes to pass."

"Then why are you doing this?"

"To verify that your story—your memory—matches the record."

It wasn't what Damian meant, but it was interesting, even if the words took a few seconds to sink through his anxiety. Before he could inquire further, the one on his right repeated, "When did you lose faith?"

So he told them, as Alena had phrased it, when he made the conscious decision to push back against what he'd grown up believing. For the sake of transparency, he left out no details, though he flushed at telling them of lying in bed with his girlfriend, like a teenager explaining to his parents the noises they'd heard late at night in his bedroom.

"Alena said it took time," he said after describing the sudden certainty that no one, omniscient or otherwise, was listening to his nightly prayer. "Everything I experienced after leaving Minade led me to that realization."

Another wave of queasiness hit him, an upset of his equilibrium, as those memories surfaced. Since university, he'd concluded that nothing supernatural awaited after death. Interactions with the world outside rural Minade were all the proof he required that no greater consciousness pulled the universe's strings. Of course, that certainty and the confidence on which it relied, which hadn't been easy to establish, were now swept aside. *Not only is there an afterlife, but there are multiple universes!*

"Why did you question me?" he asked, fighting to calm his tumultuous emotions. Tears streamed down cheeks, and his breathing grew labored. "Why'd you take me and Colin after our deaths? We have a million things in common. Boys. Nerds. School. Eye color."

Do you remember the pact of our youth?

"I don't understand!" His body strained against the restraints as his mind flinched from a burst of memories. *We were just playing Xbox!*

The Gray Ones, who had hitherto allowed his rant, appeared to stare at one another. *As much as swirling masses of dirt can.* Then the one looming before him solidified. Not into one of the beautiful nurses. Not even as one of the eyeless old crones. The new shape was even more hideous than their natural state: a horned creature, covered in black fur with red flecks, and green eyes that blazed at him. Armed with clawed hands and sharp, gleaming teeth, it stood on hoofed feet. Flames and smoke billowed around it.

A demon!

The two creatures at his sides also took solid forms. Mercifully, they were the old crones. They spoke in unison. "Satan is attempting to infiltrate the Celestial City with an evil soul."

If the demonic shape hovering over his head hadn't shocked him, the other's proclamation certainly did. "Satan? As in the devil?"

He didn't know why that surprised him. He'd given little thought to the enemy of good for many years. When confronted with the reality of the Afterlife, even when Alena said he'd made it to the good side, he hadn't seriously considered a repository for the bad.

The crone to his right whispered with vehemence, "You were a prime candidate for the evil soul."

The one on his left followed suit. "As was Colin Eugene Cherry. A common thread connects you and him and the other candidates. We believe the opposition exploited that similarity."

They're getting downright conversational. The nausea and dizziness passed, leaving his body chilled. He shook violently. Strapped down, he felt naked and vulnerable. Questions swirled around his head, though he was certain they'd ignore them all. Still, he asked again in a calmer tone, "How are we connected?"

It was the demon-clad creature who answered. In her usual voice, too, which, while unsettling, lessened the dire visage. "We are prohibited from saying to the unauthorized."

"I'd think telling me any of this would be a breach of security." He half expected them to bristle, to explode outward into a storm of grit and rage. *The demon's about to tear my face off with its fangs and claws!* Instead, the ghoulish figure shrank back into a crone, and they all stared at him with hollowed eye sockets. The light still circled between them, but at a leisurely pace.

None of them appreciated his wit, so he tried, "Why *are* you telling me this?"

"We see all that comes to pass," one of them repeated.

Another added, "We see much more, too."

"The future?"

"No! The future is closed to all but the Creator," they said in unison. "For the sake of your future, give weight to our words when making decisions."

The crone to his right, the one Damian thought of as the trio's leader, said, "Satan's influence has been felt within the Celestial City before, even long after the banishment of the opposition. If an agent of evil is let loose within the wall, the damage wrought could be catastrophic."

"You may have been a prime candidate for the evil soul, Damian Craig Hartter, but we do not see malignancy within you," said the one to his left. Despite her words, the heat and menace in her voice did not abate. "The thread that binds you and the others may be the key to stopping Satan's machinations."

The Gray Ones stepped back and fell silent. The light increased its rotational diameter, continuing to circle around them, and Damian realized the room's facade had fallen away. No more televisions or linoleum tiles. All that remained were stone walls, the scent of mold, and *bleeps* as water dripped from stalactites and pooled on the floor.

The straps around Damian's limbs and forehead suddenly fell away. He jumped out of the chair and leaped for the door. He pulled it open, stepping into the hallway. While his body no longer required oxygen, he filled his lungs with fresh air, grateful for mobility.

Before ascending the stairs, he glanced back into the room. What he saw saddened him: three women so ancient their skin sloughed off in dusty heaps at the slightest movement. The solitary light above them only illuminated their blindness and piteous nature.

The door slammed shut.

The stairwell leading to the Embassy foyer was as unending as the trip down. As he reached ground level, the fear over the encounter seeped out of him. The details didn't slip away like a dream this time, but they retained the same ethereal properties.

"How'd it go?" Colin rushed over from the strange carousel when Damian emerged into the foyer.

Damian gave two thumbs up. "Passed, as far as I know. They didn't throw me in a dungeon, at least."

"Did they tell you anything?"

"Only that your department's purview is much more literal than I imagined." He considered going into detail about what he learned, but thought perhaps the information was for his ears only. "What's their story, anyway?"

"No idea. They're immune to my charm." Before Colin said more, a young man appeared from the other side of the carousel. Damian would've taken him for a young Jim Parsons. He wore similar clothes and a bushy mustache.

"Internal post, sir," the man told Colin with a wide smile. He handed over a rolled-up parchment, then disappeared behind the spinning planks.

Colin unraveled the note. His eyes widened as he read.

"What is it?"

"The head ambassador wants to see me in her office right away. We're gonna have to cut the tour short, I'm afraid. She doesn't like to be kept waiting."

After going through all that? Damian was prepared to be furious, though the interrogation had been draining. *A nap sounds good.*

"I'm really sorry. I'll contact you tomorrow to reschedule. Or maybe..." Colin glanced down at the parchment. "Maybe the Embassy will reach out to you."

"What, did the head ambassador watch the interview?" Damian reached for the letter, but Colin deftly rolled it up, slipping it into his pocket.

"Picardia Knutt would never do such a thing. She knows that conversations with security are personal. The Gray Ones are efficient at writing up reports, though. Knutt probably had their insights into your mind before you got up here." The usual mischievous look returned to his eyes. "Must've been positive if she's looking to me as a personal reference."

"What? Really?"

Colin took his arm and led him toward the front entrance. "I jest, I jest. I need to go, though. You look beat. Take a moment to rest on the front stairs. Can't leave you unattended inside. Let the Guardians on duty know if you need anything."

"That was an inordinately quick tour," said Athan, surprising Damian as he walked out onto the stone steps. Neither of the Guardians had moved, intimidating gargoyles scaring off trespassers.

The comment stuck out to Damian, as though Athan was attempting humor. "I think I made it through security, but Colin was called away by the head ambassador."

"It pleases me that you were approved. Many find the Gray Ones to be...disconcerting."

Damian nodded absently, still collecting his thoughts. "What's with the odd light following them around? Is it alive?"

The Guardian's head shook. "It is no more sentient than one of your eyes, for that is exactly what it is. The light gives sight to the Gray Ones, though only to one at a time."

"Sounds inconvenient." Damian looked from Athan to Mai. "Does your work and that of the Gray Ones overlap? Both deal with protection."

Actually, I've mostly seen the Guardians open a lot of doors.

Somehow, without budging in the slightest, Athan appeared to bristle at the question. "Protection of the Celestial City is not work. It is the purpose of the

Guardians. The purview of the Gray Ones is limited to the Embassy, though management charges them with special assignments from time to time."

I know all about their special assignment.

"Mai and I are not guarding the Embassy, per se, but are keeping watch over the Bridge."

"I didn't notice a Bridge." Damian immediately realized how stupid the comment was. He'd seen only two rooms in the massive building.

"Not *a* bridge. *The* Bridge," Athan specified.

Mai moved for the first time since Damian emerged, waving a hand. The air around the Guardian birthed tiny golden lights. Like the ones used during the Orientation of the Dead, the radiant particles swarmed their commander before forming a small version of the Celestial City. One by one, the thin disks that represented planes of reality appeared.

"Every universe intersects here in the city," Athan reiterated. "The exact point at which they all meet is the Bridge. It allows for passage between realities."

"Where would you keep that kind of device?" Damian asked.

"You have already seen it." With another elaborate hand gesture from Mai, the golden lights rearranged themselves into countless long planks, spinning in a circle alongside one another.

"I never would've guessed its purpose, or that it was so important," Damian said, recognizing the display from the foyer. He leaned closer to the facsimile, wondering how detailed it was. Each miniature panel contained its own unique inscription. Even the keyholes lining the tops were clear as day. He squinted, noticing something he'd missed earlier. "These keyholes along the top...some of them are turned sideways. Does that mean they're locked?"

Athan nodded. "Indeed. While all realities intersect here, the path between has been barred for many."

"Really? Which ones?"

"The domain of Satan, naturally," Athan said. "And the one you hail from."

Damian straightened, looking up at the Guardian. "What?"

"The Bridge was closed to your reality many thousands of years ago after humans dissented against the Creator." Athan pulled a massive key from a hidden pocket. "Locked it myself."

Is the myth of our expulsion from the Garden of Eden actually about the Celestial City? "If the way is shut, how do our souls get here?"

"Some time after the path between the Celestial City and your plane of existence was closed, a new one was created to host your expired souls. When humans die, their consciousnesses are transported there along other means," the Guardian explained. "In your previous form, however, you could not travel between universes."

It occurred to Damian that just because he died, he couldn't assume the same for all the strange and wondrous creatures seen around the city. Many were likely in the prime of their lives. *Death may not even be an element of existence for some of them.*

"Always learn something new from you, Athan." Not to be rude, Damian gave Mai a polite nod. "I think I'm good to continue on home."

"Always at your disposal, Damian Craig Hartter," Athan said.

With a wave, Damian descended the stairs, all the while feeling the Guardians' eyes watching him. After crossing the lawn, he made his way back down the road, past Messie Bessie's, and returned to the Camaro. Behind the wheel, he kept an appropriate speed as he traversed the streets—keeping an eye out for green blobs—and peregrinated home.

The mountainous vista surrounding the house calmed any remaining frayed nerves. Damian breathed in the pine-scented air, letting go of the day's troubling events. *No need to worry about anything until I hear from Colin or the Embassy.*

As he stepped through the front door, though, a new tension sprung upon him, and he instinctively knew his days of rest and relaxation were over.

The second upstairs door, the one tucked away on the far side of the landing, stood open.

"Is that you, Damian?" Alena's voice came from further in the house. "I've got good news!"

CHAPTER EIGHT

THE LAKE SURFACE RIPPLED. Something stirred beneath it, creating a massive wake. Though unseen, the object swam at an incredible velocity. Water bulged upward as though a creature was attempting to escape.

Damian watched from the shore, staring out in awe. His legs twitched, encouraging a panicked flight back toward the house and Alena. His curiosity stilled him, the desire to discover and understand the unseen overriding instinct.

After a tremendous struggle, the unknown thing broke through the surface. Waves of water cascaded in every direction, droplets acting as prisms in the morning light. Damian's resolve to stay rooted on the sandy beach weakened as the entity pivoted and swam straight toward him. Never had he seen a creature so immense. Not in life or media—not even the ones about dinosaurs.

Yet, as the goliath rushed across the lake, he couldn't tear his eyes away. Its anatomy bore a resemblance to a blue whale, but it was much larger and had a striking reddish-orange coloration that had Damian squinting. He kept looking, though, as there was one detail he couldn't make out: the identity of the person standing on the whale's back.

"19-22-15-11 14-22, 23-26-14-18-26-13," the individual cried out as they neared the shore. Damian didn't recognize the voice. He could barely make out the sequence of numbers amid the crashing waves, though there was a sense of anguished urgency behind the strange message. "11-15-22-26-8-22 19-22-15-11 14-22."

Why are they shouting out numbers? Damian wondered. *They make no sense!*

At the shoreline, the creature opened its mouth to reveal a cavernous hole. Its depth and darkness blotted out the amber sky. Damian's base instinct to flee finally won out over curiosity, but it was too late. Gravity shifted, and he sagged forward, toppling into the abyss.

Damian's body hit solid ground. He remained still for several moments, senses on high alert.

"Mr. Hartter?" came a nearby voice. Unlike the one he'd heard seconds ago, he immediately recognized who spoke.

"Mr. Parsons? What're you doing here?" Damian jumped to his feet, scanning the surroundings. Sand fell from his shirt. The lake water was smooth, reflecting the mountains and trees on the opposite shore. No whales bore down on him. Alena slept on a nearby beach chair. Aside from her soft breathing and the chirping of birds in the nearby woods, all was quiet.

A dream? he wondered as he waved for the mail carrier to follow him a few yards down the beach away from his sleeping wife. *I've never had one so vivid.*

Jim's handlebar mustache bobbed with extra enthusiasm as he trailed behind Damian. "Didn't mean to wake you, Mr. Hartter. Apologies for not announcing myself farther up the path. I was admiring your view. My home is surrounded by desert."

Damian tilted his head as he glanced at Jim.

"What can I say? I like it dry."

"You didn't have to come all the way down here," Damian said, allowing the serene lake to chase the frightful details of the nightmare from his mind. "You could've left the mail back at the door."

Mr. Parsons shook his head, his facial hair swaying wildly. "You've got a message from the head ambassador! Those are top priority and must be delivered in person."

After rifling around his leather messenger bag for a few moments, Jim produced a sealed letter. It appeared nearly identical to the one Colin had sent: a simple white envelope with Damian's name neatly written in the center. He took it gratefully.

"Can I get you anything? We can brew some fresh coffee."

"Another rain check?" He pointed to the bag. "I have another top-priority message to deliver, and those can't wait. We'll get to that cup of java one of these days!"

"You're always welcome." Damian watched as the old man ambled back up the path and disappeared around the house. A minute later, the rattle of the ancient Model A's motor sounded, cutting through the tranquil scene until the mail carrier peregrinated elsewhere.

The lake lapped at Damian's ankles as he slowly trod back toward Alena. He stared at the envelope, its simplicity confounding him. *Is it a good or bad sign?*

Though Damian's mood had soured upon returning home the previous evening, he'd poured all the excitement and exaggeration he could muster into retelling the day's events for Alena. He bought into his own enthusiasm, an easy feat after his wife's face lit up.

But am I really all that excited? Is this what I want to do? How I want to spend the next century or two?

Much of his doubt, of course, stemmed from what Alena had shared the night before.

"Is that you, Damian? I've got good news!" she'd called out to him. Moments later, she appeared from the kitchen. "Would you like some ice cream? It never melts, you know."

"And always remains cold," he muttered, staring up at the second-floor landing. The door—the one he had yet to step through—was ajar. He wasn't sure why, but it made his stomach queasy. "Actually, maybe just a cup of that tea you always drink."

"Sure thing." She disappeared from view, off to gather the ingredients.

Damian plodded across the foyer and into the kitchen. "How was work?"

A smile graced her face, so genuine Damian knew it'd been an extraordinary day for her.

"Today was the culmination of months of hard work." She took a deep breath. If they'd been back in their Chicago apartment, Damian knew it would've been a sigh of exhaustion. "I told you about the rules keeping kids in childcare until a relative arrives. About how they can't mature until that happens."

"Of course I do." He nodded, watching her fill a tea infuser with various herbs. "I'm sure you bring them a lot of comfort."

"Actually, I haven't seen the children in a while." Alena placed the infuser in a mug, then poured in hot water from a whistling kettle. "I've been meeting with several ambassadors over the last year, gathering support to petition the Embassy to change those rules. Stepped on a few toes while making a name for myself. If Colin didn't tell you about it, you'll hear soon enough."

Damian grunted, beginning to understand what he had meant.

"Let that sit for a minute, then take out the infuser," Alena said, sliding the mug over to him. "My persistence has paid off. The Embassy is letting me launch a pilot program. If successful, it'll affect the entire soul intake process. More children will find homes and grow up."

Damian had moved to remove the herbs, but his hand hovered above the cup as his brain simultaneously saw the dots *and* connected them. "What exactly does this program consist of?"

"One baby selected at random will go to an adoptive family. Once outside the confines of childcare, their mind and body will mature. Preliminary projections show it'll take approximately one year for a baby to grow into a self-sufficient adult. At that point, they'll decide what directions they'd like to take—basically work through the same questions you are right now."

Alena stopped, seeming to realize she'd been pacing in front of the kitchen sink.

"Speaking of which," Damian had said, finally picking up his tea, "I may have found some of my answers!"

"Open it," Alena said, sitting up on the beach chair.

Damian blinked, looking up from the piece of mail in his hand. Just like him, she still wore yesterday's clothing. They'd come down to the lake after he finished recounting his interview with the Gray Ones. "Sorry. Didn't mean to wake you."

"No, no," she said, rubbing sleep from her eyes. "I want to know what the head ambassador has to say."

A knot formed in Damian's chest as his fingers traced the edge of the envelope. He shifted his weight from one foot to the other, feeling the sand compress under his toes. "Before I do, I'd like to talk about last night."

"Oh?" She leaned forward in her chair, looking like an expectant schoolgirl.

"I wanted to apologize for hijacking the conversation. For discarding your good news for my day's events. I didn't even let you finish talking about the...about the..."

"The pilot program?" Alena finished for him.

"Yeah." Damian shifted his weight again, the knot in his chest tightening. "You said a baby would go home to a family. Do you know who that family is?"

"Of course I do," she said, staring at him fixedly. "*We* are that family."

Damian never liked children. In high school, he had a penchant for tasteless baby jokes. His favorite was "What's red and orange and looks good on babies?"

"Umm, a jumper?" was the typical guess from anyone gullible enough to answer him.

"No, fire!" Maniacal laughter always followed the punchline. All who heard it told him how revolting he was and that he should never have children. This, of course, was what he'd sought all along. External verification that he shouldn't be a father.

Then he would question why he had trouble making friends.

Even after he learned to keep his offensive jokes to himself, Damian would watch in horror as parents tried to hush bawling babies or keep their sticky fingers from infecting every single item within reach. He found it repulsive how they slobbered over everything—especially their own hands.

As wretched as those displays were, they weren't the genuine reason he didn't want children. Nobody *really* knew the truth. It'd taken him time to figure it out himself.

Damian had misgivings about his mom and dad's parenting techniques. His father's aloofness and inward focus made it difficult to connect, and his mother took the meaning of overbearing to a whole new level. Isolated and alone, Damian rarely felt loved—or at least couldn't recognize their parenting attempts as expressions of affection.

Deep down, he knew they loved him. He loved them too. Yet his misgivings stuck with him. He never wanted to treat another human being like that. To leave them alone to stew in doubt and teenage hormones. Especially not his child.

What concerned Damian even more than expressing affection in a way that wouldn't traumatize a kid was the thought of not *having* the love to give. And if he couldn't feel for his own children, he would end up hating himself.

It was better not to take the chance.

There is *one person who understands me. Or at least I thought she did.* Another knot formed in Damian's stomach. Alena had seen things in him he never knew existed. She'd realized his struggles and rarely pushed the parenting issue. Desperately wishing for a family of her own, she'd waited until circumstances were in her favor. He was an interloper, stumbling into her plans.

"Is this the right time?" His voice cracked as he asked the question.

Alena cocked her head, her dark eyes studying him. "There's never a perfect time."

"I know." Damian's shoulders slumped. The envelope felt heavier, the weight of its contents more pressing. "It's just... Have you paid attention to what's happened on Earth since you died?"

She shrugged, as if the idea of peeking over the shoulders of the living had never occurred to her, then nodded at him to go on.

"It was hard to get along without you, though I'm glad you didn't have to see what the world was shaping into. Our so-called leaders used all the power granted to them—and any power they could grant themselves—to turn their ideas into reality. People like Colin live in fear of their basic rights being stripped away. Hate and violence have become so commonplace it no longer fazes anyone when schoolchildren are gunned down."

Damian sighed. Even Minade, a community haunted by decades of quiet boredom, had been rocked by two violent murders in recent years. One involved a high schooler stalking a volunteer bus monitor. The student eventually broke into her home and stabbed her while her child slept down the hall.

Alena's hand twitched as though she wanted to make a counterpoint. She remained silent, though, waiting for him to *make* his point.

"There are lots of reasons I never wanted children," Damian said. "They're gross and they stink, sure, but it also seemed ludicrous to start a family in a world where every issue is simplified to black and white, right and wrong."

Damian took a deep breath. He hadn't spoken so openly in a long while.

"The moment I woke up in the Afterlife, I knew this place was unlike anything taught in church. On one hand, I find that refreshing, because it means there's a place for you, me, and Colin." Damian held up the envelope. "On the other, I fear this is just another version of our previous lives. A powder keg waiting to erupt. The Embassy, this...Department of Satanic Investigations, reminds me of all the things I dreaded on Earth."

Alena stood up and embraced him. "I'm sorry that I left you alone in the world. I know things have been dark. The people being attacked are strong, though. Don't underestimate what those like Colin might've added to the conversation." After giving him a tight squeeze, Alena stepped back. Her eyes remained locked on his. "The Afterlife differs from what either of us expected.

Mostly that it exists at all! Imagine your mother's reaction if she knew we're together again—that you hung out with Colin!"

Damian gave a reluctant chuckle. "She'd have an absolute fit."

"I understand your concern for those back on Earth, but there are also things that must change here in the Afterlife. Without people willing to take the first step, it will never happen. Remember that we'll be here for eternity. We'll reap the benefits of our actions or else suffer the consequences. Either way, we won't be able to escape our decisions."

Alena took his hand. It was a tender gesture, but also meant to brace him. "This pilot program is my attempt at creating positive change for a group of people I care deeply about—that we should *all* care about. I've been working on it well before you arrived, and your presence will not alter my plans. We are adopting a child, Damian. Not because it's something I want, but because it's the right thing to do."

The two knots within Damian threatened to join forces and rip him apart. Alena squeezed his hand, which helped release the tension. "I know you're hesitant about working, especially for a place like the Embassy. I'll support you if you want to relax and write that book you always wanted to." She winked at him. "I wouldn't mind having an extra pair of hands around the house to help raise a kid."

Alena pointed at the envelope in his hand. "Whatever that letter says, you are more than qualified to work for the Embassy. You are *aware* of what concerns you. Now, please open your mail!"

Damian felt her hand fall away. She was giving him space to consider her words, even if it left a cold void against his palm. Like stones being dropped into the lake, her arguments created waves that crashed through his mind. *I still don't want to adopt, but what can I say? That it'll take too much time, or that I fear the thought of becoming like my parents?* Those reasons paled against Alena's convictions to help others.

While her points about the Embassy were true, they struck a familiar chord. His parents' voices echoed from the past: *Study something practical. Something you can live off of. You can always write in your spare time.*

This felt different, though. Unlike his younger self, who'd given in to parental pressure, he now had a choice. A real one. The Embassy—his friend, Colin—needed help addressing actual threats.

"You're right," he said, looking up at his wife. The knots in his chest and stomach were still there, but they lessened. "About all of it. I want to help make things better here. Like you're doing. Maybe that starts with what's in here."

Damian tried to open the envelope cleanly along the upper crease but ended up making an ugly tear. He frowned at that, thinking there should be more ceremony to correspondence from an Embassy official. He wasn't certain how leadership in the Afterlife equated with Earth. *Is the ambassador like a governor, president, or monarch? Does each plane elect its own head ambassador, or is there only one?*

"Go ahead," Alena urged him.

Damian pulled a piece of parchment from the desecrated envelope, straightened it, and read aloud.

Damian Craig Hartter,

I am pleased to learn of your interest in working with the Embassy. The Gray Ones have granted you provisional security clearance—full access will be given upon your acceptance of a job. Please consider the Department of Satanic Investigations, headed by Ambassador Wendell Klinekole. They could use the help, and he has requested that you stop by at your earliest convenience.

We are all looking forward to your many contributions here at the Embassy.

Working for you,
Picardia Knutt, Head Ambassador

"I'm in," Damian whispered. He wasn't sure why, but the knowledge helped him relax.

"Of course you're in, babe. Congratulations." Alena gave him another hug, then stepped toward the house. "I'm going to put on some coffee. You should drink some before going in."

Damian blinked, then called back to her, "I didn't say I was going to the city today!"

"Mhmm" was the only reply.

I still have a choice. I'm more relaxed because the opportunity is available, but I can decide against it, he told himself, following his wife. *Unlike this pilot program. But that's only for a year. I can do that for a year.*

CHAPTER NINE

Coffee in hand, Damian took the time to go upstairs and change into different clothes. The letter from the head ambassador hadn't specified a dress code, but he wouldn't show up wearing the same outfit as the day before. Colin would definitely point that out.

After finding stretch slacks and a polo in the spacious bedroom closet, Damian returned to the kitchen and rummaged for a quick breakfast.

"Are you actually hungry, babe?" Alena sipped tea from the island, a glint of amusement in her eyes.

"Well, no, I guess not." Damian bit his lower lip. "Force of habit, I suppose."

"You'll never be hungry again. We eat only for pleasure here."

He patted his stomach. "I've always eaten for pleasure."

"No time for that now. The Embassy waits for no one." Alena swiveled the barstool to the side and hopped off. Damian noticed she was wearing her preferred work attire just before she launched herself at him. As her arms wrapped around his torso, he tripped over his own feet. He fell backward, the kitchen disappearing into a kaleidoscope of colors. He barely had enough time to recognize the whooshing sound of peregrination before he landed on his back in a patch of lush grass.

What the hell? While Damian knew Alena had initiated the travel for him—which, overall, seemed like a gross violation of personal agency—he wasn't sure exactly where she'd sent them. For a moment, he thought he'd returned to his broken body in Minade's central park.

A figure appeared overhead. *Is it the concerned woman or the elderly gentleman with the wooden cane?*

"Good morning, Alena Isabel Hartter. And to you, Damian Craig Hartter."

"Morning, Athan," he said, recognizing the gaunt face and sunken eyes of Athan peering down at them. The oppressive edifice of the Embassy stood behind the Guardian.

"Let me help you up." Athan stooped and offered a hand.

Damian took hold, allowing the Guardian to lift him off the ground, then assisted Alena to her feet. "I hope *your* wife didn't scare you into another afterlife before you left home."

Athan did not respond. Out of the corner of his eye, Damian saw Alena cringe.

"What?"

"Guardians don't have spouses. At least not as you and I understand." Alena looked up at Athan for confirmation.

Athan considered her for a moment, then added, "We were created in such haste that no consideration was given to gender. Anatomically, we Guardians are all alike, and while we enjoy each other's company, we do not procreate. Those of us you see have always been."

"I'm sorry for the misunderstanding." Damian tried to shake off images of what intercourse between Guardians would look like. "I'll be more mindful of my words in the future."

"I took no offense." Athan stretched out a long arm toward the Embassy's entrance, where Mai was opening the door for a billy goat. "I hope both of your days go well. And that you accept the job, Damian Craig Hartter."

"You know?" He and Alena followed the Guardian up the front steps. "I learned about it an hour ago."

"I know most comings and goings at the Embassy." Athan resumed the same position as the day before, standing tall and forbidding. "Why else would you return after yesterday's ordeal?"

"Good point," he said as Mai opened the massive door. "Oh, and Athan? You can just call me Damian. The entire name sounds like a mouthful."

"You honor me." The Guardian bowed, the jeweled crown looming over his head. Mai scowled impatiently.

Damian hurried through the door, his eyes taking only a moment to adjust to the dim light of the foyer. He thought he saw the goat vanish down a hallway. Turning to Alena, he said, "Why didn't you clue me in? I had no idea they were non-binary!"

Alena shook her head. "I thought you would've figured it out yourself by now."

"How?" he asked, gesturing to the entrance. "It's not like they're—"

"Not like they're what?" she interrupted, raising an eyebrow. "You shouldn't assume based on appearances. As a creative person, I thought you'd know not all creations fall into categories we imagine."

I can imagine quite a lot, Damian wanted to say, but he bit his tongue. "What're you doing here, anyway?"

"I have to appear before a committee to finalize details on the adoption." Her face softened. "Then they'll pull a name at random, and I'll take that child home."

"Wow," he said, feeling the knot in his chest constrict in terror or...*is that anticipation?* "We're going to be parents."

Alena hugged him—gently this time. "I've got to go. Don't want to be late. Good luck today!"

In a daze, Damian watched her hurry down the same hallway as the goat. Then he shook his head, dispelling his uncertainties, and turned his attention to the foyer's central feature. Now that he understood the importance of the Bridge, he wanted to study it more intently.

As he approached, Colin appeared from the other side. "Ah, there you are, Flame! I was wondering when you'd arrive."

"How'd you know I'd be here?"

"I know you better than you think. You may have grown up, but you've still got an inquisitive soul." Colin looked him over. "Nice clothes. Very preppy. You playing golf later?"

Damian glanced down at his polo and slacks. "This is probably nicer than what my parents buried me in."

The corners of Colin's mouth twitched, but he graciously refrained from harassing Damian. He wore a turquoise button-up and a darker jacket than the previous day, which paired nicely with the foyer's color palette. *How much thought does he put into dressing each day?*

Colin led him up two flights of stairs and down a lengthy corridor, his longer legs easily keeping him in the lead. "I'm glad the head ambassador is pushing you to consider an assignment in the DSI. I really hope you take it. Not just because you and I would make a good team. We lost an employee last week. It's just me and two others now."

Their surroundings made it increasingly difficult for Damian to focus on Colin's words. The walls of the hallway continued the decorative paneling of the foyer, though dozens of wooden doors lined each side. Mounted golden plaques announced the department that lay behind each. Some sounded serious, like the Department of Tracking or the Department of Dimensional Stability. Others were downright ludicrous. Damian's favorite was the Redundant Department of Redundancy.

Someone has a sense of humor.

"Ope!" Damian said after bumping into Colin, who had stopped two doors from the end of the hall. The plaque next to it read Department of Satanic Investigations. "Sorry. Why'd the last person quit?"

"The nature of our investigations has become quite serious. I think what was initially a cushy job turned into actual work." Colin shrugged, then opened the door. "They weren't cut out for the role."

"Huh." Damian mulled over the stress and dissatisfaction he suffered at his last job. Even working remotely from his cheap apartment in Minade, he never found fulfillment. Writing code and tracking his time for management left him depressed, with no time for writing outside of night classes.

Those dismal memories dissipated as he stepped into the office. The sheer size of the space, capable of comfortably housing twenty people, astonished him. The room looked as though several other doors out in the hallway should've afforded access to it. *Spatial boundaries aren't as set as I'm used to.*

No ornate paneling lined the office walls, and the room's furnishings clashed. What looked like a billiards table dominated the center of the room. Instead of cue sticks and balls, piles of papers and peculiar objects cluttered its surface.

Individual work areas occupied each corner. One was an ultra-modern workstation with holographic view screens. Another was an Apache wickiup. Mounds of dirt broke up the marble tile floor around the wickiup, out of which colorful flowers bloomed.

In the farthest corner was a plain-looking cubicle reminiscent of Damian's workstation in Chicago. Green fabric walls doubled as bulletin boards. The metal cabinetry appeared beat up, and the chair well-used. What appeared to be dirt—not the kind used for gardening—darkened the surrounding floor. Little decor provided clues to the owner's personality—*certainly isn't Colin's*—though a metal fan lolled back and forth. In the soft breeze was a hint of smoke and tobacco.

"That's Kasee's desk." The disdain in Colin's voice was palpable. "She's out investigating some case or another. Let's wait for Wendell over here."

Colin led him over to the neatly organized workstation equipped with holographic displays. Extra seats invited company, and there wasn't a speck of dirt to be seen. No personal knickknacks or mementos adorned the desk, the only commonality shared with Kasee's. Not even a small pumpkin to liven up the otherwise sterile environment.

He's not a teenager tending his parents' gardens, Damian reminded himself. *He's moved on from that hobby to a successful career.*

"What's that?" Damian asked as he took a seat, pointing to a softball-sized sphere hovering above the surface of the table. Tiny waves of holographic light emanated from the desk, dancing across its stony, dull-gray surface.

"This," Colin said, plucking the ball right out of the air, "is the Sphere of Doom. Rather, it *looks* like the sphere. It hasn't actually done anything."

"Is it supposed to?" The object appeared only slightly more dangerous than an actual softball. Instead of leather wrapping, glyph markings covered its surface, inlaid with slivers of metal. Damian didn't recognize them.

"According to myth, the Sphere of Doom is a relic left behind by Satan when they were banished from the Celestial City. It moves—no, it rolls around at incredible speeds, never remaining in the same place long. It randomly shrinks everything within a hundred yards to minuscule size. While it's usually dormant, it's been acting up recently, creating a lot of work for several Embassy departments."

Damian leaned back in his chair. "Is it safe to keep this Sphere of Doom here?"

"No!" Colin's eyes widened. "The damage it'd cause if it activated within these walls is unfathomable!"

With a sigh, he tossed the object back onto the desk. It bounced heavily before it resumed hovering a few inches above the surface. "But this isn't the true sphere."

Damian eyed it suspiciously. "How do you know?"

"The myth leaves out important details. Four decoy spheres were created and released at the same time as the one they imitate. The markings on the decoys are identical to each other but altered from the true sphere. This is the third one we've found." He pointed to a secured cabinet against the wall. "It matches the other two in our possession."

"Details no one outside the Embassy should know, and very few outside this department," said a measured voice from behind them. The two jumped out of their chairs, turning to see a tall wiry man with long dark hair draped over his shoulders. Instead of scrutinizing them with the same disapproval lacing his words, he gazed past them to the floating orb.

"Sorry, Wendell," Colin said, looking down at his feet. "I keep thinking Damian's already a member of the department."

"No such paperwork has crossed my desk." Wendell's hard features softened as his eyes swept over Damian. "So you're Damian Hartter? Colin won't stop singing your praises."

"Ambassador Klinekole." Damian nodded. "I received a letter from the head ambassador this morning, asking that I stop by as soon as possible."

"Wendell will do here, Damian. With the serious cases we explore, a first-name basis provides a source of levity."

The ambassador wore a collared shirt and slacks, though of a more modest cut than Colin's, and no jacket. Despite the professional atmosphere, the man hadn't offered a handshake during the introduction. Damian guessed Wendell was not himself a fount of levity.

"I sense hesitation in you, Damian. Have you not decided?"

"From what Colin has said, I feel this department carries a lot of responsibility, that you demand a lot of time and energy from those who work for you. The work intrigues me, but it's a lot to take on so soon after arriving." Colin stuttered a protest, but Damian spoke over him. "No, I haven't decided."

"Very good." Wendell offered a hint of a smile. With a sideways glance at Colin, he added, "We don't allow nepotism within the Embassy. I would hate to think you only wanted in because of your friendship."

"Of course, sir—Wendell."

The ambassador walked over to the large table in the center of the room. While it had the raised sides and green felt of a billiards table, the expected six pockets were conspicuously absent.

"We have a departmental meeting first thing tomorrow morning. If you decide to join us before then, it would be a good opportunity to catch up on our current cases." Wendell plucked an untidy stack of papers from the mass of similarly organized material on the table. "In the meantime, would you do me a favor and deliver these to Mrs. Ulrich at the Celestial Library? She's the head librarian."

"Right away, sir."

He waved his hand dismissively. "Take your time. Colin tells me you enjoy reading and writing. You might find some material at the library that piques your creative interest."

"Thank you, sir."

Wendell gave him a strange look before heading to the wickiup. Damian glanced questioningly at Colin, who was trying unsuccessfully to stifle a chuckle. "What?"

"Right away, sir. Thank you, sir," Colin mimicked. "We're not used to such formal language here."

"Ah," Damian said. "Comes from having a business degree."

He peered over to see Wendell tending to a plant in the garden before disappearing inside the wickiup. The man's stern demeanor had caught him off guard. The details he knew of Damian, even more so.

"You'll grow out of it," Colin said, clapping him on the back. "Let me show you out. How about you and Alena come over for dinner soon? Day after tomorrow? I'll cook!"

After getting directions from Athan, Damian set off on foot to find the Celestial Library. A plethora of visual stimuli captured his attention. Intelligent species bustled through the streets, varied shops and eateries enticed him with smells, and the complete absence of shadows constantly reminded him he was no longer on Earth.

I feel like I'm in the Emerald City, ruled by a mysterious wizard few ever see face-to-face.

The lack of the Creator's presence nagged at Damian. He never bought into the idea of souls worshiping their gods on bended knee day after day, the deities sitting leisurely or judgingly upon a grand throne. Both parties would grow bored.

Felt rather clinical to schedule an appointment for a moment of the Creator's time, like going in for a routine dental cleaning. Damian shuddered. *I still need to think of my one question.*

The massive castle dominating the city's heart, complete with its ramparts and defensive towers, maintained vigil across the whole of existence. Damian pondered the need for such security. Tradition accounted for many elements, like the Guardians keeping watch over an impenetrable diamond wall. Other entities, like the Gray Ones, were more troubling. Their purpose was to keep evil out of the Embassy. *Which means evil lurks outside it.*

Lost in thought, Damian almost walked past the Celestial Library. It took a passerby with an armful of books bumping into him to redirect his focus. He surveyed the building, finding it no more or less impressive a structure than others around it. Shaped like a grain silo, its outer walls formed a wide cylinder reaching halfheartedly for the sky. A domed roof topped it off.

Somehow, I expected more. Damian pushed through the ordinary front doors...and gasped.

The interior of the library proved to be unlike any other he'd seen. He would've been content with a musty atmosphere, dim lighting, and cramped spaces between towering shelves. Such places were familiar territory. But the main floor of the library was stark in its austerity. At the center of the circular space was a cluttered desk, the only piece of furniture in sight. Around the perimeter, ladders granted access to a loft.

It was there that Damian spotted what he'd expected. Hundreds of shelves were built into the wall, packed tightly with novels, magazines, and manuscripts. Multiple figures stood around, each absorbed in their own tome or parchment.

For the second time that morning, what he saw disoriented him. Outside, the building looked only four or five stories. Within, it felt infinite. He had to squint to make out the ceiling. *Another case of extreme spatial distortion.*

"May I help you?" asked a croaking voice from atop the central desk. It took Damian a moment to locate the source among the clutter of books. What he'd originally assumed was a garish trinket—a glassy purple toad with a tuft of curly white hair above its beady eyes—leaped up into the air to attract his attention.

I'm talking to a toad, Damian thought to himself. *Do not laugh at the intelligent toad.*

"Um, I'm looking for Mrs. Ulrich," he said, slowly approaching the desk.

"She is me," the toad said, hopping closer. She wore tiny, frameless spectacles, complete with a fine granny chain wrapping around her thick neck. "You must be Mr. Hartter."

"That's right," Damian said, brow furrowing.

"Ambassador Klinekole told me to expect you," Mrs. Ulrich croaked. The sound reverberated around the unadorned room. She glanced at his hand, a thin tongue flicking out and moistening her lips. "My papers?"

Damian held up the documents—the librarian jumped back as though afraid he'd swat at her—and placed them on top of a stack of books.

"I must say," Mrs. Ulrich said, black eyes peering over the top of her spectacles at the untidy collection. "I'm rather surprised Ambassador Klinekole finally returned this to me."

"Oh?"

"He checked this out years ago. Whenever I broached the subject of late returns, he claimed the papers weren't suitable for a library." She gave a disapproving expression. "I don't think the ambassador understands the purpose of the Celestial Library."

"What is its purpose?"

Mrs. Ulrich croaked, appalled at the question. "The library contains every piece of literature ever written across all creations. You can find the magical Barrien works of my culture, or the lurid romances of yours. This"—her moist eyes glanced at the manuscript—"is from Earth. Written by the Iranian prophet Zarathushtra, it details his temptation by Angra Mainyu."

"Is that another name for Satan?" Damian guessed, though he was unfamiliar with the prophet.

"Yes and no. Much like the Creator, Satan wears many faces and uses many names. Now, granted, folks don't check out material like Zarathushtra's every day, but if someone has need of it, they can usually rely on us to have it. We have everything, thanks to Ambassador Klinekole's kind return." With two flicks of her filamentary tongue, the manuscript disappeared into a desk drawer. "The ambassador mentioned you like to read. I invite you to have a look around."

Damian looked up at the loft, shelves upon shelves of books beckoning him. He could lose himself for days browsing for one perfect text to read. The desire to sit in the armchair at home with a cup of coffee and a good book tugged at him.

Still time to back out of the Embassy. Leave the DSI to experts like Colin. Just enjoy your time doing what you want. Get some reading and writing done.

As he pondered how to reach the upper shelves—the ladders only went from the main level up to the loft, and hundreds of bookcases stretched toward the domed ceiling—Mrs. Ulrich interrupted with another croak.

"Perhaps what you're looking for is over there." Her shiny, purple head tilted back, directing his attention to a small podium against the far wall. He'd overlooked it before, which surprised him because upon it rested a weathered, leather-bound book so thick and tattered it rivaled the Grand Book of Appointments.

"What is it?"

The toad's head relaxed into its normal position. "The *Book of History.*"

He had an idea that all the books he'd read in his life amounted to nothing here. "My wife showed me my autobiographical series. Is this similar?"

Mrs. Ulrich nodded. "The *Book of History* faithfully records an unbiased account of all events across all planes of existence, including the Celestial City."

Including the Iranian prophet? He wondered if every article in the building could be reduced to a single volume.

Damian nodded his thanks and walked over to the podium. He stood still for a moment, eyeing the gold lettering spelling out *The Book of History* across the front cover. Then, feeling foolish—*was I expecting the book to read itself aloud?*—he reached forward and opened it.

The first page, as with most books, was blank. The next, usually reserved for copyright information, was also free of any text. *Makes sense, I guess, if it automatically records every event.* Flipping forward, though, showed that none of the dusty pages contained inscriptions.

Stupid magical book, he thought.

Cheeks burning, he was about to turn and consult Mrs. Ulrich for guidance when, without even a subtle breeze, the pages fluttered and turned on their own. Damian stared as they eventually settled. Words bled their way onto the page. As the title at the top became legible, he questioned how the volume knew what he wanted to learn.

A Brief History of the Embassy – Earth Branch

Human civilization began forming approximately twelve thousand years ago. Their advancement did not warrant a branch in the Embassy for another six thousand years, when the Creator's ultimate plan for them took shape. Once chartered, the Earth Branch was not unlike any other, existing to foster positive relations with other planes of existence. Between the time of the War for Heaven and the Great Ascension, however, the Earth Branch took a more active role in the everyday lives of those it looked after. It instituted laws and regulations, as well as several social programs beyond its original purview. These ensured Satan never transgressed what authority the Creator granted them in human matters.

Except for the occasional grand ambassador with an overly analytical personality—most of those being from the Aurelio Creation—the Embassy has always run smoothly, even as other branches adopted similar policies as Earth's. In the year 2008 CE, when the entire organization collapsed, everyone worked together to bring all infrastructure back online. Head Ambassador Picardia—

"Wait a minute," Damian said aloud. "What's this about the Embassy collapsing?"

Again, the pages flipped rapidly back and forth until they established a new location. More words appeared. *This time with a more eye-catching title.*

The Fall of the Embassy

On April 19 of the year 2008, after a decade of relative calm in the Celestial City, all critical infrastructure necessary for the Embassy's operation ground to a halt. No one could enter or exit the main building or any of its ancillary offices. With no access to the Bridge, communications and travel between all planes of existence ceased. Employees couldn't work and, more importantly, the disruption interrupted the monitoring of realms of interest.

The downtime lasted two hours. Under the capable leadership of Grand Ambassador Julianne, all branches and their associated department heads cracked their way back into the Embassy and repaired their respective cogs of the greater machine. All infrastructure was fully functional within a day.

The cause of the fall of the Embassy is currently unknown. Thus, only a handful of facts about the entire event are documented. Intelligence discovered that several bad actors from realms of interest took advantage of the blackout period. Satan, for example, used the time to infect an individual on Earth—a clear violation of their sentencing.

The grand ambassador created a new department in the incident's wake to prevent another such occurrence. Ambassador Ruphius Dolip has headed up—

"Wait a minute," Damian said again, waving his hands at the book. "I want to know more about this infection."

The pages remained still. He asked several more times, each iteration with different phrasing, but the paper did not so much as flutter under his breath.

"Mr. Hartter," Mrs. Ulrich interrupted after his seventh attempt. "The *Book of History* is a telling of known historical facts. If it doesn't answer your question, it means nothing is recorded on the matter or you don't have clearance to view it."

"Oh," Damian said with a heavy sigh. The book had given him a glimpse of the larger picture, but it had also introduced more questions. *What could bring down the Embassy? How many other bad actors are out there, and what are these realms of interest?*

Mrs. Ulrich croaked, her tiny head motioning for him to approach. "What were you reading about, if I may ask?"

"The Embassy's collapse," Damian said as he sidled over. "Something about an infection during the downtime, though I didn't get much on the latter."

The librarian's eyes bulged, an impressive feat given their prominence. She placed a webbed finger up to her mouth, though Damian couldn't tell if she was silencing him or her own quivering lips. "Do not speak so loudly about that matter! It's classified information."

Taken aback, he said, "If it's classified, why is it in a book in the library?"

"The *Book of History* contains many built-in security precautions. It allowed you to view classified information because the Embassy had granted you clearance to see it. Otherwise, it would've omitted the knowledge."

Damian suddenly realized he wasn't merely doing Wendell a favor by returning an untidy stack of papers. Zarathushtra's writings were a sacrifice to get him here. *Does he think me so curious that I'd refuse a job offer before answering these questions?*

"Why do you have clearance?"

"I don't. Not directly, anyway." She gave him a sly look. "As head librarian, I am tied to the book. It is me, and I am it. Despite that relationship, I am also simply me. That's important to you because, while I can't tell you facts the book doesn't contain, I can convey *other* details."

Damian's head spun as he struggled to keep up with her words. "Such as?"

"General suspicions, if you'd care to hear."

He kept his excitement in check, but he could tell his interest was the highlight of Mrs. Ulrich's day. "Yes, please."

"Well," she said, licking her lips. "We know Satan is a cunning entity, and they certainly took advantage of that little snafu at the Embassy. It's believed they sought one person on Earth, one individual who was certain to make it to the Afterlife. They took a soul from their realm, the soul of someone wholly evil, and hid it within that one good person. Now, when that individual dies, it's hypothesized that the evil soul could gain access to the Celestial City. Once here, it could do anything it pleased. Most likely, it would work to undermine every plane of existence."

Some of the puzzle pieces came together in Damian's head. The Gray Ones had spoken of Satan attempting to infiltrate the city with an evil soul and had told him he'd been a host candidate. They hadn't elaborated, and he'd been too caught up by their mention of Satan to ask.

The Gray Ones are searching for this soul, and the Department of Satanic Investigations aims to stave off further attacks from dark forces. Still doesn't explain how or why the Embassy collapsed.

"How does this concern all planes?" he asked. "I always thought Satan had eyes for Earth only."

"Oh, you are mistaken." Mrs. Ulrich's beady eyes narrowed, and her green skin darkened. "While Satan was granted limited charge over Earth, the issue concerns the entire multiverse. They are an extremely powerful creature with a dark agenda. They were cast out of the Celestial City for leading a mutiny. After thousands of years locked away in a separate realm, no one doubts they haven't changed in the slightest—unless it's for the worse. If this evil soul can grant them access to the city once again, havoc will be unleashed. If Satan was to actually take over all of Creation, as is certainly their goal, what do you think would happen?

"No, Mr. Hartter. This concerns far more than your world. If it's true, and this dark soul succeeds, it could mean the destruction of all we know and take for granted."

CHAPTER TEN

SOME REVELATIONS COME AT *a steep price*, Damian thought. The sentence wasn't perfect. A bit cliche. He wrote the words down anyway. *Even while I have every reason to rejoice, a heavy burden weighs me down. Knowledge of imminent destruction has that effect on people, and I am not immune.*

A garbled babble broke Damian's focus. He looked up from the writing desk at which he'd been scribbling notes. In the middle of the home library, taking up more space than he considered necessary, was a playpen. Within its confines sat a plump, cheerful baby.

"I do have every reason to rejoice," he said to the child, who only cooed back at him. "I've passed the inquisition of the Gray Ones, and I feel like my usual self. The evil soul isn't within me. You died hundreds of years ago, so you're safe. Safe enough, anyway."

The baby stared at him with watery eyes. It thumped its fat thighs with tiny fists.

"You're right. I can't write off Alena and Colin yet." He and Colin were members of a select group the Gray Ones welcomed into the Afterlife. The common element between them was still a mystery, though he felt it should be obvious. He jotted down a reminder to follow up on the thought later. "It's far more likely that the infected person is still on Earth, living out a happy life, unaware of the troubles they carry."

That individual was the reason for the Embassy's secrecy and paranoia. The Gray Ones and the DSI were only parts of an overall strategy to weed out and stop the evil soul from entering the Afterlife, keeping Satan from invading the Celestial City again. After the revelations uncovered at the Celestial Library, Damian had reluctantly committed himself to that agenda. The bureaucracy of the Embassy still bothered him, but the threat they faced had the potential to affect the well-being of those he loved both in the Afterlife and on Earth. If anything happened to Alena because he selfishly stayed home and wrote books, he'd never forgive himself.

The baby babbled again, a stream of saliva dripping from its chin.

"What?" he asked, donning an innocent face. "Look, we just met. I barely know you!"

"As I live and breathe," Alena said from the foyer, startling Damian. She was dressed for work, a conjured cup of tea in hand. "Are you actually talking to Bennett?"

"You heard nothing." He picked up his pen and focused on his notes. "I was thinking aloud."

"What're you working on?" She set her tea next to Damian's coffee and freed the drooling child from its colorful prison. "I thought you'd sleep in until the last moment before heading into the office."

"Just jotting down some thoughts about my experiences here so far. I took the Embassy job, but that doesn't mean I have to abandon my creative side. This is only my sixth day here, and I feel like I have enough material to write a trilogy."

"That's a great idea." She beamed at him. "Thanks for bringing Bennett down with you. It's good for the two of you to interact."

Damian watched as Alena swayed back and forth, the baby carefully tucked into one arm. The act conveyed a loving tenderness, especially as she poked at his chin and nose with her free hand. When he'd carried Bennett downstairs after waking, it was with two hands held out as far as possible.

We did all sleep soundly, he noted. *And aside from salivating all over himself, he hasn't bothered me this morning.*

"I'm remaining open to the possibility of, you know, liking the thing."

Alena stuck out her tongue as she retrieved her drink. "I knew you liked him the moment you came home yesterday."

In actuality, Damian had been dubious when she'd met him on the front porch, carrying their new charge. Bennett wore a happy, wet smile that initially agitated him. Then Damian looked into his light brown eyes, finding intelligence in them. In that moment, he forced himself to recognize that this was a human being, not an uncomfortable construct.

The child's history, which Alena recounted with a dramatic flair, fascinated him. Born in 1357, his family lived in La Rogue, located in the Dordogne region of southwest France. It'd been a tumultuous period. The Dordogne River formed a divisive line between French and English forces during much of the Hundred Years' War. La Rogue inadvertently found itself in the middle of a dispute between the two sides, and many perished. Bennett's home had caught fire during a skirmish. No one survived.

Only a few months old. Thankfully, he won't recollect any of it. Damian shivered at the thought of burning to death. He considered the child's birth parents. About the type of people they'd been that neither were here in the Afterlife.

"I'm heading to work in a minute, but I should return by midafternoon," Alena said, finishing her tea while disappearing around the corner. Damian froze, suddenly aware they'd made no accommodation for Bennett.

Surely no harm would come to him if left alone all day. It certainly wouldn't paint us in a positive light, though! He again reconsidered his decision to take the Embassy job.

"Thankfully, work provides daycare," Alena called out from the kitchen. "And Bennett is already familiar with everyone there."

Obviously. Damian sighed in relief, grateful she had work benefits to take advantage of. *It's a wonder the Embassy wanted to hire me.*

"We're all doomed," he muttered.

He got up, tucking his notes away into a desk drawer—except the one with *common element?* scrawled across it, which he tucked into his pocket. Alena met him in the foyer for a hug and kiss. Damian waved goodbye to Bennett from a distance, watching as they disappeared to the childcare facility.

"Just might end up liking him," he said aloud, shaking his head in mock disgust. Then he too peregrinated to work.

Damian hurried up the steps of the Embassy and through the front door. He was unfamiliar with the pair of Guardians standing watch, so he felt no pressure to make small talk. Ascending two flights of stairs and moving down the hall, he arrived at the second door from the end. Then he walked into what was to be his second home.

The office looked almost the same as it had when he'd left the day before. Wendell sat outside his wickiup, shuffling through a stack of papers. Colin leaned back in his ergonomic chair, the decoy sphere in hand.

A new desk sat adjacent to Colin's. It too was ultra-modern in design. A holographic screen hovered a few inches above the silver surface, itself free of any papers or artifacts. More than anything, its cleanliness was attractive to Damian.

"Hey, Flame!" Colin said, tossing the sphere back to its customary levitating position. He hopped up and pulled a chair out from behind the new desk. "Take a seat!"

"Is this mine?" Damian asked, traversing the wide room. The desk seemed too much for a new employee.

"Of course it is." Colin gestured again for him to sit. "It's a specialty item, but I pulled some strings and had it made for you overnight. Arrived an hour ago."

"Avenger..." He used the nickname to show his appreciation. "You shouldn't have. It must've cost—"

"It cost nothing more than a few favors. Remember that we don't use money here." Colin paused, scratching the side of his head. "No worries if you don't like it. We can get you something else or modify this however you want."

"No, I love it!" Damian accepted his invitation and sat in the seat. It looked simple enough: a high-backed office chair with armrests, made of high-end fabrics he'd never been able to afford. His body sank into the materials, its comfort unrivaled. "Oh, wow. You expect me to get work done in this?"

Colin pushed him closer to the table. "Try it out."

Damian peered at the holographic screen above his new desk. Other than a spinning logo—a design that looked suspiciously like the Bridge—it was blank. He wondered how he was supposed to interface with the system, but the answer presented itself as soon as his fingertips touched the surface. A keyboard lit up under his hands.

"Is this another projection or part of the desk itself?" Damian asked. He moved his hands across the table, fingertips still at the ready, and the keyboard followed.

Colin smiled, pleased with the reaction. "The whole desktop is actually an interactive screen. Let me show you."

Damian leaned back as Colin's fingers danced across the desk. The hologram of the Bridge flickered and disappeared, replaced by a directory of information. His eyes widened at the unfamiliar operating system—and the number of files listed.

"You have access to just about every bit of information the Embassy has," Colin said. "Don't worry. It may look like an advanced system from the future, but it's actually rather intuitive."

"I'm sure I'll get used to it pretty quick..." Damian's voice trailed off as he stared at the screen. Or rather, *through* the screen. In the far corner of the room, sitting in the plain-looking cubicle, was a red-headed teenage girl wearing an oversized hoodie, ripped jeans, and unlaced sneakers. She sat back, feet propped up on the metal desk as she casually smoked a cigar.

Damian blinked a few times and moved his head back and forth, wondering if he was hallucinating or if this was something the screen was showing him. *No, she's really there, blowing smoke into that rotating fan!*

"Who's that kid?"

Colin stepped back and looked across the room. "Hmm? Oh, that's Kasee Lang. She's rough around the edges but a great field investigator with a network of resourceful contacts. Wendell relies on her ability to turn over new information, which is why she's frequently out of the office."

"Do you know what Wendell had the kid doing three days ago?"

With a frown, Colin walked over to his own desk and took a seat. "Stop calling her a kid. Looks are often deceiving. Kasee was born in the same year we were. Died in 2010. For all you know, she could've arrived here over a thousand years ago."

Damian nodded, properly chastised.

"Anyway, she took that day off. Why do you ask?"

"Because I caught her peeping through my library window."

"What?" Colin swiveled around in his chair to peer at Kasee. She either didn't notice his outburst or didn't care. She remained focused on the cigar, not glancing their way. After turning back, he repeated more quietly, "What?"

"And when I saw her, she climbed on a bike and cycled away."

"You're sure it was Kasee?"

Damian pursed his lips as the girl tapped a column of ash onto the floor. "Do you know any other girls who bike around while smoking cigars?"

"No, no," Colin said. "She has a passion for cycling and is the only person I know who smokes. Still a nasty habit, even if it won't kill her. Let me ask her why she was at your place. I'll let you know."

More perplexed than before, Damian leaned back. He wanted to march over and ask Kasee what her game was, but the last thing he needed was to overstep on his first day on the job. *Even if this isn't a traditional workplace.*

The office door swung open, revealing a sickly woman standing in the frame. She wore a charcoal-colored suit, white button-up shirt, and black tie. Most extraordinary, though, was the top hat precariously perched on her head. At least two feet tall and sitting at a forty-five degree angle, gravity should've driven it to the floor.

"Ah, you're just in time." Wendell got up from his seat in the garden. "Everyone to the center."

Both Colin and Kasee immediately vacated their desks and headed for the cluttered table in the middle of the room. Damian rose more slowly, trailing behind Colin. He studied the strange woman as she, too, stepped farther into the office, her black shoes clicking against the marble floor. As they gathered together, he saw why she appeared so ill. Her skin possessed a blue hue.

Is she human or from another species?

"Everyone, please welcome Damian Hartter to the team," Wendell said once they all stood around the felt-topped table. The man appeared slightly more at ease than the day before, though he still gazed past Damian rather than looking him straight in the eyes. "Damian, you already know Colin, of course. Have you met Kasee?"

Damian nearly jumped when the ambassador gestured to his left. So distracted was he by the blue-skinned newcomer that he hadn't noticed the other girl standing next to him. Despite her smooth skin, vibrant hair, and grunge style, her weary eyes matched the blistering cigar in her hand. *They've witnessed events that weigh on her soul.*

"Haven't had the pleasure." After a moment of hesitation, he offered his hand. Kasee only shook it after a grudging inward battle of her own.

"Glad you finally made up your mind and joined us." Her voice had the deep, gravelly quality of a longtime smoker. Even more than Wendell, she refused to look him in the face.

"Damian, this is Odd Man Blue." Wendell turned reverently to face the woman. She was so short that even the top of her absurdly tall hat barely reached the ambassador's nose. The weave of her suit appeared nice—not that Damian knew what constituted quality fabric—though it hung loosely on her frame. "She doesn't technically work for the Embassy, but she has complete and unfettered access. She'll occasionally stop by to see how things are going and perhaps give us unique insight on a case."

"Pleased to meet you." Damian extended a hand across the table. She stared at it for a moment before reciprocating. Her palm felt cool, and the handshake was firmer than he expected. "Odd Man Blue. That's an...interesting name. I bet people don't confuse you with others often."

The top hat swayed as her head wobbled back and forth. "I often confuse others."

Her voice was deep, though not a typical baritone. It sounded like the petite woman, shuffling around in an oversized suit, housed an entire plane of existence. In a corner of that universe was a galaxy, and in that galaxy an even more remote planet. The voice came from way down on its surface, up and out of Odd Man Blue's mouth. Remarkably, it was a soft voice.

"Now that we're all acquainted," Wendell said, turning to Colin. "Are there any updates on the Sphere of Doom?"

Colin gave a curt nod and slowly looked around the table as he spoke. "I'm happy to report that the Department of Dimensional Stability successfully reversed the shrinkage of Dr. Carroll's pasture the other night. Any permanent damage to his land is negligible. Thankfully, Dr. Carroll and his family weren't present at the time of the shrinking, though their seven dairy cows and flock of sheep disappeared."

"Any living creature or soul caught in the sphere's influence is lost. Dozens of people are still unaccounted for," Wendell said for Damian's sake. To Colin, he asked, "Were you able to glean anything from the decoy orb recovered?"

"Unfortunately, no," he said, shaking his head. "I've already told Damian that it's identical to the previous decoys we have in our possession. The true sphere was long gone by the time an investigative team arrived at the pasture."

Wendell placed both hands on the side of the table, leaning in and staring blankly at a stack of papers. "So, no leads."

"Not necessarily. By charting the sphere's recent path, I may be able to pinpoint its next target."

All eyes turned to Colin. Even Odd Man Blue's eyebrows raised a quarter of an inch. Colin's professionalism still threw Damian. The adult stuck in a teenager's body. *Everyone's focused on him, just like he always wanted.*

"I thought the time in between shrinkings varied," Wendell said.

"They do, but I've still been able to discern a pattern to the attacks."

Colin gestured to the center of the table. Out of the mountain of manuscripts rose a holographic model of the Celestial City. It was a perfect miniature, even including the shimmering diamond wall. Four glowing red dots shone on the outside of the fortified barrier.

"You'll notice that each of the four shrinkings occurred approximately five miles from the Celestial Wall. I thought that was too precise to be random chance, so I ran them through a pattern recognition program. This is what it came up with."

Several lines cut their way across the model, overlaying each other at several points. Once they became stationary, having formed a cohesive picture, nobody moved or spoke for several seconds.

"Keep in mind that two attacks have yet to transpire to create this symbol," Colin said once the dramatic silence sunk in. "I may be getting ahead of myself here."

"I doubt it," Wendell said softly, leaning closer for a better look. "A six-pointed star, and the Celestial City at its center."

Colin nodded. "I believe the sphere's attacks are a kind of countdown. That there's an endgame to this."

"Have you considered," Kasee said, "this may be some type of joke?"

"If it is, it's in poor taste." Colin scowled, and Damian wasn't sure if it was from Kasee's thought or Kasee herself. "If you saw the affected areas, you'd know there's nothing funny about these events."

The table groaned as Kasee leaned against it. Cigar in hand, she said, "The Western world has long associated six-pointed stars with the occult, but the symbol also has many positive meanings."

"Kasee's right. There's no evidence to support the claim that the star is a powerful mark of Satan," Wendell added. "Or that they have any use for such sigils."

"The only power a symbol has is in the messages we let it convey," Kasee said. "It's possible that someone is capitalizing on this negative association to stir up a little fear."

Damian frowned, thinking that was awfully familiar to what the Gray Ones had said about the Afterlife. *Much of what you perceive and experience here is of your own making.*

"Who would find humor in this?" Colin bristled.

"Not everyone's sense of humor is the same. Even good people find amusement in awful circumstances." Wendell's stony face conveyed no humor.

"That's beside the point, though. The whereabouts of dozens are still unknown. And if Colin is correct, the sphere's current trajectory proves that it's not a joke."

"How's that?" Damian asked.

"When left to its own devices, the sphere engages in its devilish business at random places and intervals," Colin said. "Though erratically timed, its attacks don't appear to be indiscriminately placed. That means it's being controlled."

"Two conditions must be met for the device to be employed. The controller must have some association with Satan," Kasee said. Then, with a blatant glance at Damian: "They must also be on a plane with access to the Celestial City."

"Since both Earth and Hell cannot access the city, this means the evil soul is likely already among us," Wendell concluded. He turned to Damian. "Are you familiar with what we're talking about?"

Everyone turned to Damian. He stuttered at first, not used to being the center of attention. *Unless it's from the Gray Ones.* Then he told the others about his visit to the Celestial Library. He relayed the information the *Book of History* had imparted, focusing on how an evil soul reportedly infected someone on Earth while the Embassy suffered a mysterious collapse in its infrastructure.

Even while Damian talked about how Satan's malicious plan could end all things bright and beautiful, Wendell gave the tiniest of smiles at the mention of Mrs. Ulrich. Damian guessed the man had a soft spot for the old toad.

"Mrs. Ulrich knows her material," Wendell said. "She left out one important fact, though. A piece of information that hasn't been released to the public."

The piece of paper Damian had stuffed into his pocket earlier crinkled as he shifted his weight. "The commonality Colin and I share," he thought aloud, then flushed when he realized the others were still listening to him. Colin beamed with admiration.

"Exactly." Wendell pulled a sheet of paper from under a pile of others, causing yet another stack to topple over. "For a spirit to enter a human body, the person's consciousness must be completely shut down following a terrible experience. If I remember correctly," he said, tracing a finger along lines of text on the paper. "You and Colin were involved in a car accident during the Embassy's downtime."

Damian's jaw dropped. *Of course! April 19, 2008. How did I miss that?*

"While more people than we like to believe suffer at any time, it limits the number to a group the Embassy can manage and monitor," Wendell continued. "It seems, however, that all measures put in place to stop the soul from entering the Celestial City have failed."

"Is it possible the soul took hold of someone who subsequently died during that time?" Damian asked. He pointed at Colin. "Say it had taken him during the car accident, then he died within minutes of his injuries."

"It's possible. Approximately fifteen thousand people entered the Afterlife during the downtime, though only a fraction of that number were under duress. The Embassy questioned and examined them to rule out any unauthorized entrance."

The conversation stilled as all eyes turned back to Wendell. He, too, was quiet as he stared down at the paper in his hands. Finally, he took a deep breath and said, "It was wise of us to bring fresh eyes to the team. We need new perspectives on cases like this. Someone who hasn't been dulled by the facts and details. I want Damian to focus his attention on uncovering the evil soul."

It took only a moment for the weight of responsibility to settle on Damian's shoulders. When it did, he opened his mouth to protest—*I've barely sat down at my desk!*—but both Colin and Kasee beat him.

"But, sir!" Kasee growled, almost dropping her cigar. "I've already put hundreds of hours into this investigation!"

"You can't just take it away from us!" Colin added.

The ambassador held up his hands in defense. "You will all still be involved in the case. Colin will continue the search for the Sphere of Doom, and Kasee's talent for uncovering evidence across multiple planes has proven indispensable. Damian will simply narrow his attention to the evil soul."

The two dissenters reluctantly stepped back.

"Are you sure, sir?" Damian asked, finally getting a word in. "Being so new, I'm bound to miss something."

"I've been delegating tasks like this for a long time, and I've never handed a case over to someone who couldn't handle it. Trust me on this. I expect you to be on top of things by the end of tomorrow."

While Kasee grumbled, Colin put a steadying hand on his shoulder. "Don't worry, Flame. You're not alone. We've got your back. I'll gather all of our material and show you how to access it from the computer."

"I do have one question," Damian said before the conversation could move on. "I've heard about this evil soul a couple of times now, but I don't exactly know what that means. Would it be the soul of someone sent to Hell? Or one of Satan's demons?"

Wendell nodded. "Most intelligent creations have a soul of some kind, and many of them vary between good and evil. Technically, I believe even the soul of a Guardian can dwell within a human."

"Entirely possible," Blue said when the ambassador glanced at her for confirmation. "Messy business, though. Never ends well for the human."

"Earth is closed off from the rest of Creation, though," Colin said. "So while Satan can exert influence over humans, the Fallen cannot actually go to Earth. This is why it's believed Satan sent a human soul back during the Embassy's downtime."

Odd Man Blue abruptly gestured at Wendell to move closer. The ambassador froze at first, then squatted so she could whisper into his ear. He nodded in deferent silence at what he heard. She then gave a low bow to the group, her hat remaining fixed upon her head.

"Goodbye," she said in the same powerfully soft voice as before.

As the strange woman exited the office, Damian stepped back from the table. He already felt in over his head, and he didn't want to attract additional attention. He listened as the group discussed other cases. Kasee gave an update on a herd of subsuming cerulean cows—mysterious and worthy of investigation, but she doubted a malevolent force lurked behind it.

"I've heard rumblings from multiple contacts about an upcoming transaction," Kasee said. "Or an exchange of information. No time or place for when it's supposed to occur. I'm still verifying the legitimacy of these rumors, but I wanted to warn you all in case I have to rouse you out of something."

Colin asked if she had any idea what the subject of the exchange regarded.

"I don't. Could be nothing." She shrugged. "Or it could be the key to everything we're facing now. I'll let you all know when I learn more."

Silence fell over the group. It reminded Damian of the daily meetings at his old job. Everyone provided an update on their projects, though nobody paid attention because the caffeine hadn't kicked in yet. Even if it had, nobody really cared or wanted to be present. He was certain that, even if he enjoyed this new job, he'd never learn to appreciate meetings.

"I have nothing else to share at the moment." Wendell shifted his weight from one leg to the other, suddenly looking uncomfortable. "Damian, the head ambassador is hosting a party for the Embassy next week. Odd Man Blue asked that I extend you an invitation, since actual invitations were sent out before you joined. Picardia Knutt and her husband would love for you and your wife to attend."

Damian found himself mimicking Wendell's movements. Parties were never his thing. He glanced over at Colin, wishing they could just hang out and play some Xbox. "We'll be there."

CHAPTER ELEVEN

"So, Damian, how were your first days at the Embassy?"

Damian stared over his bowl of potato leek soup and across the lavishly decorated dining table at Anthony, Colin's boyfriend. The room—the entire home—reminded him of the house in which his friend grew up just outside Minade city limits. The Cherry family had impeccable taste, and they could afford the nicer things in life.

Apparently, Colin's style followed him into death, too. The condominium was in a tower a few blocks from the castle. *This place would cost a fortune in Chicago.*

"They've been good. Colin has helped me out a lot, walking me through the department's policies and procedures. Got me a cool desk that automates all the boring paperwork, which is great because Ambassador Klinekole already put me in charge of a big case."

"On your first day, no less." Alena raised her water glass for a toast. Light reflected off the crystal, splashing colors across her green sweater. "I have faith you'll solve all the mysteries you're confronted with."

"I hope so." Damian lifted a glass of wine. He spoke slowly, careful not to share classified information. Colin had said it was impossible to divulge any, but he didn't want to take the chance. "I'm still learning how the Afterlife works. Multiple dimensions. Mythological creatures. Babies."

Bennett burbled gleefully from somewhere beneath the table.

"You'll catch on quick enough," Colin said, taking a sip of his drink. "And you've got us to help you."

Damian peered over at Anthony again, who seemed satisfied with the answer. *Or satisfied that he'd contributed to the conversation at all?* He was unsure whether he liked Colin's boyfriend yet. The kid was pale and willowy and had shoulder-length brown hair that hadn't seen a brush in days. He wore long sleeves and pants, both of which were old, patched, and a size too big. Compared to Colin, still wearing the day's navy-blue work attire, and the spacious, beautiful condo the two lived in, he looked a little—

Don't say it, he told himself. *You grew up poor and owned worse clothing than he's wearing. The only difference is that you fill out everything you put on—including this polo.*

Appearance aside, Anthony's demeanor was skittish. He barely touched his food and constantly tugged on the sleeves of his shirt. When he spoke, which was rare, it was with an air of cattiness.

Either he doesn't want us here, or he doesn't want to be here himself! Anthony seemed a better match for Kasee than for Colin.

"What do you think of Ambassador Klinekole?" Anthony looked down at his soup, stabbing at it with his spoon.

"I like him. He's professional and encouraging. I think I'll be able to learn a lot from him," Damian said, watching as globs of potato soup splattered across the wooden table. "It's weird—he rarely looks me in the eye."

Anthony smirked. "Yeah, me either."

"It's a cultural thing. Nothing to do with you." Colin set his wine down. "Wendell comes from the Mescalero Apache people in New Mexico, though I'm not sure it was a state when he was alive."

Anthony's smirk faded as Colin spoke. He pushed his bowl away, barely having tasted the soup.

"To us, staring or pointing can be perceived as rude. To the Apache, even direct eye contact is impolite. They're not big on expressing affection, so don't give Wendell a hug. Doesn't mean he dislikes you."

Alena wiped the last remnants of soup from her lips with a napkin. "How did you and Colin meet, Anthony?"

Anthony tugged at his sleeves again, eyes darting to Colin. "In a bookstore on the outskirts of the city."

"A bookstore?" Alena's face brightened. "What's it called? I'd love to visit."

"It's not exactly the kind of bookstore you're thinking of." He fidgeted with a loose thread on his shirt. "I wasn't there to read."

"I'd say that's enough embarrassing memories involving me! Everyone done with their soup?" Colin pushed his chair back and stood up. "Damian, would you help me prepare the main course?"

Damian was reluctant to leave Alena alone with their other host. *He's such an impressive conversationalist*. She nodded at him, though, so he collected their bowls and followed Colin. As they left the room, he heard her ask Anthony, "Would you like to hold the baby?"

Like their desks at the Embassy, the kitchen was ultra-modern, impeccably clean, and monochrome. Whereas Damian found the design helpful for focusing at work, he considered its implementation within the home cold and impersonal. It made him miss the kitchen Alena had crafted for them, which possessed a warmth that encouraged congregation and cooking.

"So, how do you like Anthony?" Colin asked, placing their bowls by the sink.

"He's...nice." It came out as more of a question than a statement. Damian wasn't exactly lying, but he found it difficult to stretch the limits of truth.

Colin laughed as he removed a stack of plates from a cupboard and set them on the counter. Then he opened the oven, removing their main course. The scent of cooked chicken and sage filled the room. Damian's mouth watered. "He's not everyone's cup of tea, but I find him irresistible. Absolutely love having him here. I'm sure you'll end up liking him. The two of you are similar."

Damian winced while Colin eyed the food critically. He couldn't think of any way they were alike. Anthony was practically anemic and needed a haircut—or at least a shower. Damian was perpetually overweight and far from the most stylish individual in any gathering of people. *But at least I'm clean.*

"After the accident, while I was recovering, I often shared rooms with other patients," Colin said, cutting into the chicken. "Do you remember a middle-aged construction worker? He was injured on the job. Stuck around for a week or so. The doctors thought he'd survive his injuries, but I knew otherwise. The man wanted to die—*decided* to die—and grew more upset when he kept waking up day after day. I asked a nurse why he didn't just let go. You know what she said?"

Damian shook his head, wondering how this related to Anthony. The man sounded vaguely familiar, but Colin had never told him these details.

"She told me, 'He hasn't found the doorway out yet.' I considered it bullshit at first. Something you say to comfort other people. But two nights later, the man startled me awake. He called out, 'Ah, there it is!' A few moments later, he added, 'I've been waiting for you.' When I woke the next morning, the man was gone."

From the dining room, Bennett let out a riotous laugh. *Not the time, kid.*

"In the months between that man's death and my own, I often wondered if I'd see a door and, if so, who might wait for me on the other side. The people I loved, you and my parents, were still alive. Every time I went into surgery, a part of me despaired. I didn't believe in an afterlife, and I'm certain the door this man saw was a hallucination. It was such a comfort to him, though, and his voice was joyous when he called out. I kinda wanted that."

Damian put a hand on his friend's shoulder. "Did you see a door at the end?"

"No, I didn't." Colin wiped at teary eyes. "When I met Anthony, though, I finally felt the joy I'd desired. That's how he makes me feel, Damian. Happy to come home every day. Sorry for the touchy-feely, roundabout way of explaining that."

"Don't apologize," Damian said as Colin straightened and headed to the refrigerator. He pulled out a large bowl filled to the brim with a colorful salad. "Like you said, Anthony may not be everyone's cup of tea, but knowing how he makes you feel makes me appreciate him."

"And I appreciate *you*," Colin said with a cheer meant to dispel the somber mood. He plated four thinly cut chicken breasts topped with prosciutto, smoked mozzarella, and sage. Next to each piece of meat, he added a portion of the salad. "Oh! I spoke with Kasee earlier today. You were right. It was her outside your house."

"She told you that?" Damian asked, picking up two of the dishes.

"Didn't even try to evade the question." Colin took the remaining plates and led them back toward the dining room. "She wouldn't tell me why she was there, though. Wanted to explain it to you herself."

Damian grunted. "I'll make a point to cross paths with her tomorrow."

"It's no secret Kasee and I aren't the best of friends. I'll never invite her over for a game night—I sure miss those. All the soda we consumed." Colin chuckled. "She knows her stuff, though. Don't let my feelings affect your relationship with her."

"I don't think I'll be *inviting* her over soon."

"The best part is, he may not hate the experience," Alena was saying as they reentered the room. Anthony was holding Bennett. Neither seemed to care for the situation. "Damian seems taken with him."

"Taken hostage, maybe," Damian said, setting Alena's food down in front of her. Anthony gently placed Bennett on the floor. They all watched as the baby crawled along the ornate rug, disappearing beneath the table. "Do you think he's grown a few inches?"

"He absolutely has. Gained a few pounds, too. Thankfully, we don't have to buy new clothes every few days!" Alena cut into her chicken. "Colin, this is delicious!"

Colin beamed as he reached across the table, refilling everyone's wine glass—except Alena, who felt uncomfortable imbibing while responsible for a child, even if there was no risk. "It's an easy recipe. I'll write it down before you leave."

"Have you considered the repercussions of taking in the child?" Anthony abruptly asked. He leaned back in his chair, leaving his chicken untouched.

"Excuse me?" Alena gave him a sharp look.

Colin was less polite. "Shut it, Anthony."

"I'm just asking if they've received any...feedback yet." He shrugged. "I meant no offense."

"I'm confused," Damian said. He'd picked up his fork and knife before the conversation chilled. They were now frozen above his food. "Why would we be getting feedback about Bennett?"

"Because you're bucking the system, trying to change the rules," Anthony said, his manner calm. The tone contrasted so sharply with his appearance, Damian almost would've preferred a tantrum. "We don't know what might happen by letting these children loose in the Afterlife."

"People are afraid of change. Of the unknown. They'd rather push back against it than experience something new." Nonplussed, Alena turned to Anthony. "Yes, I've already received feedback—in the form of anger and threats. I will gladly continue to be the shield between Bennett and the narrow-minded."

Damian's fork clattered to the floor. "What? Who's been threatening you?"

"People pushed back against this pilot program long before you arrived here." She reached over and squeezed his hand. "Some people are assholes, no matter how justified they feel. They can't do anything. We're not in any danger."

Damian looked over at Colin. "Is there anything the Embassy can do?"

"You want to control people's opinions? Or their ability to express them?" For a moment, Damian thought Colin glowered at him. "That's not what we do here."

"Isn't it?" he asked, certain Colin's response would be nasty. *I won't let him deter me from defending Alena.* "Ever since the Orientation of the Dead, I've noticed a distinct lack of temper or annoyance. In myself and in those around me. As Athan put it, it should seem unnatural to act contrarily. So why are others able to express anger at Alena for helping children?"

The dark cloud that had gathered around Colin suddenly dissipated. His body relaxed, and he leaned forward. "You're right, Damian. That makes no sense. I'm sorry for defending a system that's clearly been unsupportive." Looking at Alena, he asked, "Can you forgive me?"

"Nothing to forgive," she said, though her posture was straighter than usual.

"Wonderful!" Colin clapped his hands. "Then eat up, everyone. I've prepared something special for dessert!"

Anthony obeyed immediately, finally showing an interest in his food. Alena and Damian glanced at one another, and then she too returned to her meal. Remembering that he'd dropped his fork, he leaned over to retrieve it. Much to his surprise, Bennett sat beside him on the floor. The child had picked the fork up and was lifting it toward Damian.

"Thank you," Damian whispered, taking the utensil. He didn't know what else to say except, "Good baby."

He's not a dog.

Wiping his fork clean, he finally cut into his chicken.

"Colin tells me you were killed in a pen-related accident," Anthony told Alena while chewing on his first bite. "How did that happen?"

Alena laughed. "It was the weirdest thing. Damian had given me a fountain pen a few years beforehand as an anniversary present. I was—"

An urgent knocking at the door interrupted her story. They all stared at one another.

"Who could that be?" Colin said aloud. He got up, threw his napkin on the table, and left the room.

Damian heard the front door open, followed by a smattering of hushed but serious voices. When Colin returned, Kasee followed close behind. She looked displeased, though he doubted it was because she hadn't been invited to the dinner party.

She might actually enjoy the discourse.

"We have to go, Damian. The rumblings Kasee mentioned during yesterday's meeting...well, they're happening right now."

CHAPTER TWELVE

DAMIAN AND COLIN RECONSTITUTED on the Embassy lawn. Rather than wait for their coworkers in the DSI office, the two walked the perimeter along the wrought-iron fence. Kasee had disappeared outside Colin's building, off to collect Ambassador Klinekole.

"Calm down, Damian. They won't be long," Colin said as Damian marched forward, arms swinging widely. "If you're concerned about Alena and Bennett, don't worry about Anthony. He's harmless—and really very nice. Doesn't talk much about his life, but I think it was challenging. He really needed someone to help rein in some of his more abrasive behavior."

"I'm sure they're fine." Damian waved a dismissive hand as he slowed his pace. They would be fine, too, though Alena had shot him a look that said, *You're leaving me alone with this emo teenager?* "She'll help clean up and then take Bennett home. I'm more anxious to find out where we're heading."

They continued circling the lawn. It was well after normal work hours, and the only other individuals in sight were the pair of Guardians watching over the entrance. The quiet unnerved Damian, especially with the usual amber light radiating across the sky, mimicking daytime. Without even a breeze to rustle leaves in the trees, the block possessed an air of abandonment. Doubly so, standing beneath the massive stone edifice, windows like tombstones.

To break the eerie silence, Damian said, "Do you remember passing notes back and forth in school?"

"Of course!" Colin laughed. "Didn't we encode them? Like, in case a teacher or classmate intercepted them, no one could read them? We thought we were hot stuff."

"Do you remember what the code was?"

"Something simple. I think we numbered the alphabet in reverse. *A* was *26* and *Z* was *1*." He stopped short, forefinger on his chin. "Why do you ask?"

"I had a strange dream a few nights ago." Damian told Colin about the fantastic red whale bearing down on him, and the individual on its back desperately trying to communicate. "The person spoke in random numbers. Or what I assumed were random numbers. Might've been my subconscious trying to tell me something—I remembered our secret code when I got your invitation to Messie Bessie's."

"Do you remember the sequence?"

Damian shook his head. "You know how dreams are. Most of the details slipped away when I woke up. You think it means anything?"

"Probably not, but I'm more concerned that you're having dreams at all. It's not a normal thing in the Afterlife." Colin scratched the back of his head. "I haven't had a single one."

Taken aback, Damian wondered if he should speak to someone about it. *Are there doctors in the Afterlife? Therapists?* Before he could ask, Kasee and Wendell peregrinated into view a few yards away.

"Good. We're all here," Wendell said once they gathered together. Like Colin, he still wore the dark collared shirt and slacks from earlier in the day. Damian wondered if either of them changed into casual clothing or pajamas. After what he learned about the ambassador over dinner, he looked at him with even greater respect—while avoiding direct eye contact.

"What's this about?" Colin asked. "Kasee would only say the transaction is happening."

"Yes, she's verified her informants' reports with additional resources."

The ambassador looked to Kasee, who appeared especially glum with her hands jammed into the pockets of her baggy pants. Damian wondered who would willingly divulge sensitive information to her. "I still haven't uncovered the nature of the trade, but I was told half an hour ago that the meeting was about to take place."

"Where at?" Colin asked.

Kasee looked down at the ground, kicking at the grass with her sneakers. Any blades she displaced immediately righted themselves. "The Dungeon of Darkness."

A shiver made its way down Damian's spine. *I knew I'd go there soon enough!*

"My sources tell me three individuals have entered the dungeon over the past hour, each arriving at a different time."

"As if to avoid suspicion." Colin crossed his arms. "Inadvertently raising it. Amateurs."

"Then that's where we're headed," Wendell said. He tilted his head toward Damian. "Our primary objective is to observe and collect evidence. Do not confront anyone without my approval. We don't have the authority to make arrests. That's work for the Guardians."

"Have any of you been to the dungeon?" Damian asked. No one answered. "It doesn't sound like the happiest of places. Do we know what to expect?"

Wendell considered for a moment. "The Creator constructed the dungeon to temporarily hold Satan and their followers at the conclusion of the War for Heaven. Since their banishment, it's been used to imprison those who threaten the stability of Creation. Thankfully, it hasn't been used or maintained in several thousand years."

"Is it here in the city?"

"Nobody except the Creator and the Guardians knows exactly where the dungeon is located," Wendell said. "But we can still peregrinate there."

Damian's brow furrowed. Kasee caught the expression, returning it with disgust. "Could you point to the Celestial City on a map, or even walk here from your house?"

"No," he said under his breath. In a moment of uneasiness, he realized he also didn't have a clue where his home was.

"It's the same with the dungeon," Wendell said. "We may not recognize where it is, but we can still get there through the magic of peregrination. Okay, does anyone need gear from the office?"

No one spoke up, so Wendell nodded. "Then let's go." He disappeared from view, followed quickly by Colin and Kasee.

Damian stood alone on the lawn for a few moments. *My first time out in the field, and it's the dungeon!* The logical part of him hoped no dark activity was taking place. That Kasee's informants were playing a joke on her. His creative, childlike side couldn't help but thrum with excitement. He couldn't wait to partake in the adventure, hoping he wouldn't make a complete fool of himself.

Closing his eyes, he concentrated on the idea of the Dungeon of Darkness.

The inexplicable force of peregrination tugged at his body as he traveled, air whistling in his ears. It took longer than usual for the journey to complete—or so he thought. When the warbling failed to fade, he cracked his eyelids to discover himself already standing next to his teammates. In contrast with every other location he'd yet visited in the Afterlife, strong gales blasted at his face. The sky above was deep red, only a shade or two lighter than the fine red dust the wind kicked up from surrounding dunes.

Colin grabbed hold of his shoulder, his other hand instinctively protecting his eyes. He shouted, "We're not in Minade anymore!"

The four formed a tight protective circle, blocking the worst of the crimson grit.

"We're clearly in another plane of existence," Kasee shouted. "Lucky it's hospitable to our forms."

"That's up for debate," Colin added. "A lot of effort to house a prison, though."

"Is this actually the prison itself?" Damian asked, suddenly regretting his excitement. *This is worse than a Midwest winter!*

The ambassador pointed to a large rock formation protruding from the ground a hundred yards away. Damian immediately recognized it from his Orientation—the monolithic golden display stretching up to the ceiling. "There should be a door at the base of that mount."

"Just a door?" Damian had played enough games with Colin to know entering a dungeon shouldn't be so easy. "No moat or sentries or puzzles?"

"Why would anyone want to enter the dungeon?" Kasee said. "Leaving is the challenge. Don't worry, though. We'll be fine."

"Follow me." Wendell waved a hand as he broke away from the group. "Don't get lost in the sandstorm."

Colin fell in line, followed by Damian and Kasee. If there was a path, the wind had eroded it away long ago. Their feet sank into red dust with each step, like walking through heaps of snow without the biting cold. The temperature, only a few degrees warmer than Damian preferred, was an improvement. However, the sand cut into his skin.

Even if our bodies are representations of our souls, these forms probably obey the laws of whatever plane we travel to. Damian winced as the moisture in his eyes evaporated, replaced only by sand. He'd gone a week with no discomfort. It amazed him how accustomed he'd grown to that.

About fifty yards out, a lone figure took shape ahead of them. It didn't move, but Damian was convinced a sentinel blocked their path. They'd have to defeat it with a combination of strength and intellect before gaining access to the dungeon itself.

Another ten yards, and the figure turned out to be a wooden sign hammered firmly into the red, grainy earth. The wilted remains of a carved pumpkin sat on top, decaying teeth leering at them. Damian squinted to read the sign.

Beware all those who enter here
You should know what you endeavor
For if not, and you embark
You could end up here forever

Colin turned around and yelled into Damian's ear. "Like you said, it's not the happiest of places."

They hiked forward, step by step, hands held up against the wind, for what seemed a quarter of an hour. As they neared the rocky mount, a door appeared at the base. Made of heavy metal, an iron ring hung on its side in place of a handle. He'd expected the entrance to be imposing, but it wasn't any bigger than his bedroom door.

Without hesitation, Wendell grabbed hold of the ring and wrenched the door open. It swung noiselessly and with ease, which Damian found incredible considering its probable weight. They all hurried inside, out of the storm.

"Keep the door open." Wendell shouted, but the roar of the gale didn't permeate the threshold. Even with the entrance wide open, the winds mere feet away, the silence that engulfed them would've been deafening if not for the ambassador's reverberating words. He lowered his voice to a conversational level. "It's the only light source we have at the moment."

Damian wasn't sure what he'd expected the new domain to be like, but he *had* expected to see something. The reddish light fared little better than the noise, and he could barely make out the others' faces. The space behind them was pitch-black. They might've been standing in a narrow hallway or an enormous cave.

"I'll light a match," Wendell offered.

Colin scoffed. "I'll do you one better with a floodlight."

Several seconds passed in continued darkness. Finally, Colin apologized. "I'm having trouble thinking up objects."

"We're in a different universe," Kasee reminded them, wheezing from exertion. "We don't have any of the abilities afforded to us in the Afterlife."

"Then it's a good thing I always carry matches," Wendell said in a self-satisfied tone. There came the telltale noise of a match head striking rough, powdered glass and the hissing of erupting flames.

Light, however, did not appear.

"We have a problem here."

"Quick, back to the door!"

They all turned toward the entrance. In their distraction, it had either silently shut or disappeared altogether. The door was lost to them.

"Let me try peregrinating out of here," Colin said. A few seconds later, he reported, "It appears those privileges have also been taken away."

"Of course, you can't just pop out of here. It's a prison," Kasee said. "Known for its darkness."

"Everyone to me," the ambassador said. "I've found a wall."

Damian held his hands in front of him, walking slowly toward Wendell's voice. The floor beneath his feet felt smooth and level, though he still feared tripping over an unseen obstacle. *I don't want to break a bone. Do I even have bones?* When his fingertips finally met a flat wall of stone, he breathed a sigh of relief. The other two joined after a few moments.

At Wendell's order, they followed the wall toward the metal door—or at least where they believed it to be located. When they failed to come across it within a few minutes, they doubled back and tried the opposite route. A quarter of an hour later, with no success, they took turns walking away from the wall to find other avenues or obstructions.

"I've got something." Kasee's voice wavered, and Damian guessed she wasn't a fan of the dark. *Possibly claustrophobic. Our fears and anxieties are returning full force. Is that my heart pounding?* "Seems like another wall. I think we're in a wide hallway. We should continue on in the same direction from each side, see where it leads."

"Good idea," Wendell said. "Damian, go with Kasee. That way, if we get separated, no one is on their own. The last thing we want is to lose someone in this place."

Damian wandered across the dark gulf until his fingers once again touched smooth stone. He tried to visualize the rocky formation they'd seen from the outside, wondering how far the hall—if it was a hall—could go. Then he remembered that the DSI's office dimensions were far larger than the outer hallway indicated. *Depending on this plane's laws of physics, the dungeon could run miles in each direction.*

"Ow!" he yelped when Kasee poked him in the side.

"Go on," she said. "The others have already moved ahead."

Damian heard Colin making observations, his voice growing steadily fainter. "The air is dry here. Temperature probably in the upper seventies. I always imagined it'd be cold and wet." Left hand against the wall, he moved forward, trying to catch up.

"Theoretically, if we continued along one wall long enough, we'd eventually find the door," he said, trying to reassure Kasee that their situation wasn't hopeless.

"Sure. And while we're at it, just as likely to bump into those we're here to observe," she replied. "Do you think they'll give us directions?"

Damian rolled his eyes as he grunted in response. He continued inching forward, listening for the voices of their coworkers. They were conversing, sounding farther ahead than he preferred. He picked up his pace.

"Colin says you saw me outside your window," Kasee whispered. He almost didn't catch the words, even in the dungeon's silence.

"Of course I saw you. You had your face pressed up against the glass." It surprised him she brought up the subject now, though he supposed she needed to keep her mind occupied. "I would've recognized you in the office, but the cigar was a dead giveaway."

Kasee let out a heavy sigh. "I left my cigar at home. Had I known we'd get stuck here...but we'll be fine."

"Why were you at my house?" Damian pressed. From the scent of smoke wafting off her clothing, he would've sworn a cigar was on her person. "It was creepy."

"Best watch yourself, or you'll end up just as creepy."

"What do you mean by that?" Damian kept his voice low, his attention split between her confession and tracking the others. Wendell's voice was much closer now.

"I take my job seriously. Evil lurks among us, closer than you think. I feel a responsibility to stop it." Her voice was defiant, as if daring him to ask why she felt uniquely qualified. "Colin told us a lot about you before you arrived. Wouldn't shut up about his best friend. I...believe you and I share some qualities. Maybe not the creepy thing. I was just talking shit."

"I'm not sure how to take that." Damian wasn't sure about anything she said.

"Anyway, checking up on people like you is part of my fieldwork. At Wendell's request, I work with the Gray Ones to verify the validity of good souls coming into the Afterlife." She lowered her voice as they caught up with the others on the opposite side of the hallway. "I'm pleased to say my visit to your home uncovered nothing incriminating. I don't imagine evil sits at home reading about its own boring lives."

Even in the darkness, he knew she wore a creepy smile.

The answer wasn't what Damian had expected. In fact, it was rather anticlimactic. *Were you hoping to be at the center of a grand conspiracy?* He would of course verify the story with Wendell or the Gray Ones. He shuddered at the idea of descending the stairs to their office.

Kasee doesn't know me well enough to know if I take my work seriously, which I certainly didn't do on Earth. He didn't care for the insinuation that he and the cigar-puffing kid shared similarities, though he recognized he was perpetuating Colin's feelings toward her. *And she's not a kid. She's the same age as you.*

"I found something," Colin called out. "A break in the wall. A corner, or maybe a side hall."

Damian's fingers discovered a similar feature on his and Kasee's side. A sudden sharp corner, and the wall continued back at a 135-degree angle. On a hunch, he continued forward, arms flailing until he found what he expected. Another corner, this one around forty-five degrees, and the hall they'd been traversing continued onward.

"What do we do?" he asked. "Move forward, go back, or go down one of these new corridors?"

"Stick to our current path," Wendell said. "It must lead to the center of this prison, like a labyrinth. The other halls are likely a maze, meant to confuse, and we'd become easily lost."

"As if we weren't already?" Kasee said under her breath.

They continued further down the hall, deeper into the dungeon. Damian thought the floor possessed a minor slant and that it gradually descended underground. The stone walls occasionally gave way to additional hallways, all angling back like the first.

Do those corridors have offshoots of their own? In his mind, he envisioned the entire layout of the dungeon unfolding like a tree, and they were walking down the trunk. *Are there holding cells for prisoners somewhere, or is this intricate combination of paths enough to keep criminals contained?*

"Ugh," Kasee grumbled after tripping over an untied shoelace. "I've never missed my sight so much. We'll be fine."

"Quiet!" Wendell hissed. "Do you hear that?"

Damian froze, left hand firmly pressed against the wall to steady him against the dark. His ears didn't pick up anything other than the rush of pumping blood—*that's new*. Then a low, monotonous tone wafted up the tunnel like a breeze. *The most boring breeze*, he thought, immediately recognizing the singular inflection as that of a Guardian.

"...mean that they know about Gehenna? This is bad. We will have to bring in additional souls for quarantine."

Damian felt Kasee push at his back. They crept further down the passage, trying to catch more of the conversation.

"If we fail to do so, everything we have done will have been for naught. Should we apprise her of the situation?"

"No need to tell her. She is already aware. You know that. Events shall pass as we see fit, just as they always do." Damian stifled a gasp as he recognized Athan's bored-sounding voice.

"What course of action do you propose we take?"

"We will do what the Creator made us to do," Athan responded. "We will kill them all."

The wall gave way to another corridor as Damian choked at Athan's words. Surprised, he fell over onto the floor. Behind him, Kasee clapped a hand over her mouth.

"I heard something," stated the first voice.

The sound of metal rang through the air, and a blinding light filled the caverns. Before shielding his eyes, Damian saw Kasee leap into the corridor next to him and, across the hall, Colin and Wendell drop to their knees in a similar alcove.

"Do you see anything?"

"No," Athan said. "But I heard something too."

Damian poked his head around the corner, peering through his fingers. The main corridor ended another twenty yards ahead, leading to a vast room. Athan and their companion stood in the middle of the circular space, looking in the opposite direction of the interlopers. The crown upon the unfamiliar Guardian appeared more polished than Athan's, and their robes were burnt orange.

Downright ostentatious for a Guardian, Damian thought.

Each of them held long, jagged swords pointed toward the ceiling. White flames streaked out of the blades as though they were stars, casting long shadows of their owners. The light danced off the colorful garb of Athan's companion.

"I see nothing." Athan's head swept from left to right. "It may have been a small creature."

"I do not know why the Creator deems them worthy of existence," the other said.

The pair turned around, and Damian ducked back. He struggled to tear his eyes away from his first clear view of the Dungeon of Darkness. As his fingers had hinted, solid stone made up every surface. Far from a tunnel hacked and chiseled into existence, it displayed craftsmanship rivaling the finest buildings in the Celestial City. Polished stone surfaces met at perfect angles, supporting a cathedral ceiling so lofty only the light emitted by the Guardians' swords could properly illuminate it. Delicate grooves ran parallel to each intersection of the walls and ceiling. They appeared to be ornamental, though Damian didn't understand the flourish in a place no one could appreciate.

"It is not safe here," the flamboyant Guardian said. "We should leave."

The two sheathed their weapons, plunging the space back into inky darkness.

Athan said, "I will contact you tomorrow."

Damian pressed his back against the wall as heavy footsteps headed toward them. The Guardians—*can they see in the dark?*—swept past them and up the hall. He expected to hear their footfalls for several minutes, but was surprised by the sound of an iron ring being used to pull open a metal door.

It can't be! He risked a glance around the corner, catching the silhouettes of two Guardians slipping through a door and into a raging red dust storm. *It's not even thirty yards away!*

"What was that all about?" Colin asked once the door was shut.

"I haven't known Athan long," Damian said. "I would never have believed they'd be involved in criminal activity. Who was the other one?"

"That was Bai." Wendell's voice sounded further away. He'd slipped into the circular room. Taking hold of Kasee's arm, Damian stumbled to his feet and felt his way toward the ambassador. "The Guardians don't officially have a leader, though Bai is universally recognized as their representative. I've known them both for hundreds of years. Despite what we've heard, we mustn't jump to any conclusions."

"How do you explain that conversation?" Colin asked as they all congregated in the center of the room.

"It could've been anything, really," Kasee said.

"They're going to kill someone," Colin retorted. "We've got to get back to the Embassy."

"I agree," Wendell said. "If it's true that there's evil among the Guardian ranks, it hasn't been heard of since..."

"Since the War for Heaven," Kasee finished. "This could indicate a new faction gaining—"

The screeching of metal interrupted her, so harsh that Damian covered his ears.

"Everyone out of here!" Colin shouted. Damian barely understood. They all blundered back to the exit. A hard clang shook the chamber before they reached it, then the noise ceased.

"Cell door," Colin said as their clamoring hands felt thick, circular metal rods. Spaced a few inches apart, they blocked the exit.

Must have come down from the ceiling, Damian thought.

Wendell sighed, sitting on the ground. "Now we must wait."

"For what?" The panic in Kasee's voice rose audibly.

"For someone to come along and let us out. The Guardians walk through here once a month—legitimately, I mean."

"Then we might be too late to stop Bai and Athan," Colin argued. "They might kill whoever—"

Another metallic note resonated throughout the dungeon. It was more akin to a Guardian's sword being drawn than additional cell doors falling shut. Damian shielded his eyes, but no light burst forth. Footsteps followed, though, coming toward them. He found himself gripping Kasee's hand, and he wasn't sure whose grasp was tighter.

The approaching steps halted just beyond their cell, followed by a blade's swift slice through air and a muted impact as it found its mark. A moment later, an object thumped to the floor and rolled against the iron barrier.

The group remained frozen in place for several minutes, listening intently for any movement outside their room. No footsteps echoed down the corridor. No more swordplay.

Damian, screwing up his courage, let go of Kasee and lowered himself to the floor. His whole body trembled as he reached through the iron bars, groping for the fallen item.

"What is it?" Colin whispered. "What's out there?"

Damian's hand brushed against a coil of thick, coarse rope. He pulled at it, the fibrous strands gradually loosening, its width increasing. Then his fingertips felt cold metal, hammered into a precise curve. He grabbed at it, but the metallic piece rolled away, beyond his grasp. He turned his attention back to the rope, fearing the worst.

"What?" the other three asked in unison when he suddenly choked in disgust. He rolled away from the bars, wiping his hands on his pant legs.

"It's... It's a head," he stammered. "Someone beheaded a Guardian."

CHAPTER THIRTEEN

"GUARDIANS ARE THE ONLY creatures native to the Celestial City."

Ambassador Klinekole's words startled everyone. The hour they'd spent in darkness had been quiet. Colin paced the round room, palming the stone walls and shaking the iron bars. Damian had initially joined him but eventually gave up and sat in the middle of the chamber beside his boss, believing their quest for escape was hopeless.

"I didn't know that." Colin's voice echoed off the round walls and high ceiling. "It explains why they look so old and ga—ARGH!"

"You okay?" Damian asked, already knowing Colin had tripped over Kasee and fallen face first onto the ground. She'd withdrawn to the side of the room opposite the door, isolating herself from the source of their imprisonment. With Colin venturing around every few minutes, it was a fruitless effort.

"The Guardians look exactly as they always have." Wendell ignored Colin and Kasee's grunts and shoves as they untangled from each other. "Just because they're not aesthetically pleasing to you doesn't mean they aren't to the Creator. That said, I wasn't aware of that fact until now."

"Oh? How'd you figure it out?" Damian asked. *Is the ambassador losing it?*

Wendell was quiet for a few moments. Damian pictured the man's chiseled face staring at the cathedral ceiling as he collected his thoughts—*or his wits.* Finally, he said, "Because I can see in the dark."

"You're telling us this now?" Colin asked, tapping on the iron bars. "Is there a way outta here you've been keeping from us?"

"I misspoke," Wendell said. "I can't see you or the walls or floor, but I can look *into* the dark."

Yup, he's totally lost it.

Kasee emerged from the far edge of the room, scooting across the cold stone floor until she, too, sat next to Wendell. "I see it too. Didn't recognize it for what it was until you said something, but now I can't unsee it."

"What are you two talking about?" Colin asked, continuing to strike the bars with his knuckles.

"My parents were...not great." Kasee spoke slowly, begrudgingly, as if relinquishing information she'd rather not. "They'd lock me in the basement for long periods. No windows, no lights. Just me and the dark for days. I screamed myself hoarse the first time. By the fifth, I'd learned to entertain myself."

Damian frowned into the obscurity where her voice originated. *And I thought my parents were terrible.*

"I'd make up stories in the darkness. Started noticing little pinpricks of light—you know, like when you rub your eyes too hard? Those sparkles became characters in my tales. Tiny glowing heroes fighting battles across the walls of my mind."

"You're saying those lights in your eyes weren't random?" Colin asked.

"No, they totally were. I used them to look into the darkness, even if what I saw came from my imagination," Kasee said. "What I'm seeing now, though, isn't random at all."

Wendell cleared his throat. "Many cultures speak of creatures that don't just exist in darkness but can manipulate it."

"Folklore?" Fragments of mythology lectures surfaced in Damian's memories.

"That's right," Wendell said. "The Inuit described shadow beings that could pull things—or people—into darkness. Celtic folklore also talks about creatures that lived in a realm only accessible through deep shadows."

"You're saying there's something in here with us?" Colin's voice had risen an octave.

"Not with us. *Around* us." Kasee sounded calmer than she had in hours. Damian supposed that having something to focus on helped, even if it was based on an awful childhood trauma. "It's not alive, I don't think. More like words imprinted onto paper."

"Darkness isn't empty space. It's a boundary. A membrane between here and somewhere else," Wendell said. "It's possible the dungeon's previous inhabitants learned of a way to tap into that liminal space and leave a message."

Damian rubbed his eyes, producing pinpricks of light in his vision, and squinted. At first, he saw nothing like what Kasee and Wendell described. Just blackness. Then—*is that a shimmer?* The tiny bright spots moved subtly, like ripples on water.

"I don't know," he said, not convinced he wasn't imagining it. "I think I see a snake?"

Kasee grunted in agreement. "I see all kinds of reptiles. Huge snakes slithering across...a battlefield? Some have limbs, even wings, and they're carrying different weapons."

The ambassador drew in his breath, and Damian heard revulsion in the man's voice when he said, "The Forti."

"Who are they?"

"One of the first creations, and deadly smart. Their purpose was to clear a path through the cosmos for future projects. They never lost a fight, and they became more ambitious as their successes stacked up. Confident in their right to rule, they launched a surprise attack on the Celestial City."

Damian kept staring, willing the creatures Kasee had described to appear, but all he saw was a simple snake. He wondered if he lacked a special ability. *Kasee's tough past and Wendell's knowledge of different myths might give them an edge.*

"I don't understand," Colin said. He'd moved away from the bars and sat down next to Damian. "Why would anyone invade the city? *How* could they do it?"

Damian imagined the defenses of the Celestial City as he recalled them. The palace stood at the center, surrounded by the Guardians stationed at key locations. The Celestial Wall encircled it all, diamonds glittering under the amber sky. Outside the wall, he saw groups of creatures gathering in the forest. They were tall, bipedal lizards with powerful bodies and shiny scales that caught the faint light filtering through the trees. Their eyes glowed with cold intelligence.

The vision expanded, showing more creatures hiding in the trees. Their numbers increased quickly as the army gathered, preparing for war.

Damian gasped, realizing that what he was seeing was no longer his imagination. "I can see it now! The Forti. They're planning something."

"Good!" Wendell said. "Notice the city looks different. While it was to be the hub of all existence—the Bridge was already in place—construction was far from complete. Not even the wall was done. It stood no chance of holding off an invasion of such scale."

"Couldn't the Creator have simply swept them aside?" Damian asked.

Wendell chuckled—a deep, somewhat unsettling sound. "Humans worship the Creator in various ways. Some pray to omnipotent and ruthless deities. Others look to gods and goddesses who differ from us only in their immortality. According to some lore, the Creator doesn't care about mere humans."

"Now imagine other worlds—all the other planes of existence," Colin added. "Entire societies live in fear of their gods, supposing them to be angry and destructive. Others have no concept of a higher power, whole generations living and dying none the wiser."

"How powerful is the Creator?" Damian asked.

"Nobody actually knows," Wendell said. Damian sensed wonder in the man's words. "That's part of the great mystery."

Kasee sighed, a noise that spooked Damian by its proximity. "What did the Forti believe?"

Damian didn't need the ambassador to answer. He watched as light and shadows—none of which illuminated the prison they were in—unfolded the beginning of battle. More Forti peregrinated into the woods. *I can see them now! The horns protruding from their draconic faces!* They waited while their force grew in number, only emerging and storming the multiverse's epicenter once victory was assured.

They believed in themselves. It's hard to grasp the strength of their armies, spanning across universes. They believed *they could take the Celestial City and install themselves as gods.*

Intent on slaying the city's inhabitants, the Forti attacked anyone in their path. Their weapons ranged from jagged blades to laser technology, much of it built into their armor. Some wore amulets around their necks, capable of channeling destructive magic.

"They tried to kill those who'd already died?" Damian asked.

"Not everyone who lives in the city has died," Wendell reminded him. "Remember, all planes intersect there, and the Bridge allows most to interact with one another."

"And there are things worse than death," Colin added.

"What does this have to do with the Guardians?" Kasee asked, more engaged than usual.

Colin shushed her, having also caught on to seeing in the dark.

Storm clouds gathered over the city, towering formations that shamed the Midwestern cumulonimbus clouds Damian was used to back home. The unfinished palace, lacking its bastions, barbicans, and buttresses, was still magnificent. *It was meant to be a place of beauty, welcoming to all.*

Thunderbolts flashed across the sky, destroying enemy aircraft and exposing huge flying creatures. The strikes intensified as wreckage and bodies fell. Spears of electricity hit the ground—*a bit too close for comfort, even if this isn't real*—creating deep craters. Within minutes, a thousand bolts struck the battlefield. From each impact emerged a Guardian.

"That's how they were created, born with weapons and special gifts," Wendell said as the strange images stalled out. Damian blinked as the dark grew even blacker. "Guardians surpassed the Forti in every conceivable way. They could wield Celestial Light, allowing them to destroy anything."

"Really?" Colin mused. "I've only met a handful of Guardians. If there were a thousand, what happened to them all?"

"The conflict that took place in the city was a mighty one," Wendell said. "A thousand Guardians against *tens* of thousands of Forti."

Damian rubbed at his eyes again, forcing the dark to reveal its secrets. Rows of enormous armored snakes emerged. They terrified him, and he inched backward reflexively. Then the Guardians came back into view, and Damian saw no chance for the Forti. The new defenders, armed with brilliant swords like those carried by Athan and Bai—*was that Celestial Light we saw earlier?*—quickly cut down enemies with basic blades.

Bright beams of energy lit up the front line, shadowed by the storm above. Where the Forti didn't use ammunition and lasers, magic ripped apart reality. The Guardians divided into small groups, breaking through enemy lines and using their Light to dispatch the invaders.

"Both sides suffered heavy losses, leaving only a hundred fifty Guardians."

"What a brilliant battle!" Colin exclaimed.

"I agree," Wendell replied. "The Guardians had in their midst the most ingenious strategist of all time."

"Who?" Damian and Colin asked together, leaning forward in the dark.

"The Bringer of Light."

Through the blackness, they stared at him.

"Lucifer."

Out of the nebulous air stepped a single Guardian. Tall, stern, and stoic, they looked like any of their brethren. Their long robes were emerald, and the crown on their head reflected the Light burning off their sword. No hint of arrogance or pride graced their face. Just grim determination to protect the city and the Creator.

It suddenly dawned on Damian that Lucifer—*the* Lucifer—once trod the halls of the Dungeon of Darkness. Had dwelled in the room they now sat in. Learned to leave behind this historical record. He wondered if the Bringer of

Light, who inspired so much poetry, prose, and absolute fear on Earth, was as terrible as everyone believed, or if humans had only scratched the surface of what evil they were capable of.

Kasee broke the stunned silence following Wendell's revelation by clumsily rising to her feet. "How does that surprise you? Your job depends on intimate knowledge of Satan. You should know their past. Know they used to be a Guardian."

"Of course we should," Colin said, ignoring her scathing tone. "Which is why we're learning about it now. It's a great story."

"But it's not a story, Colin. It's history, and you should be familiar with the details of Satan's entire life." Wendell tsked, but it was an exaggerated sound. "I'll give Damian a pass, since he's only been with us a few days."

Kasee huffed, and Damian heard her step away from the group. He wondered if she often did that in the office, escaping tiresome coworkers to her safe, albeit dirty, workspace. Without her cubicle to retreat to, however, she shuffled back and sat down again.

"We know the Guardians defeated the Forti," Wendell said once his audience quieted. "The surviving offenders returned to their original plane, and the pathway in or out was locked on the Bridge. No one has seen them since the attempted coup."

The image of Lucifer changed. They now sat next to the Creator—*the Creator!* But while the figure of the Guardian was pristine, the other's was blotted out as though the artist had spilled ink over it. Even more, Damian knew the disfigurement was purposeful, done in hatred. Anger washed over him, spilling out from the impression.

"For their part in protecting the city, Lucifer won great prestige." Wendell's voice wavered, and Damian knew the others experienced the same waves of resentment he did. "They became the Creator's right hand, enjoying sway in decisions made throughout the multiverse. Whole worlds were theirs to control and watch over. They even had a seat in the Celestial Palace."

Were they strictly professional, keeping their conversation to the business of running Creation? Or were they friends, finishing each day with a beer and laughs? Did either of them have any concept of how their mythos would play out?

Damian heard Colin lean forward. "What changed all that? What led them down—"

A collective gasp erupted from all four of them as the darkness rippled. Invisible tendrils reached out and touched them. Damian felt something intrude into his consciousness. Not a physical touch, and not a thought, but a gaping void of nothingness where feelings should exist.

"What the hell?" Kasee choked out. Damian's hand instinctively clutched at his chest.

The emptiness spread through him like ice water. His mind pieced together what was happening—*or what had happened so long ago.* In the Creator's haste to forge warriors against the Forti threat, they'd not granted Guardians the intrinsic ability to *feel.*

Time seemed to stretch around him. Damian's consciousness expanded, aging over eons. In the darkness, he saw Lucifer alone in a small room, practicing facial expressions that meant nothing to them. Confusion, anger, joy—just empty mimicry.

Lucifer reached out and touched objects, creatures, and even the walls of their room, trying to understand the strange reactions of others. While the other Guardians accepted their lack of emotions, the Bringer of Light rebelled in secret. Through sheer force of will and countless experiments conducted in shadows, Lucifer prodded at the void within.

Then came the breakthrough—a tiny flicker that was impossible to ignore. Joy. It was the first emotion ever felt by a Guardian, born not from the Creator but from Lucifer's relentless determination.

"They taught themself to feel." Damian gripped his knees as the vision continued. "And once they found that first emotion..."

"The people they watched over thrived. The joys of those worlds became their own." Wendell sounded weary. "Thousands of years later, Lucifer grasped sadness. After a short time of expressing sorrow through natural disasters, most of their peoples continued to lead happy, productive lives. No one likes misery. Not even Lucifer."

Damian continued to watch—to feel—Lucifer's self-discovery cascade. Curiosity. Desire. Jealousy. Each new perception carved a path through the Guardian's consciousness. With each new emotion came understanding and questions.

Why had the Creator withheld this gift? The question wasn't Damian's, but he understood why they'd asked it. The Guardians were among the few intelligent beings with such a limited range of emotions. *What else had been kept from them?*

"These questions..." Wendell took a deep breath before continuing. "This was around the time the Creator was focusing on a new project, one that thrived on evocative passions."

"Humans," Damian said as a new sensation consumed him: envy.

"The wide range of emotions humans experienced sparked powerful resentment in Lucifer." The ambassador continued to talk. Damian supposed the waves of emotions overwhelmed the normally detached man, and talking helped distract. "They requested guardianship over Earth and its creatures, but it was denied. Already bitter about the Creator's absolute authority, anger took root at how such power and emotion weren't shared with them."

Damian watched as the master strategist spent centuries devising a plan to seize control of the Celestial City and install themself as supreme ruler. During that time, they recruited a hundred of the remaining Guardians to their cause. They encouraged the others to experiment with feelings, focusing on jealousy, anger, and hate.

The coils of emotion eventually withdrew from Damian's mind, and the shadows returned to their more cinematic format. He saw the day Lucifer's plans unfolded. Much like the Forti had done before, they sent a small army to cover strategic locations throughout the Celestial City, now resembling a bustling metropolis. Then, flanked by several followers, Lucifer marched into the palace to depose the Creator. Not only were they met by their target but also by an opposing group of Guardians who matched their numbers.

Damian heard Colin rub his hands together. "Now *that* must've been a brilliant battle."

"On the contrary. There was no battle at all," Wendell said.

"What?" Damian asked. "Why not?"

"The Guardians' power, especially their ability to wield Light, comes directly from the Creator. Lucifer didn't realize that opposing their master severed their access. The dissenters had essentially built a wall between themselves and the Creator."

"Something we humans do, too," Damian said. Lucifer and their followers had fallen into the same trap as the Forti, unable to appreciate what they possessed, lusting after the dominance they lacked. Unlike the previous attempt, the second assault on the city was short-lived.

"Facing extinction, the enemy forces had no choice but to surrender," Wendell said as the shadows retreated into the folds of darkness. Damian suddenly felt blind again, even though there had been no actual light. "Now, only fifty Guardians are left in the city."

"Why were the traitors locked away here, in a separate plane of existence?" Colin asked. "Still think it makes more sense to do away with them and be rid of the threat."

Wendell grunted tacit agreement before saying, "In dealing with the insurgents, the Creator did three things. Since they could no longer wield Light, Lucifer was stripped of their very name. The conspirators, now known as the Fallen, were banished to an isolated universe—what we commonly refer to as Hell. In a surprising arrangement, though, Satan was granted something they coveted: the ability to exert influence on Earth."

Both Damian and Colin gasped. Kasee remained quiet—and annoyed.

"The human project had stagnated," Wendell explained. "The Creator wanted to shake things up. Make things more interesting."

"And now the devil rules our planet," Kasee said.

"Co-rules," Colin corrected. "They can only apply as much leverage as the Creator."

Damian felt the heat of Kasee's quiet frustration. *I bet she's craving nicotine more than ever.*

"I can't decide if what happened here—the murder of a Guardian—complicates or simplifies our investigations." The ambassador's tone had changed, no longer in story mode.

"How so?" Damian couldn't see how the transgression might be tied to the Sphere of Doom, though he had yet to fully immerse himself in the history of his new assignment.

"Here's a riddle for you," Wendell said. "The only beings known to kill Guardians have been the Forti. However, the Guardians can destroy anything in all of Creation. Does that mean a Guardian can kill one of their own kind?"

"You think one of the Fallen is still in the Celestial City?" Colin jumped in. "That'd be one of the biggest reveals since Satan announced their intentions!"

"Could it be a recent recruit?" Damian thought aloud. "One who has a romanticized view of Satan's ideas?"

"Here's another problem." Kasee scraped her shoes against the floor. "Wendell, how many Guardians are still in the city?"

"Fifty."

"And how many did Satan sway?"

"One hundred. Why—oh!"

Damian closed one eye as he tried to visualize the discrepancy. "Math was never my strong suit."

"We know a hundred fifty Guardians survived the Forti invasion," Kasee said. "If Lucifer gathered a hundred, that means a hundred and *one* were exiled, leaving forty-nine behind."

Colin was once again on his feet, pacing around the group. "Are you sure your numbers are correct?"

"They're not complicated," Wendell said, perplexed. "I've seen them several times from multiple sources. Lucifer gathered a hundred, and fifty remained behind in the city. I can't believe such simple math evaded me for so long."

"So who remained?" Damian asked. "And why?"

"We need to figure out which Guardian was killed here." Before they'd settled down, and much to the disgust of everyone else, Wendell had reached through the metal bars of their prison and placed his hands upon the severed head. They initially theorized that if they knew who was in hand, either Athan or Bai, the other must've been the killer. "Honestly, it could be *any* of them. One or more could've been hiding in any of the hallways we passed by earlier."

"I wish I hadn't lost the crown."

They'd each attempted to retrieve the diadem, stretching their arms to their limits. Since they knew the attributes of those the two Guardians wore, it would be easy to deduce the victim. Unfortunately, it was as lost in the darkness as they were.

"But it has to be one of those two, right?" Colin paced behind Damian. "With the conversation we overheard, one of them must have belonged to Satan's legion. And now they're turning others."

"I don't think so." Damian surprised himself by refuting his experienced friend so quickly. "We saw them draw their swords, which shone brightly with Light. Whatever they're up to, they haven't completely lost their way."

"Good point." Colin sounded impressed.

"Don't forget what my informants told me," Kasee said. "They saw three individuals enter the dungeon."

"Right. Maybe it's Gehenna?" Damian asked.

"What?"

"Gehenna. Bai said someone knew about Gehenna, and that it was a bad thing."

"It's not a person, but a thing. Gehenna is often referred to as the Lake of Fire." Damian heard Wendell lie down and imagined the ambassador staring up at the high ceiling while recalling lore. "In ancient times, it was basically a celestial garbage dump. Dead planes of existence or defunct projects were thrown in and incinerated. When the Creator locked the Fallen away in Hell, they tossed in Gehenna as well. No one really knows why, but it has since become a symbol of judgment and destruction. For souls who get on Satan's bad side, it can be a second and final death."

"Hmm, if everyone already knows Gehenna is an awful place, perhaps I misheard." Another thought popped into Damian's head. *Maybe this is relevant to my investigation!* "If it's true there's an evil Guardian in the city, could they be controlling the Sphere of Doom?"

Colin's feet audibly skidded to a stop. "Yes! Anyone can influence the sphere so long as their intent is malevolent."

"We've been so busy trying to keep wicked souls from entering the Celestial City that we've failed to address the potential evil living here for millennia," Kasee growled. "The individual the Gray Ones have been screening for may still walk on Earth."

"Let's not jump to conclusions." Wendell's voice silenced them. "We obviously failed to account for these scenarios in our previous analysis. Let's not make the same mistakes again. Once we are released from this place, we'll investigate this properly."

The mere mention of escape sparked a new urgency in Colin. Damian heard his footsteps hasten and then once more circle around the room. Colin slapped at stones, shook metal bars, and tripped over Kasee.

A rectangle of red light bloomed in the distance on the other side of their prison gate. The color was so soft, so muted, that Damian wouldn't have registered it under normal circumstances. Yet after sitting in absolute darkness for so long, his senses immediately alerted him to its presence.

"Hello?" a voice echoed down the hallway. A blurry silhouette darkened the rectangle. "Is anyone in there?"

"Yes, we're here!" The entire DSI crew jumped to their feet, rushing the metal bars of their cage. "We're trapped down here. Let us out!"

The rectangle—the gateway to and from the Dungeon of Darkness—increased in size until it appeared to stand only a few dozen yards away. Nowhere close to the distance they earlier traversed. Damian watched as several human shapes passed through, as well as a Guardian.

"Who's there?" the same voice asked, now much closer.

"This is Ambassador Klinekole, head of DSI," Wendell called out. "To whom am I speaking?"

"We're with the Department of Tracking. We've had a few missing persons reports. Is there a Kasee Lang with you?"

"I'm here!" Kasee called out. In a smug whisper, she said, "I told you we'd be fine."

"Funny. Didn't stop you from being afraid of the dark." Colin cried out when she hit him in the arm.

"Peregrination logs also place a Colin Cherry and Damian Hartter within the dungeon's vicinity," the DoT official said. "Are they present?"

"Yes, they're here," the ambassador said.

They track our movements? Damian thought of George Orwell's *1984*. *I'm grateful for it under the current circumstances, but that should be something they tell you at the Orientation of the Dead.*

He wondered who had called in for Kasee, then remembered how her secret sources had pointed them to the dungeon. *Of course. If they'd noticed some Guardians entering, they'd surely note four more humans.*

"We'll send Athan down to get you," said the voice.

"Athan?" Colin whispered. "Should we be concerned?"

"Just act normal," Wendell said. "Don't mention what we overheard, but don't lie to—"

Light flooded the room. They all turned to see Athan standing statuesque on the opposite side of the bars, sword drawn. They appeared unperturbed—if not mildly inconvenienced—by their presence. *Certainly doesn't look guilty of murder.*

"It has been many centuries since a human wandered into the dungeon," the Guardian said. "I hope the Embassy takes greater pains to warn others away from here."

"It'll be our first order of business." Colin gave a half-hearted salute. "How long have we been here?"

"Almost two days."

Damian's jaw dropped. It had *felt* like an eternity, but he didn't actually think they'd been locked up for more than five or six hours.

Kasee kicked at the ground. "Can you get us out of here?"

Athan stared down at them. The sword's Light cast flickering shadows across their grim face. For a moment, Damian thought them more demonic than angelic. Then, gripping one of the metal bars with their free hand, the Guardian pulled the entire gate upward with ease. When they let go, and bars' upward momentum continued until they disappeared into the ceiling.

No longer trapped, the four humans immediately stepped out of the circular room. Wendell said, "Athan, a terrible crime has been committed here."

"Yes, the death of a Guardian," Athan said. They motioned toward a crumpled form on the floor behind them, a pile of emaciated limbs and colorful cloth. "Do you know where the head is?"

Wendell pointed to the side of the hall. The disheveled head of a Guardian stared back at them, eyes as emotionally vacant in death as they were in life. The long hair, once tied back in a braid, was now askew, the knot that had held it in place cut off by the blade that separated head from body. A crusty brown substance—*blood?*—matted their face and, Damian noticed, his and Wendell's hands.

A polished crown lay next to the pile of burnt orange robes.

Despite having known a murder took place here, Damian still gasped at the sight of it.

"The remains of Bai." Athan's voice was as monotonous as ever. The Guardian stood motionless, sword held high, their eyes shifting back and forth, surveying the scene.

"How can we help?" Wendell asked.

Athan looked back at the ambassador. "You must leave here at once. Whoever killed Bai has the power to destroy us all."

"You three go home. We'll meet back at the office in the morning. We have a lot of work to do." Wendell pointed at the exit. Kasee was already halfway there. Colin and Damian nodded, following suit. As he neared the door, he heard the ambassador tell Athan, "I'm heading to the Embassy now. I'll wait for your return."

Damian stepped through the dungeon door. The raging red dust storm hadn't abated since their arrival. Four members of the Department of Tracking stood around, refusing to enter the prison now that they'd accomplished their job. He couldn't blame them. As miserable as the weather was, at least they could see what tortured them.

"Serves you right for what you and your wife did."

The words zipped by Damian, carried along by the wind. He swung around, but couldn't make out the four newcomers in the raging storm. "Who said that? What did you say?"

Nobody answered him, and the forms disappeared into a red haze. Even Colin, standing next to him, looked over and frowned.

"Thought I heard something." Damian shrugged it off. He peered through the sandy air for Kasee, wanting to ask how she was doing. She'd already disappeared from view. *Back home, reaching for her long-lost cigar.*

"In the mood for a drink?" Colin shouted at him. "Pumpkin ale?"

"Absolutely not," Damian said, shaking his head. Before Colin could protest, he went home.

CHAPTER FOURTEEN

"I WAS WORRIED ABOUT you."

Alena reached across their kitchen island, placing a hand on Damian's forearm. He looked down at the touch, admiring her radiant skin and how she'd neatly rolled up her sleeves. Really, after two days in the Dungeon of Darkness, he was thankful he could see again.

"I hope I didn't interfere with your work by reporting you missing."

"No, it's okay." He turned his arm over and grasped her hand. "If you and the others hadn't gone asking, we'd still be rotting away in that cell."

"I should've done something sooner," she said. "I reached out to Anthony yesterday. He was so much more pleasant than at the dinner party, but he wasn't concerned in the least. Discouraged me from reaching out to the Embassy."

Damian smiled, refusing to let the mention of Colin's surly boyfriend spoil his mood. He instead focused on the rich, earthy aroma of coffee filling the air. Alena had brewed a pot shortly after he materialized in the foyer. Her concern, her touch—the coffee—were comforting. *Now it's my turn.*

"You did the right thing at the right time. I learned some valuable information about my cases." He hesitated, the image of Bai's corpse flashing through his mind. He wanted to tell Alena everything. She'd likely provide valuable insight—*she'd be better at the job than I*—but Embassy policy prohibited discussing the matter. "I also missed the two of you."

The two glanced down to the end of the island where Bennett sat propped up in a high chair, banging a wooden spoon on a ceramic plate. The baby was growing so quickly, already looking less like a newborn and more like a small child. Damian saw now how easily Bennett could become an adult within a year.

A pang of emotion caught Damian off guard as he watched their child make a ruckus. *We get only a year? That was supposed to be a selling point.*

"Everything okay?" Alena asked.

"I was concerned that my imprisonment, and how I willingly walked into it, would be seen as..." He hesitated, then forced himself to be honest. "Rather, *was* a sign of bad parenting. I've only been with the DSI for a few days, but I'm quickly learning it's a demanding job. It's kept me away from you and Bennett. I considered resigning, not wanting to be one of those fathers who's never around."

"Exactly how long did you toy with quitting?" Alena's dark eyes peered at him through the steam of her tea.

Damian chuckled, picking up his coffee. "Two, maybe three seconds? I still don't want to change diapers and clean up barf."

Alena raised an eyebrow. "Have you pooped once since getting here?"

"No!" Damian said after a genuine laugh. He looked at Bennett again, who was now gnawing on the spoon. "About what you said at Colin's place. I'm not happy you didn't tell me about what we were getting into, but I also received some blowback from our decision. I'm sorry you had to fight so hard by yourself for so long."

"What happened?" Alena asked, setting down her mug.

"Nothing big. Just some vague whispers in the background." Damian shook his head. "My time here has dispelled any illusions that the Afterlife is fun and games. Like you said before, our actions have consequences we'll live with for the rest of eternity. I can't help but feel I have to protect Bennett from what's out there."

"You're already an amazing parent." Alena squeezed his hand again. "We're both lucky you're here."

"I don't know about all that." He grinned back at her, hoping she was right. *For all my fears and conceptions of fatherhood, Bennett is my responsibility.*

It startled Damian how resolute he was in that conclusion.

Perhaps...I always wanted a child?

"No," he said aloud.

"Hmm?" Alena lifted Bennett out of the high chair, preparing to head upstairs.

"Just thinking about how lucky he is we adopted him."

"I think you meant to say how lucky *we* are to have him!" She nudged him in the side as she passed by.

"You can think whatever you like." He pushed his coffee away. "Are you heading to bed? I know I shouldn't be tired, but I'm beat!"

A noise tugged at Damian's consciousness, forcing him from sleep.

"Shut up, Gregory," he mumbled, threatening to run the terrier off the roof of the building.

Then he remembered the dog was in Chicago, itself in another universe. Unless Gregory had followed him into the Afterlife to haunt him for eternity—*Who am I kidding? That dog is going straight to Hell. Satan's right-hand pooch*—something else had dragged him back to the waking world.

Damian rolled onto his back, rubbing his eyes. He'd been dreaming of the Chicago apartment he and Alena used to live in. The rooftop specifically. The same spot he so often imagined punting Gregory out into Logan Square. Ethereal moonlight painted only a small corner of the gravel-strewn surface, leaving the rest cast in shadows.

A mid-century modern entertainment console stood within the illuminated area, on top of which sat the largest flat-panel television Damian had ever seen. A movie was playing without any sound. One of the old *Star Trek* movies.

Not the one with the whales—his favorite—but the sequel with Sybok, Spock's half-brother.

Nobody likes this movie, he'd thought in the dream. *Why am I watching it?*

Next to the console was a large folding table. Computer components lay strewn around it. A large case, a hard drive, memory, and wires. *So many wires.* He was building a new PC. A powerful one on which to write his debut novel. *And play some games.*

"19-22-15-11 14-22, 23-26-14-18-26-13."

Damian had jumped as a voice called out the sequence. He glanced around, expecting a giant red and orange whale to rise from the building's horizon, conveying the man—he was certain it was a man—from his previous dream. Nobody else stood within the moonlit portion of the roof, though, and no eyes stared at him from the dark.

"11-15-22-26-8-22 19-22-15-11 14-22."

The voice had carried the same sense of urgency. Unlike last time, Damian found it familiar. He turned in a circle, squinting into the shadows, trying to place the speaker's owner and location. On the third rotation, his eyes focused on the television. The Sybok character was breaking the fourth wall, glaring at him through the panel.

"11-15-22-26-8-22 19-22-15-11 14-22." Sybok harshly enunciated each number. Desperation etched across his Vulcan face.

"What're you trying to tell me?" Damian asked, feeling foolish for talking to a television. He tried to memorize the numbers. Without the crashing waves of water, he could make them out. This was a dream, though, and he knew many of the details would slip away within minutes. "I don't understand you."

Sybok slammed his hands against the screen, the apparent force causing the television to rock back and forth. With great effort, he stammered, "Help me, Damian! Please help!"

Damian leaped back at the words—at least he'd tried to. The rocky foundation under his feet shifted, the tar beneath the gravel liquefying. His shoes were stuck in the sticky black substance. He was sinking. Everything was sinking. The folding table toppled over, spilling expensive components across the goop. They disappeared, falling into the apartment below.

"Help me, Damian!"

But tar and gravel had claimed Damian's feet. They climbed up his legs, weighing him down, pulling him under.

"Who are you? What can I do?" he'd asked the Vulcan as he sank down to his neck. Other than the plea repeating again and again, there was no response. Whether by the alien's beating against the fourth wall or the entertainment console falling victim to the melting rooftop, the flat panel had tipped over and shattered into a thousand pieces.

Was it the awful crashing sound that woke me? What a shame. It looked like a nice TV. Damian lay still in bed, letting the haze of dreams clear from his mind. The last thing he wanted was to get up. Not that he was tired. Sleep provided opportunities to snuggle up with Alena.

The doorbell rang.

Damian's eyes widened, then he peeked at the analog clock on the bedside table. It was just after two a.m.

Mr. Parsons, maybe? At this hour?

According to the Athan, time on this plane had no meaning. The clock next to him begged to differ, ticking away with precisely measured increments.

The Embassy observes regular work hours, so why doesn't the mail carrier? Damian wished telepathy was one of his new magical tricks. *Just leave the mail on the porch. I'll pick it up while I enjoy my morning coffee.*

The doorbell rang again, this time followed by an insistent knocking on the front door.

Alena groaned and rolled onto her side. Not wanting her or Bennett—*especially not the baby*—to wake up, Damian slid out from under the covers. He considered peregrinating onto the porch, then thought better of it. Knocking on a door was somehow ceremonial. A response *involving* the door was expected. Demanded even. Instead, he jumped down into the foyer, materializing in plaid pajamas. Ceremony demanded parties on both sides of the door to be dressed.

After a quick glance in the wall mirror, Damian pulled open the door. Harsh words for Jim Parsons were on his tongue. Yet instead of the jovial mail carrier, he found a middle-aged Black woman and a much younger man with wispy red facial hair. Both were dressed in black suits, solemn expressions on their faces.

"Er, may I help you?" he asked.

"I'm Rebecca Vacca, and this is Gus Green. We're with the Department of Death," the woman said, peering at him with soulful brown eyes. "Are you Damian Hartter?"

Damian let out a protracted "Yes," during which dozens of reasons the DoD was at his house raced through his imagination. *Is this about the ongoing investigation into Colin's death? Or perhaps they made a mistake on my own. Maybe I'm not supposed to be dead yet, and they're gonna send me back to my mangled body. Worse, they've caught on that the good side is the wrong side for me, and they're sending me to Hell!*

"We're so sorry to disturb you at this hour." Rebecca glanced at his pajamas. "We thought you'd want to be informed as soon as possible."

"Informed of what?"

The woman hesitated, then asked, "May we come in?"

"No. The baby is sleeping. What's this about?"

Gus stepped forward, speaking for the first time. "We regret to inform you that your mother, Denise Louise Hartter, has passed away."

The mounting dread within Damian dissipated, and he beamed at the pair. "You sure know how to put on a show! When do I get to see her? This is my first time welcoming someone to the Afterlife, so I'm not familiar with the process."

Rebecca's eyes shifted, and Gus retreated, preoccupied with his feet. Damian knew it was technically possible the man was older than his counterpart, but he got the distinct impression Gus was new to the department—and was suddenly questioning his career choice.

"I'm so sorry, Mr. Hartter, but you won't be able to see her." Rebecca spoke slowly, her voice low. "It seems Denise Hartter wasn't a good person. She wasn't...good."

The dread returned, manifesting as weight in Damian's chest and face. Pressure built up behind his eyes. "I don't understand. I don't get to see her?"

"She's in Hell," Gus blurted out. His face reddened.

Damian stared at the two. Other than a withering glance from Rebecca toward her partner, he received nothing else. "I don't understand. There must be some mistake. My mother believed in this. She had so much faith."

"Many have a firm belief in a religion," Rebecca said, pulling an envelope out of her black jacket. "But beliefs don't make a person good."

"What's this?" Damian asked through labored breaths. His arm automatically reached out and accepted the letter, but his numb fingertips felt nothing.

Gus spoke up, eager to redeem his blunder. "Anyone sent to Hell gets to write one letter to someone here. Your mother wrote hers pretty quickly, but we've been holding on to it while we investigated the incident."

Both Damian and Rebecca looked at him sharply.

"Incident? What happened? How'd my mother die?"

The woman moved as though she was going to place a hand on Damian's shoulder, but ultimately decided against it. "It was an accident, Mr. Hartter. The same car accident that killed you."

Damian drove north along Main Street, heading into Minade's downtown block. After spending years among skyscrapers representing decades of architectural history, the aging brick facades hailing back to the 1930s Midwestern take on the American Dream had a certain charm. Dried cornstalks decorated lampposts. Squash and gourds sat in the large window displays of shops. Fall was in full swing, and the city hoped for a high turnout at the upcoming festival.

"I hear Cheryl has an entry in the pumpkin contest. Supposed to be a record setter."

Damian glanced over at his mother, sitting in the passenger seat of the Buick Century. "Oh? Since when did you take an interest in Cheryl?"

Cheryl—Mrs. Cherry to Damian—was Colin's mother. She'd cultivated Colin's interest in gardening, even paying him to produce contest-worthy pumpkins. After a brief hiatus following Colin's accident and death, she continued the hobby. Whenever Damian stopped to visit, which wasn't often, a pie was always close at hand.

"I don't." His mother stared out her window as they passed by a consignment shop. "Just heard it through the grapevine."

Out his own window—rolled down so the shared space with his mother felt less confining—Damian noted the florist, an office for the Republican party, and a Hallmark store. He wondered how many businesses each building had held in its long history. The structure Hallmark took over to hustle cards used to be a theater.

How many times did Mom go to the movies before I was born? He tried to imagine his parents holding hands and sharing popcorn.

"Why'd you come with me, Mom?" he asked as he brought the Buick to a standstill at the only stoplight in town. Unlike the lampposts, which were at least designed to fit in with the quaint surroundings, the glaring red light looked unabashedly modern. "I'm going home. *From* your house. Do you expect me to drive you back across town at your leisure?"

His mother's head spun. "My leisure? With all the worry you put me through—moving away...moving *on*—I never have time for *leisure*. And now you talk about dying and expect me not to be concerned?" She gestured to him. "You aren't even wearing a seatbelt!"

The light turned green. After a moment's hesitation, fearing movement would set off another tirade from his mother, Damian proceeded through the intersection. The county courthouse, constructed of gray sandstone and mounted by a domed clock tower, loomed over them. Hidden away in its shadow was Minade Hospital.

"I didn't choose my words well, and I'm sorry for that. I may not be my best self at this moment, but I'm not suicidal. Please believe that." He rolled his eyes. Partially at his mother, though more so at a storefront they passed by. The owners had placed an enormous flag in the window. Written on the flag, in language he doubted the church condoned, was a message calling for the impeachment of the country's president.

That has to be breaking some kind of law or ordinance.

"We're never going to see eye-to-eye on many things." His mother placed a hand on his right arm. "But I hope you know I love you very much."

It was Damian's turn to jerk his head around. His mother's touch, reserved for awkward birthday and holiday hugs, was unexpected. As was her declaration. Damian could count on one hand—and have fingers to spare—the number of times she'd verbally expressed her feelings.

More surprising, though, was her need to say anything. They had their disagreements and gave each other a hard time. But she was his mother. She'd put aside every dollar she could to buy him the Buick. Helped pay for expenses while he was in school. Believed he had a soul, and prayed for its everlasting salvation. The behavior that drove a wedge in their relationship stemmed from a desire to be in his vicinity—to annoy him—for eternity.

Damian knew she loved him.

"Of course I know that, Mom. I love you, too. No matter what."

Sentimental eye contact was too much for his mother to hold, and she glanced out the windshield. Her eyes widened, and her body tensed like a frightened caged animal. "Look out!"

When Damian saw the hulking combine harvester in front of them, he wondered how both of them had missed it. As it was, once his eyes focused, he could read a small, dirt-smudged sign affixed to its back.

"Damian!" she screamed as he jerked the car to the right. They both leaned away from the metal monstrosity as the Buick bore past it, barely an inch between.

With the farm equipment behind them, Damian let out a breath he'd been holding. Slowly at first, but then it rushed out in a soft, puzzled "ope" when his vehicle jolted up over the curb. Then they decimated a giant display of pumpkins at the entrance of the city park, the location of the upcoming fall festival.

Did I just take out Mrs. Cherry's award-winning pumpkin? Damian gritted his teeth as, through the mass of gourd guts and seeds, he saw the sharp elevation of a grassy mound.

The Buick went airborne.

Weighing in at a ton and a half, the car expeditiously returned to the ground. With its momentum and cockeyed angle, it overturned several times down the other side of the mound. The centrifugal force ejected him through the side window.

Then, if only to outdo itself, the car he'd so actively despised for years rolled over him before coming to rest upside down.

A fall breeze rustled the grass Damian lay in. He coughed blood—a lot of blood—but he suffered no pain. He thought he should. People were screaming. Several approached hesitantly, faces twisted as if the sight of him caused *them* pain.

But all he felt was warm wind and lush grass upon his skin. It was pleasing to be outside. He rarely had time to appreciate nature. It was sublime.

At least until the angels descended, with all their horns and bright lights.

Damian rolled his head, the vertebrae in his neck audibly popping, and took in the sight of the Buick Century. Though the engine still ticked, he doubted it would come to life again. Grime clouded the windows, but he found his reflection—no, his mother's form. She stared blankly back at him.

As the harsh lights faded and sirens dulled, Damian closed his eyes for the last time.

Damian opened his eyes, his face plastered against the cold tiles of the foyer floor. He saw Rebecca and Gus's feet on the opposite side of the threshold shifting back and forth.

"Everyone always told me how much I looked like my mother."

"Sir?" Gus said. The lanky man bent over and picked up the envelope, which Damian had dropped in a haze.

"I thought I was looking at my reflection in the car window," Damian said, standing up. His legs wobbled, threatening to fail him again, so he made his way into the library and fell into a reading chair. The two DoD officials stepped into the house, peeking around the corner at him. "I was seeing her. My mother. I...I forgot she was in the car with me."

Rebecca came over, this time placing a hand on his shoulder. He looked up into her soulful eyes as she said, "Mr. Hartter, you have our sincerest condolences on the loss of your mother. Do you have someone who can be with you during this difficult time?"

"My wife is asleep." Damian looked toward the staircase.

"Should I call for her?" Gus asked, already making his way out to the foyer.

"No!" Damian was so abrupt that Gus almost tripped over himself stopping. "Let her sleep. She'll be awake soon, anyway. I think I just want to sit here for a while."

"Of course, Mr. Hartter." Rebecca straightened up. On her way out, she removed a card from her jacket and placed it on the table in the foyer. "If you have questions, you can contact us at any time."

Silence fell upon the room, so deafening Damian thought the two had left. Out of the corner of his eye, though, Gus slipped into the room and gently placed the envelope on the arm of his chair. Then the pair exited, shutting the door behind them.

I can go back to bed. Pretend this was all a bad dream. Other than the letter beside him and a card in the foyer, it would be easy to feign ignorance. *But dreams are not normal around here. Or at least, Colin says.*

With trembling fingers, Damian ripped open the envelope and pulled the enclosed paper out. The pressure behind his eyes worsened as he read the surprisingly brief text.

The end is always harder when brought about by a friend.

"What does that mean?" he said aloud. *Is she accusing me? Why would she call me a friend? We were never friends, but this feels so personal.*

The letter's vagueness made it feel coded and intimate, as if he should be able to read between the lines. *But there's only one line.* His mother didn't possess the capacity to be ambiguous in life, always delivering her thoughts with sharp curtness. He doubted she'd softened much in death.

A low, anguished howl burst from Damian. Wet eyes bulged as his mouth widened, the wail continuing strong until all the air left his lungs. He took a deep breath, trying to regain composure, but he howled again. He drew his legs up onto the chair, close to his chest, and hugged them as he let out continuous pained moans.

"Damian?" Alena called out from the upstairs balcony. "Where are you?"

"I'm here," he said, his voice raspy. The skin of his face stretched under dried tears—tears he hadn't realized he'd let loose. *When did that happen?* A glance at a clock revealed the time to be nearly four thirty, over two hours since the knock on the door. "In the library."

A few moments later, Alena poked her head around the corner, peering into the dim room. "What are you doing in here? What was that noise?"

Her eyes found the note still clutched in his hands. The way her face fell told Damian she was familiar with the process.

"Who?" she asked.

"My mother."

"No!" Alena sank to her knees by the chair. She gripped his legs, staring up at him. The two women had never been close, had probably been in each other's presence a dozen times, but Alena thought similarly of his mother than he. Denise Hartter was rough around the edges, perhaps a little *too* devout, but a genuine believer at heart.

"Oh, Damian, I'm so sorry." Alena reached up, cupping the side of his face with a hand.

"I don't understand it," Damian blurted out. He wanted to press his face into her palm, to embrace her, but he could feel another wail building in his chest. "How are you and I here, but she's not?"

"I don't know. It's not fair. It's really not."

"I—I killed her." He grasped her hand, needing her security. "She was in the car with me when I died. I didn't remember, and she wasn't supposed to be there. She was worried I'd kill myself."

"She was being a mother." Alena moved to the chair's arm to be closer to him. "You didn't kill anyone. It was an accident."

Damian thrust the letter at her. "Then what's this supposed to mean?"

Alena took the paper from him, reading the words several times. Her eyebrows furrowed deeper each time. "This makes no sense. The DoD gave this to you? They're sure it was from her?"

"What do you mean?"

"I've read your mother's words. A card for our wedding. Several letters begging me to loosen my grasp on you." Alena shook her head. "I never told you about those. This note doesn't read like anything I've received from her. It seems like there's a double meaning."

"I thought so, too."

She got up from the chair. "Let me tell work I won't be coming in today."

"No, don't." He grabbed her hand. "I'm going to the Embassy."

"What? Damian! You shouldn't have to leave the house today."

Damian took a while to compose himself, to find the right words. "I fell apart when you died. Wasn't much better when Colin left. I don't want to get stuck in that kind of headspace again."

"You're allowed to grieve. To take some time."

"I know. I will." He got up, taking the letter back from her. Folding it up, he tried to tuck it into a back pocket but realized he was still wearing flannel pajamas. "I just need to focus on something. Follow up on the incident at the dungeon."

Alena gave him a look. "Can I at least make you some coffee before you leave?"

"I'm going to need every bit of help I can get," he said, pulling her into a tight hug. "I mean that."

"Say goodbye to Bennett while you're upstairs."

"I will." Damian wanted to smile, to give an encouraging laugh, but he couldn't muster that type of energy. "I'll be back tonight. We'll talk more and...plan something for Mom."

CHAPTER FIFTEEN

DAMIAN PEREGRINATED ONTO A vacant Embassy lawn.

It was late when I was here last, Damian thought as he walked toward the entrance. Without Colin by his side this time, it was especially lonely.

Mai stood alone at the door. It was odd to see a solitary Guardian, and Damian briefly entertained the idea of questioning them about Athan's whereabouts over the last several days. *Could I get any information out of them, even if they don't speak?* Other than perfunctory nods at one another, though, the two exchanged no words. Mai pulled open the heavy wooden door, and Damian stepped into the building.

The Bridge rotated slowly under the central chandelier, drawing his attention. He made his way over, soft footfalls echoing throughout the room. The space seemed especially empty now. Desolate, like a dying institution.

The spinning carousel was no mere mechanism. It was alive, overseeing the passages between universes. Damian sensed heat emanating from it as the decorative panels floated by. Most were unlocked, allowing inhabitants of the planes they represented to visit the city. He estimated fewer than one in ten sealed panels.

What does it say about humanity, Damian considered, turning to the stairwell, *that the Creator commanded our world to be locked away?*

Colin was already in the office when Damian walked in. Curtains covered the tall windows, blocking the ever-present light of the outside world. Colin was leaning back in a chair at Kasee's cubicle, rifling through papers. Kasee's desk, but he'd wheeled over his own seat.

The amount of dirt and ashes forever trapped in the cushioning of hers...

"What's up?" Colin greeted, peeking over the manuscript he'd been studying. He'd removed his customary jacket, leaving it folded neatly on his desk, and rolled up his shirt's sleeves. "Couldn't sleep either?"

"Why are you here so early?" Damian sat at his own station. The holographic screens sprang to life, but he waved them away.

"Anthony was being a bit feisty. Decided to leave him alone for a while to cool down."

Damian grunted, swiveling back and forth in his chair. *Has Wendell spoken to Athan since our release from the dungeon? Did any further evidence come to light? Any conclusions?* The felt-covered table in the middle of the room was littered with papers, but he didn't possess the mental energy to sift through them in search of clues. He wondered whether entering the wickiup was against protocol.

"Colin?" he called out, knowing his friend would've already analyzed any new information.

"What's up?" he said again.

"My mother died." Damian hadn't meant to say it. The words tumbled out, taking precedence over everything else—including Satan's machinations.

Papers tumbled to smudgy marble tiles as Colin jumped from his seat and rushed over. "That's awesome! I've heard it's quite something to watch a soul wake here for the first time."

"I wouldn't know."

Colin slowed as he neared, taking notice of Damian's slumped posture. "What do you mean?"

"She already woke up," he said. *What was it like opening her eyes and realizing she was in Hell? How can anyone withstand the shock of knowing they would face the horrors they'd warned others about for decades?* "She's dead. Been dead since the accident. But she didn't wake up here."

Colin stood as still as a Guardian, eyes flicking back and forth as though rereading Damian's words. As the meaning of those words took hold, his jaw fell and eyes widened. He made to drop into his chair. It was still back at Kasee's desk, which he remembered at the last moment, so he instead leaned against the edge of his own.

"I'm so sorry, Damian. I don't know what to say. This...I never would've thought." He scratched anxiously at the back of his neck, never taking his eyes off Damian. "I knew your mom. She could be a bitch—sorry—but she was such a strong woman."

"I know what you mean." He'd been through all this before. With Colin's unexpected passing, then Alena's run-in with the pen. That he still felt such emotion, that overwhelming grief existed in the Afterlife, disheartened him. "She blames me for where she's ended up."

"What?"

Damian pulled his mother's letter from a pocket, sliding it across the desk. Colin picked it up and, just as his wife had done, read through the single sentence multiple times. Seemingly satisfied, he laid it back down, though he immediately leaned over and studied the page for another minute.

"This doesn't make sense," he finally said. "Your mother was never this enigmatic."

"Exactly!" Damian threw a hand into the air. "And we sure as hell weren't friends."

"Do you think she's blaming one of her own friends?" Colin walked across the office and retrieved his chair. "What good would it do to tell you? It's not like you could do anything about it."

"I know. I've thought of all that," Damian said. "Besides, she didn't have many friends. No *real* ones, anyway."

"What're you thinking? That someone else wrote you this letter?"

Damian nodded. "That's what Alena thought."

Colin leaned back in his chair, staring up at the ceiling. "I'm not familiar with Hell's soul intake process, but that'd be a serious accusation. Though I don't suppose their mail delivery service is secure. They're not exactly famous for obeying protocols, right?"

"If that's the case, how many people get cheated out of sending their letter?" Damian sighed.

Nodding, Colin said, "I'm sure it happens more than we'd like to think. A single individual circumventing the system to send several notes."

"What a defective system." Damian gave a wry grin. "At least this way, she can't get the last word in."

Colin, who'd suffered dinners at the Hartter household, laughed aloud. "Doesn't explain why someone else would send you this letter, since they'd presumably be able to send a message to anyone. They're evil, not inept."

The weight of reality fell upon Damian once more. *I'll never see her again.* For the first time, he regretted walking out of his parents' home the day he died. How angry he was with them. How much he'd left unresolved. He'd assumed he'd see them again in a few days. Even after he died, in the back of his head, he *knew* it was only a matter of time before they were all reunited.

Not sure if Mom would be overjoyed I made it here or mad I beat her to it, Damian thought, trying to relieve the emotional pressure. It was a useless endeavor. *Not only is she gone forever, but some idiot fool squandered away her last contact with me for this cryptic joke.*

"Damian?"

"It wasn't supposed to be like this!" he shouted. Snatching the letter off the table, he crumbled it up and threw it aside. The balled-up paper bounced off the nearby metal cabinet before coming to rest on the floor. "It was supposed to be perfect! Everything was so close to perfect."

A moment later, the fuel that lit Damian's anger melted away. He crossed his arms and leaned back, pushing the soles of his feet against the edge of his desk.

For his part, Colin waited an appropriate amount of time before speaking again. "What do you mean by *perfect*?"

"That I woke up again after death, and it was in a world of reasonable security," Damian said. "My wife was waiting for me, and I got to hang out with my best friend."

Colin nodded. "The quiche was quite good."

"I've only been here eleven days, but I grow more anxious each hour." Damian gestured at the room. "Why does this department exist? How am I having dreams if that's not normal? And why...why do I *feel* this much pain?"

For the first time, Damian conjured up a simple item. A tissue coalesced between his fingers, and he used it to wipe away fresh tears.

"Perfection is a strange subject." Colin's voice was low, laced with sympathy. Then, to Damian's surprise, he stood and turned to leave the room. "Follow me."

"What? Where are we going?" Damian was reluctant to vacate his chair.

"Have you been to the Hall of Hands?"

"No."

Colin nodded, holding the door and waving for Damian to follow. "Makes sense. Most people haven't heard of it."

"Well, what is it?" Damian heaved himself out of his seat.

"It's a place that'll help you understand Creation. At least in terms of perfection."

Rather than peregrinating, Colin led Damian out of the Embassy and down the street on foot. This suited Damian. The *immediacy* of events was grating on him. As a millennial, he found this surprising.

Even without the need to breathe, the open sky cleared his mind and lightened the solemn mood hanging over him. Colin remained silent during their walk, allowing Damian an opportunity to process the last few hours. It was rare for Colin to remain quiet for an extended period, and Damian appreciated the gesture.

It was soon apparent why Colin had opted to walk. Only a few blocks short of the Celestial Library, he stopped in front of a building not unlike most others. Whitewashed walls and smooth curves did nothing to distinguish the structure from its neighbors. Affixed to the wall above the doors was a small plaque on which extremely small lettering identified the place as the Hall of Hands.

Though the library shared similar austere qualities with the hall, Damian thought the plainness of this building was purposeful. Sandwiched between two other bland structures, few would give it a second glance, let alone bother entering.

Colin ascended the short flight of stairs leading to the doors, then pushed his way inside. The hinges creaked ominously.

After a moment's hesitation—darkness shrouded the interior—Damian followed Colin.

The small vestibule he found himself in was dimly lit, but not sinister. Two pedestals stood in the middle of the room. A pair of oversized sculpted hands rested on top of them. A sign-in sheet rested in the palm of the right hand, and the other poised as if it held a pen or quill, although no writing utensils were present.

"Nobody ever comes in here." Colin stared up at the lobby's single light source, a dusty chandelier. Bits of abandoned webbing, disturbed by the shifting air, wafted downward.

Damian conjured a fountain pen and signed them both in, noticing *Colin Cherry* in the previous two entries. Then he handed the pen over to the other sculpture. "No kidding. Does anyone manage this place?"

"I doubt anyone's desperate for this level of isolation." Colin walked around the two pedestals to another set of doors. He pulled them open, revealing yet another space engulfed in shadow. "You ever see the movie *Westworld?* I think your favorite author directed it."

"Michael Crichton, yes. Wrote the script, too." Damian strained his eyes as he entered the dark. In the film, Westworld was a fantastical theme park populated by androids that looked, moved, and acted like human beings. It was a blueprint for what would arguably become Crichton's most famous novel, and Damian's favorite: *Jurassic Park*.

"Well," Colin said. "This place reminds me of that movie."

Dozens of chandeliers burst into flames. Not just the candles they held, but the entire metal fixtures. Thick chains connected them to the ceiling a dozen floors above, each supporting two or three stacked chandeliers. The chains too went aflame, illuminating balconies. Cobwebs and dust sizzled as the fire incinerated them.

Light was abundant, though the ground floor seemed to push back, refusing to relinquish its secrets. Damian had to squint to make out anything in the shadows, and what he saw made him gasp. Hundreds of shadowy pedestals, each with a pair of hands perched on top. The displays didn't surprise him. *This is the Hall of Hands*. Their designs took him aback.

In *Westworld*, the only way to differentiate between the androids and humans was by their hands. The human extremity was an intricate design. The park's engineers hadn't been able to replicate them for their creations. Fingers were thicker, with deep ridges lining the knuckles. Unnatural, and certainly unsettling.

Before Damian were innumerable variations of hands. Each iteration came in all colors, including shades found in no rainbow. The skin on many was like that of old leather: dried up, cracked and flaking. Others were soggy with moisture. Dozens had fur of various textures and consistencies. Some possessed only two or three digits, while others sported up to eleven. The display closest to them held a pair gifted with crusty, brittle nails two feet long.

Colin led the way through the center of the hall, commenting on his favorites. Pointing to a metallic, three-fingered claw, he said, "Imagine if we ended up with those."

"Who *did* end up with them?" Damian shuddered. When Colin looked at him in puzzlement, he said, "These are the hands designed for each project, right?"

"Many assume that, but it's a misconception. One that neither the Creator nor the Embassy is keen to shine a light on." Colin shook his head. "This place should really be called the Hall of *Human* Hands."

"So, what, these are the prototypes of what we ended up with?" Damian flexed his fingers, staring upward at the additional floors. If each contained a couple hundred examples, there'd easily be over a thousand pairs. "And here I thought we were made in the Creator's image."

Colin snorted. "The Creator has many images, none of which likely portray reality."

Many of the appendages intrigued Damian, drawing him in for a closer peek. He gazed at a slender pair with no fingernails, glimmering silver and gold under the firelight. *How much time would I have saved without nails to clip?* Purple scales graced another duo, along with filed, pointy claws at the tip of each digit. *A beautiful but deadly addition.*

For every set of hands catching his aesthetic eye, another existed that was difficult to look at for more than a second. Bloody and pulpy masses twisted in pain. Jagged bones poked through ragged skin. Carapace covered others, making them appear like bugs. As awful as they were to see, they forced Damian to ponder how his life would've differed if he'd possessed them.

Colin pointed out a pair that looked nearly identical to their own. Only a sixth finger on each hand set them apart. "This version was to be the production model, but was recalled at the last moment because of technical issues. They still pop up every once in a while."

They'd reached the end of the hall, the path leading to an elevator. Damian eyed it warily. Rather than the traditional modern elevator he was used to, hidden away behind sliding doors, the carriage resembled an oversized birdcage. Gilded round bars kept passengers from falling out during transit, meeting at a single point on top. Stepping inside, he saw an ornate panel with twelve triangular buttons. Colin pressed the top one. With an unnerving clang and jolt, they ascended.

"Can you create something in your own image?" Colin asked as they trundled upward.

"You mean kids?"

Colin gave a wry smile, gazing out over the hundreds of hands before them. "No, I'm talking about artistic endeavors. Sculptors like Michelangelo. People like that strive to create human facsimiles from stone and bronze."

"They're still inanimate objects. Lesser versions of what they imitate." Damian looked at his own hands, knowing he didn't have the creative talent to match Michelangelo. The best he could do—*hopefully*—was write something that would capture the human experience. Literature was fraught with humans creating things in their image. "You're saying the Creator is like an artist?"

"Exactly." Colin stretched his hand out over the displays below. "Like any artist, the Creator has to hone their craft. Practice makes perfect, and plenty of mistakes are made along the way."

In his younger, more naïve days, Damian would've considered Colin's words blasphemous. To consider the Creator less than perfect, let alone say so aloud, was downright sinful. Even before he strayed from religion, the imperfections of the world and the humans who lived in it became painfully obvious.

"If you think about it," Colin said, sounding almost mournful, "it calls into question everything else the Creator has done."

The elevator slowed to a stop on the top floor, the metal doors swinging open. The circular balcony was as spacious as those below, but only one pedestal stood on the opposite side of the building, illuminated by a fiery chandelier. As they walked toward it, Damian saw on display the most perfectly crafted set of human hands. Proportional finger length and width. Exquisitely cut and polished cuticles and nails. Damian wasn't one to notice small physical details, but even he knew these were beautiful.

"You grew up with firm views of what the Afterlife would look like. Tailor-made to whatever you wanted it to be," Colin said as they stepped up to the pedestal.

Damian nodded, remembering his church service daydreams.

"And I take it your experience hasn't lived up to those expectations. That perfection, as you considered it back on Earth, is illusory."

Again, Damian nodded. "Figured my vision was selfish."

"The Afterlife isn't for the individual. It's inclusive. As such, it's a system, an institution, and a complex one at that."

The bump in logic. On the ground floor of the hall, Damian had imagined the Creator as a grizzled man in an old wood shop, working tirelessly but lovingly to piece together his next project. *Such a simple idea.* He glanced over at Colin, the hall suddenly feeling more confined. "I'm not sure what you're getting at."

"Do you know of any system that's not inherently flawed?"

The chain supporting the chandelier creaked above them. Both men instinctively looked up.

"The Celestial City is exactly the same. It's a complex system, and it runs like a well-oiled machine. Underneath its shiny veneer, though, are conflicting ideas and principles."

Damian considered the negative reactions Alena had faced in her fight for children to mature and think for themselves. Of the hate and fear behind the jeers thrown her way. *Does Colin face the same racist and homophobic attitudes here that he did on Earth?*

Uncomfortable, Damian leaned forward to take a closer peek at the sculpture in front of them. It was a faultless specimen, the crowning achievement of the old man in the wood shop. Dust had settled on the pair after being ignored for so long. He tried to brush away a bit of the grime, succeeding only in creating a dirty smear. A long, dark streak now marred the piece's left forefinger.

"How is this supposed to make me feel better?" He turned away from the display, wiping his fingertips on his shirt.

"It's not. You expected a perfect existence in the Afterlife because your upbringing led you to believe a perfect being had created it. But in a perfect world, the ones you love always end up by your side, and children never grow up without their parents."

Damian felt his body sag at the thought of his mother. *Things certainly didn't turn out as she believed.*

"The Afterlife is deeply flawed." Colin peered into the shadows of the surrounding space. More quietly than before, he said, "And the Creator may be, too."

Damian took an involuntary step back from Colin, nearly tripping over his own feet.

"Either way," Colin added in haste. "The world you dreamed of so long ago doesn't exist outside your own mind. Your mother may have fallen victim to a faulty system, being wrongly found guilty of whatever crimes that landed her in Hell. It's possible she's completely innocent."

CHAPTER SIXTEEN

THE JOURNEY BACK TO the Embassy was as quiet as the trip to the Hall of Hands. Colin had made his point about the Creator's supposed perfection—*practically handed it to me, really*—and was letting Damian mull over the new information. His mind, humming with fresh surges of fury, was anything but quiet.

Damian had spent a lifetime actively disliking his mother. He'd curse her under his breath whenever she intimidated him or spoke ill of Colin. Even stewing in teenage anger, though, a voice in the back of his head assured him that one day the ill will would fade. He'd appreciate and even be thankful for the upbringing he disdained. One day he'd genuinely love her, and she'd love him too.

The moment had come, the two of them sitting in the Buick Century. An authentic conversation passed between them. A touch. Understanding. And then they died.

The accident only widened the gulf between mother and son. Her soul was now in a plane of existence locked away from all others, making certain a reunion would never occur. If Colin's insinuations were true, it was the ineptitude of the Creator that had stolen her.

The voice of reason whispered to him again, though the words didn't bring comfort. *In all the years you spent maintaining a grudge against your mother, it is you who lost so much time with her.*

So much of the Afterlife ran contrary to Damian's expectations. As that polarity allowed him to live with his wife again, he'd largely left the faulty lines of code unquestioned. The idea of his mother enduring eternal punishment for sins she never committed was too much for him to turn a blind eye to. It drove him mad.

Chin held high, Damian picked up his pace, once again driven toward work. Not to distract himself, as he'd felt when he left home earlier, but to figure out the situation. If not for his mother or himself, then for Bennett.

The thought was like a splash of cold water to the face, and he almost froze on the sidewalk. He barely knew the child. Fought against the adoption. Now he was trying to build a better future for him.

"Hmm," Colin grunted, drawing Damian out of his thoughts as they neared the Embassy. Ahead of them, the lawn was no longer deserted. Throngs of creatures from a multitude of universes peregrinated onto the grass. The front doors barely accommodated everyone clamoring to get inside the institution. Mai towered over the sea of bodies, silently struggling to maintain order.

"I've never seen so many people excited about work." Damian glanced at Colin, whose lips were pursed and eyebrows furrowed. "What's wrong?"

"I'm not sure, but people only act this way when they're afraid."

The pair quickened their pace, joining the horde. Bodies jostled about, seeking the best path inside, and they bumped into Damian several times. Growing impatient, he used his size to forge a path through the crowd. Within a few minutes, he'd fought their way up the front stairs and into the foyer. They dashed up to the third floor and raced down the hall, jumping around those whose pace didn't match their own.

"Where were you two?" Wendell demanded once they entered the DSI office. The ambassador rushed out of his wickiup, a trail of papers floating to the flowerbed behind him.

"The Sphere of Doom struck again," Kasee said from the corner.

A holographic display of the Celestial City once again floated in midair above the conference table. As Damian approached, he noticed a fifth dot glowing devilishly red alongside the previous four. Its location fit perfectly on a tip of the six-pointed star Colin had proposed, an outline of which was superimposed over the city.

"When did this happen?" Damian stared at the display, pangs of guilt running through him. The sphere was his case. Other than reading about its history, he'd made no progress in finding either the relic or the evil directing its destructive actions. "We were here an hour ago."

"You just missed it, then." Wendell spread his notes across the table. "I received notice at home around forty-five minutes ago."

"What was hit?" Colin asked, gawking at the new dot.

Kasee appeared beside them, jabbing at the hologram with her cigar. Smoke clouded the image. "The sphere activated in a remote region of the planet Irvin, located in a plane known for its gelatinous life forms. I'm told Damian interacted with one of their kind a few days ago."

Face reddening at the memory of hitting the green blob with his Camaro, Damian stared at the map. Not for the first time, he grappled with understanding how the Celestial City existed within a multitude of universes. The latest strike by the sphere didn't happen in the same plane as the previous attack. *What was it...Dr. Carroll's pasture, with cows and sheep?* He'd assumed the doctor lived in the Afterlife—and erroneously accepted all shrinkings occurred there, too.

"One household was within the affected area," Kasee said. "Embassy officials from the Irvin branch are already on site, along with any others willing to help."

"It shouldn't have happened yet." Colin paced the length of the table. When Damian looked at him, he said, "Time between the previous incidents varied, but they never occurred within three weeks of one another. It's only been eleven days since the last incident. I thought there'd be more time for you to catch up."

"We don't have any more time!" Kasee slammed a fist on the table, crushing her cigar.

"Enough." Everyone fell still at Wendell's firm voice. "We haven't had time to recover from our trip to the dungeon. The Embassy still hasn't released a statement regarding the death of Bai. I suspect there's a connection between the Guardian's murder and the Sphere of Doom. I don't consider Athan the guilty party behind either front, though I suspect they know something."

The ambassador looked across the table at Damian. "Athan has taken a liking to you. Schedule some time to talk with them. See if they'll divulge any information."

Damian nodded. *Not sure what constitutes "liking."*

"Kasee is right. We no longer have the luxury of time with our various investigations. Even in this department, it's easy to become complacent, to fight evil between lunch and a nap." Wendell glanced over at his garden. "We lost a member of our department, but Damian has stepped in and strengthened us."

Damian felt his ears turn red.

"We need to pool our resources and focus on what's happening on Irvin." The ambassador pointed again at the holographic diagram. "Considering the evidence supporting Colin's theory, it is the opinion of this department that the forces controlling the sphere are malevolent. Whatever the endgame is, their plan is escalating. The next—and possibly final—shrinking could only be hours away."

"I could ask the Guardians to stand watch over the last projected target." Colin sighed. "If only we knew in which plane it'll happen."

"Could be any of thousands," Kasee said.

"Even if we discard those that've been locked?" Damian asked.

Colin sighed again. "Still thousands. And only forty-nine Guardians—one of whom may be the perpetrator."

"Ask your contacts if they've heard of anything. *Anything*," Wendell said, pointing at Kasee. "The rest of us will go to Irvin."

"Yes, sir."

"What exactly are we doing on Irvin?" Damian asked.

"The Department of Dimensional Stability is already attempting to reverse the damage and discover whether anyone disappeared."

"Our top priority is to find the sphere. It may still be in the area, or left a clue as to where it's headed next. Otherwise, be open to the smallest of details." Colin looked at Damian. "Fresh eyes might be exactly what we need."

"Questions?" Wendell asked. "No? Suit up. Irvin is an inhospitable planet."

Damian watched Colin snatch his jacket from his desk. He paused at the office door, sliding his arms through the sleeves. "I'll go speak with Mai. See how many planes the Guardians can feasibly patrol."

"Let's meet on the lawn in ten minutes," the ambassador added, following Colin out.

Uncomfortable in the quiet room, Damian stepped away from the table and the sinister hologram. The silence—even ten minutes of it—would invite depressing thoughts and memories into his mind. *I'll just wait outside for everyone.*

"Wendell was being literal about the suit." He jumped at the sound of Kasee's gruff voice. Still at the table, she glared at him through the haze of a new cigar. "Irvin's atmosphere would dissolve your lungs in about three seconds. You'll need protection."

Damian swallowed hard. "That's... What?"

"Follow me." Kasee turned and walked to her desk.

"I didn't think we had lungs to burn." He patted his chest. "Aren't these bodies just representations of our souls?"

Kasee rolled her eyes as she rummaged around her desk. "Within the Celestial City and the Afterlife, yes, but those rules don't apply to all planes of existence. I'm sure you noticed the effect of gravity at the Dungeon of Darkness."

He recalled the sharp pain of sand against his skin and the rush of blood in his ears.

"The dungeon's universe is compatible with our forms. We can experience discomfort there, perhaps minor injuries, but we wouldn't starve. The cosmic forces that hold us together here won't everywhere, including the planet Irvin." She pulled open the top right drawer, rifled through it, then slammed it shut with a frustrated grunt. "If you peregrinated over there without a suit, you'd effectively die again. Only, you wouldn't wake up in your house by the lake."

"But this suit can protect us? Keep our lungs from dissolving?" Damian imagined walking around an alien planet in a clunky space suit.

"Yes." Kasee ran a hand through her short red hair before moving on to the next drawer. "More of a bracelet than a suit. It projects a force field around your body, encapsulating you in a little pocket of our plane, protecting you from hostile environments."

Damian waited as she pulled open a few more drawers and tipped over a stack of to-go boxes from Messie Bessie's. "I can see how a bracelet would be easy to lose."

"Tech isn't perfect. You'll still suffer some effects." She wavered for a moment, as if some recollection unnerved her. "But you'll live through it. I know I have extras somewhere."

"Bottom left drawer?" Damian asked. It was the only one she hadn't opened yet.

Kasee paused her search and glanced down. "That one's been jammed since I started. Can't open it." To demonstrate, she reached down and jiggled the handle. It rattled, but the drawer didn't budge.

"Don't we have a maintenance department?"

She shrugged. "I've told Colin several times. He had it made for me when I started a few years back."

"Hmm," Damian grunted, surprised. The two never seemed friendly toward one another. *Doesn't mean he didn't help a new employee feel at home in the department.* He looked at the shoddy desk. *Didn't try too hard, though. Glad he put in more effort for mine.*

Wondering about those Kasee did get along with, he asked, "Who are the contacts you keep going to for information? Unless you can't reveal them."

Kasee shrugged. "You already know I work closely with the Gray Ones. They gather a lot of information through their screening process. They also put me in contact with others in our community, who continue to look out for one another."

"I see," Damian said. Then he shook his head. "Actually, I don't. What community?"

"The queer community." She said it as if Damian should've known better. "You, me, Colin, and his boy toy."

He shook his head again. "But I'm not gay—or even queer, as I understand it. I've got Alena, and she's the only person I've been attracted to."

"Oh, sorry. I must've misunderstood." She raised an eyebrow at him as she moved another stack of papers. "The way Colin spoke of you, I thought you two had a history."

"No, we don't," he stated. "I mean, I loved him...as a friend, but I was never *in* love with him."

"I said I'm sorry." She lifted a stone ashtray filled to the brim. "Ah, there it is."

Kasee handed him a wide silver bracelet. It was cool to the touch and, other than an engraved symbol of the Bridge on the top side, devoid of ornamentation. Damian slipped it over his wrist, watching as the metal device reshaped to fit him.

"Tap it once to activate—to suit up," Kasee instructed. "Three times to turn it off."

"Got it." He pressed a finger against the symbol. A blue mist spread out across his body, disappearing from view once it encapsulated him. A small amount of pressure built up in his ears. "I won't run out of oxygen?"

"You don't need to breathe!" She rolled her eyes again as she marched toward the office door. "Just don't deactivate it by accident. Good luck on Irvin."

The idea of a shrinking was one Damian found intriguing. He imagined a smear of colors both stretching and compressing as they overlapped each other. Not dissimilar to the visual effect of peregrinating, though his mind inserted miniature buildings, cows and sheep, and tiny waving people spinning around as if in a tornado.

Tiny waving people who have yet to be found.

The reality of a shrinking was devastating, a truth that hit Damian the moment he and his coworkers peregrinated into the designated safe zone at the edge of the disaster on Irvin. When the Sphere of Doom had activated, it ravaged everything within a hundred yards. The ancient device hadn't so much shrunk anything within its field, but *stretched* everything toward the center. A black mass hovered there, a place where all things fused together.

The sight was breathtaking in its horrific beauty. A shimmering globe—he assumed it was a globe, the bottom half hidden underground—of semitransparent, fluidic colors flowing inward, shimmering.

Or shuddering.

The inner makings of the sphere flowed and undulated, like a giant marble composed of mirror shards, glitter, and fraying strands of colorful yarn. The kaleidoscopic colors swirled and refracted light, creating a hypnotic display that both captivated and unsettled Damian.

"Practical joke, my ass," Damian wanted to say. Instead, a wave of nausea overtook him. He fell to his knees and dry-heaved.

Colin patted him on the shoulder. "I thought the same thing when I first saw one of these. Try not to puke in the suit, though."

"Nothing could've prepared me for this," Damian said between gasps, fighting the dizziness threatening to topple him over.

"Let's split up and search for any sign of the sphere," Wendell said after taking in the scene. "Damian, walk in circles around the affected area, making your way farther out. I'll go out a quarter mile, then do the same walking inward. We'll meet in the middle."

Damian tore his gaze from the anomaly, focusing on their other surroundings. As Kasee had reported, the area appeared remote. Mostly fields of grass and patches of trees, broken up by winding strea—

"The Celestial City?" His eyes bulged at the distant but familiar skyline, tucked behind a wall of diamond.

"Of course. It's the center of every plane." Colin exchanged a knowing look with Wendell. "And these events have all taken place about five miles outside the wall."

"It took me a while to wrap my head around how the multiverse works." Wendell massaged his forehead. "Still gives me a headache if I think about it too much."

"I'm going to speak with one of them." Colin pointed to a cluster of Embassy employees at the edge of a makeshift camp, scrambling to set up instruments. "See if anyone's found a clue. I'll join you afterward."

The ambassador headed out, looking more at home in tall grasses than Colin appeared in his suit jacket. Damian took in the scenery again. Other than two suns hovering in the sky, the area was surprisingly Earthlike. It wasn't unlike the countryside surrounding Minade.

No blobs on Earth, though. He spotted small groups of wobbling creatures—not just green, as Damian was familiar with, but all colors—throughout the surrounding fields. Embassy officials of the Irvin branch rolled between clusters, keeping the natives from nearing the shimmering orb.

"I wish they wouldn't do that. They might erase the sphere's beaten path," Colin said. He motioned to Damian. "Follow me."

"Slow down a bit." On top of the dizziness, Damian wheezed as he caught up with Colin.

Colin turned back, nodding as he eyed his friend. "Our bodies are truly physical here, susceptible to natural forces like gravity."

"No wonder I feel heavier."

"Hey, Colin!" a voice called out. Damian took a deep breath, then straightened in time to see a young woman running up to them. Her face was strained and covered in dirt, a testament to how the last hour had gone for her. The slightest hint of humor still glimmered in her eye, the kind only someone like Colin could bring out. "About time the DSI showed up."

"Sorry, Grace. We were in the middle of breakfast with Head Ambassador Knutt. I was making a golf joke when we got the news. Ruined my punch line."

"Affairs of state." Grace managed a chuckle.

"Have you found anything?"

"We've photographed and recorded everything in the immediate vicinity of the shrinking. I'd like to say we've gathered evidence, but there's not much. Someone from the Department of Health found a broken path." Grace pointed toward a distant field, then let out a heavy sigh. "He didn't block it off, though, and I'm sure others have trampled any clues out of existence. I'm sorry, Colin."

"Not your fault. We'll follow up. How's the reversal going?"

"Should have the area back to normal within the hour." She shook her head, looking exhausted. Damian could tell the incident weighed on her mind as much as the planet pulled on his body. "The fabric of reality here will be bruised, just like in the other occurrences. It'll take time to heal."

"Kind of like a nuclear bomb," Colin said, turning to Damian. "Even when the visible signs of the catastrophe disappear, it can be years before the land can sustain life again."

Looking back at Grace, he asked, "Was anyone around to witness the event?"

The woman turned back to their camp, using a hand to keep the suns overhead out of her eyes. "Over on the right. There's a booth set up for translators. You can see a group of blobs."

"I'd like to talk to them."

"You can try," Grace said. "You know how disoriented others have been after an event."

"Have to start somewhere, right? Thanks for your help." As Grace hustled away, Colin pointed Damian toward the field. "You should see if you can pick up on the trail like Wendell asked. Likely a fool's errand, if it even existed."

A few minutes later, Damian was clomping through a field of tall grass bordered by some woods. With his back to the anomaly, everything seemed tranquil. The melodies of songbirds drifted down from leafy branches. Water from a nearby creek burbled against rocks. A foxlike creature scurried further into the thick grass after catching wind of his presence.

Life on this planet isn't so different from that on Earth. The birds overhead cut the air with four wings instead of two, and the fox Damian frightened flicked multiple tails. If he scrutinized the vegetation, he was certain it'd reveal astonishing growth patterns and textures. Still, a gentle breeze stirred the grass stalks, which swayed to a soothing cadence. It was a pristine, idyllic scene.

Perfect, he thought.

Yet, despite the serenity of the surroundings, Damian still sensed the discordant presence of the shrinking like a lingering ache. It was an invasive force, a malignant tumor devouring what was once an immaculate, faultless design.

You're just thinking of your mother. I can't believe it was only this morning that Gus and Rebecca were knocking on my door.

The emotions of that moment, of reading the letter they'd handed him, manifested as weight in his chest. Whatever forces the Afterlife used to temper negative emotions didn't apply in a universe populated by blobs. Misery seeped through the invisible barrier of his suit. He felt as emotionally spent as Grace had appeared.

Damian paused mid-stride, bending over with hands on his knees. He narrowed his eyes, telling himself he was listening to the hushed whispers of the grasses and not being overtaken by exhaustion. With a deep breath, he straightened up and forged on, angling his trajectory toward the trees. Their leaves provided cover from the suns and might provide cover for the sphere.

Despite the reminder that he should've exercised more in life, Damian enjoyed the walk. The fields and forest reminded him of traipsing through the woods behind his house as a child. Even though he detested spiders, snakes, and mosquitoes, he'd spend hours every weekend exploring the forest, walking deer paths, and building makeshift forts. Until Colin befriended him, Damian lost himself in nature.

The woods—calling them a forest would've been generous, as there were only a few acres separating the edge of town from farmland—taught him several early life lessons no school could. He'd once watched a deer carcass decay over a summer, the hide melting over skeletal remains. As he'd visited the spot over the next couple of years, the bones scattered into an unrecognizable pile.

Once, when he was ten years old, Damian had stepped into a clearing, where a red fox sat in the middle of the trampled grass. He froze, not wanting to scare away one of his favorite animals. The creature, unaware it was being watched, licked its butt. After a few moments, Damian decided he didn't want to remember this beloved creature giving its private areas extra attention—*still can't forget it*—so he rustled the grass under his foot. The fox had glanced up and, taking notice of his presence, darted away in embarrassment.

Damian chuckled as he walked through the trees. He'd forgotten how much he loved being out in nature. It could be so peaceful. Spiritual. *Mostly, it got me away from my mother.*

A few yards into the woods, the ground declined sharply. Lost in the past, Damian almost didn't notice. When his right foot nearly gave out from under him, he steadied himself against a tree. Then he froze.

At the bottom of the hill, some twenty feet away, a softball-sized stony sphere, covered in silvery markings, spun slowly. Like the fox from Damian's past, the object didn't appear to notice him. Other than rotating, disturbing a bed of dried leaves, it made no attempt to escape.

Damian remained still, not making the slightest noise. Like coming across the biggest, hairiest spider, he feared movement or sound would scare the sphere into a hidden or inaccessible haven. To look away was even worse. It provided the enemy with the easiest avenue of escape.

Long seconds passed by. Damian couldn't decide on a course of action. Unlike the fox, he wanted to catch his find.

Taking a slow, deep breath, Damian stepped forward. He put his full weight down on his right foot, careful not to snap a twig or crush dried leaves. He took another step. The sphere kept whirling around in place.

Another step. It kept rotating.

The gentle breeze that'd been rocking the tall grasses picked up. It wasn't strong enough to knock Damian off balance, but it swept through the trees like a predator chasing down a meal. His body, in the middle of another move forward, tensed at the disturbance and adjusted for balance. His foot came down two inches from where he'd intended, scraping the side of a stone.

The sphere stopped spinning.

As quickly as it had arrived, the wind stilled. The forest was deathly quiet. Still ten feet from his foe, Damian dared not breathe—which the suit *barely* made unnecessary. His eyes darted around, seeking a method of trapping the sphere.

A net! He spent the next several seconds attempting to conjure a simple net. Then he remembered he was no longer in the Afterlife.

As if sensing Damian's desperate frustration, the sphere started spinning again. This time, it edged in the opposite direction.

Screw it. He dashed forward, yelling at the top of his lungs, hoping others would hear and come help.

The sphere accelerated to a speed Damian had no chance of competing with in this or any other universe. It rolled deeper into the woods, toward another hill steeped in shadows.

"No!" Damian yelled out, ignoring his labored breathing as he crashed through the underbrush. He imagined his mother. Not as she might be now, writhing in Hell, but as she was during his childhood, wielding a frying pan in the kitchen. "Don't you roll away when I'm talking to you!"

Just before the sphere slipped over the next hill and out of sight, Colin leaped out from behind a tree. He'd removed his jacket, holding it in his hands like the net Damian couldn't conjure.

"Whoa!" Colin jumped, arms outstretched, and landed so forcefully he rolled over several times before coming to rest against another tree. He thrashed around and, for a moment, Damian thought the tumble had injured him. Then he realized Colin had caught the sphere and was struggling to control it.

Damian glanced back, seeing several officials running or rolling into the woods. "Over here!" He jumped and waved his hands. "Bring a container!"

While the struggle between Colin and the relic was fierce, Damian also found it comical. Colin stumbled to his feet, arms wrapped around his chest. The sphere twisted around in the jacket so that the fabric almost ripped from his hands.

"They're coming." Damian rushed over. He kept his own hands at the ready should one of the garment's seams rip and their enemy slip out. "Sit back down if you have to. Just don't let that thing go."

"Of course," Colin grunted. "Not my first sphere."

"Great catch, by the way. Took me by surprise."

Damian held his breath for the next minute as Colin continued grappling with the object. The other officials surrounded them, armed with nets, and closed in. Wendell appeared, pushing his way through to their side, carrying a heavy box made of thick metal.

"In here," the ambassador ordered, opening the box's hinged lid and shoving it under Colin's tiring arms.

With a heavy thunk, the sphere dropped into the container. Wendell slammed the lid shut. He pulled a padlock from his pocket, locking the box tight. Several harsh clunks sounded from within as the relic spun around, testing its new environment. Suddenly, it fell silent.

Colin leaned against a tree for several moments, catching his breath. Then he threw the shredded remains of his jacket to the ground and slammed his hand against the rough bark. "Shit!"

"What?" Damian asked, alarmed by the outburst. "What's wrong?"

Colin turned and stalked back toward the clearing, brushing past a couple of their startled coworkers.

"Colin!" Wendell's voice boomed through the woods.

"That isn't it." Colin stopped at the edge of the forest line, shoulders slumping as his head hung low. The light from the field framed his silhouette. It appeared diminished.

"What isn't it?" Damian asked.

Colin turned around, pointing to the metal box in Wendell's hands. "That's not the Sphere of Doom."

"How can you tell? You haven't had time to examine it properly."

"But I've had plenty of time to study the other decoy spheres," Colin said, walking back over to them. "The markings on all of them are similar and, if lore is to be believed, completely different from the actual sphere."

"And?" Damian pressed when Colin fell silent.

"I noted symbols on this one similar to those on the other decoys. Ones that shouldn't appear on the true sphere." Colin paused for a moment, eyes shifting back and forth. "I think we were close, though. Whoever is controlling the sphere is using this decoy to mislead us. It's possible they're close by, watching us."

The group fell silent. Everyone scanned the area, searching for any onlookers amid the trees. No strangers stood among them.

"Should we keep looking?" Damian eyed the others with suspicion.

The forest shadows suddenly grew longer, darker. Damian thought his suit was failing, and he was succumbing to Irvin's atmosphere. Then a bright pinkish light flashed from somewhere in the distance. Momentarily blinded, everyone covered their eyes, turning away from the source. Several seconds later, in his peripheral vision, Damian saw braver souls peek back as the light faded.

"It's the shrinking," someone declared. "Its effects have been reversed."

"Run!" Colin yelled, breaking into a sprint. As the remnants of the pink luminescence dissipated, a brighter blink of white light flashed. Everything went quiet.

The lengthy shadows quaked along the leaf-laden earth as Colin tackled Damian, throwing him to the ground. Trees shook, branches cracking off and falling to the ground. Many trees fell over, swept away in a shockwave, the aftermath of the unshrinking.

"You okay?" Colin asked moments later. He scrambled to his feet, his demeanor no longer that of a sulking boy.

"I think so." Damian let Colin pull him up. He looked around, this time out of concern rather than suspicion. Everyone looked a little dazed, but otherwise okay. *A miracle, with all the heavy branches now strewn across the forest floor. And we still got the decoy sphere locked away.*

"I'm going to check it out," Colin called over his shoulder, running out into the clearing. "Make sure no one was hurt!"

"What about the actual Sphere of Doom?" Damian turned to Wendell. The ambassador's long black hair, which usually flowed neatly down his back, was now askew and covered in twigs and broken leaves. "Should we keep looking for it?"

Wendell shook his head, handing the box over to Damian. “I’ll keep looking. If the decoy was a distraction, there still might be another path close by. I want you to take this back to our office. Store it with the others. They’re in the cabinet next to Colin’s desk. Then focus on meeting with Athan.”

Damian nodded, hefting the heavy container in his hands. When he looked back up, Wendell had already wandered off, examining the ground for evidence of another path.

Good luck after that shockwave.

Damian walked out into the clearing. With the shrinking gone, the area once again looked more or less normal. The sky was clear, and the suns shined bright. Birds chirped in trees full of leaves, which Damian considered quite a feat after the commotion. Even the crowd gathered around base camp looked like picnickers.

Still, Damian felt it. The underlying damage to the fabric of reality. A hidden pain that would take time to heal. If that time was available.

What will become of this place if the evil soul carries out their plan to fruition? Damian wondered. *What happens if the sphere strikes for the sixth and final time? Will the Celestial City itself shrink, disappearing everyone within? With no governing body at the center of the multiverse, will everything fall into chaos? The possibilities are endless.*

That they didn’t know what would happen—other than something awful—scared him in particular.

Metal box firmly in hand, Damian peregrinated to another plane of existence. Back to the Embassy.

CHAPTER SEVENTEEN

DAMIAN PEERED INTO THE armored cabinet in the DSI office. The reinforced locker, as heavy as his Camaro, appeared sufficient to contain the mischievous behavior of the Sphere of Doom. Three decoy stone orbs sat dormant on the shelves. The fourth remained in the thick metal box, which he'd placed at the bottom of the cabinet.

We've got all the decoys. That's something worth celebrating. Damian counted and recounted the contents within. The spheres produced an anxiety within him that persisted until he closed the locker doors, ensuring they could no longer cause chaos and confusion.

The true cause of Damian's apprehension, the actual sphere, was still at large. If Colin's working theory was correct, it had only to attack once more to reveal its endgame.

Damian walked over to his desk and sat down, rubbing his arms. The holographic display sprang to life, awaiting his command. He was unsure of how to proceed. *How does one interrogate a Guardian?*

On a whim, he said aloud, "Can you show me material I wrote in the past? When I was alive?"

The words sounded hollow in the empty office, but the screen jumped into action. It listed hundreds of documents scrolling by at a fast pace. He recognized private emails to friends, some code he'd written for work, and simple assignments from elementary school.

"Please filter for high-school writing assignments. Probably during my junior or senior year."

The floating lights above his desk twinkled again, this time showing only a few dozen files. He scanned through the names, the title *Fall of a King* sparking a memory. He asked the computer to open the document, then spent a few minutes skimming the short story.

Minade High School's history curriculum focused on North America, glossing over its relations with the rest of the world. After receiving criticism from alumni, the district revised coverage of World War II. Rather than relying on a single class to convey the horrors of war, all subjects took part in the program. Students read books from the period, learned of scientific advances—including the gruesome methods of experimentation used—and even integrated history into mathematical equations.

Some of it was a stretch, he remembered.

English teachers tasked their students with drafting short stories based on the war. It was a brave assignment, asking students to summarize all the lessons they'd learned over the course of the program in a creative narrative. Damian didn't envy those who had to read and grade the end results.

Throughout the program, Damian grew captivated by Hanns Scharff, a German interrogator. Known as the Master Interrogator by his peers, he opposed the physical abuse of prisoners for information. Instead, he excelled at lulling his subjects into a false sense of security. He acted as a friend, soothing prisoners' fears and gaining their trust. It worked so well that his subjects often accidentally gave up information without being directly asked for it.

For his short story, Damian created a narrative about a wealthy nation led by an even wealthier king. A character named Ludwig Luxe, a stand-in for Scharff, infiltrated the king's court. Over the course of two years, Luxe became the royal's closest friend and most loyal adviser. He gleaned enough intelligence for his true masters, a rival nation, to wage war with minimal losses. Luxe disappeared from the king's court shortly before conflict broke out, none the wiser.

Once the kingdom was subdued, another interrogator named Harper Harrison—*where did I come up with these names?*—was tasked with uncovering its riches. Harrison's methods were more direct and potentially lethal, extracting his victims' fluids with needles and tubes, then forcing the targets to drink them. The beloved king died after a long period of torture, taking his secrets to the grave.

In the end, the enemy won the war, but forever lost the kingdom's vast treasury.

Damian stared at the text on the screen, wondering what point he'd been trying to make—what exactly he'd learned from the World War II curriculum. *That war is ridiculous? That people's lives are worth more than treasure? Even if some people are truly awful?*

Of course, the best interrogators Damian knew were the Gray Ones. Those swirling clouds of terror were the true experts, capable of inflicting horror and extracting answers simply by being in the same room as their subjects. The very thought of them sent shivers down his spine.

Damian lacked the skills possessed by the interrogators, real or fictional. He wasn't scary or combative, shying away from most conflict. He possessed neither the patience nor the time to wait weeks to gain Athan's trust, and the Guardian's body didn't look capable of relinquishing any fluids.

All I have is myself. He leaned back in his chair. *If Wendell is right, Athan has already taken a liking to me. Maybe that's enough.*

With a quick gesture, Damian dismissed the holographic screen. Then he stared at Kasee's corner of the room, imagining a thick cloud of cigar smoke hovering above her desk. *I'm dedicated to finding the truth—just like her. That's something the two of us have in common, though. It's something we all have a personal stake in.*

Standing up, he left the office to discover the whereabouts of his subject.

"Athan usually spends this hour of the day meditating in the Castile's gardens." Damian didn't know either of the Guardians on duty at the Embassy's entrance. The one who spoke wore mustard yellow robes and a bronze crown. They glanced into the sky as if a hidden sun revealed the time.

"The Castile?"

"The dwelling place of the Guardians." They turned their gaze toward the center of the Celestial City. To the left of the palace was the smaller castle Damian had previously noticed. Its high, reclusive walls matched those of its neighbor, but it lacked the aesthetic of every other building. In another environment, its unadorned stone facade may not have caught the eyes of passersby. In the city, though, it stood out like a sore thumb.

"We have occupied the Castile since our creation, back when most of the Celestial City was made of plain stone," the Guardian continued, as if reading Damian's mind.

"Loath to make creative changes?"

The other Guardian, dressed in drab gray tones, turned to him. "Humans have failed to appreciate the artistic ventures of Guardians. That said, we do not allow our home to be renovated or updated. It reminds us of who we are. Why we were created."

Damian nodded, choosing not to draw out additional scathing comments, no matter how subtle.

"Athan's room is on the seventh floor of the tower. Should they not be in the gardens, you would likely find them there."

With a nod of thanks, Damian hurried down the steps and out onto the lawn. The Castile was only a few blocks away. Under normal circumstances, he would've enjoyed a leisurely stroll through the streets of the city, popping into a new restaurant or confectionary along the way. After witnessing the shrinking on Irvin, though, he felt that time was of the essence.

The Romanesque architecture of the Guardian's home struck Damian when he peregrinated to its entrance. He'd expected the ramparts to run uninterrupted, devoid of embellishment. Instead, the doors were nestled into a recess and topped by a semicircular stone arch. No windows populated the wall, though rounded towers broke it up, themselves linked by decorative arcades.

I'm surprised there's no drawbridge.

Behind the rampart, Damian saw the rooflines of shorter buildings and, toward the back, the massive tower the Guardian had spoken of. Even with the Celestial Palace next door, the keep loomed over the city. It wanted its presence felt by the residents. Windows dotted the tower, tall but narrow. He imagined a Guardian behind every one of them, witnessing all that transpired between the Castile and the Celestial Wall.

Was Bennett born in the shadow of such a fortress? Damian thought the structure would've fit nicely into Crichton's *Timeline.*

"May I help you?" a Guardian asked when Damian pulled open one of the heavy wooden doors and stepped inside. The unadorned vestibule was small, lit only by a circular window in the ceiling. Feeling cramped, he wondered how the inhabitants managed.

"I'm looking for Athan. I was told they'd be here—likely in the gardens."

The Guardian pointed to a narrow hall on the right. "The second door on the left exits onto a cloister overlooking the gardens. I hope you find what you are looking for, and that you take the time to appreciate your surroundings."

Yes, these are some well-cut stone blocks, Damian thought as he entered the dim hall. He imagined the gardens to be akin to those his childhood neighbors tended in their backyards. Corn, beans, and the like. Perhaps a pumpkin patch like Colin's. The Guardians were utilitarian, and he expected their endeavors to follow suit.

Stepping out onto the cloister, a parade of colors and scents dazzled Damian's senses. The walkway surrounded a square garden, the corners of which were dominated by giant topiaries. Several routes provided serene views, each lined with bushes both wild and sculpted. Ornamental trees bloomed, vibrant petals drifting lazily into a creek that wove a path among enormous trunks.

At the garden's heart stood a towering tree, dwarfing the surrounding flora. The soaring height of the specimen reminded Damian of California redwoods—*not that I've ever been to California.* He found it strange that the enormous tree had escaped his attention from outside. Or at least, the white light radiating from its leaves.

A squirrel scrambled down one of the stone pillars supporting the cloister's canopy. It leaped over Damian's shoulder and out into the garden, eventually climbing a tree with pink fronds.

"I often question the worth of such mindless creatures."

Athan's voice snapped Damian's attention back to why he was there. Just beyond the squirrel's new haven, the Guardian sat on a bench, hands clasped on their lap.

"They help stabilize complex environments, but why those complexities exist and are so prevalent is beyond my comprehension. It is frivolous, especially since the Creator can keep them simple. They possess no qualities a Guardian lacks."

"Except, perhaps, frivolousness." Damian traversed a small bridge over the creek. Like the lake behind his house, the water was crystal clear, and several varieties of fish swam with the current.

Athan raised an eyebrow as Damian approached. "Humans possess and often employ frivolity. You enjoy many traits, though, that raise you above squirrels. They make you superior to most Guardians."

The bench Athan sat on was too tall for Damian to even consider climbing upon—*makes me look like a child*—so he leaned against it instead. "Our emotions?"

The Guardian peered at the central tree with glowing leaves. "It was not long ago that humans, theorizing their emotions evolved through natural selection, considered them unnecessary. My kind appreciated this school of thought—yes, some of us do think highly of ourselves."

"I took an intro to psychology class in college, so it's been a while, but I believe experts now think our emotions are an essential element of our intelligence." Damian redirected a floating pink petal away from his face. "Emotional sensations are so entwined in the human experience, it's impossible to separate them."

"They are complex. I am amazed your race has survived them."

"Not all of us do." Damian closed his eyes, sensing the soft white light of the central tree against his skin. He was fortunate enough not to know anyone who'd taken their own life, but he'd suffered enough in his brief life to recognize the need.

"Guardians considered emotions to be the antithesis of reason. The Creator explained the sensations were actually the next logical step—that fear, anger, and happiness were systematic responses to observed facts." Athan's voice lowered to a whisper. "We embody all things systematic and factual, but we refused to believe ourselves inferior to the human project."

"Inferior?" Damian scoffed. He recalled the image of Athan and Bai unsheathing their swords in the Dungeon of Darkness, appearing frighteningly majestic bathed in light. "Your kind can change—can evolve—just like mine."

"Certainly." Athan nodded their head, light glinting off their crown. "Though it was Lucifer who made us aware of how much we could change. And how quickly."

"How so?" Damian knew he risked a long and detailed narrative with such an open-ended question.

"Lucifer sought to be greater than they were, an evolutionary step in itself. Witnessing the progression, a hundred Guardians swore allegiance to them in return for emotional instruction."

"How does one teach emotions?"

Athan spread their long arms open. With the robes hanging loose, they looked like a stern wizard. He thought the Guardian was casting some magic or summoning the glittering lights for a demonstration, then realized they were indicating the surrounding garden.

"It took thousands of years to create this garden. So much time and patience. So much effort, and we Guardians are protective of it." Athan lowered their arms and looked down at Damian. "As I understand it, human puberty can *feel* like an eternity. For the Guardians under Lucifer's tutelage, it took centuries to understand and employ emotions. Much like the plants you see here, it took many cycles of trial and error before they reached their goals."

Lucifer had stressed what the Guardians already knew, and what Damian had alluded to earlier: every human sense and perception—every thought—carried an emotional connotation. Experienced as positive or negative, they were rarely neutral.

"They were to analyze each of their thoughts, actions, and words—to find the positive and negative factors and ask themselves why they were so. Over time, they built upon those factors, leaning into them. Once they tasted the delicious fruits of their labor, they desired more."

An eloquent metaphor. Damian peeked up to see if their face portrayed an equal measure of passion. It did not. "But emotions can be manipulated. We watch scary movies for a fright. Companies vie for consumer loyalty. Politicians sway opinions for power grabs."

Athan nodded. "The Guardians did not realize Lucifer was shaping them with purpose. At the pinnacle of their strength, Lucifer made a bid for total domination."

Damian's imagination interlaced Athan's accounts of the fateful day Lucifer dropped their pretense with what he'd seen in the shadows of the dungeon. Flanked by a hundred outraged compatriots, they marched through the streets and stormed the Celestial Palace. Frightened shopkeepers locked their stores, cautiously peeking through shuttered windows.

No one stood watch at the palace entrance, and Lucifer wasted no time racing to the throne room on the uppermost level, intending to start their reign immediately. In their greed and lust, they all failed to understand they couldn't hold power by emotion alone. They were so wrapped up in their resentment that they hadn't realized they'd lost their greatest asset.

"I was in the throne room when the battle began." Athan's voice remained the same, but Damian *felt* more from their words. "Lucifer stood tall and proud, and gave a brief speech about how weak the Creator was and how the Guardians' time of oppression was at an end. Then Lucifer drew their sword, intending to unleash a deadly burst of Light."

The Bringer of Light failed to produce so much as a soft glow. The power of the betrayers, which made them superior to other creations, was gone.

"The look of horror on Lucifer's face made it clear they were experiencing a new emotion. A most unpleasant one." For a moment, Athan sounded smug.

"The Fallen were cast away from the city into a new plane of existence, one created specifically for them and their particular transgressions. There, they suffer all the emotions they have ever desired."

"What side are you on?" Damian asked.

Athan's head cocked to the side. "Pardon?"

"There's a truth so simple it took no effort to hide." Damian stepped away from the bench and faced Athan. "One hundred and fifty Guardians survived the Forti assault. One of them recruited a hundred others for a rebellion. Once defeated, the Creator banished them to Hell. That should leave forty-nine behind, but there are fifty. Or, were fifty until Bai was murdered."

Athan nodded, agreeing with Damian's arithmetic. Then they abruptly stood and strode away from the bench, heading toward the cloister connected to the lofty tower.

"One of Lucifer's ranks remained behind." Flustered, Damian followed behind Athan, struggling to keep up with the other's long stride. *Can't let them get away without asking the easiest question.* "Are you that one Guardian?"

The Guardian opened a door at the tower's base, paused, then stared down at Damian. Their stony face never flinched. "Yes, I am."

Damian stepped back, despite Athan's inward gesture. Stunned by their frank disclosure, new questions exploded in his mind. *What does Athan know about the death of Bai? Are they familiar with the evil soul? Do they know where the Sphere of Doom is?* Overwhelmed, he could only whisper one word. "How?"

"Perhaps I, this *one Guardian*, am not exactly what you think." Athan continued to point inside the tower. "It is best not to speak of this in the open."

Damian considered his options, wary that no one was around to witness him following Athan. *Do I really distrust them, though? Wendell still has faith that they're good, even if they're hiding something.*

After a few seconds of hesitation, Damian went in. The door closed behind him with a solid thud that echoed through a stone corridor. Athan took the lead, ascending several flights of stairs. Each landing they passed was identical to the last, mirroring the vestibule—cramped, dim, and unadorned.

On the seventh floor, they proceeded down a hallway. Athan pulled an iron key from within their robes and unlocked an unmarked, unassuming door. Damian braced himself for more austerity—*a monk's cell with a simple cot and wooden chair*—but stepped into a spacious chamber that surprised him with its vibrant colors. Elaborate rugs in deep blues and crimson covered the floor. Plush cushioned chairs, tables of polished wood, and bookshelves crammed with leather-bound volumes filled the space. Art hung on the walls. Some were abstract, while others depicted landscapes he'd never seen.

Like the gardens outside, the room carried the unmistakable mark of centuries of careful curation, each piece selected to create perfect harmony with the others.

"I should start at the beginning." Athan moved toward a small stove in the corner, where a kettle was already whistling. They grabbed ingredients from a shelf above, sprinkled them into a delicate teacup, and poured steaming water over them. "The Bringer of Light was not always one to be feared. They were a prominent leader, and the worlds they oversaw prospered. Many worshiped Lucifer as a god even before that was a desire. They were a source of inspiration, even to those not easily inspired."

Athan offered Damian the drink, but he politely declined. With a shrug, the Guardian sat in one of the plush chairs. Damian hopped up onto another on the opposite side of a coffee table.

"When Lucifer was first recruiting, there was no reason to suspect foul intentions. They offered knowledge and wisdom in return for secrecy. The jealousy and hatred now associated with the Fallen developed over a long period. By the time they rallied behind Lucifer's true cause, their minds had been warped."

Like boiling a frog in water. "And you were one of those recruited?"

"I was enthralled by the promise of knowledge. Indeed, I experienced many happy decades." The words seemed odd coming out of Athan's mouth. Their lips twitched, and they lifted the teacup as though to hide it. "Eventually, like the others, I grew depressed at my apparent shortcomings. However, while they grew angry at being held back by their Creator, my depression only grew. I had lost my purpose."

"Your purpose?" Damian asked. "To protect the Celestial City?"

"Yes. We Guardians were created for that single purpose, and that task brings meaning to our existence."

"What did you do?"

"I went to the Creator for counsel."

"You *spoke* with the Creator about Lucifer's plans?" Damian got up and went to the room's single window. It overlooked the garden, but the Celestial Palace was also in plain view, a constant reminder of who was in charge.

Athan shook their head, saying they'd initially held to their promise of secrecy. They met with the Creator several times, though, walking away from each occasion feeling more like themself. The depression had eventually subsided to the point that Athan could analyze the entire situation objectively. It was then they realized the deceitful nature of Lucifer's actions.

"Of course, I immediately revealed everything." The Guardian's eyes glazed over, recalling the event. "I was ashamed of what I had become and was racked with guilt for what could yet happen. I fell to my knees before the Creator, begging for forgiveness."

Athan fell silent. Damian pressed them to continue. "And?"

"I was forgiven." They set the teacup down on the coffee table. "The Creator already knew everything."

"What?"

"Little escapes the attention of the Creator. Lucifer's intentions were known from the beginning, and plans were already in place to counter them. I was given a task. It was the hardest thing I have ever done, and it affects me to this day."

"What was it?" Damian returned to his chair opposite the Guardian.

"To continue following Lucifer as though nothing had changed. My mission was to learn and report on the plan of assault. It was an arduous task, lasting over a hundred years. Not only did I have to...pretend...to support the enemy, but I continued to learn and master each emotion thrust upon their followers. I suffered much during this time, but I did not fall back into depression. I had regained my purpose."

In the end, Lucifer announced the insurrection mere hours before it took place. Athan had barely enough time to alert the palace before the opposition marched through its halls. "I was most...gratified...when the betrayers discovered they could no longer wield the Light while I still did."

"It must've been a relief to put an end to the turmoil," Damian said. "I can see how that'd still affect you."

Athan shook their head. "The Creator forgave me for my part in the conspiracy, and I have forgiven myself. The raw emotions Lucifer taught us still boil within me, though. Even after all this time, I am not accustomed to them."

Damian blinked. He never would've guessed such depth dwelled behind the rigid exterior of the Guardian. "Can you be cured of them?"

"Certainly. The Creator offered such a reward once the Fallen were tucked away in their new home. I have thus far refused."

"But that would ease your suffering and allow you to focus on your purpose!"

Athan stood and checked the door, peeking out into the hallway. "It is for my purpose that I stay how I am. Your numbers do not tell the complete story."

"My numbers?"

"The one hundred that Lucifer recruited." Athan shut the door and turned back. "The number of *known* recruits is a hundred, but there could still be others. Bai's murder is proof of this. Keeping these emotions may help me discover the assassin."

Damian straightened up, cursing himself for taking information at face value, for not digging deeper. He couldn't help but recall a scene from *Jurassic Park*. One character showed how the park's computer system always reported 238 found animals because that was the expected number. When the administrator asked for three hundred, everyone was shocked when the number climbed to 292.

"None of this gets me any closer to figuring out who killed Bai or who's controlling the sphere," he said. "I don't suppose you can surprise me with those facts?"

"Unfortunately, I cannot." Athan shook their head. "But I will reveal what knowledge I do possess concerning those subjects."

CHAPTER EIGHTEEN

DAMIAN SLID INTO A worn wooden chair at Messie Bessie's. The scent of the day's tea and quiche still lingered in the air. Warm low light, provided by sconces on the walls, cast flickering shadows of the thick beams overhead. The other members of the Department of Satanic Investigations already sat around the circular table, their faces dark with concern.

"All right, spill it." Colin tapped the tabletop with his forefinger. Neither he nor the ambassador had changed clothes since returning from Irvin. It was odd to see dirt smears on his friend's shirt and twigs poking out of Wendell's long hair. "What did you learn from Athan?"

"You're sure we can talk here?" Damian glanced around the room, half expecting a Guardian to step out of the shadows.

Wendell jutted his chin toward the front windows. Someone had drawn shades over them, creating the illusion of night. "I called in a favor with the owner. It's after hours, and we have the place to ourselves."

Damian took a deep breath, looking over at Kasee. "It's worse than we thought. You uncovered the mathematical discrepancy, but it turns out the number of *known* Guardians Lucifer recruited is a hundred."

"You mean there could be more?" Kasee's eyes widened. If she'd been smoking her cigar, it would've fallen out of her mouth. Thankfully, it wasn't present to ruin the tearoom's aroma.

"A lot more." Damian told the team how Lucifer had seduced Athan and others with promises, and how their friend—*if you can call a Guardian a friend*—eventually became a double agent and helped the Creator bring a quick end to the coup. "Athan believes Bai's murder proves it. Assuming the Forti haven't discovered another way into the city, then only a Guardian can kill another Guardian."

Wendell stared up at the shadows dancing across the ceiling, thick eyebrows furrowed. "Who can we trust if not the beings created to protect the Celestial City?"

"And how do we ferret out the corrupt?" Colin asked. "Would the Gray Ones work on them?"

"In theory, it should be easy," Damian said. "A Guardian only needs to show they can still wield Light to prove their allegiance to the Creator. It's a personal connection, though. Not something anyone can just ask of them."

"Given the circumstances, I'd think they'd understand," Colin said.

"And if you encountered one that failed the test?" Wendell asked. "The lack of a connection doesn't make them any less deadly. We don't want to provoke an attack—or a spontaneous coup."

Damian nodded. "Athan thinks they've got a plan on how to uncover the enemy. Was going to run the idea by Mai before proceeding. They hope to get back to me tomorrow."

"Another day of waiting." Colin started tapping on the table again, earning a glare from Kasee. "You're sure we can trust them? What about the things we heard them say in the dungeon?"

"I asked Athan about Gehenna, and the need for additional souls for quarantine." Damian paused. He trusted Athan, but he wasn't sure how to relay the Guardian's answers without making them sound complicit. "Those subjects are top secret. They're getting the Creator's permission to discuss them with me. Again, hopefully by tomorrow."

"Then let's hope tomorrow is a quiet day otherwise." Colin seemed to notice his tapping and placed his hands in his lap. "You put the decoy sphere in our cabinet?"

"Of course," Damian affirmed. "What about the true Sphere of Doom?"

Wendell shook his head. "I found no more tracks on Irvin. It's gone quiet again. Could be anywhere. Did Athan have anything to say about the sphere?"

"They recall its creation, as well as the immense power poured into it. They're not surprised by the chaos it's caused, though questions the hexagram pattern."

Colin's eyes narrowed. "Except it *is* creating a six-pointed star."

"Right," Damian agreed. "But Athan doubts the pattern itself will invoke anything."

"Fear." Wendell leaned forward and clasped his hands in front of him. "My people don't communicate with snakes. It's considered a bad omen to have contact with them. Even the representation of one provokes fear. The hexagram is similar. It may not be an integral part of a corrupted Guardian's machinations, but they'd know the superstitions others associate with it. Don't discount fear."

"Fear, or simply a distraction," Kasee pointed out.

Damian turned to Colin, who kept looking around for something to fidget with. "What about the shrinking? Did you find out anything else?"

"Other than frayed nerves, no one was hurt by the reversal and its shockwave," Colin said. "Other than the one household, the area was otherwise uninhabited. Thankfully, no blobs were home during the attack. No one is missing."

All eyes turned to Kasee, who shifted uncomfortably in her seat.

"I spent most of the day at the Celestial Library."

Colin's eyebrows shot up, and a grin spread across his face. "The library? I didn't know you could read."

"Not the time, Colin," Wendell said as Kasee gripped the table, poised to leap at her coworker. "Were you able to uncover anything useful?"

Kasee's youthful face—even the scowl—fell. "Not really. My informants insist there's a connection between the fall of the Embassy back in 2008 and the sphere's endgame, so I tried to find evidence in the history books. Turns out anything that might help in our investigations, the facts behind all the lore we know, is classified. For the Creator's eyes only."

"What about Mrs. Ulrich?" Damian squirmed at the interconnectedness of events. *It can't be a coincidence that the Gray Ones interview everyone under duress during the Embassy's collapse.* "She's mentally tied to the *Book of History*, and might tell us more."

"I spoke with the old frog. She wanted to help, but like Athan, she'd need the Creator's permission to talk." Kasee shrugged, slumping back in her chair. "It's beyond all of our pay grades."

The group fell silent, the burden of their limited knowledge settling over them. Damian glanced around the tearoom. Even though nothing was being served, even with hunger nonexistent, his stomach growled with desire. He'd only been to the restaurant once before, yet the place evoked a sense of homeliness and comfort. He hoped it would never change.

It struck Damian how ludicrous it was that the actions of a small group of individuals—of one in particular—could radically alter the landscape of reality. *If the evil soul or Guardians complete their mission, if the Sphere of Doom strikes its ultimate target, if Satan makes their way back into the Celestial City and, against all odds, deposes the Creator... What would happen?* He doubted the shakeup in power would be subtle. With eons of bottled hatred and an agenda incompatible with what the Creator had built, the fate of thousands of planes of existence lay in the balance.

Damian feared the worst for all of them, especially those who refused to accept Satan's supremacy. *I suspect Messie Bessie's decrepit hostess would fight back.* Stomach grumbling again, he hoped he'd have the opportunities to sample every quiche and tea on the menu.

"Everyone should take a few hours to go home. Rest up and enjoy your families." Wendell scooted his chair back. "I know we don't have a lot of information to move forward with, but we'll reexamine everything with fresh eyes when we return to the office in the morning."

"What about the party?" Colin asked.

The ambassador sighed. "Yes, don't forget about the head ambassador's party tomorrow night. Seems an awful idea to me, and I've said as much to her. She's set on moving forward, however, and we're all expected to be there."

With a huff, Wendell disappeared from view, peregrinating to wherever he lived. Damian stared at the empty seat, having a hard time imagining the man anywhere other than the wickiup. Kasee vanished a moment later, not bothering with any pleasantries.

"Give my regards to Alena." Colin nodded goodbye as he stood up.

Damian gave a half-hearted wave. "Say hello to Anthony."

Alone, Damian gazed around the empty restaurant once more. He wondered if he should check and make sure the front door was locked, then realized how silly that was. If they could peregrinate out, then anyone could peregrinate in.

The level of trust we place in one another here...is it earned?

After inhaling the delicious aromas one last time, Damian went home.

Damian materialized on the front lawn of his home, wanting to take a minute for his frayed nerves to calm before entering. The serene lake and majestic mountains immediately drew his attention. He inhaled deeply as he gazed at the snowcapped peaks, the stress of the long day melting away.

One hell of a long day.

Damian turned to go inside, his eyes sweeping across the property once more, taking in the scenery. When they finally focused on the porch, he froze. Crude, angry letters defaced the front door. His jaw dropped as he read the hateful words spray-painted in garish red: *YOU BELONG IN HELL.*

Damian's stomach lurched as yet another piece of the Afterlife's tranquil facade broke and fell away. He sprinted toward the door, mind racing. *Who would do this? And why? Is this about my investigation? It couldn't be about...Bennett?*

Bathed in the ever-present amber light, he suddenly felt exposed. He glanced around after he reached the porch. The once-comforting view was now a field of potentially hidden threats. *They did this in broad daylight!* Hand trembling, he pressed a fingertip against the graffiti. It came away red. *Still fresh!*

"Alena!" He threw open the door, dreading what he'd find inside. "Where are you?"

"In the kitchen," she called back. Her voice sounded at ease, relaxed.

Damian ran across the foyer and into the kitchen. His wife sat on her usual stool at the island, reading a book and sipping tea. "Are you okay? Where's Bennett?"

"Everything's fine, babe." She put down her book. "Bennett's in the library. Are you okay?"

Damian turned on his heel and leaped back into the foyer, moves he never could've pulled off in life. At the entrance of the library, he froze for the second time in a minute.

"Bennett?"

A child of around seven years sat in a reading chair with a book in his lap. Curly dark brown hair cascaded down over wide, light brown eyes. The boy glanced up and said, "Yes, father?"

Damian stood dumbfounded. The boy, dressed in a plain shirt and jean shorts, possessed a semblance of the toddler he'd watched Alena place in a crib the night before. Much of the baby fat was gone, replaced with knobby knees and elbows. His bare feet stuck straight out, legs not yet long enough to fold over the chair's edge.

For reasons Damian couldn't fathom, tears threatened to spill down his face. "Are...are you okay?"

Bennett nodded vigorously, flashing a smile, then propped the book up on his lap to continue reading. Damian saw it was called *Sphere*.

An excellent selection. Nothing like a romp through the nature of human imagination. Damian nodded back at the child. He stepped away, but bumped into Alena.

"What's gotten into you?" she asked.

He motioned toward the door, still ajar, then took her hand and pulled her out onto the porch.

"Not again!" Alena exclaimed when she saw the spray-painted words.

"This has happened before?"

She folded her arms across her chest, performing a visual sweep of the lawn. The Camaro was in the driveway, its aggressive design having done little to dissuade would-be artists. "Yes, once while you were trapped in the dungeon."

"Why didn't you tell me?"

She shrugged. "I'm not sure. You were already so stressed with work and trying to find the peace you expected here. I didn't want to add to that anxiety. Especially over something you didn't want."

Damian stared at her for several moments, grasping at disparate thoughts. Then he pointed toward the library window, the one Kasee had peered through a week ago. "Having a kid wasn't something I ever expected to happen, but Bennett is our child now. *Our* responsibility. I know you can handle any situation, but this..." He gestured at the door. "This is happening to *us*."

Alena stood silently for a while, folded arms tightening. For a terrible moment, Damian thought he'd pissed her off—*wouldn't be the first time my mouth got me in trouble*—but then her face crumpled, her eyes glassy with tears.

"I was afraid, Damian." She grappled with the effort to get words out. "Afraid I'd never see you again. That you wouldn't make it to the Afterlife. But I built this place for you with the hope we'd make a home out of it."

Damian reached out and grasped her forearms. "But I made it. I'm here, and we're building a true home, continuing on from where we left off."

With tears finally falling, she wrapped her arms around him. "I'm still having a hard time believing we're together again. That it's real, or that there wasn't a mistake. Every time Jim Parsons comes to the door, I fear a letter informing me they're sending us away. And when you went missing..."

"I know. I'm sorry," Damian said, his own tears falling into her hair. "They're not sending us anywhere. They gave me a job at the Embassy, and *they* gave us a child."

With his left arm, he waved at the words written across their door. "Others can say whatever they want, but we deserve to be here."

Alena smiled at that and rested her head against his shoulder. The two stood on the porch for several minutes, locked in their tight embrace. Damian felt her tension melt away and, in doing so, his own dissipated.

Eventually, his gaze drifted back to the library window. Bennett's silhouette was visible, still absorbed in his book. He loosened his hold on Alena and nodded toward the house.

"When did he grow up?"

"Took me by surprise, too. After you left, I climbed the stairs to find a three-year-old crawling out of the crib. He's gone through four pairs of clothing throughout the day. I knew to be prepared for the unexpected, but Bennett's maturing so fast." Alena let out a soft laugh, and Damian heard love in it. She paused too soon, though, her expression growing thoughtful. "This is what others fear. The unknown."

Damian nodded. No one knew what would happen once Bennett and the other children like him aged. He'd known the baby they took in would grow up over the course of a year, but the difference within a day was staggering. It was so far outside the norm, and many fought to protect the status quo.

Normality can be comforting, he thought, realizing with a pang of guilt that he'd been as resistant to change as others. *At least I didn't paint my door.*

"I don't want to be one of those fathers," he said, his voice thick and raspy. "The kind that's always absent, always working, then resentful when the time to help raise a family has passed. I hope I can spend more time at home soon—though *soon* may be too late."

"Don't worry about that. I know you aren't running off to work to escape us." Alena squeezed his arm, then stepped back. "More importantly, Bennett knows that. He's read through parts of our autobiographies—don't worry, I edited the sexy parts out. I think he understands us. Maybe even loves us."

Raising a hand to the front door, she smeared away the painted words. They disappeared with surprising ease, and when she'd gently wiped away each letter, it was like they'd never been there. "Do you want to plan something for your mother?"

"Soon," he said, staring at her hands, clean as ever. Then he opened the door and ushered her back into the foyer. "I'd rather think of something more pleasant. Want to pick out our outfits for the party tomorrow?"

CHAPTER NINETEEN

Damian considered the home Alena had created for them to be grand. The two-story house and picturesque landscape would've been the envy of Minade—except perhaps for the Cherry residence. It would've cost a small fortune in central Illinois, and an ungodly sum in Chicagoland.

Head Ambassador Picardia Knutt's estate was on an entirely separate level of grandiosity. Or at least, Damian expected it to be. As he and Alena, dressed in their finest, stepped out of the Camaro on the border of Knutt's property, an enormous barrier blocked their path. It was reminiscent of the Celestial Wall, though made of twinkling obsidian stone instead of diamond. Two Guardians stood silently by a passage through.

Alena stepped toward the sentries, refusing to be intimidated by their towering forms or the wall. Damian scrambled to catch up. He didn't recognize the Guardian on the left, but he'd encountered the other in the Castile's vestibule. Each wore robes of luxurious red cloth, and the crowns perched atop their heads glittered along with the obsidian behind them. The pair looked extraordinarily uncomfortable.

"We're here for the party." Damian stepped carefully, afraid he'd scuff his dress shoes. "I work with the DSI."

The Guardians peered down at them, and the one on the left asked, "Names?"

"Damian and Alena Hartter."

The Guardians' red robes rippled as they glanced at one another. It was a knowing look, though Damian couldn't decipher its meaning. Clearing his throat, he asked, "Do you know Athan?"

"All Guardians know each other," one said.

"There are so few of us left," the other added.

Damian wished Athan—*or even grumpy Mai*—was on duty. Already feeling out of place next to a glimmering wall, dressed in a suit and bowtie, the familiar gaunt faces would've provided relief. As it was, he didn't know who to trust.

What is Athan up to, anyway? He hadn't heard a monotonous peep from the Guardian since their talk in the garden the previous day. Not even a note to say they were still exploring avenues to uncover the corrupt.

"Strange to hold the party here instead of at the Embassy." Alena stood with her hands clasped behind her back, staring at the top of the wall. "Though I suppose it's lovely."

The Guardian Damian recognized cleared their throat. "The Embassy lacks sufficient space for all employees. Even though this gathering is for the human branch, there are representatives from all universes attending. Some of them are quite large."

Damian nodded, recalling various beings he'd passed by on the streets of the Celestial City. Some towered above even the Guardians while others barely reached his knees. It would've been a cramped gathering in the Embassy's foyer.

Couldn't they have conjured a bigger room? He thought of how his office and the library were larger than their exteriors led him to believe.

"Head Ambassador Knutt designed this estate to welcome all peoples," the other Guardian said. Their voice remained dull, but Damian picked up a tone of condescension.

Designed to show off, more like it. He'd not yet met the head ambassador, but anyone who built a massive wall around their property likely possessed an ego to match.

"You may proceed." Each Guardian grabbed hold of a handle and pulled the entrance open.

Rather than opening onto a party, the gateway revealed a winding stone path disappearing into a dense forest. Gilded lampposts lit the way under the canopy. A fine mist hovered above the ground, offsetting the constant light in the sky and giving the place the feel of twilight.

"Was this necessary?" Damian gestured at the elaborate walkway. "It's not too late to turn around and go home."

"I think it's charming," Alena said, pulling him along the path. Her heels clicked sharply on the stone. "They even have live music."

Damian tilted his head, listening past the crickets rubbing their thighs together among the trees. Stringed instruments sounded off the path. Through the thick foliage, he noticed clusters of three or four musicians sporadically huddled around sheet music. Each group played in sync with one another. Damian didn't recognize the piece, but the display was impressive.

Less extraordinary were the murals lined up alongside the path. Chunks of obsidian, leftover pieces from the wall's construction, lay beside every lamppost. Rather than having images chiseled into them, the head ambassador had somehow manipulated the glittering bits within to twinkle a scene. The murals depicted a beautiful young girl, presumably Picardia, growing up in Victorian England.

Seems that tuberculosis or bronchitis got her, Damian thought, analyzing one image of a bedridden woman.

Upon waking in the Afterlife, Picardia struggled against societal pressures—*which continue to follow us after death*—and worked her way up through the Embassy's management.

Appears self-congratulatory. Damian refused to look at the last several displays.

"It feels weird to leave Bennett at home alone. We've only had him a few days," he said, pulling his wife away from another mural. The child appeared two years older than he had the night before. He'd finished *Sphere* earlier in the day, and they'd left him in the middle of Neal Stephenson's *Seveneves.*

"He's not alone. The neighbor is watching him."

"I haven't met the neighbors." For all Damian knew, they'd painted the graffiti on their door. "Do they take cream in their coffee?"

"That's an odd question." Alena glanced at him peculiarly. "But no, they don't. And you may not know them, but I do. I didn't spend my time hidden away before you arrived."

"Of course not." Damian squeezed her hand apologetically. Then he pointed ahead. "I think we've finally arrived."

The path continued forward through thinning trees, giving way to a grand courtyard. Corinthian columns, decorated with bolts of white cloth intertwined with holly, formed an artificial barrier around the gathering space. Hundreds of individuals composed of dozens of different species sat around tables in one corner, conversing with one another, laughing and eating. Bodies of all shapes and sizes stood in another space, swaying to the same melodic instrumentation that had accompanied them along the path.

At the center of the courtyard, a massive wooden hen sat on a bed of straw. Though constructed from hundreds of slats of wood, long, layered feathers covered much of its body. Mounds of eggs spilled out from under it. Even from a distance, Damian could make out the intricately painted peacock colors.

"Are they for eating?" Alena asked. "Or maybe they contain party favors?"

Damian was curious about that too, but his nose had redirected his attention to yet another corner of the arena. Additional tables held food of all varieties. He saw actual hens interspersed among ham glazed with brown sugar and pineapple, prime rib, and carved turkey. Bowls of garlic mashed potatoes sat next to boats of brown gravy. Green beans mixed with bacon rested next to corncobs dripping with butter.

A veritable Midwestern buffet! Damian eyed mountains of dinner rolls in woven baskets. *Butter. So much butter.*

"There you are, Damian!" Colin emerged from the crowd around the wooden hen, embracing him and Alena. "Isn't this magnificent?"

"If you say so," Damian said. Alena elbowed him in the ribs. "I mean, it's quite a display."

Colin pointed over his shoulder. "I would love to have a look inside the house."

Damian followed his gesture, not seeing anything but more festivities. Beyond the courtyard lay more dark trees and, he assumed, small groups of musicians. Then he looked up—way up—and his jaw fell. Behind the party, well beyond the cloth and holly, a hill rose above the forest canopy. On its side sat a mansion.

Now that he saw it, Damian wondered how he had missed it before. Built of white stone, it gleamed like a gem under the perpetually bright sky. Squinting his eyes, he made out towering marble columns lining the front facade, supporting a triangular, carved pediment. It sprawled outward in perfect symmetry, its wings appearing to reach out to the party below like the arms of a stern matriarch.

"Quite the statement piece," Damian muttered. He'd hoped that in the Afterlife, leadership would be less ostentatious. More egalitarian. Instead, Picardia Knutt had built herself a palace rivaling ancient Rome. Whispering in Alena's ear, he said, "Makes our place look like a shack."

"Don't judge the head ambassador too harshly," Alena said, though her eyes traced the long path between the house and party. Wide steps cascaded down from the entrance, flanked by additional columns and statues. "We could conjure up a home as opulent as this if we wanted."

Damian nodded. *This might be nothing compared to Kasee's place—though it likely smells much better.*

"I just want a tour of the place!" Colin threw his hands up. "Anyway, who's hungry?"

"Eating sounds great!" They walked over to the tables laden with food, keeping an eye out for stray dancers. Damian's mouth watered at the spread.

"One of the many perks of being dead," Colin said, piling his plate with lobster tails. "No need to count calories."

"You did a lot of that back in Minade?" Damian rolled his eyes, but also sucked in his belly. The platter in front of him held thick slices of prime rib that fell away under the knife. He moved down the table, adding crispy Brussels sprouts and au gratin potatoes. Alena piled her plate with grilled asparagus and creamed corn. She winked at him while adding a few cinnamon rolls.

With plates weighed down and glasses of wine in hand, the three waded through the crowd, searching for an open table. Damian spotted Wendell and Kasee sitting at a round table draped in white linen. The ambassador had adopted Colin's style with a trendy suit, though he looked far less at ease in it. Kasee wore a denim jacket with—*you gotta be kidding me*—a T-shirt with a tie printed on it.

"Join us!" Wendell waved them over, standing as they neared. Damian saw that the man had already worked his way through most of his meal, with a generous slice of chocolate cake lined up for consumption. "The food is exceptional, though I expected nothing less from our host."

After a quick round of introductions, Damian pulled out a chair for Alena before settling in beside her. He noticed Kasee's plate remained untouched. Instead of eating, she leaned back in her seat, chewing on an unlit cigar, and stared up at the mansion on the hill.

"Mrs. Hartter," Wendell said, leaning forward. "I wanted to congratulate you and your husband on the adoption. I think the changes you've encouraged are commendable. Let me know if you need any help dealing with political roadblocks as you continue the fight."

"Thank you, Ambassador Klinekole." Alena speared an asparagus. "We're learning even more than we expected. I've documented every moment."

As Alena filled Wendell in on the details of the previous night, Damian turned back to Colin. "Where's Anthony?"

"He's around here somewhere," Colin replied dismissively. "With all that's been going on, I've had a harder time keeping him in line. His behavior is getting erratic. Was on his third glass of wine the last time I saw him."

A mouthful of food saved Damian from having to comment on Colin's situation.

"I really should find him." Colin glanced around the vicinity. "He gets...interesting...after a few drinks, and I don't want to subject you to that kind of display again."

As Colin scooted his chair back, a horn sounded, silencing the courtyard. The conversation died, and the ethereal music cut out mid-note, all eyes turning toward the wooded path leading to the mansion. Other than a few birds taking flight, nothing happened for several long moments. Damian shifted in his chair, forked vegetables hovering inches from his mouth.

Movement stirred in the shadows beneath the trees, then a procession emerged onto the courtyard. Guards in ceremonial armor flanked distinguished-looking individuals, several of whom Damian recognized as Embassy ambassadors. *Why isn't Wendell among them?*

In the middle of the entourage, dressed in a white toga, walked Head Ambassador Picardia Knutt. Damian blinked, taken aback. Based on the murals they'd passed by earlier, he'd pictured someone imposing. In this, reality did not disappoint. Rather than cutting a proud figure, however, it was her bulk that was so dangerous. Picardia's face was flushed with exertion—*probably from the walk down the hill*—yet her skin gleamed as though freshly moisturized. Elaborate black braids coiled atop her head like a crown, and manicured nails caught the light as she raised a hand and waved.

Behind the woman, nearly hidden by her frame, walked a slight man. Though his clothes, a more modern business suit, were of a fine cut, nothing about him suggested importance. He could've been any Embassy employee. The man peeked up when the crowd applauded Picardia's entrance, and Damian saw sharp, calculating eyes.

"Who's that next to the head ambassador?" Damian asked, watching as the guards escorted the officials to a platform on the side of the courtyard, on which was an elaborately set dining table. Picardia stood behind the central seat, overlooking the festivities, while the small man stationed himself to her right.

"That would be Julius," Wendell said, clapping politely along with everyone else. "Her husband."

Colin leaned over and said more quietly, "Some think he's the power behind the curtain."

"Who do you think those empty seats are for?" Alena pointed to the far end of the table. The guards had lined up in front of the platform, and everyone else in the procession now stood behind a chair. Three vacant seats, complete with place settings, remained.

Damian shrugged as Picardia spread her vast arms wide. Her deep, booming voice carried across the plaza. "Welcome, friends and colleagues. Tonight, we celebrate our continued success in maintaining peace across realities. Please eat and enjoy each other's company."

The crowd applauded as the head ambassador took her seat. Conversation, music, and the sounds of cutlery on plates resumed around Damian, but he kept staring at the empty chairs. Picardia—or perhaps Julius—had meticulously planned every detail of the event. Empty seats at the main table felt wrong.

He lifted his fork again, thankful the vegetables hadn't cooled, but sudden movement caught his eye. Additional figures emerged from the shadowed path. Three ancient women, swathed in plain gray robes, glided over to the table.

A clattering sound tore Damian's attention away from the newcomers. He'd dropped his fork.

"Are those who I think they are?" Alena whispered. The entire crowd had quieted to a murmur.

Damian nodded, looking up at the Gray Ones. Their garments swayed despite the lack of wind. *It's not the robes that are billowing, but the dust-ridden forms underneath.* Even more disconcerting were the women's eyes. Instead of the hollow sockets that haunted his imagination, each sported a pair of gleaming eyes set deep in their weathered faces. He was certain they were illusions. Perhaps a visual aesthetic demanded by Picardia. Their *actual* eye orbited their heads like a tiny moon.

The Gray Ones took their seats at the end of the table without explanation or acknowledgment from the head ambassador. Attendants soon delivered food to everyone on the podium, and Damian watched as the old crones picked up utensils with gnarled fingers.

"I didn't know," Alena said, her face gray. Hers wasn't the only one. Damian noticed many in the crowd rubbed at their forearms or pressed fists against their mouths, cheeks puffed out. "I'm sorry I doubted your experience."

"I can't approve of their methods." Damian shuddered, but he wasn't sure if it was for his experiences with the Gray Ones or everyone else's current encounter. "But they serve an important function. I'm sure their invitation honors that."

Conversations slowly rose across the courtyard, and Alena was soon talking to Colin about Bennett's exponential growth rate. Damian munched on his food. His taste for the savory meats and crunchy vegetables had soured, however, and he put his utensils down.

"I'm going to get some wine." He grabbed his glass. "Anybody need anything?"

"I'll take a piece of pumpkin pie," Colin requested. The others shook their heads.

Damian stood and wound his way through the crowd, pausing as he passed the giant wooden hen. It towered above him, its painted beak facing the head table.

How many events has this hen showcased? Somehow, he knew Knutt had commissioned the piece specifically for this gathering and that nobody would ever see it again.

Movement beneath the wooden creature caught his attention, and he leaned in for a closer look. The decorative eggs heaped up around the centerpiece rocked back and forth. A soft tapping came from inside several of them, as though chicks were preparing to hatch.

Quite the party favor. Unsettled, Damian backed away and continued toward the buffet tables. Wine bottles were located sporadically around the food displays. His knowledge of wine began and ended with the fact that it came in different colors, but he'd noticed people pairing reds with beef and whites with fish and poultry. Back in the Midwest, on the rare occasions he socialized, he'd stuck to light beer.

After touring the spread twice, he finally spotted a collection of merlots. A particular bottle drew his attention, and its description mentioned notes of cocoa. Finding a clean glass nearby, he poured himself a generous amount.

Drink in hand, Damian leaned against one of the columns surrounding the courtyard and stared out at the clusters of people chatting and laughing. Some swayed to the music. Even the Gray Ones didn't appear displeased, though it was hard to decipher their ever-changing faces. Despite the gross indulgence on the property, the sight of hundreds of individuals enjoying themselves charmed Damian. *The Afterlife isn't all dark conspiracies.*

He pushed off the column, ready to return to Alena. Before he took another step, a figure came around the pillar and stumbled into him. Red wine sloshed over the rim of his glass, staining the white fabric draped around the stone.

"Oh hey, Dam-man!" Anthony's words slurred together as he grabbed Damian's shoulder to steady himself. He wore a nice suit that paired with Colin's, though the sleeves were too long. The stench of alcohol rolled off him, ruining Damian's curiosity about the merlot. "Some party, huh? I think they're running low on the good stuff."

"I think you've had enough of the good stuff." Damian backed up, trying to avoid the worst of the fumes.

"What're you talking about?" Anthony blinked at him, swaying back and forth. "I'm fine."

"Sure." Damian forced a smile. "Why don't you go find Colin? He was looking for you earlier."

"Colin can wait. What's the rush?"

The slight man drew close, slamming a hand against Damian's chest. *Was that supposed to be a sexual advance?*

"He told me all about the pact of your youth."

Damian's head spun as the childhood promise coalesced within his mind. Its contents blurred into a drunken haze before he could make any sense of them. He allowed the memory to slip into oblivion.

"What did you say?" He set his glass down on the nearest table, deciding instead to hunt down some coffee.

"Huh?" Anthony gaped at him.

Damian sighed, glancing at the stained white fabric hanging from the column. "Look, I need to find something to get this wine out."

"Seriously?" The drunk man snorted after following his gaze. "You're worried about a little spill? You think anyone will notice?"

"It's not a little stain." The wine had continued to spread downward. "And it's not our home."

"Wine lives longer than we do," Anthony said in a moment of lucidity. "We still hold sway over it, though."

He stepped—stumbled—toward the column. Damian expected his companion to puke, to add to the spilled wine, but he instead waved a hand over the fabric. To his surprise, the stain vanished.

"There you go." Anthony gave a smug grin. "*Cleaning* is a simple task. No need to find anyone."

Don't tell my mother that. Damian stared at the clean fabric. "I didn't know we could do that."

"There's a lot you don't know." Anthony gave him a wink before wandering off into the crowd.

Damian watched him go, wondering if Anthony wasn't as drunk as he appeared or if the effects of alcohol wore off quickly in the Afterlife. Then he shook his head and set out to find Colin a piece of pie.

A bolt of blue lightning seared across the sky, penetrating the mist, and struck the wooden hen. The creature exploded, sending large splinters and colorful eggs into the crowd. The light blinded Damian, and his ears rang as screams filled the air—at least until a ground-shaking thunderclap swallowed them up.

He staggered back against the column, squinting into the swirling dust where the hen had sat moments earlier. As it thinned, a slim figure emerged. Dressed in the same charcoal suit and top hat as before, Odd Man Blue looked even more ill than usual.

How'd she do that? Damian hadn't thought of the strange woman since his first DSI meeting.

"What's the meaning of this?" Picardia Knutt's voice cut through the lingering echoes of thunder. She'd vacated her chair deftly, springing up faster than Damian thought possible. "You've disrupted our celebration!"

"As was my intention." Odd Man Blue's voice was steady and cold. "Urgent news cannot wait for decorum."

The chill in her voice found its way into Damian's body. He feared he knew the tidings she brought.

"The Sphere of Doom has struck again."

A collective gasp went up from the crowd. Damian's stomach dropped. He looked back at Picardia, whose face turned a shade paler.

"Where?" she asked, her tone still commanding but laced with concern.

"About five miles southeast of the city." Damian was certain that location completed the hexagram pattern they'd feared.

The gasps devolved into a sea of rumblings that crashed into Damian as he made his way back to the table where he'd left Alena and the others.

"We must act swiftly," he heard Picardia declare. "This attack is a deliberate threat against us. Everyone report to their respective ambassadors."

Now it's an emergency? What about the souls missing since this began? The murmurs continued, though few people moved to find their department leaders. *This attack could be the beginning of a grand finale. Nobody is eager to return to the city.*

Wendell was already assigning tasks when Damian reached their table. "Reach out to your connections, Kasee. See if they've been holding back any information about the sphere. Anything about this specific attack or what the endgame is."

Kasee shook her head. "I'm not sure I can squeeze any more out of them. They don't trust the Embassy—or any positions of authority."

"*Make* them trust you. If you don't, there may be no one left to trust," Wendell said. "Colin and I will head out to the latest attack site. The sooner we get there, the more likely it is we'll find the sphere. Not sure what that'll accomplish now, but I'd still rather have the device under lock and key."

"I think I should go to the Embassy." Colin pushed back from the table. "To prepare for when you bring in the sphere."

"No. Your tracking experience gives us the best shot at finding it. I need you with me."

"Okay, but what about—"

"I said you're with me." The finality in Wendell's voice cut through the surrounding chaos. The ambassador turned to Damian. "Go to the Embassy. Act as a liaison between departments. Provide ambassadors with any pertinent information they request."

"Yes, sir." Damian watched as Colin's face twisted in frustration. He understood Colin's reluctance. If the culmination of the sphere's behavior was upon them, the enemy would likely target the Embassy. "Don't worry, Colin. I'll prepare for your arrival with the sphere."

Colin's scowl deepened, but he agreed. "Thanks. Just...be careful."

The team dispersed, heading toward the distant obsidian wall to peregrinate to their respective destinations. Damian stayed put, finding his and Alena's hands clasped together.

"Where did that strange woman go?" Her voice sounded distant, as though she was trying to make sense of the last few minutes.

"Odd Man Blue?" Damian turned toward the hen, now a pile of smoldering wood. No sign of the sickly woman remained. "No idea, and I don't know how she got onto the property." He wasn't sure if traveling by lightning counted as peregrination.

"What's going on, Damian?" she asked. "What's happening?"

"I don't know." He wasn't sure how much he could tell her. Even if speaking openly about his work was allowed, he still didn't fully understand the ramifications of this new shrinking. *Satan may be attacking the Celestial City right now, or the shrinkings might all have been a grim joke.* He pulled Alena in and hugged her. "It's probably nothing, but go home to Bennett. Make sure he's safe."

Alena's face tightened, but she nodded. "Be careful, Damian."

"I will." He squeezed her hand, then ran off toward the entrance.

The shouts and clamoring of the crowded courtyard faded as Damian raced back down the winding pathway. Despite most of the partygoers being Embassy employees who should've been jumping into action, he found himself alone in the trees. They'd stayed behind, in shock or hesitant to respond.

The forest blurred around him as he sprinted. Mist still clung to the ground, and it felt like he was running through the woods at night. *At the very least, I'm not running short on breath.*

A figure stepped out of the trees as he reached a bend in the path. Damian skidded to a stop, recognizing the nebulous silhouette of a Gray One. Eyes once more missing, her face was inscrutable as it phased in and out of solidity. She extended a bent hand toward Damian—not directly at him, as the floating orb that provided her sight was nowhere to be seen.

"Take this." Her raspy voice sounded like the crunching of dried leaves. It took a moment for him to notice a small pouch made of rough fabric in her hand.

Damian hesitated, reluctant to take anything from one of the nightmarish women. Her figure expanded, looming over him threateningly, and he took the proffered bag. It was heavier than it had appeared. "What is this?"

"It isn't for you," the crone said, backing into the shadows of the forest. "Though it may be of use. Do not lose it."

"I can't take this now." Damian hefted the rough burlap bag. Its contents were still—*thank goodness*—but unidentifiable. "We don't have time for your vague mysteries."

The woman was gone, though. Her form had evaporated amid the trees.

"Great," he said aloud. "Just great."

Pouch firmly in hand, he continued his sprint toward the obsidian wall.

CHAPTER TWENTY

Damian took the stone steps to the Embassy's front doors two at a time. The mysterious pouch gifted to him by the Gray One was in his tight grip. Its contents bounced against his hip, though he barely noticed. Mai was the sole Guardian presence at the entrance, appearing harried and displeased at the influx of humans reporting for duty.

Strange to see a solitary Guardian on duty. Mai's posture stiffened as he approached. "Have you heard from Athan yet?"

Mai bowed their head, which Damian interpreted as a yes.

"Are they here?"

The Guardian shook their head and sighed heavily, an audible reaction that would've been unremarkable from anyone other than a Guardian. Then Mai pointed into the distance, somewhere beyond the wall.

"They went out to investigate the new anomaly?

Mai nodded. Even with no words spoken, it was more communication than Damian had ever seen the other convey before.

"Any other news?" he asked, stepping aside as members of the Department of Health pushed their way inside. "Since Odd Man Blue crashed the head ambassador's party, I mean."

Shaking their head, Mai pulled one of the massive doors open for Damian. Two impatient individuals cut in front of him before he finally made his way inside. The foyer was still cavernous, but the floor now teemed with life. Representatives from all of Creation scurried around in panic, working to piece together the meaning of the sphere's actions.

At the center of the foyer, the Bridge continued rotating under the chandelier as though nothing of consequence had occurred. Damian walked over to it, weaving his way through crowds of individuals talking animatedly, and examined the cryptic symbols etched on each panel. He still couldn't decipher them. Didn't know which of them represented Hell.

Where my mother is. Don't tell her that cleaning here is a simple task.

He pushed the thought aside, examining the keyholes atop each panel. They all appeared intact. No signs of tampering, though he hadn't a clue how the Bridge functioned.

The surrounding conversations pressed in around him as he completed his inspection. He worried about the congregation of so many people when the Celestial City—the Embassy, in particular—was an obvious target if Satan successfully launched an offensive.

The history of the Forti battle, the clash between great serpentine beings and the Guardians, came back to Damian. So much greed, hatred, and *permanent* death. The thought of fresh blood being spilled on the Embassy lawn tightened his focus and hastened his ascent to the third floor.

The hallway leading to the Department of Satanic Investigations was less populated, and Damian speed-walked to his destination. He'd expected a long line outside his door, people requiring his expertise. *Such as it is.* To his relief, no one was waiting for his arrival. The usual sounds of shuffling papers and clacking keyboards permeated the walls, so he knew he wasn't alone in the far corner of the building. The silent emptiness of the DSI office greeted him once he pushed open the door.

"Hello?" He didn't expect a response, and the unsettling silence didn't disappoint.

On the opposite wall, his and Colin's desks faced each other. Without their holographic displays running, they looked like any other desk. The polished gray surface, which reflected warm light streaming through the windows, would've fit in with the sea of similar desks at Damian's old office in Chicago.

Better prepare for Colin and Wendell's arrival. Damian walked past the stations to the secure storage cabinet. He flipped the lock and swung open the armored doors, the metal cold against his free hand. The contents appeared exactly as they had the last time he stood there: Three orbs sat upon the shelves, the fourth locked away in a heavy box at the bottom.

Damian reached out to touch one of the decoy spheres, then stopped. They were harmless, he knew, but the memory of Colin struggling to overpower the last one on Irvin gave him pause. The last thing he needed in the middle of the current crisis was to let loose these spheres, instigating fresh chaos within the Embassy.

The pouch in Damian's hand suddenly felt heavier. He'd almost forgotten he held it, but now its weight was cumbersome. He took a step back from the cabinet, intending to open the burlap bag, but his dress shoes scraped against something gritty. With a grunt, he kneeled down and saw scattered granules of red sand coating the otherwise pristine marble floor. It led straight to Kasee's cubicle.

Damian followed the mess over to the other side of the room. Coffee stains dotted the fabric of her chair, and food crumbs and cigar ashes had been ground into any groove or indent. He set the pouch on the cleanest portion of the desk, which bore similar signs of teenage slovenliness. Rather than taking a seat, he settled for leaning against a corner of the table, careful to avoid a sticky patch that might've been strawberry jam.

Despite how filthy Kasee can be, she usually keeps it contained in her area. What's with this sand? His gaze settled on the department's entrance as he worried over how the others were doing, especially Alena and Bennett. It suddenly dawned on him he hadn't seen or held a phone since dying. How odd it was not to feel naked without one in his pocket. Right now, he just wanted to text his wife. Know his family was okay.

Colin missed the smartphone craze. Would've been obsessed. He's already so invested in the sphere investigation, exhibiting an intensity that borders on mania.

Damian considered how Colin's hyper-focused attention affected his personal life. The strain in his relationship with Anthony showed in their interactions. Colin's irritation with his boyfriend. Anthony's sarcastic responses and his drunkenness.

Heavy footsteps thudded down the hallway. Damian looked at the door, waiting for it to swing open. He wanted his coworkers to charge in, the object of their troubles in hand. They'd throw it in the cabinet, cheer each other over a cup of hot tea—*with a splash of something stronger*—down at Messie Bessie's, and move on to lighter and happier cases. The door remained shut, and the footsteps moved along down the hall.

With a sigh, Damian lowered his head and stared down at the dirty floor. His eyes eventually settled on the desk drawer that refused to open. The specter of drunk Anthony appeared in his imagination, waving a hand over the stained white fabric hanging from a column, disappearing the wine stain.

"We hold sway over it," Damian said aloud. He recalled the Orientation of the Dead. Athan had materialized a hammer, lecturing that everyone could create simple, practical items out of thin air. The more intricate the piece, the more likely they'd have to rely upon another to build it.

The same rules must apply to repairs and cleaning, judging by Anthony's ability to wash up that spill. Damian doubted there was a thriving desk repair trade in the Afterlife.

Careful not to touch the floor with his bare hands, he kneeled and pulled at the drawer. The handle was loose, and the cabinetry itself rattled, but it didn't open for him. After verifying there was no locking mechanism, he tugged harder. The desk itself shifted, but the drawer didn't budge.

With a sense of silliness, Damian placed the palm of his hand against the drawer, *willing* it to be fixed. He waited several seconds and then tried to open it again. It remained steadfast in its stubbornness.

Damian then closed his eyes and visualized the inside of the cabinet. Since it had no lock, the most complicated part of the apparatus was the rails the drawer slid back and forth on.

Could they have worn down or rusted over? he thought. *Except objects don't just break in the Afterlife, and this desk was a gift to Kasee when she started here.*

He closed his eyes once more, trying to picture the mechanism. *A small object might've fallen, lodging itself between the rail and the frame of the cabinet.*

Hand still firmly pressed against the metal drawer, he imagined himself removing such an obstruction. He felt ridiculous kneeling beside Kasee's desk in the middle of the night, all alone in the DSI, while others worked fervently throughout the Embassy in reaction to the sphere's attack.

"Come on," he said. "Just work."

No movement. Just the persistent silence of the office. With another heavy sigh, Damian opened his eyes and made to stand up, using the drawer handle as leverage. The cabinet slid open with ease, catching him off balance, and he fell onto his back.

A tumble like that in life would've left me rolling around in pain. Damian rubbed an elbow that'd struck the floor, more embarrassed than anything. *Just wait until I see Kasee. I have half a mind to—*

The rest of the thought died in his mind as he sat up and peeked into the drawer. It contained only one item: a softball-sized sphere. Its surface bore the same stony gray color as the others in the armored cabinet across the room. The silvery etchings carved into it were the same, too.

The exact same. Damian's mouth went dry, and the office walls closed in around him as he sat staring at the relic. Only Colin could claim to have studied the decoy spheres for dozens of hours, but Damian had examined them long enough to recognize the refined markings. *A fifth decoy sphere? Why is it here?*

A heavy thump sounded from across the room. Damian's head turned, his eyes retracing the path of red sand back to the armored cabinet. He saw nothing at first, but then the heavy box he'd placed at the bottom the previous day lurched up and fell with another loud thud. The padlock Wendell had affixed glowed red and melted off the front.

Damian sat frozen as the box's lid popped open and blue light spilled out. The stone orb within levitated into view, covered in runes. The markings were like those on the decoy spheres. Not identical, though. They were more refined, the inlaid silver more sinister.

It was the Sphere of Doom.

Blue light thrummed along the silver markings as Damian scrambled backward across the floor, dirtying his palms in the dirt of Wendell's garden. He stared at the weapon that'd caused so much trouble. Five attacks across multiple realities. *Gearing up for its sixth.*

"No, no, no." The single word tumbled from his lips as he pushed himself to his feet.

The sphere pulsed brighter, each groove along its surface filled with brilliant silver luminescence. Damian continued to retreat, his back now flat against Wendell's wickiup. He wanted to flee the office, to get outside and return to Head Ambassador Knutt's party. His legs shook violently, though, threatening to give out.

The light was so bright he could no longer see the sphere. It trickled lazily out of the cabinet like a buoyant fluid. A mixture of colors seeped through, glittering like broken shards of glass.

Just like on Irvin, Damian recognized. *Whatever is happening in the southeast has everyone focused on the wrong place. It's a trick.* This *is it. The final offense. Its endgame.*

The beautiful, terrible kaleidoscope of colors crept across his and Colin's desks, dripping onto their chairs. Damian's muscles tensed as he gathered the courage to bolt for the door. He didn't have to return to the party. If he could make it through the entrance of the Embassy, he'd alert Mai. *The Guardians will know what to do. They're as eager to end this evil as anyone else. They've lost one of their own over it.*

Damian's legs finally responded to his commands, and he spun toward the door. The light behind him cast his shadow across the walls, stretching it into twisted, unrecognizable shapes. He made it three steps.

The air crackled as tendrils of light exploded outward from the cabinet. They whipped through the room like the arms of an angry sea creature, wrapping around anything they found purchase. Chairs splintered as the ethereal ropes constricted around them. Kasee's metal desk shrieked in protest, the open drawer popping out completely, spilling out the newly discovered decoy. The armored cabinet groaned as its surface warped.

Cold bands of light strung around Damian's arms. He screamed, expecting his limbs to snap like twigs. Rather than break him, more tendrils snaked around his legs, their touch both burning and freezing. His knees buckled in terror. The floor rushed up to smash his face, but the light pulled him away. He wriggled in their grasp, fighting against their pull. Suspended in air, he was helpless to stop them.

The Sphere of Doom was now a vortex, a growing marble of fraying color. It yawned before him hungrily.

Damian struggled, but the coils pulled him higher into the air. His stomach lurched as gravity reversed. Desks and chairs scraped against the walls and ceiling. Colors strobed around him. Silver, gold, crimson, and azure. They blended together, separated again, twisting impossibly.

The tendrils released Damian, and he fell directly into the heart of the churning maelstrom.

He fell—and continued to fall.

CHAPTER TWENTY-ONE

TRUMPETS SOUNDED IN ALARM, dragging Damian back to consciousness. He lay on his stomach, blades of grass tickling his nose. As his eyes opened and focused, he found himself surrounded by a lush meadow, plants swaying in a warm wind.

Where are the lights? They were so bright. Damian's mind clumsily pieced together the past and present. *Are the angels still descending?*

With great effort, he rolled over onto his back. He expected to find the Buick Century a few yards away, overturned, its warm engine ticking. The body of his mother, still strapped in by her seatbelt, would stare back at him. *Are her eyes filled with the love from our last conversation? Or have they reverted to their usual disappointment?*

Neither the Buick nor his mother was in the vicinity, and the sky above told Damian he wasn't lying in Minade Park. *I'm not at home or even on the Embassy's lawn.* Instead of azure or amber, the atmosphere appeared emerald. As in the Afterlife, no sun hung overhead, so he didn't think he was far from familiar territory.

Damian found breathing laborious, but he *was* breathing. *Is it required here?* He lifted his hand, checking his forearm for a silver bracelet like the one Kasee lent him for Irvin, and that was on—

Kasee! He sat up as memories exploded to the forefront of his mind. *Her standoffishness, the clumsy attempts at chumminess, and her long absences talking with supposed informants.* All her behaviors took on new meanings. *She hid the sphere right under our noses, masking her true nature behind a facade of teenage rebellion!*

Damian bared his teeth at Kasee's betrayal, but his anger subsided as he took in the surroundings beyond the meadow. In the distance, behind a dense forest and the top of a diamond wall, he spotted the tall towers of the Celestial Palace. To its side was the Castile. He imagined Guardians gazing out the narrow windows of their home. *Can they see past the wall, into the many planes of existence that surround them?*

A nearby groan grabbed Damian's attention. An older woman pushed herself up from the grass, tangled gray hair falling down her shoulders. He recognized her as one of the impatient officials that'd pushed past him into the Embassy. Hundreds of other people stirred and sat up across the field, blinking rapidly as they looked around slack-jawed.

Damian scanned the crowd dotting the landscape for familiar faces. *I don't think Colin or Wendell were close to the Embassy when the sphere activated, so they shouldn't be here.* Mai had been standing outside the building, but he didn't see the Guardian among the others.

The trumpets blared again, a sharp, discordant noise that reminded Damian of a tornado warning. He clapped his hands over his ears, turning toward the source. He expected it to be the Celestial City, some sort of klaxon alerting the populace to an attack.

His jaw dropped as the trumpets drew his gaze far to the left of the city, past the Celestial Wall. Another city rose from the horizon. At first glance, it appeared to be a mirror image of the city, with the peaks of the Celestial Palace piercing the emerald sky. His mind spotted the Castile and the library, white buildings trimmed with gold. On second glance, though, the structures looked off, like an amateur architect had recreated them from memory. Whereas the city's style flowed with graceful curves, the facsimile's towers and walls bristled with harsh angles and pointed edges.

What is this place? Is this where all those caught in a shrinking end up?

At the edge of the meadow closest to the curious new city, tall figures in flowing robes appeared. Two dozen Guardians, long braided hair swaying as they stepped through the high grasses, split into groups of two and spread out across the field. They moved with practiced efficiency, helping dazed humans—and a few species he didn't recognize—to their feet, handing everyone a silver bracelet. Mai was not one of them.

The trumpets ceased, and Damian let his hands fall away from his ears. His right hand brushed against rough fabric on the ground. It was the pouch given to him by the Gray One. *Was I holding it when the sphere activated, or did it come along for the ride?* He remembered setting it down on Kasee's desk and doubted he had the wherewithal to cling to it while being assaulted by the light tendrils. Glancing around, it seemed to be the only inanimate object from the office—from the entire Embassy.

His legs wobbled as he pushed himself upright, stuffing the burlap bag into a jacket pocket. *Of course, I'm on a strange new world dressed to the nines.* Five Guardians remained at the edge of the meadow, huddled together, watching as the others gathered the displaced into small groups. He stumbled toward them, thinking they might be the leaders of this rescue party. As he neared, his shortness of breath worsened, and he felt the onset of fatigue.

Definitely not in Kansas anymore, he thought, glancing back up at the green sky.

Four of the five Guardians turned to Damian when they heard his labored gasps. Dressed in robes of black and deep purple, they appeared more emaciated than others he'd seen. Their skin pulled tight over underlying bones, giving them a skeletal appearance that sent a chill through Damian's tired body. The diadems on their heads exaggerated the image, stretching upward like the spires of the nearby mirror city, tall and sharp.

Massive swords hung at their waists, polished hilts gleaming. The open display of weaponry gave Damian pause, but then the fifth Guardian turned around. They stood taller than their companions and had lustrous blonde hair that framed a heart-shaped, boyish face and tumbled over broad shoulders. Blue eyes burst with life, tamed only by thick eyelids opened barely more than a nick. Instead of a heavy dark robe, they wore one of pure white linen. It hung loosely over their body, revealing a muscular chest and a sculpted abdomen.

The creature smiled—*smiled*—down at Damian. "Are you well, human?"

"Are you...are you a Guardian?" Damian immediately regretted the question as impolite. *And unimportant.*

The smile faltered for a moment, and their eyes narrowed even further, scrutinizing him with focused intensity. "Yes. I am Adrian. May I know your name?"

"Damian Hartter. I work for Ambassador Klinekole in the Department of Satanic Investigations." He couldn't take his eyes off the Guardian. Adrian was beautiful, a being so perfect he lost his breath. *What little I have left.* He simultaneously wished Alena was experiencing the mesmerizing sight with him and was grateful he had Adrian's attention all to himself.

"Damian of the DSI." Adrian held up an expectant hand, and one of the other four Guardians hastily produced a silver bracelet from their robes and placed it on their palm. Adrian offered it to Damian. "I am familiar with Colin Cherry. Is he here?"

Of course you know Colin, Damian thought absently as he slipped the bracelet on. It resized to fit him, and he felt a pressure along his neck. "No, he and Ambassador Klinekole went out to investigate the area where the Sphere of Doom had supposedly activated. We've all been misled. I'm not sure what you know, but I believe I know who's responsible for directing the sphere."

Adrian leaned forward, looming over Damian, and raised an eyebrow. "Oh? And who is this evil soul?"

"Her name is Kasee Lang," Damian said. "She works with us in the DSI. I believe she hid the sphere in her desk, swapping it out with a decoy we'd found."

But why would she do that? Damian felt silly once the words left his mouth. *The result would've been the same if the sphere had gone off in her cubicle.*

Adrian's perfect features hardened as they turned to the other four Guardians. "Report our friend Damian's findings to the council. Tell them to begin preparations for what comes next."

The skeletal figures bowed and strode away, their long legs carrying them faster than Damian could've ever run. They didn't head for the Celestial City but toward its unsettling mirror image.

Damian turned in a circle, watching as the two dozen other Guardians gathered the displaced Embassy officials into small groups and herded them off in the same direction as the others. As he took in the scene with a sharper eye, something about the Celestial City looked off. The defensive towers and white walls appeared to shimmer behind a hue of pink. He took a step closer, seeing a transparent dome over the entire city, stretching into the emerald sky. The barrier reminded him of the shrinking's surface on Irvin. *It's different, though, like being inside the bubble looking out.*

"Where are we?" Damian asked, his chest tightening. "And what's that other city?"

"We stand outside the Celestial City, of course." Adrian flashed a wide smile. Such an expression would've been unnerving on any other Guardian, even spooky. But on Adrian, Damian found it pleasing, drawing his gaze and locking his attention. "The other is the city of Acheron."

The name struck a chord in Damian, and the horrid faces of the Gray Ones flitted across his mind's eye. He stumbled backward at the sudden image, the pouch in his pocket vibrating. Adrian's hand shot out, steadying him with a firm grasp on his shoulder.

"What's this council the others are reporting to?" The words came out in a whisper.

"The council is a group of my closest advisors. Those I trust above all others." Adrian's fingers remained on Damian's shoulder, warm through the thick fabric of his jacket. "Trust is a hard thing to come by, would you not agree? It must be earned, and it goes both ways."

"And who are you, Adrian, that others trust so much?"

Adrian's smile widened, stretching just beyond the perfect proportions of their face. For an awful moment, Damian saw the black-furred creature with horns and fangs the Gray Ones had warned him about. "You already know who I am, Damian. And where you are."

Someone shouted close by, and Damian saw a woman brush a Guardian's hand off her shoulder. The Guardian responded by backhanding her across the face. She remained on her feet, but her defiance faltered. Six other humans stood around her. In the presence of the Guardians, none offered help. Damian wanted to run over, but the hand on his shoulder pulled him toward Acheron.

"This can't be." He glanced back at the Celestial City. The pink glow surrounding it appeared more opaque. "I can see the city. If this were..." He couldn't bring himself to say it. "We can't see it on Earth."

"In the infinite space that is your universe, you think the Celestial City would be on your minor planet?" Adrian's smile turned wistful. "You are right, of course. It was—is. Just as it is at the center of all planes of existence. It is visible here because I was given partial rule over Earth. The way between worlds was not completely shut, and my influence requires the Bridge to operate." Adrian paused for a moment, looking back at the city. "Not that I believe its visibility is required. It was added, though, as a mocking symbol of what I lost."

As they closed the distance to Acheron, a massive wall rose before them. It dwarfed the Celestial Wall, though it consisted of chiseled black stone instead of diamond. It reminded Damian of Head Ambassador Knutt's estate, though this material lacked the glittering texture. The stone absorbed the atmosphere's green light into an oppressive darkness. Like a black hole, it seemed to pull at his soul.

A wide moat lined the base of the wall. Unlike the crystalline waters of the lake behind his home, this liquid was dark and oily. Fed by a nearby river, the water moved sluggishly—*or, somehow, chunkily*. Damian watched as Guardians prodded his Embassy coworkers across a massive bridge spanning the moat. It was wide enough for twenty people to walk comfortably shoulder-to-shoulder, and their shepherds used that space to force them onward.

"What's going to happen to them?" Damian's lungs burned as he inhaled noxious fumes bubbling up from the moat. He tapped the bracelet on his wrist, wondering if it was broken and the air toxic.

"They will join the others who have been transported here via the sphere's mechanisms," Adrian answered. They'd come to a standstill behind the others, watching as dozens of small groups passed through a gate in the black wall. Rather than the wooden doors of the Celestial Gate, these were fashioned from iron bars reminiscent of those in the Dungeon of Darkness. "They've been well cared for during their time with us."

"How many have you imprisoned here?" Damian refused to mince words as Adrian guided him across the bridge toward the gate. Two Guardians stood watch, swords drawn, their thin hair wafting aimlessly in the wind.

"Only a hundred or so from previous shrinkings, including non-human creatures from other planes. Those have been a source of great amusement, as we don't see many here."

Damian held his breath as they passed through the gates of Acheron. Every tale he knew of the underworld, whether religious or mythological, painted vivid pictures of torture and suffering. He braced himself for scenes of horror and depravity.

But the street stretching out before them was wide and clean. People strolled past in tailored clothing, engaged in lively conversation. A group gathered around an outdoor cafe, sipping drinks while sharing plates of pastries.

"This can't be right," Damian said. *This could be the same street on which I hit the blob with my Camaro.*

Adrian's grip loosened, and the Guardian peered down at him. "Were you expecting something more dramatic? Fire and brimstone, perhaps?"

While flames didn't ravage the architecture, what he'd mistaken for gold trim from the meadow revealed itself as brilliant orange accents. The outer walls showed visible signs of aging, though careful repairs kept everything looking pristine.

"I don't understand." Damian watched a woman in a blue sundress laugh with friends as they admired a window display of jewelry and clothing. The scene felt surreal in its normalcy. "This looks just like—"

"The Celestial City?" Adrian thrust their chest out. "Did you think we abandoned order and civilization?"

"Everything I've been told about this place," Damian said as a street sweeper walked past, clearing away debris, "none of it matches what I'm seeing."

Even the air lacks the sulfurous stench I expected. The fumes of the brackish water were absent, held back by the black walls.

"History is written by the victors." They continued to trail behind the larger group, which was headed toward the massive castle at the center of Acheron. "Those in power never paint accurate portraits of their enemies. They portray me as a demon who sought to destroy Creation. In truth, I fought only for the rights of my kind. We wanted what humans take for granted—the ability to feel, to choose, to love."

Damian looked up at Adrian, admiring the blond hair cascading down their shoulders and the sparkling blue eyes brimming with intelligence. His tongue went dry at the sight of defined abs peeking through the white robe. Then he shook his head, reminding himself who—*what*—walked beside him. *Satan. The Great Deceiver. The Father of Lies.* Every story from his Sunday school classes, every warning from his mother, crashed through his mind.

Don't trust their words. They'll say anything to make you compliant.

The two passed over a small bridge. Like the one outside the wall, it crossed over thick, oily water. Though subdued, Damian still gagged as foul odors wafted over him. It was the reminder he needed that, despite how Acheron defied his expectations—no demons prowled the streets with pitchforks, no pained screams of the damned—a current of tension still flowed through the city.

As if to emphasize his point, another trumpet blast pierced the air. Its discordant notes set Damian's teeth on edge. As the noise echoed through the streets, he asked, "What's that for?"

"They herald our victory. With the help of our mutual friend in the DSI, the Sphere of Doom has completed its work." Adrian stared at the castle, which grew larger with each step. "Now we must gather our forces and proceed with the next phase."

"Another war," Damian said. "I don't understand why."

"Of course you don't understand. You are one of the Creator's privileged, gifted with emotions and free will from the moment of your formation." Adrian spoke slowly, patiently, as though Damian were a child. Bitterness crept into their voice as they continued. "Guardians were created to serve, nothing more. No feelings, no choices, no desires of our own. Nothing but empty vessels meant only to maintain order."

"That's not true!" Damian said. "I've been to the Castile. Seen the gardens tended by Guardians for thousands of years. Your kind has found meaning beyond their original purpose. In my conversations with Athan—"

"You will never speak of them in my presence!" Adrian turned on Damian so fast he nearly fell over. "If anyone is to be labeled a betrayer, it is Athan. They will never sit on my council. It is a pity, as they showed so much promise. They have been dispatched. I can deal with them at my leisure."

"What do you mean? They should be outside the city." Damian closed his mouth, not wanting to reveal any more of what he knew.

"The trust Athan broke was repaid." Adrian gave their disarming smile again. "They are no longer a threat to my plans."

Damian's stomach churned at the memory of finding Bai's head, and his limbs shook uncontrollably at the thought of Athan being harmed. The Guardian had been kind to him since his arrival in the Afterlife, helping with the transition from life on Earth. *I never would've gotten far in my investigations without them, and they boosted my confidence enough to accept the job in the first place.*

"Do not fret." Adrian waved a dismissive hand. "Athan is not alone. They have company in your wife and child."

Acheron tilted beneath Damian's feet. He found it difficult to breathe, and pressure suddenly built up behind his eyes exactly as it had when Rebecca and

Gus informed him of his mother's death. "What? No! Please, they have nothing to do with this!"

"Not directly." Adrian's azure eyes sparkled behind their narrow eyelids. "But your son represents change in your Afterlife, a challenge to the bureaucracy of the Celestial City. He has helped prime everyone for the true upheaval that is to come."

"I'll do anything." Damian's voice cracked as he fell to his knees. *I have to get back to the city! Find and protect them!* "Don't hurt them. I'm begging you!"

"Such dramatics." Adrian's smile widened, revealing sharp teeth. Their handsome features twisted into something much darker. "While I would love to stay and watch you grovel, I must be going."

"Going where?" Damian wiped away tears. A useless gesture, as more spilled from his eyes to take their place. He looked at the group ahead of them. They'd crossed over yet another bridge and were being led through enormous doors into the castle. Darkness lay beyond. "Am I going with them?"

"No, they are joining the others. Together, they will be cast into Gehenna and purified."

"Gehenna?"

Adrian reached down and took hold of Damian's shoulder again. It was a painful grip this time, sharp fingers digging through layers of fabric and into his skin. It was a sensation Damian hadn't missed since death. "The Lake of Fire."

"No!" Damian gasped in pain. He didn't know the others. He barely knew those in his own department, aside from Colin. But the thought of so many souls being lost forever created an inconsolable panic. "They did nothing wrong. They were just doing their jobs."

"My friend, have you not heard?" Adrian lifted him up over their head. For the first time, Damian had to look down to see a Guardian's face. Adrian—*Satan*—looked him in the eyes and said, "Everyone burns in Hell."

Adrian's fingers dug deeper into his shoulder, then released. Damian plummeted, bracing for impact on the street below, expecting his ankles to snap. The ground rushed up—

The surface vanished. Damian fell through empty air, limbs flailing for purchase. A familiar tingle swept through him, similar to peregrination. The similarity ended there. Instead of the swirling colors and whooshing sounds he'd grown used to, white-hot pain tore through his body. His flesh ripped apart as though invisible blades carved him into smaller and smaller pieces. Each slice burned worse than the last. He screamed in agony—until his vocal cords separated from his neck.

His consciousness fragmented along with his body, thoughts scattering. *Wisdom teeth...car accident...losing Colin...felt better than this.* Just when he believed his sanity lost, the process reversed. Shards of his physical and mental self snapped back together, nerve endings firing as they reconnected.

Damian materialized in a pitch-black room. He gasped for breath, collapsing to the floor. Sweat poured down his face, soaking into his collared shirt and jacket.

"Unpleasant sensation, isn't it?" a familiar voice asked from the darkness.

Damian's head jerked up. As his eyes adjusted to the dim light, he found himself in a small foyer. It reminded him of the apartment he and Alena shared in Chicago, cramped and filled with shoes, coats, and umbrellas. Other than a small table pushed against the wall, this one was empty.

Nearly empty. He pulled himself back onto his feet, trying to identify the source of the voice. A large frameless mirror leaned against the wall in the far corner. He wouldn't have noticed if not for his reflection. The image wasn't twisted and malformed like a funhouse mirror, but it was somehow warped.

Then the image moved. It stepped out of the dark corner, closer to Damian. He realized he hadn't been staring into a mirror at all, but at another person. Another *him*.

"Excuse the state of the place," Damian's doppelgänger said. "We weren't expecting guests."

CHAPTER TWENTY-TWO

"PAINFUL, ISN'T IT?" DAMIAN's double said. "I'm told peregrination is a pleasant experience where you're from."

"Wh-what is this?" Damian's legs threatened to give out as he stared at his near duplicate. The man wore a tailored gray suit over a vibrantly colored shirt. He'd styled his hair, product keeping each strand in place. A metal chain hung loosely from his hand, leading to—

Damian's hands flew to his neck, finding a thick leather collar fastened around it and attached to the chain lead. Breaking out in a cold sweat, he again asked, "What is this?"

"It's a collar. Everyone of your status gets one. Helps keep you under control." The other man gave the chain a light tug. "Don't worry. Nothing kinky about it."

Damian felt the veins in his neck sticking out, pushing at the leather. His fingers clawed at it, and he gasped for breath as he stared at his facsimile. "H-how is this possible? Th-that there are two of me?"

"You really don't know?" His lips curled in anger. "Do you all live in ignorance?"

Another voice interrupted them, echoing down a dark hallway. "Craig! Is he here already? Are you boring him to death?"

The man gave a heavy sigh, but Damian's entire body sang at the intrusion. "Alena? Are you okay?" He pushed past his duplicate, dress shoes hammering loudly on the wooden floors. A figure at the other end of the hall came into view, leaning against the wall, just as he ran out of leash. With a startled yelp, he fell backward onto the floor.

"Of course I'm not fine," the woman said when he peered up at her. "Now I've got two of you to deal with."

The person slouched against the wall was Alena, but she wasn't *his* Alena. Unwashed hair hung in limp strands around her face, and stained sweatpants fit loosely around her waist.

She's not wearing underwear was all Damian could think as the woman lifted a glass to her mouth and drained it of amber liquid.

"Follow me." She pushed herself off the wall and disappeared into another room. "I need a refill."

A hand settled on Damian's sore shoulder. He jumped at the touch, fearing Adrian's return. It was only his duplicate, though. *Alena referred to him as Craig? He's going by my middle name?* Not nearly as strong as the Guardian, he gestured down the hall while pulling the chain upward. "Move it."

"I don't think I can." Damian's stomach turned, and his head felt light. *This is our old apartment. It's different, though, just like these versions of Alena and me.* He was certain he'd throw up at any moment.

"We're just going to the kitchen." Craig continued to point down the hall. When Damian didn't budge, he pounded a fist against the wall. "You're in no danger here, except maybe from the truth."

"Is that really Alena?" Damian asked, stumbling to his feet. He inched down the hall, elbows pressed into his sides. He wanted to turn and flee, to escape the nightmare, but he thought that opening the front door would instigate another painful peregrination.

"Who else would it be?" Craig huffed from behind, prodding him forward.

Unlike the foyer, dark and disused, the kitchen surprised him with its familiarity. It was larger than the one he and Alena—*my Alena*—shared in Chicago, allowing for more than one person to maneuver with ease. It lacked the decor that made the original homey, and while not dirty, the empty liquor bottles lined up along the counter kept it from being warm.

"Again, excuse the state," Craig said as they entered. "I can barely keep up with the clutter she creates, and we were only told of your arrival a few minutes ahead of time."

"Shut up and sit down." Alena pointed at a small dining table in the far corner of the room. A cheap lamp hung from the ceiling. It would've been a dismal scene if not for a small window overlooking Acheron. *Not that the view comforts me.* With her drink topped off, she dropped into one of the four seats surrounding the table. "Tell me again why they brought him here?"

"Because of what's in the basement." Craig ground his teeth, an unsettling sound that sent a fresh wave of nausea through Damian. "Deal with it. Things will be better tomorrow."

In a daze, Damian let his duplicate lead him across the room and shove him into a chair. Then Craig sat back in his own, crossing his legs and fingering the chain leash.

"Look at this." Alena leaned forward, the ice in her drink clinking as she pointed between the two of them. "Two versions of you, *both* dressed to the nines. Never thought I'd see the day."

Damian peered over at Craig, admiring how his clothes fit in such a way as to hide his stomach bulge. *My suit is soaked with sweat and covered in grass stains.* Then he glanced at Alena, who appeared so familiar—*but so, so different, like crossing paths with an acquaintance from high school in the grocery store*. "Is this a dream?"

"Oh, this is real," Craig said, letting the chain leash slip from his fingers. It fell, clattering to the wooden floor. "What do you think happens to a person's soul when they die?"

Damian shook his head, half expecting a version of Bennett to appear and climb into the empty seat. *How old does he appear now? A teenager? Probably still all knees and elbows.* The thought of his family's predicament brought tears to his eyes. "Where are they? Where's my wife and child?"

"No!" Craig said, snapping his fingers just as Alena's eyes narrowed. "I asked you a question. What happens to a person's soul?"

"I don't know." Damian forced himself to focus. "I expected nothing after death. Don't we just get sorted out to wherever we deserve?"

"You don't believe that. I know because *I* didn't expect to wake up here next to that." His duplicate pointed at Alena. "Thankfully, there are plenty of other things to occupy my attention."

"I don't understand." Damian gestured around the table. "Then...how?"

The drunken Alena slammed her glass down on the table. "When Damian—*the* Damian—died in the park, his soul got sucked up into a great big brass machine and split in two. Now there's Good Damian and Bad Damian—or Craig or whatever—and the machine sent each along to their corresponding destinations."

Everyone burns in Hell, Adrian had said. Damian tugged at his collar, suddenly twice as irritating. His mind reeled. "But I felt no more good than I did before."

"Bold of you to assume *you're* our good half!" His counterpart struck a palm against the table, then bent over and grabbed the leash. "Ever stop to consider you're not all that great, either?"

"Perhaps neither of us are our best representation." Damian pressed his body back into the chair. Watching Craig's wild gesticulations, he wanted to be on the other side of the kitchen. "Who decides what is good and evil? This brass machine?"

"No." Alena belched, then answered, "You do."

"I didn't believe in good and evil before death." Damian tried to turn toward her, but found he could barely move. The leather collar had somehow attached itself to the chair. A glance at Craig, who grinned maniacally while fiddling with the metal chain, told him there was more to the accessory. Refusing to give his other half any satisfaction, Damian endured the inordinate effort it took to turn his head to Alena. She rewarded the struggle by getting up to grab a bottle of whiskey from the kitchen counter. "Good and bad *people*, maybe, but not—"

"And wouldn't you agree people are a mixture of good and bad?" He heard the refrigerator door open and ice cubes clinking into her glass.

"Sure. I did plenty of things I consider bad through my—"

"Who made that call?" Craig stood up as well, his chair sliding back against the wall. His voice rose as he asked, "Who decided the morality of our actions? Of our thoughts? Who we were?"

Damian hesitated, shaken. The chain between them pulled taut. "We did."

"Yes! Good and evil aren't some divine mandate. They're what each person believes about themselves. What they hide. What they embrace."

With a fresh drink in hand, Alena fell back into her chair. "Did you know my family is full of alcoholics? That *I'm* an alcoholic? No, of course you didn't. I was too ashamed to tell you, afraid you'd leave me."

"No. I—I didn't know." Damian's lip—his entire jaw—quivered at the revelation.

"Thought I escaped the family curse for the longest time." She traced the rim of her glass with a finger, glaring at them both. "But then you refused to have children. Wouldn't even talk to me about it. So I found refuge in whiskey for a while. Eventually got a handle on it. Drank a lot of tea instead. But then that pen came along and killed me. Now I'm here, the manifestation of my own dark secret."

She was always so calm, so steadfast. She was my rock, but I broke her down with my own wants. "I'm so sorry."

"Don't apologize to her," his doppelgänger said. He was still standing, peering out the window overlooking Acheron. "She's also an incredibly selfish bitch."

Damian waited for her to object. *His* Alena wouldn't take the verbal abuse. Instead, she raised her glass and glanced around the kitchen. "It's true. I wanted a small place, not a big house like you. I have no intention of leaving here."

Alena fell silent, her righteousness having drained any energy the alcohol left behind. As she stared into her amber drink, Damian coaxed his head over to his double. *What parts of myself did I hide away? What was I ashamed of?*

"I don't have a good reason to be angry with you," Craig said, noticing him in the window's reflection. He turned around, pulling at a stray thread on his jacket. "It's not your fault that I'm here, or mine that you ended up in the Afterlife. Still, seeing you in person, there's nothing I want more than to hurt you for all eternity."

I recall the anger. I hated being poor, especially when my best friend was so well-off. Hated my parents for holding me back. Alena's death had sent him spiraling into a fury at the entire world. Throughout his entire life, though, he'd tamped down on his anger, afraid others would think him crazy and lock him up. *Now that side of me has done exactly that.*

"I recognize that look," Craig said with a wink. "There's more to me than anger and irritation and a better wardrobe. A lot more, but I'll let what's in the basement inform you."

"Why? What's in the basement?" A horrible thought crossed Damian's mind, and his throat tightened. "You're not keeping Mom there, are you?"

The duplicate's face went blank. "Mom? Why would she be here?"

"She died. In the same accident we did." Damian tried and failed to keep more tears from pooling on his lower eyelid. "She's here in Acheron. I received a letter from her a few days ago."

"I didn't know. Haven't seen her, and I don't care to. She deserves every terrible thing she gets." Craig shrugged, walking around the table and behind Damian. The metal chain rattled as if he wasn't sure what to do with it, then he let the length fall heavily to the floor. "If you'll excuse me, I have work to do."

Alena's glass clinked against her teeth. "What're you doing again?"

"Raising Gehenna from the deep."

"What?" Now that Craig wasn't holding the leash, it was easier for Damian to move. He turned his head so he could see the other man, who'd moved further into the kitchen.

"Raising the Lake of Fire." He said it slowly and mimicked turning a crank. "It's subterranean, sitting underneath the castle. Too hot to keep at surface level. Takes a lot of us to bring it up."

Damian attempted to push back from the table and stand. The collar kept him in his seat, steadfastly attached to the chair. "You're working with Adrian?"

"They came to me, which was quite an honor." Craig moved back toward the hallway. "Even if it's manual labor."

"You're leaving me with him?" Alena yelled after him.

"Just take him to the basement. He'll learn a few things about himself," Craig called back. "Kisses!"

The front door opened and slammed shut, leaving Damian alone with his—*our? his?*—wife.

Alena pushed her glass away, then heaved herself out of the seat. Grabbing hold of his leash, she pulled him to his feet. They both wavered unsteadily. "Come on. Let's get this over with."

"How can you be a part of this?" Damian gripped the edge of the table, hands trembling as he found his balance. "The Alena I know would never—"

"Yeah, well, my other has a child. Not sure how that happened. *And* she doesn't know about Gehenna. There are fates far worse than a true and permanent death." She gave the chain a sharp tug, and together they shuffled across the kitchen and down the hall, the floorboards creaking under their feet. "Much worse."

This close to her, Damian smelled the whiskey on her breath. Still, he leaned in closer when she muttered something about being stuck forever with someone she despised. He didn't ask her to elaborate.

In the foyer, Alena jabbed at a button on the wall beside the door. They stood in uncomfortable silence for half a minute, Damian wondering what they were waiting for. *If this is like our old place, there's a narrow set of stairs on the other side.* A harsh buzz sounded. Alena yanked the door open, revealing not a stairwell but an industrial elevator cage. Rust spots dotted its black metal frame, and the floor grating had worn thin in places. She gestured forward. "After you."

Damian stepped onto the platform, which shifted under his weight with a disquieting groan. He watched as Alena pressed a button marked *B6*. "I don't understand."

She sighed, raising a hand to her mouth before remembering she'd left her drink at the kitchen table. "What don't you understand?"

"If souls split when we die," Damian said, watching the elevator's decaying doors close, "why have I only heard from one version of my mother?"

Alena relaxed against the wall, her shoulders slumping. "Your mother is a special case. There's not a lot of her kind, but it happens from time to time."

With a grinding of metal, the elevator lurched downward. Damian almost fell forward into Alena, but caught his balance by grabbing a corroded bar. He kept a firm grip, afraid his hands might slip outside the cage. The outer wall, made up of haphazardly placed bricks, sped by at an alarming rate. "How so?"

"Listen, there's a hierarchy in Acheron." Alena went silent for several moments, closing her eyes. Damian thought she'd fallen asleep, but she eventually continued. "Adrian and their Guardians sit at the top, obviously. Then there are people like me and Craig, first-class citizens."

The elevator creaked as it continued its descent, the air growing thicker with each floor they passed. Damian saw sequential numbers painted on doors. The apartment they'd left behind was 25. "And my mother?"

"Some people consider themselves to be so completely awful that their souls can't split." Alena's eyes opened, and she stared at him. "They judge themselves to be wholly heinous. No good to separate out."

"That's ridiculous. Mom wasn't evil. Sure, she had her faults. Certainly didn't like you, but—"

"It's not about what others think." Alena's voice no longer carried its usual slurred quality, and her eyes appeared more focused. "It's what they believe about themselves. Anyway, it's people like your mom that sit right below us. Bad, but not *that* bad."

Damian quieted as the cage passed a door marked *Lobby*, followed by *B1* and *B2*. The elevator finally came to a grinding halt at *B6*. Someone had propped a chair against the door, keeping it open. He stared into the darkness beyond. "How can anyone feel that way about themselves?"

"You'd be surprised what people hide." Alena stepped out of the elevator, swiping at a switch in the darkness. Fluorescent lights flickered to life, revealing industrial metal grating lining both sides of a long hallway. She pulled at his leash, forcing him out of the cage. "Come on. There's something down here you want to see."

Damian's dress shoes—*my incredibly scuffed dress shoes*—sounded against the concrete floor. He glanced around, recalling a similar setup in the basement of their old apartment building. *The grating keeps curious residents away from boilers and ventilation systems.* As they walked along the corridor, movement behind some fencing caught his eye.

"Wait." He stepped closer. The pale face of a young woman peered back at him. She had hollow eyes and wore a leather collar around her neck. "There are people in here."

"Welcome to the bottom of the hierarchy." Alena's voice echoed off the walls. "The mistakes."

"Mistakes?"

"Good souls that ended up here by accident." She gestured at the cells lining the hall. "Like you."

Damian's flesh broke out in goosebumps as he pressed closer to the metal mesh. He found a handle, tried wrenching the door open, but found it locked. The pale woman didn't budge from the far corner of her prison. Only stared back at him. He reluctantly moved on.

Just one basement—one of at least six—in a random apartment building in Acheron. How many of these people are here, imprisoned in darkness and used for who knows what?

"How did they get here?" he asked.

"Same way you did. The Sphere of Doom has caused havoc for thousands of years." Alena shrugged dismissively. "Or the machine malfunctioned. I don't know. Souls sometimes just end up in the wrong place."

"Can't they appeal? Get transferred?"

The alternate Alena laughed for the first time. The sound was familiar, pulling at Damian's heart, yet simultaneously off-putting. "You really think Adrian cares about petitions? These people are stuck here. Forever. Unless they fall into Gehenna."

Damian's stomach churned as he looked down the row of cells. *Anyone could end up here by accident.* I'm *here by accident. Is this where I'm to spend eternity? In a dark cage in a subbasement?*

They walked on, further away from the elevator. Only two other faces peeked out from behind the grating. An elderly man stuck his weathered fingers through the mesh, and a young boy sat cross-legged, back against the cinderblock wall.

"What's going to happen to me?" Damian asked.

Alena pulled a set of keys out of her baggy sweatpants. "Adrian handed you over to us for safekeeping."

"You mean imprisonment."

"Don't be so dramatic." She stopped at the end of the hallway, selecting a key from the ring. "It's temporary. We'll be heading to the castle shortly. I'm sure they have nicer accommodations."

Damian imagined his other half, who'd likely arrived at the structure looming over Acheron, bent over a winch. *I hope he's sweating through his suit, too.*

"First things first." She gestured to the cell in front of them, then slipped the key into its lock. The door groaned as she pulled it open. "You get to spend some time with an old friend. Someone you made a pact with in your youth."

Damian stumbled into the cell, his shoulder catching the edge of the doorframe as Alena shoved him forward. She tossed the leash in after him, then slammed the door shut. He heard her turn and trek back toward the elevator.

A figure shifted in the shadows just out of the fluorescent light's reach. Damian's breath caught as another person lifted their head. Even in rags, he immediately recognized his friend Colin.

CHAPTER TWENTY-THREE

Alena's footsteps echoed down the corridor, keys jangling as she tossed them in the air. Damian barely registered her departure, focused entirely on Colin. Even outside the harsh lighting, he saw Colin's face was ashen, with dark circles under red eyes. The rags draped around his frail body appeared unwashed.

"Colin?" His tongue felt thick in his mouth. He stumbled forward, nearly tripping over his leash. "I should've known you'd end up here, too. When did you get to the Embassy? Where's Wendell?"

Eyes wide with terror, Colin pressed himself against the far wall. "No. No, you can't be here! You're not him. You're the *good* one. I can see it."

Damian paused, struggling to process Colin's words. *None of this makes any sense!* Then he heard the clinking of a metal chain as the other man inched away from the wall. It hung from a thick collar around his neck. Damian slumped back against the door. "Oh, you're not my Colin."

"I am!" The man—*no, he looks even more like a teenage boy than the other*—crawled into the light. The terror in his eyes subsided, though another fear shone through. "Or at least I was supposed to be. Why aren't you safe in the Afterlife?"

"I was an hour ago." Damian's limbs shook. He wanted to slide down the mesh door to the concrete, but the sight of Colin crawling across the ground in dirty rags kept him on edge. *It's a scene right out of a horror film.* "The Sphere of Doom transported me here, along with a hundred others. I suppose you know all about that."

"I do!" Colin nodded his head several times, an awkward movement as he stared up at Damian. "I've been told about the plan many times. About my part in the scheme. Did you get my messages?"

Damian frowned. "What messages?"

Colin tilted his head to the side, then said, "19-22-15-11 14-22, 23-26-14-18-26-13."

"That was *you?*" Damian finally let his body fall to the floor. He stared at his friend—*or what looks like my friend.*

"11-15-22-26-8-22 19-22-15-11 14-22." Colin pushed up off his hands, leaning back on his knees. "Please help me."

"It was you on the whale? And mimicking Sybok?"

"Huh?" Colin's face scrunched up, then his eyes widened. "Oh! In your dreams! I only passed along the messages and hoped she'd send them. We had no control over how you interpreted them. Couldn't even be certain you'd picked them up. It was a risk, and we took a different approach to warn you about me."

"We?" Something clicked in Damian's mind as he stared into Colin's bloodshot eyes. "It was you who sent me that letter, not my mother."

"I sent the words along." He nodded quickly again, reaching out with a shaky hand. "Are you here to save me?"

"Save you?" Damian backed up against the grating, suppressing the urge to swipe the man's hand away. "You stole my mother's last words! You distracted me when I needed to focus on more important things. I don't know what parts of yourself you considered evil, and I'm not here to save you."

"Evil? You think I'm evil?" Colin fell back on his rear, affronted. He grabbed at his collar with one hand, rattling the attached chain in the other while pointing at Damian. "Do you know what this means in Acheron?"

"Yes..." *Too much information. I don't understand. I don't* want *to understand!* But Craig's words cut through the fog: *Everyone of your status gets one.* "No, this can't be. You're lying."

"I didn't replace your mother's letter. How could I do that from here?" Colin let go of his restraints to gesture at the cell. "She was here. Snuck in. Found me and took my words."

"What?" Damian's head whipped around, scanning their dire surroundings, hoping his mother would step out of the shadows. *She's here! She's a*—he wanted to say she was alive—*well, she's not gone forever!*

"She broke our code." Colin shook his head in mock disappointment. "I gave her only the numbers, but she said she'd figured it out the last time she visited."

"How'd she get in here? What were you trying to warn me about?"

The lights went out—*Alena's heading back up to the apartment*—obscuring Colin's face. The hum of electricity ceased. All he could hear now was his own labored breathing.

"Tell me, my friend," Colin said in the dark. "Do you remember the pact of our youth?"

"That's what, fifteen wins in a row?" Colin stretched his long frame across his queen bed, arms crossed behind his head. "You're supposed to get better, not worse."

"It was only thirteen." Damian let the Xbox controller slip from his fingers as he stood up, careful not to knock over a pile of empty Dr. Pepper cans. His butt had gone numb from sitting cross-legged on the carpet for hours. "I don't even like Halo."

"Lies!" Colin laughed, the sound bouncing off the cathedral ceiling. The home's architect had meant the room—Colin's *bedroom*—to be an extensive media room above the garage. With space to hold all the tech gadgets he desired, he'd co-opted it a year ago. It had the added benefit of being farther down the hall from his parents' bedroom.

"Whatever." Damian checked his digital watch. In the low light of the room, most of which came from the television, he squinted at the faint readout. 11:47 PM. "Crap, I need to head home."

"At this hour?" Colin sat up. "There's still snow on the roads. Just crash here. My folks won't care."

"Mine will." Damian stumbled, catching himself on Colin's desk. His legs tingled as normal blood flow returned.

"You can barely walk. How're you gonna drive?"

Damian grabbed the keys to the Buick his parents had gifted him a week before off the desk. "You know my mom. She's probably already called the police."

"That's messed up." Colin swung his long legs over the bed. "They track you like you're on parole or something."

"Tell me about it." Damian shook his own legs, felt like he had control over them again, and crossed the room to the bedroom door. "If they could afford a cell phone, they'd make me call whenever I came and left, along with confirmation that your parents will be close by."

"Stay. We'll deal with them tomorrow." Colin's voice lowered. "I've got the new Gears of War game. We could try it out."

Damian's hand rested on the doorknob. He would already disappoint his parents by returning so late, but they'd be furious if he rolled up in the driveway the next morning. "Can't. You know how they are."

"I would really like it if you'd stay," Colin said, placing a gentle hand on his shoulder.

Still facing the door, Damian froze. The gesture was friendly enough, but they rarely made physical contact. *He's standing so close. So close.* Warmth spread across his back, down into his abdomen. His heart hammered loudly in his ears as Colin turned him around.

"My parents are close by, but not too close." Colin's voice dropped to a whisper. His brown eyes stared down into Damian's, the glow of the television screen turning them amber.

Damian's mouth went dry, but his palm grew slick against the doorknob, which he still gripped. He caught the scent of Colin's cologne. *Something expensive. Something his parents bought him*, he couldn't help but think, to distract himself from the physical contact. The closeness.

"You okay?" Colin asked.

"Not sure," he said. His friend was—*we are?*—crossing a line they'd drawn years ago through unspoken agreement. They'd always maintained a careful distance from one another, even during their gaming marathons. Now the line was gone.

Colin lowered his head. Their lips grazed against each other. Blood rushed to Damian's ears. His legs, so recently numbed from sitting, were now weak for entirely different reasons. Colin's presence overwhelmed him, and the room spun with possibilities he'd never allowed himself to consider.

The moment stretched, fragile. Damian's breath caught as Colin shifted closer, eliminating what little space remained between them, pressing him against the door. His fingers slipped from the doorknob, his last lifeline, finding their way around Colin's waist, pulling him even closer. Years of careful distance evaporated as heat spread between them.

Colin's fingers traced up the back of his neck and became entangled in his hair. The touch was electric, and everything else fell away as Colin deepened the kiss. His disapproving parents, his religious notions, the carefully constructed walls he'd built around these feelings. *None of it matters. This feels right.*

Colin's lips tasted like Dr. Pepper. His solid frame pressed Damian against the door, grounding him even as his head spun. Damian's fingers clutched the other's shirt, afraid to let go. Afraid the moment might end.

When they finally broke apart, both breathing heavily, Colin kept his forehead pressed to Damian's. His hand remained warm on Damian's shoulder, thumb tracing small circles that made him shiver.

"Do you wanna stay the night?" Colin asked, gesturing toward the bed with a tilt of his head.

"I stayed the night," Damian said into the dark that engulfed him and Colin. "I didn't remember—didn't *want* to remember—until now, but I stayed with you."

"Yes." Colin's voice came from across the room. He'd retreated as the memories bubbled to the surface of Damian's mind. "How about the next morning?"

Damian remained still for several moments, reaching into the past. He remembered opening his eyes, the winter light filtering through half-closed blinds. Colin's warm breath against his neck, arm draped across his chest, the weight both foreign and familiar.

"I saw our clothes spread across the floor." Damian's hands balled into fists. "I was frozen in panic. All the barriers we'd broken down were back, strengthened by fear."

"Did you regret what we did?"

Damian shook his head, realizing it was a fruitless gesture in the dark. "I think...I've had many feelings about that night in the years since, including shame. But I don't think I ever regretted it."

"Not even when you got home?"

"I was so scared, I considered driving into the ditch!" Damian barked a laugh. "Thought I could pretend I'd hit an ice patch and was unconscious all night. Didn't know how to fake a bump on the head, though."

Damian heard Colin slide across the floor again, the rough fabric of his clothing scraping unpleasantly against the concrete. "What did we talk about that morning?"

"You were great. Let me think for a while, then asked if I wanted to talk about it." Damian reached back as the memories continued reemerging, feeling like he was experiencing it for the first time all over again. "I wasn't sure what it meant for me—as a person, I mean. I wasn't gay, and I'd never thought of other guys in that way before. You...you understood. Told me I didn't have to figure it all out right then."

"And the pact?"

"You asked—and I agreed—that if I ever figured things out, found I was queer, that I'd tell you and...and we'd give it a go. Be there for one another.

Protect each other." Damian gulped. "It wasn't an 'if we're still single in ten years' type of promise. I loved you. Knew I loved you. I just wasn't sure how."

We didn't have ten years. Not even a month. Only three weeks passed before Damian climbed into Colin's BMW. Before they *did* drive through a ditch.

"I'm glad you remember." Colin sighed contentedly, as though he'd been waiting years to hear Damian say those words.

"But why didn't I until now?"

Colin's chains clanked. "Maybe you were ashamed of that night. If you were so scared of that part of yourself, it probably split off into your other half when you died."

"I was scared, sure," Damian said, the chill of the concrete seeping into his bones. "But not enough to foist it onto a separate persona. I don't think it was shame. No, it was guilt for making a pact for a future you never got to experience. The pain of your death was too much. I must've locked that part away."

"Know that I'm not angry about it. I'm glad we got that night before the accident." Colin shifted his position. "Judging by my friendly upstairs neighbors, I assume you eventually found someone to build a life with. I hope Alena wasn't anything like the version I've experienced."

"The one here is a mere shadow." Damian's heart ached at the thought of his wife and Bennett, captured and held by dark forces. He clenched his fists again, knowing he couldn't do a thing to help them. "My Alena is kind and thoughtful. I've never seen this side of her before."

"If that's the case, then I'm glad you found her." Colin's leash jingled. "We all died too young."

At the sound of the leash, Damian's stomach dropped in sudden realization. "No."

"Well, I can't speak for you, but I certainly died way too early."

"No. No!" Damian repeated, refusing to believe the reality his mind was piecing together for him. *The end is always harder when brought about by a friend.*

"What?"

"You're the good Colin?"

The metal links clinked again as Colin nodded. "Yeah."

"So the other Colin, the one I've been working alongside, sharing meals with, confiding in...is your evil half?"

"I think evil is a rather harsh term."

Damian's thoughts whirled as the implications of the truth crashed over him. *Kasee never controlled the sphere. It was Colin! He gifted her the desk with a broken drawer, a perfect place to hide the relic if need be. He* pretended *to catch a decoy on Irvin, feigning a struggle with the true sphere.*

Every moment of camaraderie since arriving in the Afterlife—the meals, the help with procuring a job in the DSI, and all the advice and condolences—had been with a corrupted version of his best friend. Colin had been intent on bringing down the Celestial City the entire time.

And Anthony? Damian saw the pale, willowy man, surly but compliant, in a new light. In life, the long sleeves and baggy clothes might've suggested physical abuse. Bruises and broken bones weren't concerns in the Afterlife, *but perhaps he'd suffered similar treatment?*

Damian's throat constricted. "No, after what Colin's done, I don't think calling him evil is too harsh."

"I suppose I was trying to be diplomatic toward myself."

"The Embassy believes Satan hid a dark soul in an individual the night of our accident. They theorized that the soul would then piggyback its way into the Afterlife upon the person's death. A twisted form of possession," Damian said, speaking more to himself than to his friend. "The Gray Ones were so focused on finding a separate entity within people like us, people under duress that night, they failed to see what was right in front of them."

At the mention of the Gray Ones, he remembered the pouch he'd tucked away into his jacket pocket. In the chaos since waking up in the meadow—*it feels like days have passed since the head ambassador's party*—he'd forgotten about the mysterious gift from the old crone.

Damian pulled out the pouch, the burlap fabric uncomfortably warm against his palms. Its contents vibrated as he unknotted the drawstring. He widened the opening, and a burst of light exploded out.

The darkness retreated, and Damian saw Colin throw an arm across his face. "What's that?"

A ball of light, the eye of the Gray Ones, floated out of the pouch. It hovered above his palm for a moment, then darted around their cell like a curious hummingbird, illuminating grimy concrete walls and the rusted metal mesh of the enclosure.

"It's okay. This thing belongs to some friends of mine." The orb completed its inspection of the prison and settled into a familiar circular pattern above their heads. He placed a hand on Colin's arm. With the light, he once again saw how emaciated Colin appeared. "How long have you been here?"

"I've only been in this basement since your wife died. She was curious about me from your stories." Colin kept a wary eye on the eye floating above them. "When she discovered my status, she made a deal to procure me."

Damian recoiled at the idea of buying and selling souls. That any part of Alena—good, evil, or anywhere in between—actively partook in the trade made him hate her for a moment.

"But I've been in Acheron since the accident," Colin said.

"Since we crashed the BMW? But you lived another year!"

Colin nodded. "April 19, 2008. I was so close to death that night. Adrian somehow initiated the mechanism that splits people's souls and forced my arrival in Acheron. When my earthly body actually died, I suspect the bureaucratic process saw there was already a soul here, assumed there'd been some paperwork mix-up along the way, and shipped my other half on to the Afterlife."

The ball of light tightened its orbit over them as if responding to Colin's words. Its glow intensified for a moment before returning to its steady luminescence.

Damian threw the burlap pouch into the corner, then slumped back against the cold metal. *I've been a fool. Not just since I died, but from the moment the BMW wrapped itself around the telephone pole. All those hours every day spent in the hospital, visiting someone I loved, a version of my best friend who would conspire to bring down the Celestial City. And now they've got Alena and Bennett held hostage.*

It wasn't just the fate of him and his family on the line, though. All of Creation hung in the balance with what would transpire over the next couple of hours.

I'm so small. Just one soul trapped in a basement cell. In Hell, of all places, one of countless planes of existence. Even if I escape this building, get out of Acheron, the path into the Celestial City is locked. There's nothing I can do.

As if sensing his despair, the orb of light swooped over him. It hovered over his shoulder, pulsing soothingly. Damian pulled his knees to his chest, making himself even smaller. *Even this gift from the Gray Ones is useless. What good is light if it can't help me reach the ones I love?*

Colin's chain leash clinked as he scooted alongside Damian, leaning back against the grating. "Remember how you used to go on about Jurassic Park?"

Damian's head jerked up at the unexpected question. "Used to?"

"You kept telling me to read it, even though I'd already seen the movie." Colin laughed. "I finally gave in and borrowed a copy from you."

"Returned it with coffee stains all over it, too!"

"Had to stay awake. Those velociraptors were scary," Colin said. "Any other good ones from that author since I passed?"

"Crichton died around seven months after you—your physical body's death, anyway." Damian lowered his head. At the time, he felt the universe was determined to take away everything that mattered to him. "Plenty of books were released posthumously, though. There was one with pirates that was pretty good."

"*Timeline* was always my favorite. Scientists getting trapped in medieval France, jousting and sword fighting, making enemies with lords."

"Sounds fitting for our situation." Damian didn't care for the parallel between the book and their current predicament. "At least they ultimately found a way to return home."

A metallic grinding suddenly echoed throughout the basement. Both Damian and Colin froze as the elevator returned to B6. The Gray Ones' single eye blinked out, plunging them into darkness. Only for a moment, as the fluorescent lights overhead buzzed to life. Through the harsh glare, Damian spotted the orb tucking itself into a shadowy corner near the ceiling.

Footsteps reverberated down the hall. Damian recognized the uneven gait. After a minute, Alena appeared before their cell. She'd washed her hair and changed her clothes, trading the stained sweatpants for a sleek red dress. *She looks gorgeous*, Damian thought automatically. A faint whiff of whisky clung to her, reminding him of who she was. He noticed strands of hair sticking out at odd angles.

"How sweet," Alena said as the two stood, legs shaky after sitting on the cold floor. Her words slurred. "I hope the two of you enjoyed your brief reunion."

"What's going on?" Damian asked as she removed her keys from a clutch.

"It's happening sooner than I thought, but I'm taking *both* of you to the castle." She fumbled with the keys, finally slipping one into the lock. Her lips curled into an unsettling smile as she pulled the door open and gazed at them. "One of you won't be making it back out alive."

CHAPTER TWENTY-FOUR

ALENA KICKED OPEN THE front door of the apartment building, the heel of her high-heeled shoe nearly snapping off, and stepped out onto the street. She held a chain leash in each hand. They rattled as she gave them a sharp yank, forcing Damian and Colin to stumble after her.

Groups of people streamed past them toward the castle, laughing and making conversation. None gave the collared pair a second glance. *They're all off to see a show, and we're Alena's accessories.*

Damian climbed to his feet. No sun shone above, but the emerald sky appeared a few shades darker. In the moody light, the buildings loomed larger, their pointed edges decidedly more sinister than before.

They were exactly where Adrian had pushed him into a painful peregrination, a few blocks away from the bridge Damian had last seen his Embassy coworkers crossing. Like the one outside the city wall, it passed over a deep moat. He hadn't noticed before, but orange light flickered along the sides of the trench. The temperature noticeably rose as they neared.

"Are you okay?" Damian asked, glancing over at Colin. *How long has it been since he stretched his legs? We must look a sight, me in a grimy suit and him in rags.*

His friend nodded, albeit glumly. "It's nice to see a sky again."

"How about you?" Damian looked ahead at their escort. Alena was having difficulty navigating the growing crowd along the bridge in her heels. When she didn't respond, he dared to peek over the side. Instead of traversing oily, lethargic water, their path crossed over raging fires. "Is this Craig's work? Is this Gehenna?"

"Not even close." Alena pulled hard on their leashes again. Damian's neck chafed where the leather dug into his skin. "Now shut up."

The castle doors stood open. It might've been welcoming if not for the darkness beyond, making the facade appear like a hungry mouth gobbling up all who entered. People fell silent as they passed over the threshold. Only a few sported *pets* like Damian and Colin, and those who did only possessed one. None of the slaves—*for that is what we are*—looked eager to enter.

"Have you been inside before?" Damian asked Colin. His friend didn't respond, and instead stared fixedly at the ground, face ashen.

Blackness pressed against them once they finally stepped inside the castle. Damian blinked rapidly, trying to adjust to the dim lighting. Unconsciously, he stuck close to Alena's side for comfort. The shapes of other people gradually emerged from the gloom, and he saw they'd entered a massive circular chamber. *It's like walking into a circus tent.* The space stretched upward, floor after floor of balconies ringing the central space. Figures leaned over the railings, features lost in shadow.

The air felt heavy. Damian heard grinding metal and labored breathing over the hushed crowd around the entrance. Standing on his toes, he saw twelve individuals operating winch wheels along the perimeter of the chamber. Heavy chains wrapped around the mechanisms, pulled up from holes in the floor. Each worker's movements were mechanical, driven by watchful Guardians standing behind them, hands resting on sword hilts.

Damian's breath caught when he spotted his doppelgänger among the dozen. He'd removed his dress clothes, which would've been impractical to wear for such labor, but had replaced them with a black rubber bodysuit. Sweat ran down his face, plastering his hair to his forehead.

What the hell is he wearing? He'd been on enough farms around Minade to know manual labor and rubber didn't mix. Many other workers wore similar garb, some entirely covered in gimp gear. *Is that sexual? It can't be voluntary!*

Though the twelve turned the winches with feverish zeal, Damian saw no evidence of their work. No fire. No lake of any kind. Just the endless turning of wheels and rattling of metal.

Intricately patterned stones made up the floor of the main chamber. There were no decorations or furniture. *No hoops, rings of fire, or dangerous animals.* A single beam of light illuminated—

Damian blinked, his skin heating beneath the collar. In the spotlight, standing in the middle of the vast room, was Adrian. *Well, one dangerous animal.* The Guardian appeared larger than life, their beauty more terrible within the castle than it'd been out on the streets. Power radiated from their form, and the smile on their face sent chills down his back.

Suddenly convinced Adrian was looking right at him, Damian fell back on his heels, behind the heads of other onlookers.

Alena pulled them through the crowd toward a bank of elevators. They were more like the one in the Hall of Hands than the rickety carriage from her apartment building. People packed the lines, clamoring to get a better view. The elevators worked efficiently, and they soon stood at the front of their line. When the door swung open, Alena shoved Damian inside. She jabbed the button for the top floor, then let go of his leash and stepped back out.

"Wait, where are you going?" Damian asked. The polished metal frame of the new cage reflected his frightened expression. *Why didn't she take me to join the other Embassy employees?*

"Slaves are stored at the top." She sneered at him, dark eyes cold. "They're encouraged to watch. Keeps them behaving, or else they'll get a similar fate."

Colin moved to enter the lift, but Alena kept his leash taut. "Nope, they've got other plans for you."

"They?" Damian lunged forward as she slammed the door shut. His arms poked through the bars, fingertips brushing against Colin's. "Where are you taking him?"

The only response Alena gave was a bitter smile. He knew with sudden certainty that he would never speak with Colin again. Their reunion was only meant to emphasize how much he'd lost—much of it for the second time.

"Avenger!" he said as the elevator ascended. "I'm sorry if I ever made you feel less than you are. I love you!"

"I love you, too, Flame!" Colin's tear-streaked face disappeared as the lift rose smoothly above the crowd.

Damian rocked back and forth as the floors ticked by, his own tears wetting his dirty jacket. He stared out into the chamber but saw nothing. Not even Adrian's figure, standing like a statue at the center of it all. When the lift stilled and a man in a crisp crimson uniform took hold of Damian's leash, he barely registered the action. He let the usher lead him along the curved balcony.

Other people—*other slaves*—already lined up along the edge, securely chained to the railing. Their condition and attire varied wildly. Some wore dresses and suit jackets in far better states than Damian's. Rags hung off the emaciated bodies of others. Leather or rubber encased a few. The majority, however, were naked. None of them made a sound. Their eyes were empty, robbed of humanity and thought.

"Here ya go," the usher said after walking Damian halfway around the chamber. As he secured the leash, Damian peered out over the circular chamber. Thousands of faces looked expectantly toward the center. "Enjoy the show."

The grinding of the winches echoed throughout the space, a steady mechanical heartbeat. Damian saw that the stone pattern of the chamber floor actually formed a glittering six-pointed star. Instead of the Celestial City sitting at its center, Adrian stood. They continued to stare at the castle entrance as the last few groups of people walked inside.

The doors eventually closed, cutting off most of the chamber's source of light. Everyone's eyes were now forced to turn toward the only illumination, the beam of light shining upon their master.

Adrian's form appeared to glow brighter as the last echoes of hushed conversation died away. They turned in a slow circle, head tilted up to take in every level of spectators. Damian's collar felt tighter as the Guardian's gaze swept past him. Even from this distance, their eyes pierced through him.

They see me through and through, Damian thought with certainty. *They're intimately familiar with every person here.*

"Under normal circumstances, this space and time would be used for our daily Orientation of the Damned." Adrian's voice carried effortlessly through the room, drowning out the winches as they continued pulling at heavy chains. "One of my fellow Guardians would stand here, explaining to newcomers the rules and expectations of their new existence. If lucky, there would be fuel to feed Gehenna's hungry flames."

Murmurs broke out across the room as Adrian paused. Damian wondered how the policies and promises—*perfection?*—differed from the Afterlife, but figured he'd eventually find out if he survived the day.

"Acheron is a beautiful city, the ideal representation of our domain. We have worked for eons to shape it as we see fit, and we deserve every bit of comfort we eke out of its existence. For all its wonder, though, it is still a prison for us all. We Guardians were first banished here, a punishment for daring to dream. To be more than what we were created for!"

Damian noticed dozens of Guardians appear throughout the crowd. Even in the low light, they were easy to spot as they towered over the other attendees. With the twelve paired with the humans working along the perimeter, he estimated all hundred were in attendance.

"You humans received a most unjust deal, too." Adrian's voice grew harder. "Over 110 billion of your souls live within our realm. Not whole souls, no. Only pieces split off from the original, deemed unworthy and tossed aside. You are leftovers. Those in the Afterlife look down on you with disgust because you represent what they hate most about themselves."

Shouts of angry agreement erupted, though the noise quickly died down. Damian's hands gripped the railing, knuckles turning white. *Nobody wants to interrupt Satan.*

"This ends today!" Adrian's voice continued to rise, booming throughout the chamber. "In a few hours, the path between Acheron and the Celestial

City will be opened. No more barriers. No more separation. You'll be free to choose for yourselves. Stay here in the home we have built. Walk the streets of the Celestial City. Venture into any universe you desire."

Adrian smiled, perfect teeth gleaming in the spotlight. "But first, we are going to force those who worked so hard—so *desperately*—to keep us locked away here to face justice."

The crowd erupted in enthusiastic cheers. The railing vibrated under Damian's hands. Even some of the vacant-eyed slaves around him showed signs of life, their faces lighting up, hoping to be forgotten by their masters.

With a flourish, Adrian strode out of the light and disappeared. A moment later, a deep rumbling shook the building. Everyone leaned forward. Damian gripped the railing tighter as cracks spread across the stone floor below. The six-pointed star split apart, five sections retracting to reveal a pit underneath.

Light erupted from the opening, bathing everyone in an orange glow. Heat rolled upward in waves. Even on the top level, Damian immediately broke out in a sweat. His damp, dirty clothes stuck to his skin.

The grinding of the winches grew louder. As the flooring disappeared, Damian saw what the workers had labored to raise: an enormous bronze bowl suspended by twelve thick chains. It reminded him of the weight plates on an old-fashioned scale. *Only this one's large enough to hold everyone in attendance.*

Instead of precious metals, fire raged inside the bowl. Flames licked hungrily at its rim, which glowed red where the fire touched it. *This castle is a well, the bowl a bucket.* Perspiration dripped into Damian's eyes. *This is only a small portion of Gehenna, drawn from an underground lake.*

Once the tips of the fires reached ground level, the workers secured their winches, preventing the heavy chains from slipping back. Damian saw his counterpart, drenched in sweat, glance at his Guardian overlord before sitting cross-legged on the floor. The chamber quieted again, except for the crackling of flame.

Movement near the entrance caught Damian's eye. A line of people emerged from an antechamber, many of whom he recognized from the meadow outside Acheron. They wore expressions of confused panic. Others had clearly been around longer, dressed in ragged clothing covered with filth. Some even had collars like his own. These individuals held their own chains, eyes filled with a mixture of fear and relief.

Guardians herded the group of nearly a hundred onto the section of flooring that hadn't retracted, which looked like a jagged shark tooth against the fire beneath. Damian stepped back as understanding struck. He'd thought the mechanism had failed to withdraw, a blemish on this choreographed production. *It's not just part of the floor. It's a stage. A plank. And they're being forced to walk off it.*

The prisoners huddled together on the tooth-shaped platform, their faces illuminated by the fierce orange lighting. Some wept openly, their tears sizzling as they splashed onto the hot ground. Others stood frozen in terror. A few tried to break away—*where would they escape to?*—but the Guardians forced them back with the tips of their swords.

Damian choked, unable to look away from the horror unfolding. It wasn't a performance, or an inconvenience like being locked away in the Dungeon of Darkness. This was a cruel and meaningless sacrifice. It was death. And nothing awaited these souls on the other side. *They've already suffered and died once. Now they're being erased.*

As the damned clustered along the edges of the plank, the first couple lost their footing and toppled over. They shouted in surprise, hands grasping upward, seeking help. None came, and their shouts turned to screams as they disappeared from view, tendrils of fire wrapped around their bodies.

The crowd roared in approval as the Guardians continued pushing the group back, their swords glinting red. A woman stumbled, her heel catching on the edge. Her arms windmilled as she fought for balance. A nearby Guardian gave a gentle push against her chest with their blade. She disappeared with a shriek.

Her fall triggered a cascade. Other prisoners scrambled away from the advancing Guardians and their terrible weapons, but there was no place to go. Bodies tumbled over the sides. Their screams echoed off the chamber walls, joining the roar of the flames.

Damian's legs shook, and bile rose in his throat. He wanted to look away. To close his eyes and block out the disgusting scene unfolding below. But he forced himself to watch the slaughter. *Someone—someone good—needs to remember this atrocity. Someone has to bear witness to their last moments.*

A dozen remained on the platform. An elderly man fell to his knees, hands clasped before him. "Please! I have grandchildren I want to see again. Show mercy!"

A Guardian's expression remained impassive as they kicked the man into the inferno.

The screams of the last few people echoed and faded as they, too, fell to the crackling flames. Silence fell over the chamber. The crowd leaned over the balcony railings, waiting for whatever came next.

They just witnessed the murder of a hundred people. Their own kind. And they want more.

Another figure emerged from the antechamber, and the crowd burst into frenzied cheers. Damian's stomach dropped. Still dressed in rags and wearing the leather collar, Colin stepped out onto the platform. The Guardians moved aside, lining up as the lone human soul walked to the pointed edge.

"No!" Damian screamed, but the cheers of the onlookers drowned out his voice. He lunged forward, grappling with the railing. Only the part of his brain that strove for self-preservation kept him from jumping over.

Colin turned his face upward, finding Damian on the top floor. A grim smile crossed his face as he stretched his balled-up hands out, moving them up and down in a circular pattern. *Like he's driving a car.*

Colin stepped off the edge. The flames swallowed him.

As the world exploded into a raucous uproar, Damian howled. He yanked against his restraints. The collar dug deeper into his flesh with each desperate pull, his leash gouging the railing every time he pulled it taut. He didn't care if he broke his neck. His best friend, the one person he could lean on in this dark, twisted plane of existence, had walked into oblivion.

By the time the crowd calmed, Damian had collapsed to the floor in exhaustion. He no longer possessed the strength to yell, though fresh tears continued to stream down his face. The other slaves around him sensed his pain—*likely understood it more than me*—and bowed their heads to him in commiseration.

Silence crept over the chamber. Through his grief, Damian sensed the restless energy of the crowd. Their leader—their *god*—had given them a rousing speech and promises of a bright future. Adrian had then walked offstage. The people came for a gruesome spectacle. In that, they were not disappointed.

But those promises now hung in the air, unfulfilled. Even though Adrian had said the state of the multiverse would change over the next couple of hours, the masses expected immediate results. With nothing happening before their eyes, they shifted toward boredom, whispering uncertainly to their neighbors.

Two Guardians opened the entrance, allowing emerald light to blend with the orange of the flames. The oppressive heat of Gehenna's fires still raged, but the bloodthirsty fervor of the spectators had dulled to disappointed mutters. People filed toward the exit.

The crimson-uniformed usher worked his way along the balcony, unlocking souls from the railing and leading them back to the elevators. Some of the captives' owners appeared to collect their property personally, leading them away with tight grips on their leashes.

Probably wondering how their stock is faring against others. Damian remained motionless on the floor, his chain still secured to the rail. His muscles ached from fighting against the restraints. His whole body hurt, but the pain felt distant, unimportant.

Footsteps approached, and a shadow fell across him. Damian lifted his head, expecting to see the usher. All the other slaves were gone, the relative emptiness of the space surprising him. He'd lost track of time in his despair, the surrounding events transpiring outside his awareness. Now it was just him and—

"Get up." Alena's voice cut through his fog of misery. She stood over him, arms folded over her red dress as she studied his tear-streaked face. A mixture of disgust and pity warred across her face, and her eyes appeared glassy.

Is she...sad?

Alena opened her mouth to speak again, but the only sound Damian heard was a harsh metallic *CLANG*. His wife's eyes rolled back, and she crumpled to the floor. Behind her stood another woman. She was taller and thinner than Alena, dressed in a long skirt, and wore her hair up in a tight bun. Clenched in one hand was a frying pan.

"Mom?" Damian's voice faltered.

"I must admit I've always wanted to do that."

The pan clattered to the ground, the sound echoing through the now-empty chamber. Damian stared at his mother in disbelief as she rushed forward, fumbling with a ring of keys.

"We don't have much time." Her hands shook as she tried to fit different keys into the lock securing his leash to the railing. Her sharp features, now even more angular than he remembered, were tight with concentration. "And I need to return these keys to the usher before he wakes up."

"How'd you find me?" The groaning of metal almost drowned out Damian's question. The twelve human workers had resumed their work at the winches, lowering the bronze basin holding a portion of Gehenna—*and Colin's remains*—back into the depths.

"I'm your mother. I'll always find you." She bit her tongue as she stared at the lock, trying another key. It clicked open, and she yanked the chain free of the railing. "Got it."

"I'm so sorry, Mom." Fresh tears wet Damian's cheeks as he stumbled to his feet. "The accident. I killed us both."

She towered above him but held his face between the palms of her hands, a familial gesture he was unaccustomed to. "Oh, Damian. It *was* an accident. You didn't kill anyone."

"But you're here."

"It was my decision to come to Acheron." She drew him into an embrace. It was another token she rarely doled out, but he fell into it weeping. "I did it to protect you. And Alena."

Despite the situation, Damian barked a laugh. His wife's crumpled form a few feet away made for a compelling counterargument. "And Bennett."

His mother stepped back, peering down at him with curious eyes. "A grandchild?"

Damian nodded. "It's hard to explain, but we adopted him a few days ago and he's already grown into a teenager. You'd like him. He's so skinny, just like you. I...I love him."

"I'm so proud of you, Damian." She gripped his shoulders. One was still sore from Adrian's firm grasp earlier, but he ignored it. "I wasn't good at showing it, but I've always been proud of you. I wish I could join you and your family."

"They've been captured." He glanced over the balcony. Not only was Gehenna being lowered, but the tooth-shaped sections of the stone floor were sliding back into place, preparing to hide evidence of any atrocity. "They're being held, and I can't do a thing to help them."

"Do you know where they're at?"

Damian nodded again. "I'm pretty sure I know exactly where they are."

"Good." His mother pulled him close again and whispered into his ear. "I'm sorry it had to be this way, but we're out of time. Know that I've always loved you. I always will."

Then she shoved him backward. Damian felt his body smash into the railing. His momentum carried him over, and he plummeted toward the bottom of the chamber. Above him, his mother peeked over the railing, sorrow etched across her face. A hand reached out, and a bright ball of light soared after him.

As his body turned, Damian saw empty balconies pass by him, then the scorching flames of Gehenna between the narrowing sections of the floor. He screamed as he sailed right into one chasm, missing the jagged edge of a moving slab by a foot, and fell into the fire.

CHAPTER TWENTY-FIVE

Heat seared through Damian's body. Muscles seized, and he steeled himself at the prospect of flesh burning away, revealing bones before they disintegrated into ash. His lungs filled with—

Damian sneezed. He cracked an eyelid, finding himself once more lying face down in a field of grass. Like the park in Minade, the grass was short and dotted with dandelions. The seeds of a mature plant, a puffball, were floating down upon him, tickling his nose. He propped himself up on his side, head throbbing as though he'd spent a long night out drinking. A hundred other people sprawled across the field in various states of consciousness.

A wall enclosed the area, high enough to keep prying eyes away. Beyond it, the familiar spires of the Celestial City's skyline rose into an amber sky. The towers of Acheron were nowhere to be seen.

"Please remain calm." Several Guardians traversed the field. They wore their typical stern expressions, but gave no hints of aggression. None of them brandished a sword. "You have returned to the Afterlife and are safe."

"Questionable." Damian pushed himself into a sitting position, the pain behind his eyes lessening. To the side of the Celestial Palace, around where the

Embassy would be located, he saw the recognizable pink hue of a shrinking. *It hasn't been reversed yet.*

A nearby woman retched into the grass. Damian recognized her as the one in heels, the first to fall into Gehenna. She cowered as a Guardian approached her, offering her a cup.

Damian scoured the meadow, finding other familiar faces in the crowd. *If we're all here, then Colin should be too!*

"Water?"

Damian jumped, then looked up at a Guardian offering him a cup. He accepted it with trembling hands. His throat burned as he swallowed, washing away the lingering taste of smoke.

"Where are we?" he asked, allowing the Guardian to help pull him to his feet. His voice came out raspy.

"We stand outside the Celestial City, of course."

The answer gave Damian pause. The sight of the city did comfort him, though. No transparent dome encased it, barring his entry.

"I'm not dead?" He stretched his muscles, the fatigue that'd plagued him for several hours melting away. The chain leash no longer weighed him down, and the leather collar had vanished. On the ground next to him, the bracelet Adrian had given him lay broken.

The Guardian shrugged. "A mere technicality. Someone from the Department of Rehabilitation will be along shortly. They will answer your questions."

Damian watched as the Guardian moved on to another person, materializing a fresh cup of water in their hands.

I don't know how, but we're back in the Afterlife. Colin has to be around here somewhere. Damian scanned the surroundings again with a keener eye, looking for his tall friend. While plenty of those around him wore tattered bits of clothing, the familiar outline of Colin wasn't among them. He spotted a gathering of humans huddled around some tables in the middle of the field, though, all dressed in decidedly cleaner clothing.

I can save Alena and Bennett! The joyful thought energized him, and he ran toward the group. His body no longer weighed him down, and he didn't have to breathe again. Only minutes ago, he'd been holding his breath, falling into smoke and fire, looking up at his mother... *Can't think about that now. She knew what she was doing.*

"Thank you, Mom," he whispered.

A man stepped toward Damian as he neared the group, holding out a blanket. "Welcome back, sir. Can you tell me how long you were gone?"

"Only a few hours. I was part of the Embassy group." He waved away the offered blanket. "Department of Satanic Investigations."

"DSI?" A woman with a sharp jaw and yellowing hair came up behind the man. "Do you know how you ended up in Acheron? That the Sphere of Doom pulled you in?"

When Damian nodded, she pulled him into the middle of the group, out of earshot of the other victims in the field. "I'm Ambassador Houch of the Department of Rehabilitation. Can you tell me about your return passage? Has Satan figured it out, or is it still a secret?"

"I'm not sure what you mean, but I fell into Gehenna just before ending up here." *No, my mother pushed me in.* "The flames should've destroyed me."

"Gehenna isn't exactly what everyone thinks it is." Houch glanced around, lowering her voice. "It's actually a portal. In creating Hell, the Creator suspected Satan would dispose of any good souls who may have accidentally found themselves in the wrong place. In providing the Fallen a method with which to dispose of those souls—"

"A secret escape route." Damian's eyes widened as he imagined the countless number of innocent souls the portal might've saved over the years. "And this is where it leads. Oh, this is the quarantine!"

"Precisely." Houch narrowed her eyes at him. "My department was set up to help souls coming through Gehenna acclimate to the Afterlife. It's a highly guarded secret, which is why we've walled off the entire area."

"Are all the Guardians aware of this?" Damian recalled Bai's murderer was still at large, likely the same Guardian who had removed Athan as a threat to Adrian's plans.

"No, only a handful. If Satan ever discovered they'd been sitting on an open door into the Afterlife..." Houch shivered, shaking off the nightmare scenario. "Do you know if they've found out? Should we call additional Guardians here for battle?"

Damian shook his head. "I don't think so. Adrian is planning to attack, but I don't believe they're aware of the portal."

The ambassador cocked her head. "Adrian?"

"It's what Satan calls themself."

"Okay." Houch relaxed, the tension in her jaw dissipating. "Don't like the idea of an imminent attack, but we're ill-prepared here. These walls could contain a few rogue Guardians, but we'd be screwed if all the Fallen came through the portal. We can barely keep the humans in!"

"What do you mean?"

"Someone who just came through immediately got up and left. Snuck past security!" Houch had stopped whispering now that they weren't talking about the true nature of Gehenna. Some of her coworkers nodded in agreement. "I'm told he peregrinated away once outside the barrier."

Damian's chest filled with hope. "What did he look like?"

"Tall Black man. Appeared hollowed out. Dressed in scraps." She pressed her lips tightly together for a moment. Damian took the time to peer down at the dirty remains of his suit, which hung off his frame like rags. "Really wish we'd been able to get his name. Looked like he was going to need some time to work through things."

"Colin," Damian said, turning toward the Celestial City. "He's going exactly where he should be. To warn the others about Adri—Satan's attack."

Houch frowned. "The city's in a state of chaos. I've got reports saying people from all creations are showing up to provide support and help reverse the shrinking of the Embassy. If that's where your friend is headed, then he's going to have a hard time getting a hold of someone to listen to him."

If anyone can find a way, it's Colin. "Can I peregrinate out of here?"

She shook her head, looking like she wanted to tell him to sit down with the others for processing. Instead, she pointed him toward the exit. "Tell Mai that I gave you clearance to leave."

Damian gave a brief smile. "Oh, Mai and I are good friends."

As he walked to the exit, he gave a quick mental command. The remains of his tattered jacket and scuffed dress shoes disappeared, and fresh clothes materialized on his body. *I never appreciated good clothing*, he thought, glancing down at a navy button-down shirt and dark slacks held up by a leather belt.

Mai wasn't on duty, and the two Guardians that were present shrugged impassively when Damian asked about them. They let him pass through the wall without argument. Once outside, he allowed himself a moment to relax into freedom. Being inside the quarantine, even if it was in the Afterlife, felt too much like the cages of Acheron.

Enjoy it now, because it could still get a lot worse.

After taking a deep breath, Damian disappeared from view.

Damian didn't know where the Dungeon of Darkness was located. The wondrous magic of peregrination meant he only had to think of the destination to be transported. Whatever world the Creator had built the dungeon on, he still hated it.

At least it's not Acheron. Damian closed his eyes against the fine granules of sand scouring his face. It was night, and despite the winds pushing at the dunes, the sky was clear. Distant stars shone above him. With the little light they provided, he spotted the large rock formation in which the dungeon lay jutting out of the earth.

Halfway to the base of the mount, Damian came upon the wooden sign hammered into the ground. The carved pumpkin still sat atop, leering at him through rotting eyes and teeth. He passed by without giving it a second glance, though the rhyme etched into the wood ran through his head.

Beware all those who enter here. You should know what you endeavor. The DSI hadn't heeded the warning on their previous visit. They'd charged into the dungeon, chasing after an idea. The group still didn't understand the nature of the transaction Kasee's contacts had warned her about, or if it even took place at all. Damian suspected the culprits would've been evil Colin and whatever creature killed Bai. *Was Colin going to head here after our dinner, or had he canceled the meeting after Kasee's report?*

Damian vowed to get answers out of his *friend* if the Celestial City successfully rebuffed Adrian's attack.

I know exactly what I'm doing here this time, along with the wherewithal not to become trapped for days. He cut his way through the wind and sand.

For if not and you embark, you could end up here forever. A year ago, the idea of raising a child, much less holding a baby, would've sent him running. Fears and insecurities aside, the presence of children kept him on edge. He wouldn't have known what to do with one without Alena. He'd forbidden her the chance in life, and he might've done the same in death if he'd had a choice.

Damian had only been dead—*two weeks? Was I really in Acheron for just a few hours?* Bennett had been present for just over half of that time. As much as he hated to admit it, and despite the *days* of sticky fingers and garbled nonsense, the kid had wormed his way into Damian's heart. *Am I sad that all the baby stuff is behind us, that I lost so much time with him as an infant?*

Maybe the sign is wrong, and we shouldn't always understand what we begin. And sometimes forever isn't a bad thing.

Except for the dungeon. This place is awful. The wind died down as Damian reached the rock formation. He put a hand against the metal door, thinking of how Alena not only built his dream house, but had transformed it into a true home for more than just the two of them. Bennett fit in so well. It was the perfect place for him to mature and explore.

For a moment, Damian looked forward to retiring from the Embassy and watching over future grandchildren. *No grandkids, but maybe other adoptees?*

Damian's work at the Embassy had started as a distraction, a way to unravel his perception of perfection and reengage with his best friend—*that traitor.*

It wasn't about solving cases anymore, but about making the Afterlife a safer, better place. For Bennett to grow up in. For Alena to continue her work without fear of threats or persecution.

The Afterlife isn't perfect. It was never supposed to be. But at its center is family. Damian grabbed the iron ring and pulled open the door. *Time to bring them home.*

As before, the door swung open without issue, revealing absolute darkness beyond. He stepped inside, his foot catching on the threshold. Without the sound of wind permeating the entryway, the noise of his shoe echoed throughout the stone hall. Even after his previous imprisonment, the complete absence of light unnerved him.

The wind caught at the metal door, slamming it shut. Damian cursed himself for not bringing along a doorstop. He pushed it back open, scanning the hazy ground for a sizable rock. Not finding anything useful, he yanked off his right shoe and wedged it under the door.

I will not get stuck in here while Adrian destroys the multiverse.

Back inside the dungeon, he stood motionless, straining his ears for any sound. Somewhere along the labyrinth of halls, Alena waited. He was certain of it. The urge to call out, to run toward the central prison cell, surged within him, but he tamped it down. He didn't know who else or what else might lurk in the various hallways.

Colin might be here, waiting to trap me along with them. Damian's right foot chilled against the stone floor. *However, if I am going to call out, it should be from here. I can still leap out the door and peregrinate to the city.*

"Hello?" He whispered the word, but his voice echoed down the hallway. "Is anyone in here?"

Silence pressed back. Dread fell upon him, not helped by the blood pumping through his ears. *I could be wrong, and they're being held somewhere else.*

"Is anyone here?" he shouted, not caring who else heard him. "Alena?"

A distant sound, not his voice. The rustling of fabric against stone.

"Damian?" It was Alena's voice, weak but unmistakable. "Damian, is that you?"

His muscles tensed, ready to sprint down the dark corridor. He resisted. *This could still be a trap.*

"Who's with you?" His voice was steady even while his hands trembled.

"I'm here, Dad," came the deep voice of a teenage boy. *Bennett!* "And Athan's here with us. We're in the center cell."

"Damian." For once, Athan's monotone voice was music to Damian's ears. "Other than us, I believe the dungeon is empty. I have detected no other noise or movement since our imprisonment."

Relief flooded through him at hearing all their voices. Still, he held back. "How did you all end up here?"

"It was Mai," Athan said. "They have sided with the deceiver."

The answer stunned Damian. Mai's surly attitude set them apart, but all Guardians seemed grumpy to him. *Did I only notice it more in them because of their* supposed *vow of silence?*

Then he remembered what Houch had told him only minutes before. Mai was supposed to be watching the exit of the quarantine area. They weren't there when Damian left, which meant—

"They're going after Colin." He glanced over his shoulder, half expecting to see the turncoat Guardian escorting his bedraggled friend through the sandy winds to a new prison. Seeing nothing, he finally sprinted down the hall. His own gait was awkward, his bare foot slapping against stone.

"Mai showed up right after I sent the babysitter home," Alena said, her voice helping to guide Damian. *Must have left their post after I entered the Embassy.* "They said there was an emergency and that we needed to come with them, but something felt off."

"Mom tried to block the door," Bennett said. "But they just knocked it down."

The corridor seemed to stretch on endlessly. Damian couldn't tell if he was making progress or if the dungeon was playing spatial tricks again. He continued to run, hands outstretched in case he encountered a wall. "Any idea how long you've been here?"

"Hard to say." Alena sounded close. "The darkness makes it difficult to track time. Not too long, though it feels like days have passed."

"I think it's only been a few hours," Damian said. "Since the party, at least. Though I took a detour to Hell."

"*What?*"

"Careful," Athan said. "Mai embedded my sword in the floor just out of my reach. You do not want to run into it."

Damian slowed his pace, sliding his feet forward instead of stepping, keeping his bare foot behind him. A minute later, his hands found the round metal bars of the central cell. Fingers wrapped around his own. Alena's touch sent warmth through him, dispelling some of the dungeon's chill.

"Hell?" she whispered, pulling him into an uncomfortable embrace.

"A long story," he said. "We have to get you out of here. The Celestial City is under attack."

"The sword." Athan's voice conveyed urgency. "I can use it to cut through these bars."

Damian stood still for a moment, wishing he could create a pole or broom to swing around. He didn't want to wave his arms around or paw the ground. A cut from the Guardian's weapon could be deadly in any universe. He wiped his hands, sweaty from the sprint, against his shirt. *Oh! I dressed for this!*

Unfastening his belt, Damian pulled it off his waistline. Then he swung it in wide arcs like a makeshift whip. The leather strip swooshed through empty air. He took a step forward, repeating the motion. Another step. Another swing.

Clink.

The belt's buckle struck metal. Damian swung again, the leather catching on something sharp. He followed the lead, careful not to pull too hard lest the blade slice through it, his fingers finding the sword's ornate hilt.

"Got it," he said, tossing the belt aside.

Damian wrapped both hands around the hilt, bracing his feet. Energy surged through the weapon, racing up his arms and throughout his body. Every nerve ending fired, and his muscles seized. The sensation wasn't exactly painful. *More like touching a live wire, if that wire carried divine power instead of electricity.*

Despite its massive size, the blade lifted from the ground with surprising ease. It hummed, vibrating in his grip as he carried it toward the cell.

"Here," Damian said, passing the weapon through the bars to Athan. He let out a breath as his body relaxed. "Let's get you all out of there."

A moment later, white flames burst forth, illuminating the jagged sword. As Damian marveled at how he hadn't sliced himself in half, the Guardian swung it twice in wide arcs. A dozen bars clattered to the ground, allowing the prisoners passage through.

"Damian!" Alena hugged him again. She still wore the dress from the head ambassador's party. It'd fared better than his suit. "What's going on? I thought for sure this was about us and Bennett."

"No, nothing to do with Bennett." Damian looked in awe at their son. He'd continued to grow since they'd left him with the babysitter, his pajamas now several inches too small. Curly hair nearly hid his brown eyes, which peered back at him with a mixture of curiosity and pride.

"How'd you know where to find us, Dad?"

The title startled Damian. It was only over the last couple of hours that he realized how much the boy meant to him. How much he regretted not being more present while simultaneously vowing to make the future a better place for him. Still, he hadn't truly considered himself a *father*, and didn't think he was yet worthy of the designation.

"Someone tracked a trail of red sand through my office." Damian looked up at Athan. "I noticed it right before the attack. I figured whoever left it there—I thought it was Kasee at first, then Colin, now I suspect it was Mai—had also kidnapped you. The only place I'd seen sand like it was here, outside the dungeon."

Alena and Bennett stared at him in confusion. He'd forgotten how little his family knew of his work, let alone what had transpired since the party. *And Athan has been here even longer than that.*

"We need to leave." Damian turned, preparing to lead them up the hallway, and was shocked to find the exit only a few yards away. His shoe still propped it open. "Is there a safe place you can go? Somewhere not in the city?"

Alena nodded. "We can go to our neighbor's home on the other side of the mountain."

"Great. Just don't go back to our place until we know it's safe."

"Wait." She grabbed hold of his hand. "Where are you going?"

"Athan and I have to go to the city and help Colin." Damian drew Alena and Bennett into a hug. He wanted to explain everything to them, yet didn't want the weight of the situation to fall upon Bennett's young soul. "We've got to stop an attack, and we've got to do it right now."

"Where should we meet?" Athan asked.

"Are you familiar with Messie Bessie's?"

The Guardian nodded.

"Let's go see what their quiche of the day is."

Still holding Alena and Bennett's hands, Damian stepped through the dungeon's door and out into the raging winds.

The familiar scent of tea and fresh-baked goods wrapped around Damian as he materialized inside Messie Bessie's. Light filtered in through the windows, glinting off the bronzed tin panels overhead. Teacups sat overturned on saucers, waiting for new customers. From where he stood at the back, he saw that all the seats were currently empty, the restaurant vacant.

Let's hope the tearoom will open its doors again. Damian speculated about the time, unsure if the place was quiet because of the shrinking or if it was 3 in the morning. No one passed by the windows on the sidewalk.

Athan's towering form appeared before him, their stature cramping even the high-ceilinged room. Dark robes brushed against chairs as the Guardian moved between tables, careful not to disturb anything.

"Charming." Athan ducked beneath a wooden beam. "Though I do not understand its strategic value."

"For us or for the restaurant?" Damian no longer needed to eat, but the lingering aromas pulled at his attention. "I wanted to arrive without being seen by anyone, but we should get a clear view of the Embassy outside the front. Whatever's left of it, anyway."

He ran a hand along the edge of a round table. It was the one he'd sat at when he and Colin reunited. When his friend—*the evil side of him*—had pulled him into an unfolding cosmic drama. He wondered if there had been another motive behind Colin's actions. Something other than chaos and ruin.

Did he still value our friendship?

"Perhaps." Athan crossed the room with a few easy strides, reaching out to open the door. As they did, a pinkish light flashed through the window. "Though we might have saved time if—"

The blast hit like a physical wave, shattering the windows. Several wall-mounted teapots crashed to the floor. Chairs and tables overturned, throwing teacups to their doom. The force knocked Damian against the back wall.

"Are you okay, Damian?" The Guardian was already back on their feet, alert for additional threats.

"I'm fine." His head had throbbed for a moment after impact, but the pain quickly faded. Long shadows drifted across the floor's wooden planks. "The shrinking was reversed."

"The Department of Dimensional Stability has carried out its duties," Athan confirmed after peering out through the broken glass. They turned to Damian, dark eyes narrowing. "Exactly as expected."

"It's part of Satan's plan!" Damian pushed himself up, shards of glass falling off his clothing.

Athan's look of foreboding morphed into perplexity. "But how?"

"No idea." Part of Damian wanted to stay inside the restaurant. Right the tables and sweep up the broken cups. He recognized that as something he could control and fix, even if the actions meant nothing in the long run.

Colin dragged me into this mess. And now he—the good part of him, anyway—is out there trying to stop whatever is coming. I owe it to both versions to see this through.

"Let's go," he said, falling in behind Athan. "Watch your head on the way out."

CHAPTER TWENTY-SIX

Broken glass crunched under Damian's feet as he and Athan stepped outside Messie Bessie's. The last pink hues of the shrinking faded from the sky, returning it to its usual amber. Down the street, crowds of people picked themselves up off the ground, cheering at the restored Embassy.

They'd cheer even more if they knew all the employees—everyone caught by the sphere—had safely returned to the Afterlife.

"We'll never find Colin or Mai in the chaos." Damian scanned the group, made up of dozens of intelligent species. The Department of Dimensional Stability wasn't exclusive to the human branch.

"Incorrect." Athan's dark eyes narrowed. "I can see that they have broken through the crowd and are headed for the front doors."

Damian squinted, thinking he spotted a couple of blurry figures ascending the stairs. Even with perfect Afterlife vision, though, he couldn't make out fine details from this distance.

"Why is Colin Cherry dressed in rags?" Athan asked.

"Because that's not the Colin you're familiar with." Damian looked up at the Guardian. "I found out what happens after humans die. How our souls are split. The Colin we've been working with is his evil half, plotting against us this whole time. The one you see now just arrived here from Acheron. Mai must've captured him."

"Then we must act quickly." Athan's hand twitched as though it desired to unsheathe their sword and drive it through the devious Guardian's chest. "I will go to the Castile and gather my brethren. Without Bai, it may be difficult to spur them into action."

"You give yourself too little credit," Damian said. "You risked your own well-being for the safety of all Creation. I think you make an outstanding leader, Athan. The others respect you, too."

The Guardian bowed their head. "I am humbled by your words, Damian."

"Several Guardians were assisting the Department of Rehabilitation in the quarantine zone. You should get them, too." Damian glanced down the street, back toward the Embassy. "I'm going to save Colin."

"Do not engage Mai on your own. They may no longer have access to the Light, but their skill with a sword is still formidable." Athan fixed Damian with a hard look. "I will return shortly."

Without waiting for a reply, the Guardian disappeared from view. Damian closed his eyes. When he opened them again, he was on the Embassy lawn. Creatures of all shapes and sizes spilled across the pristine grass, a bustling crowd threatening to knock him over.

A line of otherworldly individuals stood at the base of the stairs. Head Ambassador Picardia Knutt was among them, her thin husband hovering behind her frame. Damian guessed the others to be head ambassadors of other branches. *Isn't there a grand ambassador?* He thought back to what he'd learned from the *Book of History*. *Seems like information I should know.*

"Please remain calm," Knutt said once another of her peers stopped talking. She still wore the same attire from her party, though it looked out of place—*even more ridiculous*—in the current scenario. Damian wondered if that showed a dedicated work ethic or an attempt to foster such an image. He decided to trust in the prior and thought better of her. "As you can see, we've successfully reversed the effects of the shrinking. More importantly, all those caught in its effect have been retrieved and are unharmed."

Bit of a stretch. Damian pressed through the crowd, muttering, "Ope, excuse me," as he squeezed between bodies.

"The building is off-limits." A security officer held up a hand when Damian neared the steps from the side.

"I'm with the DSI." He pointed at other officials hustling inside. "I need to get in."

"Sorry, only members of the Dimensional Stability team are allowed through."

Another of the head ambassadors, this one a crystalline entity, stepped forward and gave their own assurances. Their mode of communication sounded like a series of disjointed musical tones. The officer turned to listen, and Damian used the distraction to slip behind the group of officials. He kept his head down and quickly climbed the steps, trying to blend in with the Dimensional Stability employees. When the security officer turned back and spotted him ascending, he cried out, "Sir! You can't—"

The heavy doors swung shut behind Damian, muffling the exterior chaos.

The chaos within surprised him. Much like it had earlier, the foyer buzzed with activity. Authorized employees from all branches darted around, waving devices that looked like metal detectors. The equipment chirped, emitting colored lights that reflected off the chandelier. No one gave him a second glance.

Through small gaps in the crowd, Damian caught glimpses of dark flowing robes and white strips of clothing. *Mai—and Colin!* They stood near the Bridge, looking an unlikely pair. Others thought so, too. Unlike Damian, the two garnered plenty of attention.

Damian weaved through the crowd, careful not to interfere with the others' work. Minding Athan's warning, he kept his distance, careful to stay out of Mai's line of sight. He watched as they studied the rotating Bridge, pointing at various panels as they floated by.

A group of employees passed by Damian, their devices chirping. He used them for cover to inch closer to Colin. *They look like museum patrons.* Mai stretched out a hand to trace the symbols etched into one of the thin panels.

This doesn't feel right. Something's wrong. Colin appeared calm, speaking in hushed tones while Mai listened with rapt attention. The Guardian appeared *reverent* of their human captive.

"There it is!" Colin's eyes widened as he pointed at a panel.

"After all this time." It was the first time Damian had heard Mai's voice. It was higher than expected, more shrill than any other Guardian he'd encountered. "They're only a turn of a lock away."

Mai reached into their robes.

"Sword!" Damian's voice rose above the collective trilling of the strange devices as Mai's hand found purchase along their waist. "Colin! They've got a sword!"

Several nearby officials gave Damian odd glances, protesting as he pushed his way through the crowd. Someone behind him said, "Of course they do. They're a Guardian!"

The commotion drew Mai and Colin's attention. Colin did a double take, face twisting into an unfamiliar expression. When his dark eyes locked with Damian's, they contained no warmth. No compassion. No love.

"You were supposed to return to your friend's prison and rot in darkness for the rest of time." Colin's deep voice boomed across the foyer, though no one else seemed to hear. Those Damian had knocked over stood back up and returned to their scanning. "But I am glad you have returned to the Celestial City to witness this."

Colin's body went rigid, face snapping up toward the ceiling while his arms straightened by his sides. His jaw dropped open, and he let out a bloodcurdling scream. It was wet and sharp, his lips spreading wider until they split at the edges. Damian gaped, expecting blood to pour down Colin's neck. Instead, green light streamed from his widening mouth.

Though only Damian had heard him speak, everyone within view witnessed Colin's form split down the middle. They cried out in terror as emerald light flashed across their faces like blood splatter. They stumbled back as the skin and rags that had once housed part of Colin's soul fell away. A figure emerged from within.

"Adrian," Damian said. Blond hair tumbled over broad shoulders as the Guardian's perfect form stretched to its full height, towering above the crowd. The remnants of Colin's body dissolved into wisps of shadow, curling around Adrian's feet. Everyone in the foyer, even those who'd witnessed Colin's grotesque decimation, stared transfixed at the beautiful creature before them.

A wave of nausea rolled through Damian. He staggered back as his stomach heaved, gripping the shoulder of a nearby stranger for support. Certainty flooded through him that his best friend—the good half who tried to warn him of impending danger—had died before his body had fallen into Gehenna.

Messy business. Never ends well for the human. That's what Blue said. Damian struggled to stand on his own. *How could Alena turn Colin over to them, knowing what would happen?*

"What have you done?" he choked out.

"Done?" Adrian replied, brilliant blue eyes staring fixedly at Damian. "My friend, I have not even started."

The Guardian turned to Mai and held out a hand. Mai finally withdrew their own from their robes. Instead of revealing a sword, they held a large skeleton key. A glimmer of triumph shone in Mai's dark eyes as they placed the key into Adrian's palm.

"I am unlocking a new chapter in history." Adrian winked at Damian, then slid the key into the Bridge panel they'd been inspecting a minute before. A soft click echoed throughout the now-silent foyer. Though no one but Damian understood what was truly happening, everyone's eyes widened in panic.

Adrian twisted the key. The symbols etched along the panel's surface glowed brightly, and the room's air vibrated with energy. Damian felt a thrumming deep within his chest. A force pulled him—drew everyone—toward the Bridge. They all braced themselves, leaning back.

The glow dissipated, and with it went the vibrations and gravitational pull. Damian stumbled back, watching as Adrian snapped the key in half along its shank, leaving the key bit lodged within the lock. They stood tall, a pleased look on their face.

The crowd stood in uneasy silence, unsure of what to do or expect. Then, in the distance, came the faint sound of explosions.

"Welcome to your reckoning," Adrian proclaimed, eyes glinting with malicious delight. Both Guardians drew their swords and swept them in wide, horizontal arcs. The tips sliced through three individuals, their bodies turning to ash before they could even gasp in surprise.

Bodies surged back, pressing against one another as they made room for the two aggressors. The blades carved a path toward the doors, leaving behind a trail of ash. In their attempts to escape the weapons, others knocked Damian off balance. He fell, head cracking against the floor. A murky darkness swallowed him.

"Damian!"

Someone shook his shoulders. The throbbing in his head disappeared as consciousness returned. "Colin?"

He wanted it to be his friend. To wake up from this awful nightmare that kept repeating itself.

"Open your eyes, Damian," said a stern voice.

"Athan?" *If this nightmare continues, it wouldn't hurt to have an army of Guardians leading the charge.*

Damian's eyelids fluttered open. He found two individuals standing over him. Wendell was the one shaking him while Kasee examined the surroundings. Except for scattered debris, the foyer had emptied.

"I'm sorry." Damian looked up at Kasee. "I was wrong. About everything."

"What do you mean?" She reached out a hand, pulling him into a sitting position.

"I forced open the broken drawer in your desk." He winced, touching a tender spot on the side of his head that had yet to fully heal. "There was a sphere inside. A decoy, I think, but I assumed you knew about it. Thought you were the one working against us."

Kasee gave a crooked smile. "But my charming personality..."

"I'm also sorry about..." Damian paused. Whatever Colin had told him, despite the memories that returned to him on B6, he didn't *feel* any different. "I learned a lot about myself in Acheron. You were right about a lot of things."

Both Wendell and Kasee's heads snapped toward him. "*Acheron?*"

"That's where anyone caught in a shrinking is teleported. Have you discovered anything since the party?" The pair pulled him to unsteady feet. Then he remembered Wendell's last orders. Grabbing the ambassador's arm, he asked, "Where's Colin?"

Wendell flinched at the touch but remained still. "I can't find him. It's the strangest thing. We peregrinated to the site of the supposed attack, which we now know was a false flag. He ran off to do a perimeter sweep, and I haven't seen him since."

With full strength returned, Damian filled his coworkers in on what he'd uncovered as they walked across the foyer to the entrance. Adrian and Mai had apparently blasted the doors open while he was unconscious, and a broad hole in the wall now revealed a changed landscape.

Few people walked around the lawn, and the head ambassadors were nowhere to be seen. Smoke rose on the horizon, clouding the amber sky. Portions of the diamond Celestial Wall had crumbled. He imagined that the Fallen had surrounded the city after the assembly in Acheron, waiting for the shimmering pink barrier to disappear. When it had, they'd breached the wall, ready to unleash an eternity of emotion.

"I can't believe it," Wendell said. They all stared slack-jawed, lost in thought. "The devil was in our house the entire time."

Kasee sniffed. "I never trusted him for a minute."

"Learn anything new from your informants?" Damian asked.

"Nothing." Her voice sounded hollow, regretful. "They've all left the Celestial City. Disappeared into one universe or another. Saw the writing on the wall, so to speak, and took off."

Damian had a hunch they'd offered her the opportunity to join them.

"We should help with the evacuation," Wendell said as explosions lit up a series of buildings, each closer to the center of the city. The ambassador sounded defeated, and Damian realized how much of a personal and professional loss this was for him.

A contingent of Guardians materialized on the Embassy's trampled lawn. They wore their usual heavy, muted robes and jeweled crowns, though most had weapons drawn, Light barely contained along the blades' sharp edges. A fire burned in their eyes, belying the stony passivity defining their faces. *They're angry, and they're ready to fulfill their purpose.*

Athan emerged from the front of the group. Head held high, they marched over to the steps and looked up at the trio of humans. "The Celestial Wall has been breached in three locations. The Fallen are making their way to the palace."

"We saw Mai and another head that way, too." Wendell glanced at Kasee for confirmation.

"It was Satan," Damian said, watching as a sea of Guardians tightened their grips on their weapons. He supposed some hadn't believed Athan when they'd delivered bad tidings. The name of the great betrayer on the lips of another hardened their hearts. "They've returned. They must be meeting the other Fallen at the palace."

"How many?" Kasee asked.

"All of them. No reason to hold back now." Athan turned to the other Guardians, nearly a hundred in all. *Twice as many as the Fallen. There's still hope of ending this.* "Protect the palace. Keep safe the Creator."

The Guardians dispersed without question, peregrinating or sprinting toward the center of the city. It was odd to watch such decrepit-looking creatures move with speed and purpose. Instead of joining them, Athan ascended the Embassy steps. Behind them, screams echoed throughout the streets. Some were of terror, of complacent individuals surprised by the latest wave of disruption to the norm. Most were of rage, though. Pent-up anger spilling out onto the perfectly laid brick roads.

"The souls of the Damned." Athan glanced over their shoulder. "Enough to pose a significant threat."

"What can we do?" Damian whispered. The Guardian reached the top of the stairs, brushing past the trio and striding into the foyer. "Athan?"

"We must carefully weigh our options."

Damian watched as the Guardian—his friend—paused and stared at the Bridge. Amid the surrounding debris, the device continued rotating at a leisurely pace. The pane representing Acheron floated by, the broken skeleton key keeping that plane from being easily shut out again.

"I'm sorry about Mai." Damian stepped up beside Athan. "Colin's betrayal has me in shock, but you've known Mai for lifetimes. I can't imagine how you feel."

"It feels...bad." Athan's lips pursed while they nodded their head. "I did as you suggested, asking brethren to summon Light. Mai could not do so. I hesitated in responding, not wanting to believe the evidence. That wavering, my lack of conviction, provided Mai the window they needed to overpower me."

"Don't beat yourself up. Mai was your friend." Athan was too tall for Damian to put a hand on their shoulder, so he settled for what he hoped was a comforting pat on the arm. "We all want to believe in our friends."

What remains of Colin is what he considered to be the worst parts of himself. That doesn't mean I have to hate him, Damian told himself. *Even if he contrived the downfall of the multiverse.*

"At least we can close the case on Bai's murder," he said, steering his thoughts clear of Colin. "Why do you think Mai turned on us?"

"Mai was with us during the War for Heaven, or at least we thought they were." Athan peered down at Damian. "A wall collapsed on them early in the battle, pinning them to the ground. With their part in the coup still veiled, they continued their subterfuge when we rescued them afterward. The subsequent vow of silence was presented as self-imposed atonement for their failure to assist."

They've stewed in silent resentment ever since then. Made it easy for anyone to miss the darkness growing inside someone you trust.

"What's our next move?" Damian asked.

"Your next move is to find shelter," Athan said. "You do not stand a chance against my kind, and this is not your fight."

"Like hell it isn't!" Kasee walked around the Guardian, staring up at them. "This is everyone's fight."

Wendell cleared his throat. "The DSI exists exactly for this situation. We've been investigating this threat for months now. We're not sitting this out."

Another sequence of explosions sounded from outside. The floor vibrated beneath Damian's feet, and the chandelier hovering above the Bridge threatened to collapse. Flashes of light flickered through the destroyed entrance, and Athan's expression hardened as several Guardians raced toward the commotion.

"Very well." Athan turned back to the Bridge. "Then this is our next move."

In a fluid movement, Athan reached into their robes and pulled out a heavy metal skeleton key. It was identical to the one Adrian had used to unlock Acheron's panel. Damian's eyes widened as the Guardian moved closer to the Bridge, inserting the key into another locked panel.

As soon as the key met the lock, the symbols etched into the panel erupted in brilliant light. The air vibrated again, sending an electric ripple through Damian's body. He instinctively leaned back as gravity shifted, pulling him toward the Bridge.

"What's happening?" Kasee had been unprepared and was toppling forward. Athan reached out, grabbing hold of both their shoulders, anchoring them in place against the invisible forces. Wendell clung to the stairwell banister behind them.

The vibrations intensified, saturating every corner of the room with a deep, resonating hum that felt...ancient, like it emanated from the beginning of time itself. Damian held his hands to his head as the sound penetrated his body. Then, just when he was certain he'd explode at the right frequency, everything stopped. The glow faded, and silence fell upon them. Athan withdrew the key, their face no more or less indifferent than it'd been a few minutes prior.

The distant explosions and commotion faded. *Everyone felt that. Even the Fallen and Damned know something has changed.*

"What did you do?" Wendell whispered the question, maintaining a tight grip on the banister as though wary of whatever spirits had descended upon the city.

A siren trumpeted. Damian jumped at the noise, as it was identical to the one that'd blared throughout Acheron.

"Good," Athan said, striding over to the ruined door. "They have arrived."

Damian squinted into the distance. Machines rolled through the breaches in the Celestial Wall, crushing diamond debris. They reminded him of tanks, though their surfaces seemed alien, shimmering with an iridescent sheen that distorted light.

"No," Wendell said, stepping back with fists clenched. Between the armored vehicles, enormous slithering forms made their way into the city. They coiled their way through the streets with serpentine grace, scales glistening like molten metal under the amber sky. "This is a bad omen."

The cries of the Damned rose again, though the tone morphed from anger into terror. Their pain cut through Damian like a knife. He staggered back against Athan.

"Look!" Kasee pointed at a tank rolling up the street, passing by Messie Bessie's. "They're firing!"

Bursts of bright light erupted from the alien machines, tearing into buildings and scattering crowds of people. Stone and dust rained down on them like confetti. The engines moved forward, unperturbed, toward the Celestial Palace.

"Guardians are one of the strongest inventions in all the planes of reality," Athan said. "Aside from the Creator, only one other race can threaten our existence."

Damian's mouth fell open. "The Forti."

"Yes." Athan then rushed forward, long legs taking them down the steps three at a time. "We must hurry."

The three humans sprinted down after them. Damian glanced out at the chaos unfurling throughout the city. One of the squirming creatures Wendell had spotted was now fully visible. It was an enormous snake, making its way across the domed building where orientations took place. Its eyes smoldered as it surveyed the area.

"Focus!" Athan said to them, and Damian saw he wasn't the only one awed by what transpired across the city. "Do not let yourself be distracted."

"Where are we going?" Wendell asked as they filed out onto the lawn.

"Join hands," the Guardian urged. "I will take us to the palace."

Damian took comfort in the blurred colors and whooshing sounds of peregrination, knowing full well it could be the last time he ever traveled.

CHAPTER TWENTY-SEVEN

Damian had only walked close to the Celestial Palace once before, when he'd visited Athan at the Castile. Its fanciful towers had kept his eyes drawn upward. Now, as he and his companions gathered outside the walls of the Guardians' home, the closest peregrination would allow them to their destination, he saw that the palace grounds were equally impressive. A network of walkways crisscrossed the lawn. Trees created a shaded tunnel over half of them, the rest connecting open areas for congregating.

"Look there!" Kasee said, pointing toward an open patch of grass near the front of the palace. It took Damian a moment to find what she'd noticed. Flashes of Light sliced through the shadows of the covered walkways, distracting him. Then he spotted a pair of Guardians in the clearing. They appeared to be dancing, twirling gracefully around each other. Each brandished a sword, denoting the true purpose of the dance. It would end in blood.

"The Fallen approached the palace from multiple angles." Athan towered over the others and therefore had a better view of the battlefield. "Though there is only one entrance to the building."

Seems like a poor design. Damian counted ten duels taking place. It was easy to tell sides. With access to the Light, the good Guardians' weapons were ablaze.

Additional Guardians fought off hordes of the Damned clamoring up the surrounding streets. The faces of those souls bore the rage of inequity, but fear lurked in their eyes as they sensed something even darker than themselves approaching.

"Behind us!" Wendell's voice wavered. When Damian turned, he understood the ambassador's apprehension. A colossal serpent coiled along the pavement, its scales shimmering in the light of nearby explosions. It raised its head, surveying the front line, and unleashed a roar that reverberated through Damian's bones.

Tanks rolled along beside the snake, cannons intermittently firing a mixture of shells and lasers. Smaller creatures walked alongside the tanks. Others drifted overhead, held up by leathery wings. All held weapons. Damian recognized some of them. The sharp edges of blades translated across civilizations. Others were beyond his imagination, and he wondered at their magic.

"We must get inside the palace." Athan's voice regained their attention. The Guardian took off, Damian and the others sprinting after them, struggling to keep up. "Stay close!"

The group ducked down one path that curved around the palace grounds, leaving the horde of Damned and Forti behind them. Tree branches twisted together over them, creating a shadowy tunnel that cut out much of the surrounding noise. Remnants of the amber sky peeked through, creating strange wriggling shapes upon the ground.

The sound of metal on metal rang out ahead of them. As the path straightened, Damian saw a Guardian lean back in time to evade a strike from a sword engulfed in Light. The Fallen then parried, lunging at the chest of their opponent. The defender easily blocked the attack.

"Enough!" Athan lunged for the Fallen. It was distraction enough to pause the skirmish, the enemy turning to see the newcomer draw their own flaming sword. The blade pierced their side, and they shrieked in anger and pain. It was the most emotion Damian had witnessed a Guardian express. Then they collapsed in a heap, thick brown blood soaking through their robes and pooling beneath their body.

The other Guardian—Damian recognized them as the one who'd greeted him inside the Castile, then later granted him and Alena entrance to Knutt's party—paused and examined the intervening group. After a nod of thanks to Athan, they said, "You said we were fighting the Fallen, but I smell Forti in the air. We are outnumbered. We cannot hold this ground."

"Come with us, Lirael." Athan still stood ready for attack. "We must find and protect the Creator."

"It is our purpose." Lirael bowed their head, and they all hastened down the covered path, leaving the dead Fallen behind. Damian struggled to comprehend how death could so easily find a creature so ancient and experienced. He pushed forward, focused on surviving.

As they approached the palace's outer wall, Damian expected to find a moat like the one surrounding its counterpart in Acheron. No barriers kept them from the doors, though, and for all the structure's defensive features, no one stood watch. Damian glanced up. Against the shifting smoke and ash in the sky, the building appeared to be falling over onto them. *The palace itself is a warning, looming over us.*

"No watchmen?" Wendell asked, voicing Damian's concern.

"There may have been." Kasee pointed to the entrance, and Damian's heart sank. Something had blasted the front doors off their hinges, just like those of the Embassy. Debris littered the ground, fragments of wood covering another dead Guardian.

Athan led them through the ruined entrance. "Stay alert."

Damian braced himself for the dim lighting and aura of dread he remembered from Adrian's castle. As he stepped over the threshold, the vast chamber beyond caught him off guard. Pristine white walls stretched up, accented with shades of blue. Like the amber sky, light touched every surface with no apparent source, leaving no shadows.

The inner sanctum wasn't completely unlike its counterpart. His shoes squeaked against an intricate mosaic floor. Millions of tiny stones fit together to form a six-pointed star. The design appeared to shift. The floor wasn't opening beneath their feet, but seemed to pulsate like a living star.

Balconies also ringed the chamber. Rather than birdcage-like elevators connecting the floors, a curved hallway spiraled upward around the room. The craftsmanship put Adrian's version to shame.

This was the original, Damian thought. *Adrian attempted to reproduce it, but nothing comes close without the Light.*

They scanned the balconies above, but no movement caught their eyes.

"The Creator's office is at the top." Athan moved toward the hallway as a nearby detonation rattled the building. Dust drifted down, particles catching the light. "We must hurry."

"Where is everyone?" Kasee asked as they ran up the path. She'd whispered the question, but everyone heard her in the enclosed space. The pristine white walls rounded inward, creating a tunnel that reflected all sound back to the middle. It would've made for a pleasant walk if not for the muffled sounds of battle outside. "And what was that room on the ground floor?"

"The Chamber of Light." Lirael's voice carried no strain despite their pace. "In the early days, it served as the meeting place between Guardians and the Creator."

Another explosion rocked the palace. Damian shielded his eyes as cracks formed along the curved walls and debris skittered across the floor. *Closer this time.*

"As the Creator's favorite, Satan spent considerable time there," Athan said. "Used it as a base of operations, coordinating events across the domains under their care."

"Until the trial," Wendell said.

"Yes." Athan's monotonous tone dropped an octave. "The Creator passed judgment in the Chamber of Light, and Satan was immediately sent away to the dungeon."

They passed the fifth balcony and continued upward. Damian's shoulder scraped against the wall as he struggled to maintain speed around the curve. *At least I'm not wheezing like I used to.*

"How much further?" Kasee asked.

A thunderous blast cut off any response. The surface on their left shuddered, long cracks webbing across the wall. Everyone pressed against the opposite side, watching as chunks of stone broke free.

"Keep moving," Athan commanded, amber light crisscrossing their face. "The Creator's room lies just ahead."

The path finally leveled out, ending ahead of them with an ornate wooden door. Intricate patterns covered its surface, similar to those carved into the Embassy walls and the Bridge's panels. Damian wished he possessed even a basic understanding of what they meant. *Do they tell a story or are they some kind of ward?*

Before they reached the door, the outer wall collapsed. Rubble pelted the group as they ducked. Through the cloud of dust, Damian glimpsed the scaled form of a Forti warrior floating outside, held up by huge wings. It was humanoid, with a serpentine face and a long tail coiled to strike. Behind the creature, the battle for the Celestial City raged across the sky.

The Forti's hungry yellow eyes fixed on the group. A forked tongue flicked out of its thin mouth, tasting the air. Clutched in one of its clawed hands was a weapon that crackled with purple electricity.

"The Creator's den." The warrior's voice sounded like steel scraping stone. "At last."

Wendell yelped. He pushed Damian and Kasee back against the wall, using his own body as a shield. The Forti's massive form blotted out the view of combat as it moved through the hole in the wall and into the hallway. Its scales gleamed like polished armor, and it raised its head as though preparing to strike.

"Your swords!" Wendell screamed at the Guardians.

Neither Guardian held up their weapons, and the alien warrior didn't attack. The creature's gaze swept over the group again, lingering on Athan. "You summoned us to aid in the city's defense." Its speech carried a slight whistle through needle-sharp teeth. "The Fallen must fail."

Relief flooded through Damian. Wendell was more hesitant, at first refusing to lower his protective arms and let his team step away from the wall.

Athan nodded. "Let us proceed."

The Forti retracted its wings and coiled its tail around its body, making space for them to pass by. Athan and Lirael moved forward, pushing at the ornate door. It swung open at their touch, revealing a room that took away the humans' breath. Damian even heard their new companion hiss in apparent surprise—*at the Creator's den.* Light streamed through floor-to-ceiling windows, illuminating pristine white walls, a seamless marble floor, and a ceiling accented with cerulean swirls. *It's like walking through a cloud.* The entire city spread out below them, though smoke marred the view.

Where there weren't windows, bookcases lined the walls. Leather-bound volumes packed their shelves. Despite the situation, Damian immediately itched to pull one out, to peek inside. *The knowledge those books must contain. The secrets written on those pages.*

As Damian took in the chamber, his gaze caught on a plain metal lever mounted beside the doorframe. It stood out as such a mundane feature in the otherwise extraordinary room. *Looks like an afterthought, a later addition.*

A simple desk of dark wood sat in the center, the only piece of furniture other than the bookcases. Its surface was bare except for a fountain pen and journal. Behind it, perched on a high-backed chair, sat a sickly-looking individual. Blue skin appeared to glow in the ambient light. An impossibly tall top hat balanced precariously upon her head.

"You?" Damian's eyes widened. "*You're* the Creator?"

"Hello." Odd Man Blue nodded at the intruders.

I can't believe it. Damian stared in awe at Odd Man Blue, feeling his jaw fall open. *I stood at a table and conversed with the Creator. Shook her hand! I must've acted a fool.*

Through the windows, another detonation ripped through a building close to Messie Bessie's. Damian watched as the war for the Celestial City stormed on. High above the skirmishes, time seemed to stand still.

"Creator." Athan stepped up to the desk. "Satan has escaped their prison."

"I know." Blue nodded. "They are here."

It took a moment for Damian to realize that the woman wasn't nodding in agreement, but tipping her hat toward the door. The group turned in unison to find Adrian standing in the doorway, flanked by Mai and Colin. The sight of his friend sent a fresh wave of pain through Damian. Even with his face twisted in fury, lips pulled back in an animal snarl, Damian almost felt comfort in his presence.

"Step aside, Athan." Adrian's voice carried none of the warmth it had in Acheron. Raw power rippled through the air, accompanied by a ringing of metal as Adrian and Mai drew their swords. "Put down your weapon, and I will not destroy you when this is over."

"The Creator is under our protection," Lirael said, moving between the desk and the door. "You will fail."

"No matter." Adrian flashed a wide smile. "I actually would have killed you all in the end, anyway."

The deceiver lunged forward, blade raised to strike at Odd Man Blue. The Creator didn't flinch, but Athan intercepted. Two swords clashed in a burst of light that left spots dancing in Damian's vision. The two Guardians circled each other, trading blows that echoed through the room like thunder.

Mai used the distraction to take on Lirael and the Forti warrior, moving with remarkable speed and agility. Lirael blocked the initial attack in time to keep their abdomen from being skewered. The serpentine creature took a swing with its mace, purple electricity arcing between the weapons. The trio continued to trade blows, neither side gaining the upper hand.

Wendell inched his way behind Blue's desk, careful to avoid the swords swinging over his head. He planted a firm hand down on the desk so that his arm crossed over the Creator like a shield. "Stay behind me." Blue remained seated, watching the fight unfold with an unreadable expression.

What can I do? Damian watched the celestial creatures collide around him. He turned to see Colin barreling toward him and Kasee, face twisted in a fury. He barely had time to brace himself before his old friend slammed into his chest, driving him back against a bookcase. Leather-bound volumes rained down around them.

"I was supposed to be pulled to Acheron when the sphere struck, but you should've stayed there." Colin pulled back for a punch. "Would've been safer for you."

Kasee appeared from the side, ramming an elbow into Colin's ribs. He stumbled, giving Damian space to slip away from the wall.

I've never been in a fight before, Damian thought as the three squared off. *I won't be any better fighting Colin than the Guardians!*

"Two against one?" Colin kicked the books at his feet away. "Hardly seems fair. Especially after all I've done for you two."

He struck like a snake, catching Kasee with a backhand that sent her sprawling. Shocked to see Colin hit another, Damian rushed in, ducking under Colin's next swing to land a solid punch to his stomach. Colin barely flinched, grabbing Damian's shirt and hurling him across the floor.

We can't actually hurt each other. Damian rolled to his feet beside Kasee. They attacked in unison, forcing their former coworker to divide his attention. While Kasee clearly had some sparring experience, his own punches were ill-placed. Together, they barely slowed Colin down. *All we're doing is distracting each other while the others fight for victory.*

Mai screamed from the other side of the room. The serpentine warrior had lashed out with a clawed hand, opening deep gashes along the Guardian's face. Dark brown blood oozed down their face and neck, soaking into the thick fabric of their robes. The wounds didn't slow Mai's agile movements. They circled the Forti, then pivoted and slammed into Lirael. The force sent the other Guardian crashing through a tall window. Glass shards rained down as they disappeared from view.

"You betrayed me," Adrian snarled, the duel between them and Athan intensifying. They lunged forward, but Athan parried the blow. "After everything we accomplished together in training...you could have ruled by my side!"

"I have always served the Creator." Athan's monotone voice was a stark contrast to Adrian's temper. "As was our purpose."

"I create my own purpose!" Adrian's next attack went wild, and their sword cut deep into Blue's desk, inches away from Wendell's hand. The ambassador stood firm, staring back into the face of the enemy. Capitalizing on the mistake, Athan forced Adrian back toward the door.

Muted pain exploded across Damian's jaw as Colin's fist connected. He staggered backward, stars dancing in his vision, nearly tripping over a pile of fallen books.

"Don't get distracted by the big kids." Colin readied for another punch. "You were always prone to daydreaming."

Kasee circled to Colin's left. "And you were always an asshole."

"Spare me your angst." Colin easily blocked a kick. "You were dead before you could even drive."

"Old enough to see through your bullshit." Kasee feinted right, then struck left. Colin caught her arm and twisted, but she rolled with the motion.

The pinpricks of light dissipated from Damian's eyesight. "You don't have to do this, Colin. Just because you embody what *you* found evil about yourself doesn't actually make it so. It's not too late!"

"I am not a redemption arc in one of your stories." Colin released Kasee with a shove. "Just because I—*any* version of me—represent something you were afraid to embrace doesn't make me vile."

"That's not—"

"You think you or Alena are making a difference?" Colin stomped toward him. "Flitting between your little jobs and home? Your quaint house in the country is nothing but a vain attempt to appear modest. At least Adrian is honest about what they want!"

"Screw your honesty!" Kasee screamed as she tackled Colin from behind.

Across the room, the Forti warrior had Mai pinned against a bookcase. Razor-sharp claws were inches from the Fallen's throat. Mai scrambled against the shelves, then brought their knee up, connecting with the Forti's scaled underbelly. The serpent dropped its prey and fell to the ground in agony.

Mai circled the fallen creature, the point of their sword keeping it prone. With the smoke-filled sky roiling behind them, they smirked and raised their blade. The sharp edge caught what little light remained. Before they could plunge the sword down into their opponent's chest, fiery metal burst out of their own. Brown blood sprayed across the pristine floor. Mai's head tilted down, staring at the weapon protruding from their body with a curious expression.

The sword withdrew, making a horrible wet noise. Mai staggered, their own blade clattering to the floor. The Forti sprang up, hurtling into the Fallen's weakened form. Both figures tumbled backward through the broken window. Their bodies twisted in the air before falling out of view.

Through the jagged pieces of glass, Lirael hovered in midair. Massive wings of long, amber feathers beat back and forth, holding them up. Damian only glimpsed the Guardian for a second before they dove after the other two.

"No!" Adrian bellowed when Mai's blood splattered across their white robe, and again when their comrade disappeared. Sweat beaded across their forehead and their breathing grew labored as they struggled to maintain a defense. Athan showed no signs of tiring, and the deceiver's confidence crumbled with each clash of metal.

"Your ambition blinded you again." Athan pressed the advantage. Their blade moved in precise arcs, testing Adrian's guard. "The Creator gave us everything we needed."

"Except freedom!" Adrian's counterattack carried less force than before. "Except for the ability to feel!"

Athan's sword slipped past Adrian's defense, drawing a line of blood across their chest. Adrian stumbled back, eyes wide with shock.

"You were wrong about many things," Athan said, advancing. "Including my capabilities."

"You think you are special?" All signs of weakness melted from the Fallen's face, replaced by a wide grin. "You are still nothing more than what you were created for."

Adrian stepped forward. It was a graceful movement, but when their foot touched down, it was as if they'd stomped on the floor with a weight several times their own. The room shook, and cracks in the marble floor branched out from beneath them. The impact knocked Damian off his feet. What books remained on their shelves tumbled off. Colin lost his grip on Kasee, and both sprawled across the ground.

A demonic scream pierced the air, ripping through Damian's skull and setting his teeth on edge. Emerald wings burst from Adrian's back, unfurling like glorious, deadly fans of light. For a heartbeat, the Fallen's form shifted, revealing the monster the Gray Ones had shown him back in their basement chamber. Black fur rippled across Adrian's body, dotted with red specks. Green eyes blazed beneath curved horns. Flames and smoke danced around cloven hooves, and razor-sharp teeth gnashed at everyone in the room.

Then Adrian was beautiful again, their perfect form enhanced by their shimmering wings. The green feathers stretched toward the ceiling, as intimidating as they were stunning.

A soft rustling drew Damian's attention to Athan. Amber feathers sprouted from their backside, tearing through the thick fabric of their robes. Magnificent wings spread wide, appearing to glow from within, as if they contained fire.

Kasee's arm rose, obstructing Damian's view of the Guardians' transformation, then dropped. She raised it again and again, each time producing a dull thud when bringing it back down. A leather-bound tome was in her hand. Damian realized she sat atop Colin's back, the book connecting with his skull. Despite the assault, Colin sputtered and thrashed, though his attempts to buck her off grew weaker.

"Colin, please." Damian crawled closer, ignoring the winged battle above them. "This isn't you. The Colin I know never would've hurt people. He... I've already seen him die twice today. Help us. Help us save everyone."

"This *is* me!" Colin spat on the floor. "I am all that's left. The part that hated how easily you dismissed me."

Damian's chest tightened. "I was scared. But you meant everything to me."

"Liar." Colin's voice hitched as Kasee brought down the book.

"You have every right to be angry with me, but this isn't the answer." Damian held up a hand, interrupting Kasee's next blow. He reached out and touched Colin on the shoulder. "Help us stop this. Show me the friend I love."

Colin's struggles ceased, and his eyes narrowed. For a moment, something familiar crossed his face. *Doubt? Or recognition?* But then his features hardened again. "I'm done with talk."

Colin twisted beneath Kasee, throwing her off balance. As she tumbled sideways, Damian scrambled back toward the door, out of Colin's reach. Colin leaped to his feet, face contorted with anger.

Above them, Adrian and Athan's wings stirred the air. Adrian's emerald feathers flashed like deadly blades while Athan's gleamed with inner fire. Neither Guardian spoke. The clash of metal on metal said all the words for them. Each strike of their swords sent sparks cascading down onto everyone.

They're perfectly matched, Damian realized. *This could go on forever.*

"Enough."

The single word, spoken softly, cut through the din of battle. Odd Man Blue had risen from her chair, pushing aside Wendell's protective arm. Her presence filled the room as she reached out her arm, palm up. "*Enough.*"

Adrian and Athan's weapons met in one final, thunderous clash. The impact sent a shockwave through the chamber, blowing out the remaining windows and knocking Colin off balance as he reached for Damian. The two Guardians strained against each other, neither yielding ground.

Light blazed from Athan's blade, so bright Damian had to shield his eyes. The radiance grew until it blotted out the entire room. When it finally faded, the Fallen's sword lay in pieces across the floor.

Adrian fell to their knees, staring at their hands. Blood oozed from lacerations where shards of their blade had torn through perfect flesh. Their wings drooped, the emerald brilliance dimming.

"How?" they asked, voice shaky.

Without hesitation, Athan swept their sword up in an arc of light, bringing it back down behind their opponent. Adrian's magnificent wings separated from their body, falling to the floor in a heap before dissolving into ash.

Adrian screamed, collapsing onto their bloody hands, shoulders hunched where their wings had been. The anguish penetrated Damian's soul like a physical force, and he actually *felt* for the Fallen.

"My wings..." Adrian looked up. Tears fell from their blue eyes. "Why my wings?"

Arm still outstretched, Odd Man Blue's head swiveled toward the door. "Pull the lever, Damian."

"No!" Adrian screamed. They fell on their stomach, turned, and crawled toward Damian. Their image shifted again, and he saw the horned beast, fangs bared as they raked the marble floor to get to him. Behind them, Athan rose into the air, amber wings beating furiously. "No! *Please!*"

Damian turned to see the odd lever he'd noticed earlier by the door. It was within reach, and he grasped it with a trembling hand. The shaft was cold, biting into his fingers. He pulled it toward him, then down. The mechanism clicked, followed by a deep rumbling that shook the room.

A seam appeared along the floor between the entrance and Blue's desk. The gap widened as the marble fell open. *A trap door!* Damian saw the Chamber of Light far below. The six-pointed star pattern was no longer visible, as the large chamber's floor had also disappeared. A swirling pool of amber radiance had taken its place.

Adrian dug at the smooth floor, seeking purchase. Their claws left bloody gouges across the marble as they slid, small chunks of rock tumbling down.

"I will be back!" Their voice was heavy with fear. "You cannot keep me imprisoned forever!"

Adrian's legs slipped over the edge first. Arms straining, they held on for a moment before their grip failed. The Guardian plummeted through the opening, limbs flailing wildly as they fell. Their screams echoed off the walls, growing fainter until they disappeared into the pool of light. The amber surface rippled, swallowing them whole, then went still.

Instinctively, Damian pushed the lever back into its original position. He sat up against the wall as the floor retracted, hiding the light—*another portal?*—beneath them. Kasee pulled Colin to his feet. She had a firm grasp on his arms, though his face had softened, the rage melting away to shock with Adrian's defeat.

Athan's feet touched down beside Odd Man Blue's desk. Their wings folded in against their back but remained visible. "The Dungeon of Darkness?"

"Yes. We cannot risk sending Satan anywhere else until Acheron is secured." Blue gave a single nod. "Go help your brethren round up the other Fallen, Athan. Make sure Lirael and the Forti took care of Mai."

The Guardian glanced around the ruined room, eyes settling on the window through which Lirael had last been seen. Damian wanted to say something—*Congratulations? Good job?*—but choked at the raw emotion plainly visible on Athan's face. Their gaunt skin was tighter than usual, twisted into a mixture of sorrow and enmity.

With a sudden snarl, Athan swung their blade in another wide arc before sheathing it. Then they leaped through the window. Their wings unfurled, and they flew away.

Colin made an abrupt gurgling sound before falling back. A rip in his button-up shirt revealed a deep gash running along his front side. His head made a sickening crack when it made contact with the marble floor.

"Colin!" Damian scrambled across the floor, sweeping aside the array of books between them.

Colin lay sprawled on his back, eyes wide with shock. The wound on his chest was deep, though it didn't bleed. Damian cradled Colin's head, refusing to look at the laceration, afraid of what he'd see.

"I'm sorry." Colin's voice was wet and raspy. His hand found Damian's arm, gripping it with surprising strength. "I wanted you to be safe. For us all to be safe. They promised we would be."

"You're fine. You're going to be fine." Tears blurred Damian's vision. He peered up at Wendell and Kasee, but they stood frozen, uncertain in their sympathy. Odd Man Blue sat back down, offering no intervention.

"Tell Anthony..." Colin's grip weakened. "Tell him I'm sorry. I never meant—" A violent cough cut off his words.

"Save your strength. We'll get you help." Damian wiped his eyes with a dirty sleeve. He looked again at his coworkers, who stared back with hopeless expressions. Wendell shook his head. “Help is coming, Colin. You’re gonna be fine.”

Colin’s gaze fixed on something near the door. His lips curled into a smile. Not the twisted snarl from before, but a genuine, boyish grin. He pointed a finger before his arm collapsed to his side. “There it is.”

“There’s what?” Damian looked back and forth between Colin and the entrance. Aside from battle debris, nothing stood out.

“Hop in the car, Flame,” Colin said, his voice barely audible. The tension faded from his body. “Let’s get out of this dinky town.”

Colin’s eyes remained open, but the light behind them faded. His entire body went limp. Damian pulled Colin closer, pressing his forehead against Colin’s as sobs wracked his body.

CHAPTER TWENTY-EIGHT

"YOU TWO MAY LEAVE."

Damian lifted his head to see Odd Man Blue gesturing Wendell and Kasee toward the door. The pair shifted unsteadily, not wanting to leave the room but also not daring to defy the Creator. Not after what just occurred.

"What about me?" He climbed to his feet, careful to stay away from the massive broken windows. The breeze wafting through wasn't strong, but at five stories above the ground, his survival instincts kicked in. *I might not die again if I fall, but it's still not a trip I want to experience.*

Blue motioned for him to remain where he was. "You and I have an appointment."

"We do?" The words were surreal, not fitting with the deadly coup they'd just put down.

Blue nodded, her top hat wobbling. "Yes. After your Orientation, you scheduled time with me in the Grand Book of Appointments. Today at ten a.m."

"Oh." Damian's body wavered in sync with the Creator's hat. "My one question."

"Correct."

"What about Colin—" He peered down to where his friend had lain, but found only piles of books at his feet. "Where'd he go?"

"Our bodies are representations of our souls." Wendell reached out and placed a hand on his shoulder. "Without a soul, there's nothing to see. I'm sorry, Damian. He's gone."

"I can't believe it." Damian looked from Wendell's hand to his face. For once, the ambassador met his gaze head-on. "I don't *want* to believe it."

"I'm sorry," the man said again, squeezing his shoulder before following Kasee out of the chamber. "We'll be at the office when you're done."

Damian stared at the marble floor as his coworkers closed the ornate wooden door behind them. He'd held Colin in his arms moments before. Felt the life drain from him. Now there wasn't a trace of his existence.

"Why?" he asked, dragging his gaze from the floor to Blue's steady stare.

"Is that your question?"

Damian nodded.

"Then..." Blue tilted her head and wrinkled her nose. "Why what?"

"Why any of this?" He pointed down at the debris littering the floor. At the marble that'd swung open, plunging Adrian into a pit of amber light. Out at the Celestial City, where a war unfolded. "Why? Why's all this so unexpected? So utterly weird yet still so similar to life?"

Am I criticizing the Creator?

"That is more than one inquiry. At the very least, it is a very broad single question." Blue stood, buttoned her jacket, and walked over to a window. Ignoring his body's inclinations, Damian joined her, though he refused to peer down at the wooded grounds.

So strange that I'm taller than the Creator.

From their vantage point, Damian watched as Forti tanks and foot soldiers herded clusters of the Damned toward the breaches in the Celestial Wall. Massive serpentine forms glided between buildings, searching for the Fallen. The battle's momentum had shifted. However ugly the view was, they were witnessing a cleanup operation.

"They have evolved." Blue absentmindedly picked shards of glass from the frame. "The Forti. Billions of years in isolation changed them. When we locked the species away, they were consumed by hatred, by the desire to rule. Now they understand the importance of balance."

A snake-like creature—a baby compared to some of the larger ones—coiled around the Celestial Library. It yanked a lone Fallen from atop the roof. Feathers drifted to the ground as the creature tore the wings asunder. The sight made Damian's stomach turn.

"What about us humans?" He thought of Colin, his mother, and all the souls caught in the crosshairs of the ongoing conflict between good and evil. "You've kept the living from the Celestial City, too."

"Do you believe your kind has learned to control their base impulses and desires? To turn away from prejudices and judgments? To treat others—*everyone*—with dignity and respect?" Blue turned from the window to face him, eyes wide as she peeked at him from beneath the rim of her hat. "Have humans overcome their susceptibility to self-deception?"

Damian was shaking his head, about to tell the Creator that Earth still needed at least another few thousand years—*if we last that long*—but her last question threw him. "What do you mean?"

"This." She pointed out beyond the city. "A thousand planes of existence lay beyond the Celestial Wall. Including the Afterlife, the only plane I did not create."

Damian stepped back from the window. "What?"

"Many of my creations, including several Earth cultures, have considered the idea of life after death. It wasn't until the Great Ascension that one actually came to be. The Afterlife was not part of my designs." Blue pointed up to his chest. "Humans invented it."

"How is that possible?" he asked, scratching at his jaw.

"Through that same ability for self-deception, what many think of as *imagination*." Blue walked around the perimeter, taking in different views of the city. "As your civilizations grew, institutions couldn't rely on their populations to be good for the sake of the whole. So they created eternal reasons to behave.

The idea took hold, and the communal belief in the Afterlife became so strong among humans that it manifested into reality. You created and shaped it through generations of belief and imagination."

None of this was supposed to be. I wasn't supposed to exist after death. Damian thought of Alena, their house in the country, and the mountainous pile of conflicting ideas regarding perfection. In particular, he considered Bennett, and all the other children kept out of society's sight. *All the Afterlife's peculiarities, especially how it mimics our past ideologies and prejudices so closely, make sense now.* "What happens now?"

"I do not control the fate of humans. It was not my decision to split your souls, sending undesirable portions to Acheron." Blue removed her hat and held it in front of her, working her hands methodically around the rim. "You are an author. Surely you understand the act of writing one's own story."

"Huh." The realization of humanity's autonomy amid all of Creation had struck him. *I can understand how Adrian grew jealous of us.*

"I find humans impressive. Unlike the Guardians, I did not craft them to perform a specific function. Other than to survive, that is. They can follow their own paths and find joy or sorrow at the end. You can support those that lead you—or not." Blue placed her hat back on her head, then peered curiously up at him. "Do you believe in something, Damian? If so, do you follow that principle? Is your faith so strong that you could make anything real?"

Damian opened his mouth to respond, but wasn't sure how to answer. The only thing that came to mind was *family.* Alena and Bennet, his mother. Even Wendell and Kasee.

Even Colin. He looked back to where his friend—the last version of him—had died.

Instead, he asked, "Who are you?"

"I am known by countless names across all realities." Her form shimmered like heat waves rising from a simmering pavement. "Your kind has imagined me in many forms."

Odd Man Blue's charcoal suit melted into flowing robes like those worn by the Guardians. Her skin shifted from blue to gold to obsidian, and her height stretched upward until her top hat—*no, now it's a crown of iron!*—scraped against the white ceiling. Multiple arms sprouted from her torso, each holding a unique object: a sword, a scale, a lotus flower.

Damian stumbled back as the Creator's face transformed. Zeus's thunderous visage. Odin's one-eyed stare. Ra's falcon head. Shiva's serene expression. The Virgin Mary's gentle smile. The Great Pumpkin. Hundreds more faces he didn't recognize flashed by, some humanoid, others completely alien. His mind tried to process the constant metamorphoses, knowing that each form carried its own weight of cultural significance, its own story of creation and destruction.

"My people once numbered in the billions." The Creator's giant form dissipated into heavy steam. From within came a clanking and banging so loud Damian fell over and covered his ears. He watched as a mountain of pipes, lined with gauges and levers, emerged from the mist. He cowered before the convoluted brass machine, thinking this was her true form. "We spread across our universe, watching and learning, sometimes inspiring."

The steam faded as Blue settled back into her usual form. "Now we are few, stretched thin across the vastness of space and time. Many have diminished as belief in ourselves has waned. Others simply grew tired of existence and ended their watch."

Damian grabbed hold of the nearest bookshelf and pulled himself to his feet. His legs trembled as his understanding of history and existence shifted yet again. "So you're not really *the* Creator?"

"I have shaped many slices of reality." She laughed, a sound that flitted around the room with the voices of a thousand deities. "*Creator* is simply another name humans gave me. Like all others, it holds power because of belief, not inherent truth."

"Then what should I call you?"

"Blue will do." She put a steadying hand on his arm, and his entire body calmed. "It is as true as any other name I have worn."

Blue marched back to her desk. Damian turned away from the outside view—the sounds of combat were diminishing as the combined Guardian and

Forti force pushed the enemy back—and followed, keeping a wary eye on the marble floor. "What will happen to Adrian—I mean, Satan?"

"Like me, Lucifer goes by a multitude of names and faces. You may refer to them however you wish." She sat and clasped her hands together. "They and the other Fallen will be returned to Acheron, as well as the souls that escaped their dominion. Those that survive this incursion, anyway."

Damian stepped lightly into the middle of the room. "Why not get rid of them? Get rid of them all?"

"Destroy my creation?" Both of her eyebrows shot up as if the question genuinely surprised her. "Would you do away with Bennett if he broke your household rules in the spirit of rebellion?"

"That's not the same!" he cried out, horrified at the idea of snuffing his son—*my son!*—out of existence. "Is it?"

"Lucifer and the Fallen still have a part to play in my story," Blue said. "As does the human project. Over time, they will regain their strength and once again seek to depose me. One day, they will probably succeed."

Today's victory isn't even permanent. A shudder made its way down Damian's back. He abhorred the idea of reciting the last several days cyclically until the end of time. Images of future battles played out in his head. *More souls lost. More friends forever gone.*

"How can you be so calm about that?" He felt heavy, worrying that his bulk would accidentally activate the trapdoor mechanism, sending him plummeting into the chamber below. "You know they'll undo everything you've done. Reshape reality in their own image. How can you face your own death with such placidity?"

"Even gods must die." Blue shrugged. "And who is to say what I have done is right?"

After my excursion in Acheron, I will continue to fight any future where Adrian sits on the highest throne. Blue may not be the benevolent creator my parents told me about, but I don't want Bennett living in a world of injustice and hate.

"May I go?" The thought of his son had snapped Damian back into focus. To what mattered. "I need to see my family. They're probably worried sick about me."

"Almost." Blue reached into her suit jacket. The motion seemed to stretch forever, her hand disappearing deeper than the fabric should allow. When she finally withdrew it, a familiar orb of light pulsed in her palm. "You must return this first, lest you suffer the same fate as Perseus."

The eye of the Gray Ones. Damian vaguely recalled the orb falling alongside him into Gehenna, though Colin's supposed death and his mother's surprise arrival had consumed his attention. *Why did they give this to me? Was it for my benefit or theirs?*

"They are waiting for you back at the Embassy." Blue gave a slight smile. "They are quite fond of you, you know."

"Right." Damian reached across the Creator's desk, plucking the orb from her palm. He turned to the door, pausing long enough to say, "Thank you. For everything."

"Thank yourself," Blue said. "You wrote this story."

Damian's shoes crunched over shattered glass as he picked his way through empty streets. The Gray One's eye pulsed warmly in his hand, a steady rhythm that felt like a heartbeat. He could've peregrinated straight to the Embassy once he stepped off the grounds of the Celestial Palace, but he needed to see the aftermath of Adrian's—*of Colin's*—actions and betrayal.

Scorch marks scarred the walls surrounding the Castile, and explosions had dislodged the stones forming the semicircular arches above doors and decorative arcades. A Guardian's sword lay abandoned just outside the front doors, its hilt dulled with dried blood. Damian thought of Athan wielding their blade against former brethren—*against my friend*—and wondered how many times they would survive this same battle in the future.

The Hall of Hands loomed ahead, its plain facade now pockmarked with holes. Through one sizable gap, Damian saw rows of preserved hands still reaching skyward as if in prayer. He peered down at his own, thinking he would've been more helpful with one of the earlier concept models. *Something with claws or diamond-tipped nails.*

Paper scattered across the street like fallen leaves, pages torn from the Celestial Library's collection. Damian picked up a single sheet, half expecting to find the works of Zarathushtra. It was part of an autobiography, its subject an alien species. This saddened him. *If humans are one of the few creations to exist in perpetuity, then the war has reduced this individual's life to fragments floating in the street.*

In the distance, explosions still echoed, growing fainter with each passing minute. The sound reminded him of his father, whom he'd thought little of since dying. *How he must be suffering after losing his entire family.* During the Iraq War, which encompassed much of Damian's teen years, his father had sat in the living room and watched footage from Baghdad, of reporters ducking behind concrete barriers as missiles lit up the night sky.

It's one thing to see those scenes on a TV screen, safe in your home. In the years since, Damian had watched clouds of tear gas roll down city streets in his own country as demonstrators sparred with and fled from riot police. *I thought I felt it. That I understood. I was so wrong.*

Just outside the wrought-iron fence surrounding the Embassy, much of it now bent and broken, Damian glanced down the street toward Messie Bessie's. A building had collapsed, blocking his view. The chunks of stone and rebar reminded him of images from September 11th. Dust-covered New Yorkers emerging from clouds of debris, papers descending from shattered towers. The attack had been so close to home, especially compared to the ensuing conflict in Iraq, yet still 900 miles from Minade.

We can't even escape the cycle of violence in paradise, Damian thought. *Even gods must die.*

He turned to face the Embassy, its massive dome still proud against the clearing amber sky. Unlike the surrounding devastation, the building stood largely untouched. Only the front showed signs that the location was the epicenter of the assault, its doors blown off, lying on the trampled lawn.

Two Guardians flanked the ruined entrance. Neither was familiar to Damian, but each held a sword pulsing with Light.

"I'm sorry for the losses you've suffered." Damian bowed his head to each of them once he'd climbed the stairs. "Thank you for your protection."

"We have lost many today," one responded, their blade dipping slightly. "As have you, Damian Craig Hartter. Your vigilance has saved us all."

Damian's hand tightened around the orb as he fought to hold back tears. He gave them another nod and, not knowing what else to say—if there even was anything else to say—ducked inside the building.

The foyer was darker than usual. With the chandelier lopsided and unlit, Damian saw dust in the light streaming in through the windows. Piles of debris were scattered around, giving the room the look of an abandoned building. Three Embassy employees huddled near the Bridge, trying to pull the broken key from Hell's lock. They appeared to be squatters in their torn and dusty clothing.

The Bridge continued its slow rotation, oblivious to the fact it'd played an instrumental role in an everlasting war. *How many souls left Acheron? They could've turned tail and escaped into any of a thousand realities. It could take forever to round them all up.*

Damian's gaze drifted to the staircase. Somewhere above, Wendell and Kasee were surveying the wreckage of the Department of Satanic Investigations. *They'll assume the mess resulted from the battle, not yet knowing the Sphere of Doom activated above the ambassador's flower garden.*

"Sir?" One of the bedraggled employees stepped away from the Bridge. "Are you okay?"

Damian realized he'd been standing motionless, staring listlessly at nothing. "No, not really." He gave a polite nod, then turned toward the door tucked away in the far corner.

The stairwell leading down to the Gray One's office appeared much shorter than before. Damian could see the landing at the bottom the moment he opened the door, the golden nameplate denoting *The Graeae* glinting in the dark. The orb lit his path, casting his shadow in three directions as he descended, each dancing independently as his footsteps echoed off the walls.

Outside their door, he raised his hand to knock. Three voices spoken in unison interrupted him from the other side. "It is unlocked. Come inside."

Of course, they know I'm here. They're staring at me from the palm of my hand. Or into the palm of my hand? Gross.

Damian pushed the door open, finding the women huddled together in the middle of the room. They appeared as ancient, eyeless women, stringy gray hair covering bulbous shoulders. Leathery skin occasionally sloughed off their faces, disappearing into a cloud of amorphous grime. The orb shone brightly, pulling itself from his hand. It zipped through the air and spun around its masters' heads like an excited puppy. Its light revealed not their office, stone walls covered in mold and water dripping from stalactites, but his home. Not the one he shared with Alena and Bennett, nor the cheap apartment in Minade with a view of the parking lot. It was his parents' living room. The last room he was in before he died.

One stepped forward. Though he couldn't yet tell the women apart, he guessed she was the sister who'd gifted him the burlap pouch at the head ambassador's party. "You brought it back." Her voice carried neither gratitude nor reproach.

"Seemed the right thing to do." Damian reflexively wiped the palm of his hand against his shirt, as though their eye had left behind...*eye juice?* "I'm not sure why you gave it to me."

"I told you, it wasn't for you." She cocked her head, the bones in her neck cracking. "Was it—were we—at all useful?"

Damian looked down at the ground. "It made me feel...not alone. And helped bring me closer to an old friend."

"We are never alone." All three of the Gray Ones hummed in appreciation. Then the one who had spoken broke off and took the form of Damian's father. He gawked as the small, bespectacled man, dressed in khakis and a sweater vest, gave a tight grin before sitting down on the couch.

"What the hell?" Damian stared at his father's replicant, whose eyes were bright as he watched the television. The scene wasn't uncommon, though his *true* father would've turned on the television first.

The remaining two women, still in their nebulous forms, stepped toward Damian. "Until now, the only details of Acheron came from misplaced souls who found their way to the Afterlife through Gehenna. They painted a grotesque picture. While no one doubted their experiences, we needed an impartial view."

"So I was, what, your spy?"

"Our witness," his father's doppelgänger said in a correctional tone that was usually used by his mother. "By your path, we observed through our eye a reflection of the Celestial City."

Damian expected him—*her?*—to expound upon the statement, to say that the two cities were mirror opposites, one reflecting good and the other evil. He would've argued against such simplicity, having experienced both sides of the spectrum. The Gray Ones remained silent, though, and he surmised they probably agreed with him.

"You knew I'd end up there?" he asked instead. "I thought you couldn't see the future."

"We cannot," one crone confirmed. "That knowledge came from the Creator."

"Of course she knew." Anger flared in his chest. "She knew what would happen and just let it play out?"

"The Creator sees all potential paths."

"But she chose this one." He clenched his hands. *I have half a mind to march back to the palace and demand an explanation.* "She let me suffer. Let Colin die."

"No," one woman said, her papery voice carrying a sharp edge. "You chose this path. Every decision, every action you made, led you here. The Creator merely saw the possibilities."

She shifted closer, her hunched form withering away until a new face emerged. Damian now faced a younger version of himself. Unlike Craig, this one wasn't angry or agitated—*or covered in shiny black rubber.* This new form turned and took a seat in a recliner. Rather than face the television, the copy picked a book up from a side table and flipped through the pages.

Tears stung Damian's eyes as he faced the remaining sister. "You all said something similar the first time you questioned me. That much of what we perceive and experience is of our own making."

"And now you know how that is so," the remaining crone said, her hollow eye sockets staring at him. "Your imagination is a powerful tool. It is instrumental to your hopes and dreams, to your ideas of perfection."

"Is that how Acheron operates, too?" *The place is a juxtaposition to the Celestial City, but it isn't truly its polar opposite.* Many of its residents appeared happy, content, if not easily persuaded by Adrian's wants.

"No, not directly." Dust swirled around her vague body as she shook her head. "They would never admit it, but the Fallen—especially Satan—admire humans. They are so jealous of your kind that they emulate you as much as they influence you. Your desires, secrets, and expectations are laid bare to Satan, and they used those thoughts to craft Acheron as a perverted haven for your more wicked aspects."

Damian nodded, but the motion made him dizzy. He thought at first the Gray Ones were willing his body into a catatonic state as before, but when the spell faded, he guessed it was the surreal nature of the illusion they were acting out. *After the day I've had, this is almost too much.* "You told me the thread that binds would be the key to stopping Adrian's mechanisms. I know that thread was the BMW accident. Colin and I were unconscious at the time the Embassy went down. I don't understand how that was helpful, though."

"That was *a* thread," the crone said. Then all three said in unison, "There are many threads."

"Friendship," said his doppelgänger.

"Family," said his father.

"Love," said the sister in front of him.

Damian froze as the last woman's form shifted, her body dissolving into swirling mist.

"Please don't," he whispered, the tears running down his face. The dust cloud ignored his sputtering, coalescing into the sharp features he'd loathed his entire life. Even through wet, blurry vision, he'd recognize the tight bun and rigid posture anywhere. "I can't."

"You can," said the image of his mother. She appeared exactly as she had in Acheron, moments before shoving him into the Lake of Fire. "You must."

"Did she know?" The words caught in his throat. "When she pushed me?"

"Yes." His mother's voice emerged from the Gray One's mouth. It lacked the edge he expected from either woman. "She knew precisely what she was doing."

His mother's duplicate moved over to the couch, settling next to his father's form. Damian ached at the sight. *How many times did I see them just like this, watching the news and knitting?*

"Your mother is not the wretched soul you or she imagines." She pulled out a pair of jeans with a hole in the knee, along with a sewing kit. "We approached her shortly after the both of you passed. She agreed to act on our behalf within Acheron. If either of you was a spy, it was her."

"But she never..." Damian choked, and he wiped his face with the palms of his hands. "All those years, she never showed..."

"Love?" His father turned from the television. "Did you ever wonder why she pushed you toward that business degree? Why she insisted you stay close to home?"

"She was controlling. Manipulative."

"She was terrified," Damian's younger self said, glancing up from his book. "She perceived you going down paths that, in her mind, would've led to darkness. To Hell. She fought to turn you from that path the only way she knew how."

"By making me miserable?"

"By keeping you safe." His mother's form leaned forward, setting the garment aside. "Your mother's understanding of the Afterlife was flawed, and we cannot defend her actions toward you. But she was afraid you would end up in Acheron."

All three of them stared at Damian. "And you did."

"So what, you gave her the opportunity to save me? To push me into the flames?"

"To save everyone," they said in unison, sitting back into their seats. "We provided her with the tools to communicate with you."

"How?"

"Pay more attention to Alena." His mother's facsimile winked. "She's a smart one."

More tears flowed. Damian remembered her last words before the shove: *I've always loved you. I always will.* He'd rarely heard those words from her. This time, for the first time, he truly believed them.

"Will I ever see her again?" he asked.

"We are blind to the future," they all said.

The image of his mother turned to him. With a slight smile, she said, "But we hope so."

CHAPTER TWENTY-NINE

DAMIAN CLIMBED OUT OF the sporty red Buick Century, balancing a stack of boxes against his hip. The scent of eggs and cheese followed him out of the car. His stomach growled in anticipation, and he knew he couldn't resist the quiche's temptation much longer. *Can always count on Messie Bessie's to deliver.*

A line of vehicles stretched along his driveway. Parked next to the Buick was the black Camaro Alena had waiting for him upon death. His gaze admired its sharp lines and aggressive posture. *I'll never love another car as much as this one.*

The Buick was identical to the one his parents had given him in high school. Every ding and scratch matched his memory, down to the screwdriver jammed into the window. *Every defect other than the* last *one.* It was a reminder of the sacrifices his parents had made—*and continue to make*—for him.

On the other side of the Camaro sat a BMW M3, the car that had carried him and Colin on their final ride together. He'd only driven this replica once, just to make sure it performed as expected. It had, and he recognized at once how it stacked against his pony car—something he never would've admitted to Colin. *I hope you're speeding along a coastline in one right now, Avenger.*

The BMW had been a hard sell for Alena, let alone for himself. The specialists who'd traded him the vehicles for a few short stories hadn't understood why he wanted these specific models with particular imperfections. They offered new, sleeker options with fancy Afterlife add-ons. Each car represented a chapter in his own story, though. He wanted the memories, even the painful ones.

He shifted the boxes of quiche and headed toward the house, brown leather shoes crunching on gravel. A horse nickered softly from the lawn where someone had tethered it to a tree, and two bicycles leaned on their kickstands near the front steps. The gathering out back would be a mix of friends and new allies, all still struggling to make sense of recent events.

The bang and rattle of an engine cut through the air. Damian turned in time to see a Model A mail van, its ancient frame shuddering as it rolled into the driveway. Once parked, Jim Parsons' thin frame hopped out. He wore cargo shorts and a Hawaiian shirt that assaulted Damian's eyes with its clash of colors and palm fronds. It was a stark departure from the man's usual gray button-up and sweater coat. His handlebar mustache still bobbed jovially.

"Need a hand?" Jim hustled up the driveway, plucking a few boxes from Damian's stack.

"Thanks. Glad you could make it. Wasn't sure if you'd be bogged down with special deliveries."

"And miss out on that coffee you promised? Been waiting to cash in that raincheck." Jim's mustache twitched. "With all the extra time I've been putting in after the, uh, incident, I decided I could use an afternoon off."

Damian nodded. He'd invited more people to the gathering than he was socially comfortable with, knowing he'd be lucky if half of them showed up. The *incident*, and the subsequent rebuilding efforts of the Celestial City—not to mention fostering trust in its institutions—were ongoing and more grueling than most human souls were used to. "Don't worry. I asked Alena to put on a fresh pot. Dark roast, none of that flavored stuff."

Laughter drifted over the house, accompanied by the sound of splashing water. Kasee's raspy shriek pierced through the other voices, followed by the unmistakable sound of someone—*likely Kasee*—being thrown into the lake.

"Tables are set up out back." Damian nodded toward a path leading around the side of the house. "Would you mind putting those boxes anywhere there's space? I need to check something in the kitchen."

Jim's mustache bobbed in acknowledgment. "Sure thing."

"I'll get you that coffee." Damian shifted his remaining boxes. "Want a splash of something stronger? Got some Irish whiskey that'll put hair on your chest. Or take it off, depending on how much you want."

"Now you're speaking my language." Jim chuckled. "After the week we've had, a little kick wouldn't hurt."

"Head on out. I'll see you in a minute." Damian watched as Jim disappeared around the corner, then pushed his way through the front door. The house smelled of coffee and baked goods. *Alena's been busy.*

After setting the boxes of food on the counter, he grabbed two ceramic mugs from a cupboard. A bottle of whiskey waited above the refrigerator. Damian reached for it as someone walked in the back door.

"You're using the gift I got you!"

Damian smiled as he turned, bottle in hand. Bennett filled the doorway, his lanky limbs having filled out over the last few days. Maturation gave him an air of casual confidence, though the rapid transformation still caught Damian off guard. *A baby only a few days ago, now practically a man.* Dark curls fell across his forehead, damp from swimming.

"Of course I am." Damian gestured to one of the ceramic mugs he'd set down, the words *Afterlife's Best Dad* emblazoned across its surface. "The marketing is misleading, but I love it."

"Here we go again with the modesty." Bennett rolled his eyes. He grabbed an apple from the fruit bowl on the island, tossing it between his hands. "I read over the manuscript outline you left in the library."

"Already?" Damian splashed some whiskey into the two mugs. He offered some to Bennett—*it feels weird to offer alcohol to my son*—who turned it down. "I just finished it yesterday."

"Went over it this morning. Couldn't put it down, and I can't wait for you to write it." His eyes lit up the way they always did when discussing books. "The protagonist's internal conflict about faith and family is really moving."

"Think it needs a few dinosaurs?" Damian winked. A warmth spread through his chest—*and I haven't even touched the whiskey yet.* He'd spent his entire life avoiding conversations with and about children. Now he was discussing character arcs and narrative structures with a son who devoured stories as voraciously as he did.

"Every book could use a dinosaur or two," Bennett said with a laugh. "Speaking of family, Mom's trying to wrangle everyone up for food. Need me to help carry stuff out?"

Damian pointed to the boxes of quiche. "If you want to grab those, I'll pour some coffee and follow you." He made for the coffeepot, then half-turned. "Oh, and Bennett? Thanks for reading the outline."

"Thanks for writing it." Bennett paused at the doorway, boxes balanced in his arms. "And that mug? Not misleading in the least."

The back door slammed shut before Damian could protest. He picked up the mug, tracing his fingers over the lettering. The struggle to reconcile his anxiety over parenthood with the reality of watching Bennett grow into an adult was ongoing. Now guilt accompanied that feeling. Regret at not having been more present over the last few weeks.

You did help save the multiverse. They were words everyone kept telling him. *Bennett knows that. The only thing he wants from you is your love.*

And that he gave in abundance. Every time Bennett referenced a book they'd discussed or expressed a quick wit that reminded him of Alena, Damian felt a fierce pride he never thought possible.

With another splash of whiskey in Jim's mug, he finally poured the coffee. Drinks in hand, he headed toward the back door. The sounds of laughter and splashing grew louder.

Damian barely recognized anyone as he scanned the backyard. Though mostly human, creatures from across Creation were in attendance, a testament to the battles they'd survived. He spotted three blobs rolling away from the lake.

One paused at a buffet table, its translucent body rippling before it absorbed an entire quiche in one fluid motion. *There goes Messie Bessie's finest.*

Jim stood with Kasee and Anthony by the water's edge. Carefully sidestepping a pair of winged beings engaged in an animated discussion about dimensional physics, Damian made his way over to them.

"Your coffee." He handed Jim the doctored mug. "Just as you ordered."

"Much obliged." The man took a long sip, his mustache twitching. "I think I see your neighbor over there. Should ask about that cream they keep ordering."

As the mail carrier wandered off, Damian studied the remaining pair. Kasee and Anthony both sported black hoodies, torn jeans, and identical looks of disinterest. *They could be cut from the same cloth—in style, at least.* Kasee nursed a new cigar, complementing her usual scowl. Damian noticed she appeared only slightly less grumpy now that the Department of Satanic Investigations had solved their major cases. They'd turned their attention to older mysteries, like the fall of the Embassy back in 2008. Damian suspected Mai was the culprit, though it was likely they'd never officially solve the case.

"Nice spread." Smoke curled from her lips. "Your blob friends are decimating it, though."

"I can always get more food." They watched as another gelatinous creature engulfed a quiche. "Though their table manners leave something to be desired."

Anthony laughed, a genuine sound that surprised Damian. When he'd sent the invitation, he'd worried that it was too soon after Colin's death. That he'd receive an acidic response. Anthony had responded immediately, though, with gratitude for the inclusion.

"I never thanked you." Anthony raised a glass of water. "For exposing what Colin had become. Looking back, I can see how he was manipulating me. The isolation. The control. Easier to spot the red flags when you're not blinded by love, I guess."

"I am so sorry for what you went through," Damian said, shaking his head. "I know it doesn't help, but the Colin I knew—the real, whole Colin—would've hated what his darker half became. How he treated you. You deserved better than that version of him."

"We all did." Kasee flicked ash from her cigar. "But we got through it. Together."

Damian nodded, recalling how she'd walloped Colin over the head with a thick book in Odd Man Blue's office. "Together."

"Speaking of together, your more attractive half is waving you down."

Damian turned to see Alena standing further along the shoreline. She'd taken off her shoes and was wading in the shallow water. He held up a finger, indicating he'd be there in a minute.

"Duty calls." He nodded to his friends—*friends!* "Try not to let the blobs eat all the food!"

On his way over to Alena, Damian stopped by a nearby picnic table under the shade of a tree. Wendell sat, elbows on the table, still dressed in his usual work attire. For once, the ambassador appeared relaxed.

"Enjoying the party?" Damian asked. The man had two plates in front of him, though he'd only cleared one of food.

"Even more than expected." The ambassador glanced up. "Though the blobs keep trying to consume Mrs. Ulrich, mistaking her for an hors d'oeuvre."

Damian blinked, then realized that Mrs. Ulrich perched on one plate in front of his boss. He'd mistaken her mottled green skin, curly gray hair, and the gold rims of her glasses for a mixture of foods.

"They know better now." The librarian smoothed her cardigan with a webbed foot. "I may be small, but I can be very loud."

"How are the repairs coming along at the library?" Damian asked. "Last time I stopped by, the outer walls had been patched."

"Faster than expected," Mrs. Ulrich croaked, her face brightening. "Most of the shelving has also been fixed, and the majority of texts that sit on them have found their way home. Those that haven't..." She shrugged her tiny shoulders. "Perhaps it was time for some spring cleaning. The recent upheaval will certainly inspire new literature, requiring considerable space."

"Lost books aren't truly gone though, right?" Damian leaned forward. "The *Book of History* captured everything?"

"Every word, comma, and period." She tapped her foot against the plate. "Though some first editions were precious, the content remains preserved. And really, that's what matters most."

Damian smiled at that, wondering if any of his short stories had appeared in the library yet. Turning to Wendell, he asked, "Any new updates on the Embassy?"

"Not much beyond what we've covered in our departmental meetings." His expression sobered. "The Bridge has been secured, and access to the Embassy has been tightened. Half the Guardians are patrolling the exterior of the Dungeon of Darkness, ensuring Satan doesn't escape before they and the remaining Fallen are transferred back to Acheron."

"Have you heard anything from Athan?" After some deliberation, Damian had invited the Guardian to the gathering. They hadn't spoken to each other since the battle, and the invite had gone unanswered. This suited him just fine. Any time he thought of his friend, the memory of them cutting down his *best* friend replayed itself. It would take time for him to move past that action. Damian wanted to forgive Athan, but he wasn't there yet.

And they must be reeling from the emotional aftermath of that death. Of the entire event. We'll both come around.

"Mai admitted to Bai's murder before succumbing to their wounds. They were their last words, apparently," Wendell said. "Seems Athan is the Guardians' de facto leader. They'll be inheriting a lot of responsibility, especially since they've been tasked with rounding up the remaining Damned still unaccounted for, but the Castile could do a lot worse."

Despite his current feelings toward Athan, Damian still believed in what he'd told the Guardian before. *They will make a worthy leader.*

Someone walked away from Alena, heading toward the buffet, and Damian excused himself from Wendell and Mrs. Ulrich. He crossed the remaining distance to where she stood ankle-deep in the lake. Water lapped at her feet, creating tiny ripples that spread outward before dissipating into larger waves caused by nearby swimmers.

"There's my hero," she said as he stepped up next to her. She reached for his hand, interlacing their fingers.

Damian laughed. "I'd object, but Bennett already shut down my modesty."

"Good!" She squeezed his hand. Damian savored the sensation. It centered him.

"You were right," he said, staring at the rippling water. "About the pennies."

Alena frowned. "Pennies?"

"The day of my Orientation, you showed me how planes of existence interact not just at the city but along the entire line at which they intersect. I don't understand how, but I think that's how my mother communicated Colin's messages to me."

Her eyes widened. "The coded dreams?"

"Without access to the Celestial City, she needed another way to reach me." He kicked at the water, watching droplets disrupt the placid surface. "There must be places where the Afterlife and Hell meet that the Embassy doesn't monitor."

Alena squeezed his hand again. "Then you may hear from her again someday."

They gazed out over the water, watching as their son splashed water on some of his new friends. One of them retaliated by launching a blob—*a child blob, or part of an adult blob?*—in Bennett's direction. The blob appeared delighted by the development, changing shape into a translucent net before catching Bennett.

Alena breathed deeply as the swimmers continued to laugh and splash. "This is perfect."

Damian tilted his head, studying her profile. The amber light highlighted the freckles scattered across her nose, and her dark eyes sparkled. "I disagree."

"How so?"

"The Celestial City is still rebuilding. Adrian hasn't been transferred yet. Half of the Guardians and Embassy employees are recovering from injuries." His voice dropped. "And amid it all, there are still people fighting against your adoption program. I'd argue the very idea of a perfect paradise is a lie."

Alena nodded contemplatively, a strand of brown hair falling loose from her ponytail. "You're right. There will always be opposition. If not to orphaned children maturing, then to something else someone finds unnatural. Even if we succeed and every child gets placed with a family, some souls will challenge our way of thinking for all eternity."

"And you're okay with that?"

"Look at Bennett." Their son had escaped the blob net and was now perched on another friend's shoulders. They both laughed hysterically, broad smiles on their faces. "We succeeded with him. We survived the battle. Now we're here together, with friends, and we've got as many supporters as detractors."

"You're right, of course." Damian let his anxiety seep away into the water. "The Afterlife may be flawed, but this...this is authentic."

She leaned over and bumped her shoulder into his. "This isn't just about the war and Bennett, is it?"

Damian watched as a fish broke the water's surface. Its scales, of a reddish-orange coloration, flashed before it disappeared beneath the waves. "No, I suppose not."

"I'm sorry about Colin. About all of it." Alena's own voice dropped, too. "I know what he meant to you. What you meant to each other."

"Did you know?" Damian asked. "About Colin and me? About...me?"

"Of course!" She smiled at him and raised his hand to her mouth, giving it a kiss. "You told me all about it back in college. You weren't sure at the time what it meant for our relationship. What it said about you as a person."

"I don't remember talking to you about that. I must've been so ashamed." Damian had told her all about Acheron, including how everyone's souls split at death. He still wasn't comfortable with the idea of another *him* walking around in another universe, a version embodying all the virtues he hated in himself. "Was I ever into anything...kinky? Like rubber?"

Alena's smile widened. "You sometimes spoke of a desire. I was always willing to explore that with you, but you never quite got there." She raised her eyebrows. "I'm still game if you are."

If blood still flowed through his body, Damian would've flushed bright red.

"Just know that I was never ashamed of you. I've always loved you for exactly who you are—including your kinky bisexuality."

"I keep thinking about that one night with Colin. About what might have happened if—"

"Don't." Alena turned to face him. "That path leads nowhere good. Trust me. I spent years wondering 'what if' about having children. About the accident with the pen. And now about my drinking—something *I* don't remember but am immensely sorry for."

Damian pulled her into a hug. He didn't need her to apologize. Any version of Alena. He'd already decided there was nothing to forgive.

"We can't change the past, but we can shape our future." She wrapped her arms around him. "And right now our future includes a party full of people who love us, a son who adores you, and whatever food the blobs haven't discovered yet."

Large droplets of water fell over them as Bennett cannonballed nearby. Damian watched their son surface, shaking water from his curls like a dog.

She's right, he thought. *This is perfect.*

"Come on." Alena tugged him toward the buffet. "Let's get some food."

"Good idea." Damian patted his belly. "Do we have any pumpkin pie?"

ACKNOWLEDGEMENTS

IT'S BEEN FIVE YEARS since I published a book. A lot has happened in that time. *Big World* happened, of course, as to explained to Alena. But also, *My World* happened. I met and fell in love with my husband. An intoxicated motorcyclist killed my younger brother while he was crossing a road. Shoulder pain necessitated surgery. I moved across the country yet again.

In between all the happening, I finally finished *The War for Heaven*, a fantastical story I originally dreamed up over 25 years ago. Writing can be a lonely venture, but this story did not come to fruition without help. Many people were involved in elevating the initial drafts into something *much* better. My good friend Glenn Schudel has championed all my books and was an early fan of Damian. A.C. Andrews, for whom I've narrated a couple of audiobooks, offered to read the book long before I finished it. Whenever imposter syndrome got the better of me during the editing phase, I revisited his positive comments for encouragement. Matt Beard was kind enough to verify that Damian's journey was exactly as weird as I intended it to be. The *Onwards!* writing group of Austin, Texas, has provided a safe space to write, share thoughts, and make friendships. I am especially grateful to Sarah Pepin for reading my words and offering her perspective as a librarian. My editor, Kristen Hamilton, did another wonderful job of polishing my jumbled paragraphs. I relied heavily on Tim Barber to create a beautiful cover with little input and direction from myself, a task I did not envy. Conversations with Kevin Knipp helped keep my mind healthy and focused. My husband, Lane Flores, let me live in and talk about this version of the Afterlife for years. It would've been easy for them to tell me the book was great, to nod and smile, but they did what they always do: loved and encouraged me.

And finally to you, the reader! Thank you for picking up *The War for Heaven*. I hope you enjoyed spending time with Damian in the Afterlife, along with all his friends, family, and frenemies.

Now for some pumpkin pie!

Isaac Grisham
January 23, 2026

www.ingramcontent.com/pod-product-compliance
Lightning Source LLC
LaVergne TN
LVHW100511110826
845146LV00002B/592
9798991741033